Reader,

Hi! Please read
it! Please
enjoy, & share
typo-filled first-print cip!
debut novel. It's rare! It's
You are too.

Xoxo,

[signature]
Mannitters

MW00488247

BANANAS!

AUTHOR'S NOTE

This book has defied every attempt to categorize it. It is not science-fiction exactly, nor is it fantasy. It's not a satire. It's not political, and it isn't purely entertainment. It's silly at times. It's deathly serious elsewhere. It has literary aspirations, but enough nonsensical asides and bad jokes to perhaps seem more like a story told by a friend. It is admittedly bizarre. It is certainly unlike anything I've seen elsewhere.

When I set out to write *Bananas!*, I wanted to capture some aspect of the millennial experience, of growing up and adjusting to adulthood in a dizzy, oft-ungrounded world. Every day, we wrangle with technologies and forces too young and too powerful to be understood. Social media remains in its infancy; we have no idea of its true power, nor its true capacity. The planet is slowly dying of heatstroke. Grand-scale existential dread exists for us just as it did for many during the Cold War, but its every knuckle twitch is now communicated live and direct and in real-time. Hell, every millennial you know has some combination of depression and anxiety and ADHD, diagnosed or not. We all stare together into an uncertain future. And that brings me to the pandemic.

Bananas! was completed in December of 2019, which makes it an innocent book, written by an innocent author. Neither of us knew about the catastrophic illness 2020 would introduce, and thus, the millennial experience as I wrote it no longer exists. Our world, and our generation, has been forever and fundamentally altered. And so, *Bananas!* is a kind of snapshot, dealing in psychoses and schemas that I once believed were very important, stolen from a pre-pandemic world.

Yes, ours is a particularly odd time to live in, all times are, forever oscillating between various levels of it. No matter how odd your world is, my hope is there are things in this story which resonate with it, because they too are odd, because the story itself is odd, because above all else, this story understands how odd it is simply being alive.

And lastly, this is a story meant to be shared. If you find this story in your hands, I encourage you to share it, discuss it, gift it. It is my great honor to have entered your life in this way, and your sharing these words with others is a tribute I can hardly fathom. I love you. Oh gosh, I love you lots and lots.

If you do enjoy this story, I ask and encourage you to visit its accompanying website, *www.bananasnovel.com*, wherein you will find ways to support the artists, aka myself and my extremely talented graphic designer (and dear friend), Jessica Richards, who was *absolutely instrumental* in the creation of the work you hold before you. I am deeply in her debt, and it is important to me that you know of her before we begin. All these words, all the spaces in between…hell, the entire book, is as much a physical product of her genius as it is a mental product of my instability.

Please share. Please reach out if you like. And most of all, please enjoy. It means the entire world that you have decided to take this journey with me. I'm honored and humbled and, well, I'm flabbergasted beyond all belief. Thank you for all you've done for me; it is already more than you know.

Dutifully yours,
Sandy Manmittens

To Reich, champion of the underrated.

"Reality spilled out into the alley like water from an overfilled bowl — as sound, as smell, as image, as plea, as response."

Haruki Murakami, *The Wind-Up Bird Chronicle*

———————

"Maybe I don't understand as much as I should. Maybe I don't make as much sense as I should."

Marilynne Robinson, *Gilead*

PROLOGUE

There's a word for places like this. It's not hokey, not kitschy, and it's not exactly tired. And it's not that this place is uncool, it's just that, well, it's trying too hard. And as soon as they can see you trying, well that's game over for you, pal.

But it's not even 11, and nobody is going to see him in here anyways, not that it would matter much if they did. All that really matters is that this is a bar, that they serve alcohol here, that it's 99% empty, and it's dark, dreary, moody, dangerous. Like it was designed to precisely match his emotions. And my my, how fortuitously it appeared.

There he was, walking down the street, becoming one with the drizzle and the gloom of this, the first overcast, oppressive day in far too long. Ever since it happened, he'd longed for a day like this, a day that matched his mood. But impossibly, it's been sunny and cloudless, perfectly pleasant, for weeks, not the most superb circumstance if you're trying to get in touch with your inner demons. The niceness forced him to stay inside with his blinds closed, illuminated by dank candlelight, with only a few carafes of good scotch and an unannotated copy of *The Count of Monte Christo* to accompany his withering, dithering soul.

But then the weather turned sour, sour enough to match his soul, and he decided it might be nice to go off in search of a stiffie, instead of simply rolling over and retrieving one from his night-table.

The mist and drizzle performed perfectly, coating his face in dramatic droplets, allowing him to get into just the kind of properly furious headspace in which he could relive and revise what happened. Not that the former weather had been stopping him, he'd been replaying it, tweaking it, revising himself pretty much nonstop since it happened. The current version of the event goes like this: he exits the conference room, but instead of leaving in a state of shock, he waits in Pat's office, quietly, in Pat's own chair. The Big Man comes in, relieved grin on his face, sees the man in his chair, and drops his jaw. "Caleb…what… what are you?"

But Caleb doesn't give him the time.

"Alex Pepperidge? Fucking' Alex Pepperidge!?" he screams, "Pardon me, sir, but he's had his teeth in my *ass* for half a decade. Do you really think he could've done what he did if he didn't ride me up? Three months, Pat, I'll give it three months before he fucks you. You know what? Good luck. Good luck with him. Here. Yeah, here," and in his mind, he scribbles down a phone number on a post-it, crumples the thing and tosses it in a perfect parabola, hitting vaunted restaurateur Pat Trier in his wrinkled, wet forehead. "Call me when you realize how three-ways fucked you are. Maybe then, we can both reconsider." He can almost hear, somewhere past the car wheels and the thuderbolt threats, the slamming of the charred-oak door, behind him, the powerful, shaking silence of a man scorned. But of course, that isn't how it went down at all.

Anyways, Caleb went out, walking and muttering and retconning for the umpteenth time, when a vengeful car from across the street switched lanes and passed wicked close to the curb and sent a huge wave of muddy street-water crashing upon him. He stood dripping and smelly and livid on the sidewalks, imagining how good it would feel to take a tire-iron to the driver's head. But then, as if the car and the storm were in on some sick joke, the drizzle amassed power, demonstrating the supremacy of nature by beginning to come down in a fucking torrent. No matter how much Caleb had romanticized the standing in the gloom and getting drenched, it was just too extreme to stand, the reality being much less pleasant than the thought.

So, Caleb huddled himself into a nook off the sidewalk, trying to squelch the water from his slicked hair without disturbing the gel. Across the street, a brightly-lit bank sat at odds with the general melancholy of the day. Caleb stared forward and made eye contact with the dry, safe security guard standing militia-straight behind the double doors, a guy probably making only 55k a year, his dry, safe breath fogging Rorschach patterns on the glass. The guy didn't take his eyes off of him for a second.

Unconsciously grumbling under his breath, Caleb realized all at once what he must look like to a stranger. The grumbling, together with his mangy, unshaven face and wild hair made him look crazed, homeless perhaps, a madman. It suddenly became imperative that Caleb get off the street, get into hiding, get himself a drink.

And lo, kind fate had bestowed upon him its favor, for the nook he cowered in was not an empty nook, but a nook with stairs leading down, down to a door glowing red underneath a neon *BAR* sign. Strange, he didn't see the door or the sign when he ducked out of the rain, but give the man some credit, his perception of late has been clouded by drink and self-pity and rage.

Emerging into the bar was like stepping into his own head. The theme, apparently, was "Black." The long bartop over there and the floor tiles, the grout in between them, even the alcohol on the backbar all held within black vessels. Dingy, but in a sophisticated way, as if the dinginess had been designed and not devolved into. But again, troublingly on-trend. These dark, cavernous speakeasies are all the rage in the more secluded parts of the Pacific Northwest, it was only a matter of time before New York succumbed to their charm as well.

So, here's Caleb, standing at the doorway, dripping, looking around for signs of life. No bartender, even at 11am, which is amateurish. No host, no coat boy. He knows he expects too much, and steps to the bar. Over by the far wall, past a few semi-circular outposts of blood-red bean bag chairs, are two cushioned half-moon booths, low to the ground, made semi-private by pink, sheer curtains. The only other life in here, besides the noisy rats in the walls, are sitting in one. A terrifically obese man with no hair lays back like in an opium fog, casually smoking a hookah, a redhead sprawled semi-unconsciously on his thigh. Neither pay Caleb any mind. He decides to pay them the same. There's a spectral smell of things pickling.

Oh look, here comes the Bartender. Swaggering up, as bartender's do, a great lilt in his step, perhaps he's a bit drunk himself. The man runs a few smooth fingers over his bar's black bottles, admiring them and their streaks of dust, before turning to Caleb, not so much looking at him as looking in him, as if Caleb is sharing a seat with another.

"Something to drink?" the man asks.

"Yeah, something with a little bite, if you please," Caleb asks, suddenly feeling it vital to slick back his hair.

"My specialty," the bartender says, all but winking. Could he possibly be *interested*? On another day, Caleb might explore the prospect further, but for now he's content to watch the man's lower half move down the length of the bar. You can't blame Caleb for his lust, this gentleman is a truly handsome spectacle. Most dive bartenders are as chewed up, clawed and spit-slathered as their establishments, but this guy's impeccable. There's a sharpness to him, you know? Fingernails trim, nose pointed, devilish beard. Peaked lapels (though why wear a three-piece in a place like this?), skin so ghastly white it seems painted on. Dark eyes just about as black as the pupils within them, in fact, they're almost all pupil. Yeah, sure, Caleb is a little smitten, but he'll need a bit more fire in his belly, and maybe some snow in is nose, before he'd dare make a direct gesture. Best to just watch for now.

The bartender returns with two double old-fashioned glasses, each filled a third of the way with dark, amber liquid.

"Both of those for me?" Caleb asks.

The bartender smiles. "In a way," he says. Both men pick up a glass. "Cheers to serendipitous meetings at 11:30 on a Tuesday."

Here, here.

The drinks are knocked back. Bite was an understatement. It burns going down and burns long after.

"A little liquid fire to get you on my level," the Bartender adds. He asks if Caleb wants something else and Caleb says, yeah, but, you know, maybe something sippable. The bartender has "just the thing," and goes to get it. Over his shoulder, he asks, "So, what circumstances bring a man to this type of life so early in the week?"

"Long story."

"You just ordered a sippable drink. Leaving anytime soon?"

"I don't want to bore you. It's work stuff."

"Work stuff or lack of work stuff?" the bartender asks, returning with a grey drink in a snifter. He pushes it up to Caleb, who takes a whiff and winces. "This one's called Brimstone."

"Smells like it."

"It's sippable, but only just. It'll definitely put some hair on your chest. If, that is, you don't have enough already." If that's not a declaration of intent, Caleb doesn't know what is. Maybe the snow isn't necessary after all. Caleb smiles, takes a sip of the drink and shudders. It's strong and bitter and tastes like it smells. Maybe it's some putrid part of his imagination playing tricks, but, god damn, is that the pitter-pop of fresh hairs sprouting on his chest?

"It ain't good, but it gets the job done."

"Truly," Caleb says, smiling while the bartender, rag slung over shoulder, goes to rinse off glassware. "Lack of work stuff, by the way."

"Hmm?"

"About the job. Uhm, lack thereof."

"How long's it been?"

"Two weeks," Caleb says, wincing.

"Ah, a fresh wound. No wonder you haven't any dirt on your face…
or under your nails."

"Yeah," Caleb says, taking as much time as he politely can before
having another sip of Brimstone. Each one produces a larger shudder,
like the liquid expands to further limbs and ligaments within him.

"Was it something *you* did, or was it just the Boss-man shafting
you?"

"The latter, I'd say."

"Fucking bosses! Fucking corporate executives, right? Not a care
about anyone but themselves. Pardon me, I'm assuming you're corporate. But you are, right?"

Caleb suppresses a smile. He's taken pains to appear just so — the
globs of gel slicking back his hair, the tan-hide coat *and* the sweater
vest *and* the pink-checkered oxford collar — a corporate climber with
no shame about what he is. Even on such a dreary day, even with such
ignoble intentions as finding a cocktail before noon on a weekday, he
keeps the appearance. This is not an accident. "That obvious?" he asks,
knowing it is.

"I see a lot of people in this post. I'm pretty good at getting through
to the core of them." The Bartender smiles wickedly. "Mind if I pour
myself something, sidle up beside you?"

Very forward. Caleb isn't going to say no.

"Well, I'm not going to say no," he says, pulling out the seat to his
right. The Bartender takes a black mug full of a thick juice from the
backbar and brings it with him. "What's that drink called?"

"Still playing with the name," the Bartender says, "Thinking about
calling it 'Cerberus.' "I'm detecting a theme."

"A play on 'hair of the dog.' Tell me about this boss of yours."

Where might Caleb even begin? The contrived haircut? The pros-
titutes called to his office in the middle of the workday? The endless complaints via text and call and email about everything from the
ranch dressing being too thick or the servers' outfits being too tight or

the bulbs in the bathrooms not quite the right wattage? Or the late-night drunken demands?

("Caleb! Bring the God-damned Escalade to *The Stone Room*, Freedman and I have some tail waiting for us at *The Washington*."

"Caleb! You gotta go check on whatever the fuck is in my pool filter, Christina just called me freaking out and I, sure as shit, am not rooting around in there at 1:30 in the morning."

"Caleb! Stop here! Freedman's too shy to say it but he wants a fucking pizza so stop here, for Christ's sake, and go fetch us one!"

Caleb, Director of Operations for these last years at five hugely successful midtown restaurants, on the very cusp of being made Junior Vice President, could be found most nights bringing pizzas to house parties, rummaging through Great Neck wine cellars at witching hours in search of some ridiculously expensive, fiendishly elusive '86 *Chateau Margaux* or some shit. If one of Pat's mistresses wanted something, it generally fell on Caleb to provide it. Anything might edge him further towards the elusive promotion.)

Or the vulgarity? The lies? The false promises?

Unable to choose a specific area of import, he imports them all. With each new thought, his blood temperature ticks up a degree, his pitch gets louder.

"No wonder you're here before noon." A red gleam flashes in the Bartender's black, black eye. He asks, "So how did it go down? How did he let you go, exactly?"

Caleb's shoulder begins twitching, one of the many nervous tics he's developed since the firing. The Bartender asks if Caleb is okay. He replies, "Trying to be. Trying to be."

But he isn't, not at all, and soon it all comes out, with historical accuracy this time: the meeting in the big, round room, the board surrounding him, all of them licking their chops like hungry sharks, eager to finally kill this career and chomp on its bones. Pat's at the head of the table, way over there, and you can tell he's suppressing a smile, the corner of his lips just barely quivering. And then, beside his master, Alex Pepperidge, corporate shitsucker, a twig-like thing in overpowering musk with an even twitchier nose than he, smiling, *obviously smiling*, and then he leans in, *he* leans in to Patrick, whispering something that makes Patrick Trier laugh. Guffaw, even. The nerve. The audacity. The disrespect. For years the cold war between Alex and Caleb had been waged savagely but secretly. But then it became hot, hot only for a moment and suddenly over. There was Alex the Cutthroat, slaying the Golden Boy in front of a crowd. It was positively Homeric.

Caleb fought for his name, pled his case. In his daydreams, he followed Pat into his office. In his daydreams, he had a line prepared. In his daydreams, he did the thing with the crumpled-up paper. But hindsight is incorruptible, and daydreams are fleeting. They caught him by surprise. They broke him into pieces right there in that meeting. They told him he was being pathetic. They told him the decision was final. They said he could still preserve his dignity as they ushered him out. He believed them. He actually believed them. As they closed the door behind him, he swore he heard the clinking of glasses.

The Bartender prods him further.

"You mean they didn't even let you speak for yourself?

"They promoted this man, this inferior man, over you?

"Can't you see how calculated it all was?

"Don't you feel betrayed?

"Does your pride not hurt?

"Don't you feel wrathful?"

All the while, Caleb's fists clench tighter, his eyes see redder. The very bar seems to change hue, turning reddish, and the heat seems to rise, the walls seem to sweat. Pools form underneath Caleb's shaved armpits. Cold droplets drip down his torso. The Bartender is behind the bar now, pouring another drink, a drink that burns going down, and then another, and then is beside him again.

"What about your career?

"They made you a pariah.

"It's all his fault, right?

"It's all *their* fault!"

Caleb may not have thought so before, but he certainly does now. He thinks everything the Bartender tells him to. His rage is justified. Blind fury is the only proper response. This is a slight the very universe has designed; his rival and his old boss are servants of a terrible God. The universe is an unjust place —

"— ruled by an unjust God, wouldn't you agree?"

Of course Caleb agrees.

"And this isn't enough for such a God. He'll ruin you, he'll destroy you. Is that not the only way it ends?"

Of course it is!

"You must do something. These are vengeful, petty, spiteful workers of a hateful God with spiders in their hearts. They drink the prospect of your suffering like Satanists drink blood from a skull."

Of course they do.

Then the Bartender's tongue grows long and scaly. Snakelike, it enters into Caleb's ear, pulling the Bartender's face close from within Caleb's own cranium. "What if I said I could help you?"

"What if?" Caleb asks.

"What if I could bring you back to the top, give you all the success, the money, the title you've always craved, a perch so very high up you can look down and sneer upon wee Alex Pepperidge, so high up you can spit down upon Patrick Trier and have it become a fireball by the time it smashes down into him?"

"I'd say that sounds too good to be true," Caleb says, imagining his arms spread out over a smooth, black desk, knuckles hard upon its surface, the open landscape of the world's most magnificent city visible through the giant windows behind him, its meager population at his every beck and call.

"Hmm, I suppose it does that sound that way. But, in fact, all you have to do is sign," the Bartender says, pushing towards Caleb a piece of paper and an old-timey quill dripping with red ink.

"What is this?" Caleb sputters out.

"You know what it is," the Bartenders says. He flings his arm out towards the bar, and all the tops of all the block bottles blow skyward; all kinds of dark animals — snakes and beetles and bats and worms with hides black as onyx — freshly freed, slither and creep and fly out into the bar like some kind of Halloween Hellscape.

"Who — who are you?" Caleb stammers, hallucinating, surely hallucinating, just piss drunk or something.

"You know who I am." Red liquid, like that on his quill, viscous as blood, oozes out from the cracked gout in the wall, staining the words *You Know Who I Am* upon it.

"What do you say?" the Bartender asks, snake's tongue flicking outward. The fat man behind the curtain blows a huge cloud of sulfurous smoke that grows and grows and begins engulfing the bar. "Do we have a deal?"

Caleb looks at the walls. He knows exactly who this is, exactly what this is, and exactly what he'd give up in exchange for all he's been promised. He looks the Devil in his eyes, in his black, black eyes.

"You promise I'll get my vengeance?"

"Yes."

"You promise I'll be so high up I can look down on them? On everyone?"

"Higher still."

"I want to be on top of the world."

"You'll have a corner office there, with a window all your own to peer through. Your station, your advancement, your *meteoric* rise," the Devil says, his left hand absentmindedly twirling an all-black Rubik's Cube, "all that work, you will finally taste its fruits. I'm not as bad as the stories would have you believe, Caleb Swami. I'm an agent of justice. And what's happened to you, sir, is unjust."

That's all it takes to get the pen in Caleb's hand. But first, a pertinent question.

"Will it hurt?"

"Not you."

As he signs his name on the dotted line, one more question.

"How is this going to work?"

"Oh, I have an idea."

"And what is that, exactly?" Caleb asks, rather brazenly.

The Devil smiles, revealing rows of sharpened shark teeth where his molars, incisors and the like should be. All he need say is one word, and he says it:

"Bananas!"

BANANAS!

I

Miranda Swami — petulant, difficult, voice of her generation?, depends who you ask — is staring at her phone.

It's almost eight, which means that the post is already up, which means that in a thousand bedrooms and the booths of a thousand restaurants, people of power and influence are cancelling their dinner plans, calling their friends, refreshing their timelines, putting on their Sunday best and all the makeup they can muster, retweeting and reposting and regramming the news that, *Holy Shit*, Gwami the Seer's first show, long prophesied in various underground rumor mills, is happening, is actually happening, which means dropping everything, which means skipping this evening's PT session, which means calling a Black Car and griping pointlessly about the surge pricing but nonetheless making the quickest trip possible to North Brooklyn, to what an untrained eye might believe is just another dilapidated warehouse amongst hundreds, but where, if the account is to be believed, Gwami the Seer will be showcasing works that will rival only Banksy in price and clout. Those in LA curse their dedication to the sun and warmth; in Miami they're screaming at whoever charters their flights —"Well make the fucking thing fly faster, Gavin!"— and in New York City, *The Big Apple*, they commend themselves for settling in this incomparable hub of art and culture, for they know that there would be no other place in the world where

Gwami the Seer, keeper of 5 million followers and bonafide director of the culture, would choose to ascend to her perch atop the world.

And Miranda Swami, meanwhile, is an entire borough away, tapping her feet and hugging herself tight and thinking that she should've been across the harbor an hour-and-a-half ago. But when Judith LeMeur says she's coming to check out your opening and maybe even write you up in *ArtChicDeco*, there's just no even half-believable excuse for declining. You agree because who wouldn't?

So, you stay and you wait and then your professor gets a text that she isn't coming, and you say, "Wait what? Are you serious?"

And he says, "Yup, she just texted me. Apparently got caught somewhere uptown, won't be able to make it in time. I'm sorry, Swami."

"It's fine. It's totally fine, honestly, I don't even care. This whole thing was a bust from the start."

"Well, it's not, *not* a bust," says Professor Gillibrand, all sharp elbows and shoulders and tweed. "At least *they* seem to be enjoying themselves."

He's pointing to the only other two people in the cavernous, lauded, and selectively bestowed *Eldred L. Apple Exhibition Center*: a couple hanging around by the door. Miranda didn't see them come in, which is insane, because they're obviously begging for attention with all that pastel, *his* huge gauges, *her* rhinestone-choked mini-skirt, and, of course, the Bananas. The Bananas like some skin disease tattooed onto their forearms; the Banana logos splattered like Pollack paint onto any empty patch of clothing: his backpack and her earrings and the pins snapped onto his vest. Her tawny hair dyed the color of bananas, his shoes and the seat of his jeans with banana patches ironed on. One of his eyebrows is dyed yellow. The *intelligencia* of yore wore top hats, frocks and boutonnieres, now they get some dipshit Brooklyn tattooist they read about in a magazine on their Xanax dealer's coffee table to permanently etch a piece of fruit onto their necks. How could it possibly have gotten this far? How could so many people have given themselves over to it?

Breathe, Miranda, she thinks to herself. *They'll get what's coming to them. Don't let them get to you.*

Miranda Swami breathes and looks around the mammoth room, given to only the most promising students in the department, and all of that is well and good and truly humbling, but it's physically too large a space for the meager sixteen pieces that comprise her exhibit. Sixteen pieces that were the culmination of almost two years of ceaseless toil. So much time and intention went into every brush stroke, every bit of laid plaster in this room. If they'd seen all the crushed, disposed canvases, the tubes of biodynamic paint creased and leaky on the tarp in the corner of her room, well, maybe the department would have *marketed* this thing better. It's a travesty that it's this dead, that the only attendees were two girls taking Gillibrand's extra credit bait and this couple with their fucking bananas.

The pieces themselves, however, (and this is Miranda *not* wanting to drum herself up too much) are rev-o-lue-shun-air-ee. Gillibrand told her they're like Picasso got a hold of a Magic-Eye book, so enjoy imagining that. A lifetime of theory and study went into the creation of this exhibit, and standing next to her Professor, her only measly champion, in a room of this size, makes her feel like she's floating in space. She'd rather be floating in space.

Admittedly, she could have done herself more favors, played the politics game, been more forthcoming in class and more friendly with her classmates and not so damn condescending when they talked about their "uptown friends' really very exclusive openings," but it seemed better to hole herself up and commit to the actual work rather than skimping in that regard and making herself into, like, a totally loveable Mandy or a cool, edgy Miri, instead of remaining the private, unknown, aggressive Miranda she's always been. And thus, an empty room, the culmination of all that isolation.

"Miranda."

She has a name that sounds like a cartoon villain. Mer-an-duh. So many short, ugly syllables. Someone on a bus in grade school called her "Miran-*duh*" and it stuck. Such brilliance, such devotion to her craft, and still she struggles to attract ten people to her exhibition. All the while, people like the Twins are getting job offers and internship interviews left and right. It's not fair, it's not, it's unjust, it's...

"Swami."

But if all goes as planned, it won't be another week before the two are one, before Gwami's reach, and Miranda's head can work in harmony, before an end to all the secrecy and pomp is —

"Swami!"

"Professor, I actually have to run, I'm late for a group meeting.

"Oh."

So, the fidgeting Professor, who had just about worked up the unprofessional courage to ask his pupil for a drink, begrudgingly frees her from his presence, disappointed, and Miranda emerges into the night.

Night in the City is as bright as daytime anywhere else. Even the nascent fluorescent glow of the gallery couldn't prepare her eyes for the staggering brightness of freshly-lit New York. The lights from the cars and billboards and phone screens conspire mid-air to create a hazy, half-daylight. But what was once so endearing, what was so fascinating — time's inability to contain the city — now makes Miranda grumble. It's been ruined, ruined by a yellow hue, ruined by the *bananas*.

Passing taxi cabs carry banana advertisements on their craniums, and all the stores have bananas in their displays. Any restaurant with a pulse is yellow-lit and leaning into the trend, and the billboards are all gargantuan bananas spinning on a loop or otherwise just *Big Banana's* logo plastered bigger than a jumbo jet for all to see. All those city-block-spanning video screens play different versions of the same ad: someone enjoying a banana, dancing with a banana, dressed like a banana, laughing with bananas, enjoying life better with the aid of a banana.

Big Banana, the billboards say in letters big enough to crush you, *Go Bananas*.

By tomorrow though, everything will be different, God Willing. All this will lose its sheen. The masses will return to worshipping their televisions, their gods, their health insurance providers, though that may actually be worse. Well, at least it'll be different.

Wanting to preserve a visual vestige of a soon-to-be-shattered world, Miranda asks her *Uber* driver — "Mubarak, right? Yeah, for Miranda." — to take the 9A. She sheds her usual aversion to the bananaic sights that have, like some noxious wildfire, engulfed the lower City's milieu and instead deigns to focus on it all, taking in a long, last look at the horrible thing she's about to destroy.

A world gone bananas.

The very specific path Miranda has asked her driver to take runs along the south bend of Manhattan Island, a set of formerly blasé blocks at the bottom base of big banking buildings that's become, with *Big Banana's* purchasing and repurposing of the Statler-Abramson Building, a banana-themed carnival ringing day and night. Within the expanse of five-ish square blocks, affectionately called *The Big Banana Bash*, or the *Bash*, all the storefronts are painted yellow, street vendors patrol the sidewalks looking for avaricious children, and the rich and famous enter into trendy clubs — *Peel*, *Bunch*, and *Amarillo*, a Latinx spot, just to name a few. The drunk hop from tiki bar to tiki bar, drinking fruity cocktails out of commemorative mugs, everyone hoping to catch a glimpse of one of *Big Banana's* famous board members traipsing around the place, maybe even grabbing a drink themselves as they're rumored to do when feeling saucy. How much the company pays for all that real estate is unknown, but the figure is rumored to be in the low tens of billions. Is it worth it? Who's to say? But the *Bash* attracts crowds in a way the other New York City landmarks now only dream of. The Met has had to increase their entrance admission. The Empire

State Building is mulling an end to their observation deck viewings, citing the impractical cost of elevator maintenance.

"A lot of fun down here, ya?" the Driver asks, costing himself a star. Alas, it's not his fault he's fallen under the *Big Banana* spell. He's not alone, that is. The American tendency towards entrancement preceded *Big Banana's* charm, a charm the masses were wholly unprepared to resist. The populace was like some bookish, four-eyed high school boy struggling with acne, and *Big Banana* the buxom blonde from the cheer team waiting at his locker seeking a math tutor. There's a certain, ahem, power dynamic at play in such a situation.

The *Big Banana* spell...*Sigh*. *Big Banana* came along one day, a rather obscure agricultural company with an unruly mess of plantation sites in Guatemala and a killer name, and decided to adopt the Luxury Commodity Model — mimicking *Gucci* and *Supreme* and *Moet & Chandon* — applying it not to a product, but to the company itself. Their "brand" became their product. They weren't selling bananas; they were selling themselves. And where those companies did everything in their power to make their *products* cool, figuring the company would follow suit, *Big Banana* reversed the paradigm. They made themselves cool; cosmically cool, gravitationally cool. And *everything* else followed.

First, they came for the influencers, the pop stars and the Instagram models and the reality TV moguls, the offspring of celebrities who controlled the culture. Sometime early this year, all at once it seemed, they were snapped coming out of clubs, arm in arm with their latest spouse, looking out over yellow aviators and from under hats with banana prints, their clothes run over with banana tessellations, *Big Banana's* "*Twin B's*" logo plastered everywhere. Virgil Abloh and the designers at *Gucci*, *Louis*, *Chanel* were paid handsomely to collaborate with the agricultural anomaly. All those arbiters of cool, assuming fads followed only their fat fingers, got played, were manipulated into doing *Big Banana's* work for them. They didn't just make *Big Banana* a household name, they made them a premium product. Why buy

Chiquita when *Big Banana* was on the next shelf, and for such an attractive price? For anyone under the age of 40, the choice was easy. And what banana-buying business would stock their shelves with *Dole* when *Big Banana* shipments would literally produce lines out the door?

When was the last time you saw a line out the door at *Shoprite*?

A good source of potassium, colorful and possessing the capacity for risqué association, part of a nutritious breakfast and part of the trend-setter's wardrobe, what couldn't bananas do? *Big Banana* bought the rights to that Warhol painting, the *Velvet Underground/Nico* one, and proceeded to *license it out to the free market*. Ditto the *Twin B's*. Soon, everyone had unrestricted access to two of the coolest, most-powerful logos in the world, so no wonder everyone began to co-opt it.

By then, Virgil Abloh and the designers at *Gucci*, *Louis*, *Chanel*, if they wanted to sell anything at all, were forced to infuse *Big Banana's* logo into their very business plans. That was the cost of doing business.

Now, if you want to dress in all-yellow, smell like bananas, see through yellow contact lenses and spend anywhere from 30-3000 dollars doing it, you can. The beauty of the 21st century, kids: everyone has a choice on how to be exactly the same.

Miranda couldn't stand the fruit even before the brand. She found them patriarchal, phallic to the point of parody. Once they became commercialized, things soured even further. What's cool about a corporation? Nothing. And besides, what they do is so *obvious*. They partake in much wrongdoing, but no sin is greater than that.

And also, for the record, Miranda is not, as Caleb claims, an icon-oclast. She does not dislike *Big Banana just* because they're popular. She's liked plenty of popular things. Lady Gaga, for instance. Popular isn't inherently bad, but there's much bull-shit in the popular. No-body had particularly strong feelings about bananas — what was it, three months? Six months? — however long ago it was when this thing started, so why would they now? Because, suddenly, they're "cool."

Because the greatest marketing campaign in the history of marketing campaigns made them so; forget Apple, there's a new fruit in town.

Nobody was ever going to see through a ruse it's been so much dang fun to overlook. But it was all ever about profit, about control, about power. No corporation in the history of the world has ever had any other motive. To believe otherwise is ignorance, willful ignorance. *Big Banana* peddles in willful ignorance.

But that's what tonight is all about. It's about exposing the company for what they are: market manipulators, capitalistic blowhards who are only different from the rest because they don't need a fifth-floor full of data scientists to know what their audiences want, because they have, get this, actual human intuition. It's scary to see an intuitive corporation. Scarier still to see a cool corporation. It almost defies belief. It's unnatural. Unholy.

Last week, Miranda saw a line of people 50-deep outside a *Dean and Deluca* somewhere downtown, all of them lining up because they'd heard the store was getting in a shipment of *Big Banana* Banana's *the next day*. These fucking people lined up A DAY EARLY FOR BANANAS. ACTUAL BANANAS. LIKE THE FRUIT. Bananas that will taste the same, rot the same, look the same in a fruit bowl or still life as any other. Except they won't. They'll taste better, last longer, look better because they have to. Because everyone wants to believe they will.

What is one lonely little girl to do? What single person is strong enough to stand up to a force like that?

But Gwami the Seer is neither a girl nor a person. Gwami is like *Big Banana*; she's an idea, a suggestion. That's why people follow Gwami in the first place, because she's a suggestion of cool, because she's been accepted to be so. The staggering idea of Gwami is why so many people of power and influence are going to trek to some shoddy corner of North Brooklyn and stand in line to see her molt. They want to be a part of something grand and precedential and communal. Thus, it falls to Gwami to reverse all of this, to challenge the Goliath. So much power and possibility in her hands alone, Miranda practically faints from the nerves. Gwami the Succubus, Gwami the Better Banksy, ready to siphon all the cool from the corpulent company into herself. They'll write about this in history textbooks. They'll write about it on *Buzzfeed*.

The backstreets of North Brooklyn, like the furthest reaches of the Siberian peninsula, are discouragingly depopulated. Thus, they've mostly avoided the skin disease of commissioned banana graffiti and yellow window-paint that has infected the rest of New York. This is the ur-Brooklyn, the last span of the old city. It's been spared much condo development. The once disparate and desolate landscape of old warehouses and condemned buildings have only become, over the past 50-years of gentrification and coalescence, a slightly less seedy version of itself. There's no reason for *Big Banana* to market here because, well, who would see it?

"Are we, erhm, going the right way, miss?" the Driver asks, and Miranda grunts an affirmation. He'll know soon enough. In fact, he'll know right about *now*, because the camera flashes from down the street confirm that, yes, there are people here! There is civilization even here!

"This is fine!" Miranda shouts.

Four-or-so blocks down the road, Miranda jumps out, gives the guy 10 dollars in cash to leave the way he came, and watches as her will be done.

Once he's out of sight, leaving her in the dark, she opens her bag in the dark and cloaks herself. The human, Miranda Swami, vanishes under a scarf wound tight across her face and a turban pulled low over her eyebrows. Any suggestion of a specific human is soon hidden behind mottled, muffling cloth.

An initial fear of reveal, of celebrity worshippers gone mental, surrenders to general excitement as Miranda, feeling compelled to do so, approaches the line of fashionable people waiting outside the warehouse, passing them from a so-called safe distance. It's not like she can ignore them, for its one thing to see your influence in a number on a screen, and another to see it in the caliber of celebrity that waits outside a warehouse for you. The line, at least before it snakes and vanishes around the corner, is all fashionistas and men in scarves, some movie actors, an acclaimed producer or two, lots and lots of models, eye-grabbing outfits on every body, phones in every hand. This is not a place for a smart, *Giorgio Armani* suit, but a place for that suit spray-painted purple, and eyebrows dyed to match. Miranda wonders if they dress like this, hold themselves like this, when they're alone, when they're running to the Bodega for milk, when they're coaxing their cats into the bath. Miranda wonders if they aren't like her in a way, if they don't also contain a second person within them, the one they must summon, the one who *affects*.

The first of many approaching news vans, however, means it's time to go. The collective internet will most certainly rip through all of their videos, and if she's in the background, or God-forbid interviewed, she runs the risk of some intrepid, snotnose prepubescent putting pieces together on *4chan*. Before that can happen, Miranda retreats away from the line and the streetlights and heads towards a shadowy side-path she's never before taken in the dark. Streetlights don't even bother reaching over here, for whom would they be illuminating?

Miranda hates the dark and, more so, what it conceals — demons that await the tantrums of unruly children, and swamp things a-shambling, white men with torture toys. Her steps she makes tepid, her breath she controls as the light dims further. If those in line couldn't see her as she stalked and watched, well, what can't she see now? What stalks and watches her?

The lane soon obscures itself under deliberately untrimmed vegetation, leading only its most intrepid followers to a door carved into the side of the building. You'd have to know it was there, and though she does, she still must grope around for its exterior. Use of this entrance supposedly requires a secret knock, like this is a *Yakuza* meeting, but she lifted a key the last time she was here and simply won't stand for any pomp she herself didn't prescribe.

Just as she opens the door, both a wizard-sleeved arm and a rabid, rank voice reach out to accost her. "Jou're late! Late! Late! Late! Get een here, good Gawd, come on!"

She *told* him she'd be late, but with some people, the rich especially, you know it goes in one ear and out the other unless it's what they want to hear. His hand is strong and unmenacingly firm and smells like firewood as it pushes her down the hallways, this one unlit, same as the next, and finally to the brim of a door with her name on it. One of her names, that is: *Gwami the Seer*, in neon-red light on the door.

"You're going to post dee sign, yes?" he asks, dementedly. Everything said in that horrible stray-cat voice sounds demented. He looks like his voice sounds, too, with the grey hair sticking out from his ears, the John Lennon shades, the lab-coat-looking thing he wears which, from afar, makes him appear a mad scientist, though from this close you can see its intricate threading of $10,000 Merino wool. His name is Zanzibar Al-Feifel, and he's the money behind this whole shebang.

And he is not pleased.

"Yeah, yeah, I'll post it," Miranda says, affecting her Gwami voice, a gruff, roguish grumble conceived concurrently with Gwami's iconic look.

"Good, good," Zanzibar replies, his brogue vaguely Middle-Eastern, maybe also semi-French, but put on, as if it's a chore to bring his pitch to that place. "And late! Late! Too late. Jou said thirty minutes, thirty! Eet ees one hour! One hour!"

"I told you 'late!' *You* said 'thirty minutes.' Have you let anyone in?"

"No, no, they know they moost wait." he says, shooing away her complaints. "We let them een soon, get them roaming. Your entrance, no vorries, same as always planned. Now, queeck, please prepare. Time, time is not wanting to slow for you now."

Even when Zanzibar leaves her alone in the dressing room, she can feel his stress seeping through her skin. It's like an oil slick of anxiety absorbing up through the soles of her shoes.

Fortunately, Miranda has a knack for losing herself in her work, and before the night truly begins, there's work to be done. All the tools are laid out as per her instructions: the wig and the paint and the hairspray, the cans and cans of hairspray. First is the paint, white as plaster, which when applied liberally to her face, affects not just its shade, but changes its entire shape, making her appear portly and rounded. It's not easy to fake-out the cameras, cameras that come at all angles, so she scrubs it into all the folds, the glands, extra around the ears. When all is white, almost offensively so, she goes to work on the hair. The wig is a termite mound of black hair, and she attaches it to her scalp with melted glue. The hairspray helps her work the wig strands up into two curling mounds on either side of her head, Maleficent-like mounds shaped like horns and finished with these golden bangles Mother brought back for her from some Marrakeshi bazaar years ago. They were tasteless but expensive, and Miranda was glad to give them a purpose.

The transformation leaves her part-dragon and part-witch, completely inhuman, but most importantly, completely un-Miranda. That's the important part of this: she cannot appear herself. Gwami is Miranda only in the broadest sense of the word. In effect, they are separate people.

"Miranda Swami" lives in the East Village and rationalizes her decision to pursue a Graphic Design degree instead of Fine Arts as "practical," though really it's because Mother threatened to cut her off financially if she didn't "get serious." Miranda Swami has two roommates, The Twins, she essentially had to bribe into accepting her as their third, and a brother she doesn't get along with. Miranda Swami has trouble remembering her mother's birthday, but her mother has trouble remembering her's, too. Miranda Swami is a physical entity who walks on pavement and paints on canvas, who sometimes stencils and splatters spray paint on bridge-sides and building corners, who likes getting her hands and smocks dirty.

"Gwami the Seer" exists only in the superposition. Gwami the Seer has no physical form beyond Miranda's imitation of her. Gwami the Seer exists as a series of thoughts on the internet, as a set of high-profile pictures and portraits spray-painted and stenciled and splattered on bridge-sides and building corners, in posts and pictures and videos (@GwamitheSeer, like and subscribe, ya'll!) fleshing out the mind and milieu of this fantastical being, one whose keen nose for bullshit and lovingly brutal sense of humor has kept her in the good graces of a far larger part of the internet than most can even wrap their heads around. Gwami the Seer is an idea and a collection of ideas. And Gwami the Seer is, if you please, really fucking famous.

And all they have in common is this: the same mind makes both of them tic.

The mind is an engine, and Miranda Swami's engine powers two separate beings, connected only by a shared set of skills and experiences. The two cannot exist at the same time; that's what nobody would ever understand about the whole get-up, that it isn't a character Miranda is playing, but an entirely different being brought into this world.

And here she is, ladies and germs, the one you all came to see.

Whatever remains of Miranda Swami is left in a heap in the dressing room. What leaves and saunters down the hallway in a flowing black and purple robe bought at a discount Halloween store is Gwami — the woman of the hour — the Seer. And she passes Zanzibar, who nods at some security fellows, as she moves forward through a pair of double doors into her kingdom.

Her kingdom is a converted pediatrician's office, empty except for a standing lamp and a small spotlight, a desktop computer on a folding table, and an uncomfortable baby blue chair flecked with exposed rust, aka her throne.

In a darkened auditorium some 60-feet of plaster, rebar and dried rat carcasses away, influencers in all their various forms flock in finally from the line outside, looking for somewhere to put their tripod, looking for a bathroom, looking to get a quote from the gallery owner, but most of all, looking for Gwami.

They said she'd be here. She's *got* to be here. She *said*.

The warehouse is so deliberately dark, however, that these phone-faced mostly-phonies can't see the exhibits rising up like Sauron's spires in the open parts of the room. They can't see the exhibits, they can't see the curtains covering them, they can't see anything except other blue-tinged faces illuminated by their own phone screens. Soon, there's a growing anxiety among the attendees: there should be more to post right?

They expected so much more to post…

Meanwhile, Gwami logs onto a secure channel on a rinky-dink computer too decrepit to be hacked, and waits to hear the gasps and screams from the other room.

A few moments pass. Two spotlights by the warehouse entrance shoot white light through the hundreds of shuffling ankles. Somewhere on the ceiling a projector yawns to life, coughing a fat blue square onto the wall between the spotlights. Three words in its center: *dialing… dialing…dialing*.

There are the requisite gasps and screams from the other room, and Gwami enters her communion.

A little, green light flashes awake on the upper rim of a computer 60-feet away. Gwami the Seer smiles and the entire structure around her shakes with the thunderous screams of 300 people trying to make the most possible noise while keeping their camera arms steady. Unable to clap properly, they slam their open palms into their chests, like gorillas, like tribal warriors. To Gwami, watching them on a screen, they appear as nothing more than stomping white ankles and the suggestion of faces.

"Well, well, well, what a turnout on a Monday night, and on such short notice!"

The people *whoop* and holler, proud of themselves for having so stolidly braved the surge pricing. Gwami's voice booms outward like the voice of God from two dozen speakers placed strategically throughout the room. She's meant to sound like she's coming less from one specific place, and more from everywhere at once, or like she's coming from inside their own heads.

"You've all come here for a show, for a first glimpse of something that will have a lasting effect on the world you live in. And you all get to see it first. Now, let me tell you a little story.

"Once, *you* all were the people who directed our culture. You decided what was cool, what people wanted to wear, where they wanted to go...who they wanted to be. You were idols in the most religious sense of the word, and you wore that crest with pride, with a certain responsibility."

Someone in the crowd snickers loudly.

"But something has happened to you, something none of you could have foreseen because of how ridiculous it once seemed. A *corporation*, filled with number crunchers, made up of beings better than you at your own game, snuck into your beds while you were sleeping and left a mark on your necks. They manipulated you into doing their work for them, into *working* for them, without pay, without thanks, without compensation. They used you like ragdolls, and like ragdolls, you will all be tossed aside when they grow tired of you. And none of you can see it. You so love being used, being useful, that you've covered your eyes with rags.

"But that is what you're here for today: to have the rags pulled off. I hereby name the perpetrators of these crimes, the crimes of mass manipulation, of misdirecting the culture, the culture *you* all worked so hard to forge."

As she says each of the names, the names of each of *Big Banana's* Board Members, a spotlight snaps awake from the ceiling, illuminating one of the curtain-clad spires below it.

"I give you, The Devil's Row!"

A sign in red neon bearing those words lights up over Gwami's giant, disembodied, virtual head. "Adelaide Ansley, Dominic Lambrusco, Agatha Wolonsky, Jean-Paul Bundi, Derek Cassiopeia, Mary-Jane Kant, Fausto Gutierrez, Naomi Freeman-Rothschild, Cynthia Rodriguez, Arthur Haynes, Cassius Winston, Dolly Meyers, *and…* Cindi Lapenschtall."

Then, when all have been named — with varying levels of dramatism — the lights come up on the whole room. The curtains all fall. *Woooooooosh*, they sigh, adopting the prone position. There are less camera flashes than one would expect. The initial opinion of the onlookers is that the exhibition seems curiously pointless, without teeth. A gaggle of PA's run around to collect the tarps. You might note the continued lack of gasps or screams.

But they come, the gasps and screams and murmurs too, as people approach, get closer to the plastic, 3-D printed sculptures, and see what's really going on here. This ain't no weak-ass wax museum shit.

Once they *get* it, some of the less confident influencers shoot dirty looks over at Gwami's giant, self-assured head, quiet and conspicuous and watching from the wall. Others, finely attuned to popular sentiment, scramble to hide their banana earrings and forearm tattoos in their pockets. Those with no panacea from the embarrassment, wearing banana-printed shirts and shoes and lip-piercings, feel their skin heating up, the sweat pooling up and dripping through their prescription deodorant, the unflappable itches forming on their necks and cheeks and crotches. They aren't used to such humiliation.

The pieces, by the way, are structured to maximize their viewer's embarrassment. They're finely conceived traps. When seen from afar, they appear to be nothing more than incredibly lifelike and amiable statues of the thirteen members of *Big Banana's* Board of Directors. You may call them the Board. Each of the sculptures (3-D-printed somewhere in Queens for a truly staggering amount of money, but, hey, that's what Zanzibar al-Feifel can do for you when he smells dollar signs) shows the target smiling, holding a notebook or a pen or something, standing at a podium maybe, looking like the best version of themselves, and all is well and good, except for if you look through any of the numerous slits cut into the sculpture's person, slits just large enough perhaps for a phone camera to slip in.

Over there by the door is a piece in the likeness of *Big Banana's* outspoken Head of Research and Development, Adelaide Ansley. Famously photogenic, she's mid-laugh with her hands on her hips, back bent forward, whip-straight smile adorning the wood nymph face. Brown hair flowing, brown skin glistening, button nose all scrunched. She probably just finished telling a joke.

If you were to get close, however, and see through the small slits in her abdomen to her insides, you'd see that she's an automaton, full of levers and pulleys controlled by miniature figures of South American dictators, fat-chinned army generals, and white men in suits; they make her move, lengthen her smile with puppeteer strings, hold up the very nose on her face. The gist, one might say, is that Adelaide Ansley is controlled by sinister interests, that her being is entirely un-hers, that she's a congenial face for a whole lot of less than congenial folks.

Cameras start snapping.

Jean-Paul Bundi, the half-Italian, half-Tunisian CFO, is a grotesque gluttonous monstrosity when viewed from within. His real-life paunch is seen as endearing, sincere, but in his internal view, it's got its own face, a ravenous maw sucking money, money, money, wallets and old lady's purses into a bottomless black pit. Miranda likes this one, but Zanzibar thought it was too on the nose, which, she knew, it was.

Though so much went into *Big Banana's* rise, its Board of Directors were doubtless the most important part. The Board was the truly, truly impressive thing about *Big Banana*, the proof beyond all doubt that they were masters of the internet and masters of culture. They knew that whenever a new fad or business or individual moves from obscurity into the popular crosshairs, the investigative force of the internet, ravenous for scandal and outrage to feed on, will begin *snuffing* for wrongdoing, for dingy pasts, for crude comments and rank representations. And yet, car companies keep burying emissions loopholes as if nobody will find them. White, male CEO's keep groping women, as if every single thing anyone does isn't captured online and made viral. But *Big Banana* understood the game and the pitfalls of their contemporaries. They gave the internet something to consider first.

Every member of *Big Banana's* 13-member Board of Directors is a Person of Color or identifies as female or is a member of the LGBTQ+ community. Some are all three. They're all of them personable as hell and do the interview rounds like pros, each with incredible smiles and stories, speaking humbly about their struggles growing up with single or alcoholic parents, in destitution while their brothers and sisters sold drugs and served time, choosing the be the change they saw in the world, describing their ascendancy as a mark of upswinging society, something to be proud of, like they're everyone's children or something. To attack *Big Banana*, to assail the company, was to assail the very Board Members who led it, and thus the marginalized populations they represented.

They're so wrapped up in the framework and decision-making of the company that it almost seems *Big Banana* is some child's lemonade stand run out of a garage, where the product and the producers are really one entity, i.e. you're paying for the kid's smile, not necessarily the puckering juice. Or what about this: if your mother sold pies at the market, but used high-fructose corn syrup and aspartame when she made them, you'd still support her, right? I mean, she's your mum! You're not a complete asshole. Well, take that phenomenon and apply it to a grand scale. *Big Banana*, the genius laid bare.

The internet, of course, loved them from the first. Influencers and thinkpiecers lauded the company's progressivism, vocally investing in their product and their bottom line. That alone could have catapulted them into any number of Forbes articles, but when combined with the insanely effective branding? An organic banana company with a sense of humor and a catchy name led by a highly-accomplished team of underrepresented cultures and gender? The glass ceiling lay below them in shards. They were revolutionary.

But look closely at anything, and you'll see its cracks. Miranda is a product of the internet, gets her kicks there, and she *knows* that beautiful images almost always belie terrible truths. All of these people rising up from complete obscurity at once to become heads of a multinational corporation, seems fishy, right? So, she did a little digging on the Board, this Board that is so lauded and respected and beloved, and, uhm yeah, these people certainly seemed to be involved in some shady shit. After reading in some hellishly progressive message board about *Big Banana's* ruthless expansionary tactics in South America, the deals made with warlords and dictators and macho military men, hearing distasteful rumors you too can hear if you keep your head low enough to the ground, Miranda became fully convinced these people were frauds, frauds with nice smiles and lovely things to say, frauds with hidden pasts they'd just *love* to make unjudgeable before anyone could begin mulling a trial.

And *that* was the inspiration for this whole exhibition: someone needed to say something about the Board because nobody was. People don't listen to what they don't want to hear. Although the truth is unguarded, is available to anyone interested, exposing oneself to such a thing kills the very fine dream, kills the buzz, forces a horrible hangover. The culture won't destroy one of their own without good reason. Sometimes you need to strap the people down and cinch open their eyes to get them to see. Horrorshow.

Besides, compared with her schoolwork, this was a leisurely breeze. Zanzibar put up all the money, outsourced all the labor, and only the ideas and the sketching were left to Miranda. And the ideas — remember, we're talking about political art — were, ahem, easy to come by. Corporate slime has a million faces all hanging up on the wall for your perusal; all you have to do is climb up and select the correct one, fit it, and forget it.

And in 48 hours, when the world is sufficiently drunk with anticipation for Gwami's next move, when the interview offers have been crammed so tight into the mailbox it's threatening to burst, Miranda will publicly shed both of her skins — the Madonna and the Whore — and reveal the single ego beneath the two of them. Tonight isn't just about bringing down *Big Banana*, it's about burning them and Gwami both to the ground and then rising up, a fresh-faced phoenix, from the ashes.

These are the melodramatic terms of our fair heroine.

How's that for "getting serious," *Mom*?

It's just a shame, and Miranda will always stand by this, that Cindi Lapenschtall, CEO, had to get mixed up in all this. A shame. Necessary, of course, but a real shame.

Regardless of the guests' embarrassment and the guilt Miranda feels for slandering Cindi, a woman she admires and emulates, the show goes on more-or-less as planned. There are some smutty words thrown at the face-on-the-wall by angry, humiliated influencers who are soon carried out by security — great news for the next person waiting in line —, and all the hip journalists surround Gwami with their mailbag questions:

"How does this kind of success feel?"

"What are you going to do next?"

"Can we talk about the outfit? I mean, what gives?"

"Can't you give us a little hint about your next project?"

"What's the hottest brunch spot in Williamsburg?"

You can't blame them for such weak questions, they're out of their element: nobody has ever interviewed Gwami the Seer before. Each of these questions could make or break their "journalistic" careers. Let them flounder, the harmless buggers, they're trying their best.

Most of the other goers, even those wrapped in banana gear, form small, introverted groups, comparing editing softwares, discussing what kind of filters will work best over this and what hashtags will attract the widest audience, trying to diminish their embarrassment by pretending they can't feel it. A futile kind of ignorance.

And Gwami's face is laughing towards the crowd and lording over them and soon most of the goers have even forgotten what they're wearing and where they are because they're too busy laughing with the face and hanging on her words and just reveling in being one of the few special presences at this historic happening. A few lucky ones get invited at random to engage the great gaze in lively conversation. Gwami discusses elephant rearing, childbirth, the Dark Web (or what she knows of it), and Lewis Carrol. She's the belle of her own ball. And then, as if the shadows of Blitz planes appear on the ground, all goes silent.

The silence starts over at the gallery entrance and spreads inwards. By the time it reaches Gwami, it's afflicted the entire space, and even the camera flashes cease. Phones go down to hips; the incessant murmuring momentarily remains in mouths. All one hears are the galloping breaths and the soft heartbeats, the *clip-clop* of two highheels oscillating on the tile. A tangled mess of black cloth is pulled along from the gallery entrance towards its center.

Leading the black frock is a figure creamy of skin and bouncy of hair. More beautiful in person than Miranda ever could have captured in plastic, Cindi Lapenschtall, standing a majestic 6'4 in her stilettos, strolls through the place, coolly unresponsive to the attention paid to her. No security surrounds her, but nobody'd dare approach anyways. The presence of one cultural goddess is enough to incite frenzy in a population of influencers, but two? You can see the overloading amygdale rebooting. Unsure of where to lend their attention, everyone remains motionless, silent, unthinking…husked.

Now, if you don't know Ms. Cindi Lapenschtall, you just haven't been paying attention. *Big Banana* CEO; *Time Magazine's* Most Influential Person of the Year. Multi-millionaire distributor of grants, currier of bipartisan political favor, fighter for minority rights, for the rights of women, and most important of all, a Trans Woman of Color. It only takes half a brainstem to understand that Trans Women of Color are the most at-risk population in the world. 25% of all Trans people have attempted suicide, with a ridiculous 67% depression rate within the community, and that's just the start. 47% of Trans people are sexually assaulted at some point in their lives, and for Trans Women of Color the numbers are even higher. 25% of Trans people are HIV positive, but that's 56% for Trans Women of Color! 56%! And 67% of all murdered Trans People are People of Color. Ridiculous numbers, horrible numbers, medieval numbers. Humbling, damning, depressing numbers. And then onto the sordid scene steps Cindi Lapenschtall, with a mane of curly brown hair and skin the color of mocha almonds, rising high in the finance sector on the back of the genius investments she made with the dough she'd put away working three jobs, one behind a bar, one behind a desk, one behind bullet-proof glass at a *TDBank*. Suddenly, she gets a position at *Big Banana*, is named Chief Executive Officer, and in the press release, they say she's everything they ever wanted in a CEO, smart and charming, efficient and hard-working, a representation of all that's good with America.

And they're right.

More a master of marketing and public outreach than of corporate affairs, she's always on TV, on podcasts, on radio shows and on *CSPAN* lobbying for the interests of the poor and disenfranchised, donating whole schoolhouses, paying for college tuitions, stopping at elementary and middle schools across the country to talk about what being Trans is like, what it means to be different and what it means to be accepted anyways. Any way you look at it, even through the angry, suspicious lens through which Miranda seems to look at everything, she's a god-damned heroine. And she's loved and lauded as such.

Miranda has always felt a kinship with the woman. There's an authenticity in her that doesn't exist behind the smiles of the other Board Members. Thus, Miranda wasn't sure how to represent Cindi in this exhibit. There could be no takedown of the woman, nothing brutal like the others, yet she was still a key member of *Big Banana's* Board and thus theoretically complicit in any of the evil the corporation carried out. So, Miranda, in the dark on Cindi's true intentions, tried to reflect this in her piece.

So, if you look through the little slits in Cindi's smiling figure over there, you won't see a damn thing. Just darkness, emptiness, nothing. It's supposed to reflect a certain unknown about her character, as well as act as a kind of exoneration for both the artist and the subject. For Cindi, it's the artist acquiescing to her subject's *perfect* superficial face, and for Gwami, it's a bit of armor against accusations that she's desperate to find fault.

Of course, Cindi's presence wasn't planned; she's too big a fish for even Miranda to have attempted to hook, probably the most famous person in the world, give or take. And, you know, you generally don't invite someone to their own funeral. Somewhere nearby, Zanzibar starts feeling faint.

All the while, Cindi, redefining elegance and panache with every step, takes sparing looks into some of the exhibits, probably not thrilled to see her closest coworkers painted so unflatteringly. It's all a timing thing, this slow walk. She'd have to be an idiot not to know that time has slowed, waiting until she peers inside her own facsimile to regain normalcy. Content right now to meander around, however, she steps through groups of onlookers as if stepping around sid walk vomit. But the exhibition is designed as a kind of whirlpool, or an apostrophe. Every onlooker eventually makes their way to the center, and so does Cindi Lapenschtall.

Slowing, Cindi takes more than a moment approaching her Doppel. The sculpture has her fist up in solidarity, in power, a smashing fist, the kind you don't want pointed at you, that would destroy you not just with the bluntness of its knuckles but with the promise of force behind it. Cindi tilts her head, seeming to betray the slightest hint of a smile. As a peer-reviewed art critic herself, she might have feelings about the style and the shading. Then she peers through the slit in her torso, seeing within herself as Gwami sees her.

While there aren't exactly tears in her eyes when she pulls back, there's a certain shimmering wetness. Her face flashes pale white, and her mouth hangs open stupidly. Tightening her hold on the corners of her dress, she looks up at Gwami's fat, projected face, their eyes meeting for the very first time. Even though satisfied time snaps back into itself, though the room explodes with phones flying upright and cameras flashing *boom* and *bang* hither and thither, though both the CEO and the Seer are swarmed by questions and screams and reporters and photographers and fans and fans and screaming, aching fans, they two are alone in a quiet little world.

In this personal universe, neither a word nor a thought is exchanged in their stare, no understanding nor desire. They are simply two people who've affected the other, both trying to accurately gauge the extent of that effect. Like a strong acid trip, the experience in hindsight will seem to have lasted days and minutes all at once. When this world melts, Cindi will have left what feels like a burning mark on the inside of Gwami's skull. She'll wonder if she left the same on Cindi's.

Gathering herself with the same coolness with which she entered, Cindi Lapenschtall, flanked on both sides by a groping gaggle of less-influential influencers taking unauthorized pictures and holding out sharpies, exits the gallery. Her steps a little quicker, her pace brusque. Some onlookers will say they knew what was to come when they saw her face, her famously deliberate face, normally drizzled by a smile or furrowed in thought, here completely devoid of control, all wriggling and wrinkling and twitching uncertainty.

Zanzibar, fearing a riot, turns off Gwami's face and maximizes all the lights. Disappointed stragglers eventually limp out of the building, the show unceremoniously over, forced to sober up from a night of unmatchable excitement. And worst of all, the service in this part of Brooklyn is so bad hardly anyone can post. Cars threaten to take *over twelve minutes* to arrive at the pickup point. A collective tantrum is thrown on the sidewalk outside. Someone named Jezebel tells her friend Arabella they're "like, definitely going to get mugged out here."

A small miracle of foresight, camouflage, and cleverness allows Miranda to mostly evade Zanzibar's spiraling anxiety —

("But what if they speen thees? What if-vwee become untouchable? Thees pieces, very very expensive, what if-vweee don't get thee money? Even close to eet?"

"Zanzibar, calm down. They're Gwami pieces. What do you think is going to happen between then and now? It'll be fine, now please, let me change in peace.")

— and get six or seven blocks away unseen, where she finally removes her scarf, her turban, her heavy jacket, and calls a car to take her home. She allows herself to become Miranda Swami again, leaving the cloaking paraphernalia in someone's trash can. For the final time, perhaps, she lets Gwami the Seer dissipate into the ether, believing wholeheartedly she can be culled back from the nothingness whenever Miranda so chooses.

🖋 🖋 🖋 🖋 🖋

The car hits a bump in Dumbo and the crown of Miranda's head hits the handlebar above the window.

What a night she's had. Opening two galleries as two different artists, how many others can lay claim to an experience like that? If anyone remembers her, she hopes its as a pioneer in the field of identity, and how we all contain multitudes.

"Miss. Miss? We are here."

Door shut. Steps climbed. Hallway windows gazed through longingly. Home. Rest, or the promise of it, at hand.

Katie and Kathy — The Twins — couldn't be sitting any closer to the TV. Neither sees fit to greet Miranda when she walks in. Perhaps they're concerned that sudden movements will disrupt the steaming bowl of soup on the table by their knees. One of their entertainment networks is doing an evening devoted to the Gwami opening, essentially an extended breaking news segment seeing as nobody knew about the event until three hours before its start.

"Miranda, did you see?" Kathy asks without turning. Kathy and Katie, Katie and Kathy, identical twins with identical minds. Identical voices, laughs, fluttering laughs and fluttering eyelashes. Katie and Kathy, underneath two queen's nests of cropped blonde hair, live for this kind of coverage: the intrigue, the glamour, the shine. "Apparently even Kandy Wu couldn't get in. Imagine that…Kandy Wu."

"Is this the Gwami thing?" Miranda asks, stepping forward, putting her bag down. In the glint of the refrigerator, she sees there's a smudge of white paint still on her cheek. She scrubs it off, silent as she can, with the back of her palm.

"Yeah, it looked insane."

"Totally insane. Cindi Lapenschtall showed up," Katie adds.

"So weird, right?" Kathy asks.

"So weird. I mean the whole thing was like maligning her," Katie decides.

"Did a lot of people go?" Miranda asks, planning an exit from the conversation.

"Like all of Soho."

"Here, look," Katie says, holding her phone up for Miranda to come inspect. It's someone's uploaded video of the line outside the warehouse, a much longer line than the one Miranda originally saw coming in, one riddled with celebrities shoving cameras out of their faces, with turtle-necks and circular glasses, writing in notebooks while women in banana-printed crop-tops look bored from behind their sunglasses and over their cigarettes.

"That's wild," Miranda says, pouting.

After a moment, Katie asks, "Oh shit, how was your show?" The Twins share a knowing but guiltless glance. They are not as sly about it as they think.

Miranda, confused at first, realizes they're talking about *her* show, not Gwami's. Fortunately, there's a response prepared for this. "Yeah, you know, a quiet start. But good, really. Really, really good."

All millennials know the importance of everything being "good." There is no bad, there is no disappointing, there will be no tears nor angry rants about the pointlessness of it all. Everything is always "good," in homeostasis, and no amount of failure must ever reach the ego. Want to satisfy your folks, impress your relatives, and shrug off the finance majors who pollute the downtown bars? Tell 'em everything's *great*, because they'll surely be telling you the same thing. Don't want to appear lesser. Don't want to appear unsuccessful. Don't want to appear unhappy.

The Twins shrug a response; is this agreement or dismissal? Miranda hasn't the energy to figure it out. She traipses to her room without another word. Neither of her roommates seem to care.

Sleep comes aggressively. Being two people tires one out, and Miranda falls asleep without brushing her teeth, very un-Miranda, her eyes still darkened with eyeshadow.

In the black of first sleep, she dreams of drowning in a sea of bananas, the fruits taking on liquid form and melting into a goo, falling from the sky to overtake and crush her. She's in some kind of lab beaker, or else some other receptacle with glass walls. Though she bangs on them with all her might, and though a large crowd of faceless observers sit in bleachers outside, popcorn and candy and big-ass sodas in hand, there is no spare invitation to salvation. The bananas fall from the sky and turn to goo and eventually swallow her whole. She begins drowning on their sweetness. This is not their intended use.

Then, sometime in the bleakest night, a blood-curdling scream explodes outward from the living room. Miranda, ready to leave her dream anyways, instead rockets up out of it, and then out from her room.

"Jesus Christ, what, what's happening?!" she cries, heaving, panic having stolen her breath.

Katie has her face buried in the couch and appears to be sobbing. Kathy's face is pressed literally right up to the TV, and she's pleading "no, no, no, no, no, no."

Living in New York, one is always half-expecting the next great terrorist attack, so you can understand why Miranda's heart slams against her chest, sensing present danger. The TV shows a black, moonless sky behind the zenith of a luxury-apartment building uptown. At the base of the image, the red flare of ambulance sirens make it appear as if the building is falling down into a fiery, hellish pit. But it's not, Miranda is.

It's not a terrorist attack, it's somehow worse.

The chyron says it all. *Big Banana CEO Dead by Apparent Suicide at Age 32. Big Banana* CEO Dead by Apparent Suicide at Age 32.

"Cindi Lapenschtall dead by apparent suicide at age 32."

The girls wail into pillows and into their fists.

Looking out the window, so many lights that should be off are turned on; so many people pace in front of their TVs. Miranda experiences vertigo. The whole world shifts on its axis. She falls against the refrigerator.

The TV says something about a note, or, rather, a post. Something about Tumblr. Something about Gwami. Something about an opening. Miranda doesn't hear any of it. There's a screaming pain in her abdomen that drowns out all the noise and makes her vision go white. She doesn't hear the TV and she doesn't hear the crack of her skull hitting the tile as she falls.

Ask any millennial about silence, and they'll tell you that it's weird. Really weird. There's only one time any of her generation might actually expect silence: at the very end of the world.

BANANAS!

2

FOR IMMEDIATE RELEASE: 09/09/19

AN INFORMAL STATEMENT ON THE UNTIMELY PASSING OF OUR CEO, CINDI LAPENSCHTALL

At 12:18 A.M. EST, we received unimaginable news. You have likely already heard. We will say only this: losing our beloved Cindi isn't just difficult because she was a close friend, a wonderful teammate, or a guileless leader, but because of what she represented. Nay, what she continues to represent. For all women, for all people of color, for the entire Transgender community, she showed that there is a way to the top, and a place for you there, that there is no social limit too powerful to keep the gifted from excelling. Attitude, perseverance, cunning and wit, she continues to be a beacon of hope for all people, regardless of background, of stereotype, of stigma. Losing Cindi is like being shot. The wound will never fully heal. Always it will remain on our collective abdomen, a reminder of the incredible human we lost. Of the leader taken from us.

We will not sit here and point fingers. Suicide is a most awful sin, and there is never one party at fault. Not Cindi's struggles with mental health, nor any individual, regardless of what any post or note proclaimed. But we will say this: vitriol and hate are strong in the world, and those who know so little do seem, more than ever, to act as if they know a lot. We condemn vitriol and hate in the strongest possible terms. Be aware of your actions, because they all have consequences. Be aware of yourself, and be aware of others. Be kind to them and be supportive of them, even if it means swallowing your own pride, even if it means silencing your own opinion for their sake. Love your fellow humans. If you cannot understand them, or if you must indeed hate, at least communicate. Open a dialogue. All of this senseless meanness, it's too much. Let this be a lesson to all of us on how to treat our fellow human, and now, how to forgive.

If you or a loved one is struggling with suicidal thoughts or actions, even if it may not be obvious, please, please, PLEASE call the National Suicide Hotline at 1-800-273-8255. Seek help. You're too important for us to lose. And nobody, no matter how strong and smiling and brave, knows the size of the hole they leave behind when they take themselves from this Earth.

God bless us all. God bless our dear Cindi. She left quite a hole. She will be missed.

###

God, it's perfect. See what they did? They didn't name an individual writer. They didn't name Gwami either, but of course they didn't need to. Cindi did. The last communication from the departed CEO, a short and obsequious post on her personal blog, admitted in relatively transparent terms that it was Gwami the Seer's "fabulously, daftly critical expose on myself and my dear colleagues," that confirmed many of the anxieties she had about herself, that she was empty and a fraud and that, with this truth of herself laid out before her, she couldn't bear another day of looking in the mirror, at her own false, haunted reflection. Cindi's post was brutal, if maybe a tad self-indulgent. But what are we to do? Critique a suicide note? Nobody'd dare.

The post was taken down but not before it was downloaded and shared some 123-million times. If you have internet access, you saw the note. That was last night; the Press Release is this morning. If the post was a sword thrust through Gwami's skull, the Press Release is the armored body behind it, the chain mail and the shield; every-thing but the blade.

How could you hate on *Big Banana* now? How could you see them as anything but victims of a horrible, defiling act? Cindi's suicide didn't just tear the fabric of pop culture, it tore a family apart, the *Big Banana* family, the grieving and bereft *Big Banana* family. *Big Banana*: the world's first celebrity corporation now become the world's first corporate victim, worthy of all the pity and prayers you can spare. They announced a series of candlelight vigils. All the remaining 12 Board Members will attend. The vigil is being held, not around the *Bash* or the Statler-Abramson Building, but in a park in North Brooklyn, some three square-blocks from Gwami's show. Somehow, that doesn't feel like an accident.

She's been reading the press release forever it seems. Her head, bruised but not bleeding, thumps metronomically in a bastard time nobody else can hear. The Twins have been crying in their room for the better part of eight hours. A part of her, a teeny part trying it's damndest to feign *gravitas*, is telling her this isn't as big a deal as it seems, that the winds of the internet may blow roughly now, but that this too shall pass, as all storms do. But this is one big storm, and it's coming headstrong for the mainland.

For your perusal, some highlights from the internet's newfound style of speaking to/about @GwamitheSeer:

@GwamitheSeer should REVEAL HERSELF for all to see! This is a CRIMINAL. SHE MUST BE PROSECUTED!

#MurderGwami because it's what she deserves.

Let's take the evil cunt @GwamitheSeer and rip off her mask and stone her to death! No punishment too terrible for this FUCKING BITCH.

Let a pack of wild dogs tear the flesh from @GwamitheSeers corpse. Let her family feel the hurt that she made us feel. Trample the bitch and let the pigs and methheads fuck her corpse.

#UunmaskGwami and make her pay!! #UnmaskGwami!!!

She deserves to have her life ruined!!!! #UnmaskGwami then burn her alive!

#UnmaskGwami
#UnmaskGwami
#UnmaskGwami

Others are somehow even more graphic in their desire to see Gwami exposed, raped, ruined, destroyed, maimed, mutilated, burnt and drowned and suffocated and crushed to death by the hooves of a hundred mad horses. Some are explicit, some are purposefully provocative, some are even rather eloquent in their calls for an execution.

Nothing is scarier, however, than the hashtag sweeping the globe. *#UnmaskGwami* isn't as much a wish as it is a call-to-arms. The collective voice of the internet coagulated into one violent shout, hoping to reach the ears of the dormant demons that swim in the subterranean lakes under the internet.

These are the beasts, the hackers, the dark web operatives, the shadow corporations, the masters of code and data analytics. They who can find and trace and connect data from disparate sources, they who effortlessly pull off impossible capers — tearing down a Fortune 500's whole computer system, or, say, knocking out power to entire cities — can surely find and reveal the identity of some internet celebrity, do the hard work so someone with less skill and more fanaticism can take an ax or a Desert Eagle to said celebrity's newly-exposed noodle.

When her phone rings mid-daydream, Miranda nearly faints from fright. She hesitates before looking over at it, peering at the horror movie screen from between two eye-covering fingers, but it's only

Lakshmi. Thank God, actually, it's Lakshmi; if anyone knows what to do, how to proceed, what to think and how to respond, its him.

Let's allay your suspicions up-front: yes, it's *that* Lakshmi. Eric Lakshmi. Just the name can start a gaggle of preteens screaming, or streaming, lol. You might know him as @ELThunder88 (for you devotees who knew him back when he was a mere streamer, before his content-minded brain started churning out the stuff that would ignite his superstar career), @LakshmiThaTrapGod (assumedly, this is how you first were introduced to the man, with his dozens of Vines-cum-Youtube-Storylines, the handle that brought you the *Brutus and Champagne's Halloween* series, the *Desperate Times in the Back of a U-Haul* miniseries, and, most salient to our story, *Eric Lakshmi In: The Lair of Gwami the Seer*, a quaint little couple of low-production-value videos that were the public unveiling of then-unknown Miranda Swami's, ahem, rather popular Gwami the Seer character) or, if you've spent the last five years under a rock and just emerged of late, @EricLakshmandCo (his now far-reaching content brand producing all sorts of things: music videos and mini-documentaries, celebrity interviews [like that one with Gwami from the beginning of the year] and those uber-high quality, fake movie trailers that have been making the rounds).

Eric Lakshmi, who has more credit than anyone other than Miranda for Gwami's success, he the famous streamer who saw something in her wild online blog ramblings, who reached out *to her*, who nurtured the character from her inception, who put his whole brand on the line for the sake of Gwami, who's been the best friend and the best mentor — and what's it matter that he lives three thousand miles away and that they don't talk like they used to, and how he got *weird* after the whole thing a few years back, who cares about any of that? — he'll know what to do. He's here to save her.

"Lakshmi, Thank God, I —"

"Jesus, you're okay. Thank God."

"What do you mean, 'Thank God?'"

"Well, it's just…this has got to be really hard on you, and, I don't know, my mind went to the worst places."

"Look, just because —"

"I know. Please, just…I know. I'm sorry, I didn't mean to insinuate… but I just, well, it's bad. It's really bad, and I had this stupid thought that…well I just woke up and saw everything and my first thought was —"

"Yeah, I appreciate it, Lakshmi, really, but honestly, I've got a lot —"

"Don't use my name again, please. And don't use yours. Just, just let me talk, okay, we have to get right to the point because I don't know who might be listening, so I'm just going to let you know what I think you should do, okay?"

Holy shit.

"Okay."

"I saw as soon as I woke up. It's the only news anywhere. It's like 9/11 probably was. Every article that talks about Cindi talks about Gwami, and every article is talking about one of you, and, and, and, well, a ton of unauthorized pictures from the Brooklyn gallery have gone up. They're all over. It's all over. It's done. For your own safety, you have to end it."

"What do you mean —"

"You have to delete everything. Scrub yourself from everything, every page and every post and every blog, you have to delete it all. The only way people are going to forget about you is if they can't see or hear you anymore. If you have any videos or posts up, someone could, I don't know, track your IP or something and get your address and then maybe even your name and all it takes is one stupid person with Jodie Foster's voice in their head to do something really, really bad. I've been researching. This is about your safety, and honestly, it doesn't matter how popular Gwami was —"

"*Is* —"

"*Was*! Maybe you're not seeing what I'm seeing, but what I'm seeing is an apocalypse. There are mass mobs of people calling for your execution, and *nobody* is saying otherwise. Always, almost always, there are a million thinkpieces up by now, counter-arguments, you know? Every side gets a say? But there's nothing. There's only hate and it's scaring me. Really scaring me. Some of these people, they're really nasty. They've done nastier things for a lot less of a reason."

"People have been trying to figure out who I am for a long time though? Why —"

"Because *then* it was just about curiosity. It was like an Easter egg hunt nobody really wanted to win. Now it's a bounty hunt. You have to understand what you're dealing with. *Who* you're dealing with. These people, they want blood. Whatever hand you had in the suicide aside, the internet *believes* you were the primary factor. *You* might've pushed her off that building for all anybody cares. As we speak, hundreds of thousands of people are looking through everything you've ever posted, every single one of your interactions, to see if they can get a clue as to where you live, where you went to school, anything. Think of the publicity, the fame, the satiation from finding you, exposing you, letting not just the internet, but *the world*, have their way with you.

"But *you* can escape Gwami. You can delete her and destroy her. That's up to you. But if it gets to *you you*? I don't want you to have to destroy yourself. And it might come to that. Please, you had a good run. A great run. You were amazing. Now pivot, we'll do something else, figure it out. You have the beauty of anonymity on your side. Whatever your hand was in this, you can get out. So, get out."

"But I —"

"I have to go. I love you, but please, please don't take too long. Just trust me and do as I say. I know this is painful, but you have to let go of her. You're already gone from everything of mine. I had to, I'm sorry. I'm so sorry, but it's time to let Gwami die. And soon. When it's all done, call me back. Until then."

And the line goes dead. *Click*. In vain Miranda yells, "Lakshmi! Lakshmi! Lakshmiiii!!" into the receiver, but he's gone. He refuses to pick up any more of her calls. He leaves her on read.

She's actually, truly alone in this.

There are bubbles in her stomach, all acid and hot hot hot. They fly up from the melting belly bile and pop against her throat, the burning burning all over her chest and shoulders until the room is like 1000 degrees and her skin is so, so itchy she wants to peel it off just to be rid of it. Red flashes, hot flashes, red and a moment of black and then the confusion in her chest has a new brother, a just born infant brother crying a piercing cry in Miranda's ear: it's Fear.

What is Lakshmi really asking her to do? This is more than deleting an account or two or twenty, this is about murder. It's the post-birth abortion of a living, breathing person, a person more real to so many than even their closest friends. It's a murder of Miranda's entire future. This was supposed to be the time, the time when Gwami and Miranda would finally coexist in the same form, but now Gwami has to die? She has to die — Miranda essentially has to carve out a portion of her soul — or it might be the ur-Miranda, the engine, who dies in her place.

And she hasn't even had her coffee yet. Or a cigarette. But surely, the apocalypse can wait fifteen minutes.

All in all, the doing takes longer than the contemplating. Not for any reason other than the accounts all need to be deactivated individually, and across all the disparate platforms there are something like 24. Her video archives, her posts across all platforms, her pieces, her websites, her marketplaces, all of them torched and destroyed, all the advertising contracts forfeited, the dollar flow dammed. Doesn't matter anyways, the advertisers (the very few she allowed to sponsor her in the first place) fled in the night. By noon, there is no trace of her in any annal of the internet. Individual archives of her work compiled in private by former zealots are all that is left of Gwami the Seer. They'll exist onward like exhibits in a Museum, showcasing artifacts of a lost and misunderstood civilization.

Now she's supposed to get ready for class.

The Modern Millennial Woman can compartmentalize much heartache, keeping her daily routine unaffected by breakups or death or suicidal thoughts, end-times prognostication or flu diagnoses. Classes may still be attended, in which hands are raised and homework assignments are submitted on time. Insomniac bags under eyes may be hidden with tasteful and expensive makeup, and looking the part is half the battle. Perhaps a close friend would notice the dandruff and the split-ends, the malaise behind the eyes, but there are no such friends to speak of. There haven't been in years. If there were, perhaps their sweet and concerned presence might pry loose the pain from behind the Modern Millennial Woman's, Miranda's, strained eyelids, her cracked voice. But there are no such friends to speak of.

She doesn't leave her room much, but who'd notice that? The Twins, her theoretical roommates, have been off on the first leg of their new *Big Banana* internships, invitations to which were passed around with opium-pipe-languor to most of the Graphic Design students, although there were some *fascinating* exceptions. They're always getting home late from drinks with coworkers, from spons-ored events at galleries and uptown bars and the homes of well-connected execs. Miranda, though semi-curious about the exact nature of their new positions, won't bring it up, afraid that any interaction will lead to some long, painful dissection of the Cindi/Gwami debacle. Miranda is a lady with opinions after all, though it sometimes takes some finagling to get them out in the open. Not ever a fan of those gossipy, surface interactions the Twins and their ilk so love, now they may actually destroy her. Not worth finding out, if she does say so herself.

Not that she wanted one, but isn't it strange that she never got an invitation? That a yellow, banana-scented envelope never found its way into her mailbox, onto her desk, into her portfolio? She'll never admit it, and don't you dare tell another soul, but she searched. She searched in the mailbox and on the desk and in the portfolio, and all around each, thinking there must have been a mistake. There had to have been a mistake, right? Not that she cared, *or cares*, but there must've been a mistake, right?

Right?

Her meager free-time is spent mostly unmotivated. It's like she's sitting *Shiva*, giving Gwami's death the time and weight it demands, letting the universe slowly adjust her to a new reality. Only this *Shiva* looks to go on much longer than seven measly days. Only there's nobody around to bring her baked goods and casseroles, to send big flower displays that'd keep her spirit up. She sits in mourning alone, depressed as can be, replaying all of her paltry mistakes in grave, hyperbolic detail. Early on, she realized it was futile looking for a single thing that she'd done wrong. The conclusion was that she'd done *everything* wrong, that she had taken on Goliath with a measly slingshot, missed her shot over the giant's shoulder, and it, laughing, stomped her out. Outside of the Bible, this is how these stories go. She's missed her chance at beatification, at myth.

Any *motivated* free-time she spends in the gallery. Her *real* gallery. The other one, the one in Brooklyn, is impossible to even query into. It would be fatal to give Mr. al-Faifel the slightest inkling of her real identity. And with the frenzied press likely swarming on his skin, he must wish so badly he could point his finger over to Miranda's East Village apartment. "There she is! Accost her yourselves!" But alas.

The world, reacting to her sorrow, has drained itself of color. It has taken on death hues: grays and dark, ambiguous blues, blacks like voids and brown like unmentionables underneath boot-heels. A bleak, cloudy Summer becomes a bleak, cloudy Fall, and when the sun does deign to shine, it does so far away: across the bridge in Brooklyn, across the water on the steep slopes of the Palisades, slopes that fall suddenly, enthusiastically into the ocean, zealous watchmen on the edge of the known world.

She tries her hand at more painting, just small stuff in her room when the boredom of constant anguish becomes overpowering. Her hands create only thick, ugly brush strokes, and all her colors seem sapped of their vivacity. Decay has crept into all aspects of her life, like a reminder of how she should be feeling, of how worthless it is to pursue, to dream. Is this a punishment? Is this some divine confirmation that one body is to live one life, or else? It's a shame, she let her selves get too mixed-in and jumbled-up to be disentangled, a sad, theoretical pair of Siamese-twins miscarried together. Even her analogies are lacking in depth.

As she thinks more about the Great Deletion, a split-second action spurred on by emotion and friendly concern, Miranda's own life seems worthless without Gwami juxtaposed beside it. It's too late now, of course, but if she had to do it again, she'd save Gwami's life over her own. If it would spare her the experience of this current life, she would do it unflinchingly. Mind you, Gwami doesn't "exist." But Miranda'd cut off her own arm if it meant rewinding events a few weeks. Maybe a foot, too. She could survive just fine with only one ear, like that cop in *Reservoir Dogs*, who, despite his mutilation, went on crying and carrying on for the entirety of his short thereafter existence. But alas.

Alas there is no trace of Gwami anymore. She has been written from existence, and only the soft wind blown past the wisps of her vanished hair catalogues her once life. The wind carries only faint, barely perceptible whiffs of glamour, of clout, of cool, just enough for a melancholy nose to sniff nostalgia.

When Gwami evaporated into the stratosphere, she took all of Miranda's concealed cool with her. Thus, Miranda's newly wastoid slant of the shoulders, the carelessness about hygiene, the overall spike in her avoidability index. Miranda Swami has no conscious control over these things, they simply happen. Perhaps something's happened to her aura, or, you know, she's just depressed.

Maybe that's why nobody's reached out, even less nobody than usual. Historically, professors would often email, asking the star pupil's expansiveness to come fill up their office hours or place piece in some small student collection. None of that. Once, Caleb might've tried coaxing her to one of his work parties, but they haven't spoken in months. Mother and Father, forget it, they're too busy, or self-important. Lakshmi, well Lakshmi was good at first, checking in constantly. Semi-constantly. A few times. But, anyways, once he settled and saw that Miranda wasn't lurching towards lethality, he receded back into his own nervously selfish life. Don't be too harsh on him, though, he's got one of those easy minds that only recognize extremes. You're either depressed to the point of suicide, or probably fine. This is the characteristic attitude for men of a certain age.

But even the Modern Millennial Woman can only take so much solitude, and since her last remaining companions — the sixteen pieces hanging in the *Eldred L. Apple Exhibition Center* — aren't speaking to her anymore, that means nobody is. Solitude doesn't have to be a physical sensation, you know; this isn't jail. Ask any suicidal and they'll tell you: company can be right beside you yet be nowhere at all.

The solitude creeps into Miranda's bones, into her bloodstream. Always kind of a solitary cat, she nevertheless had this best friend hitching a ride within her for the brunt of her adult life, a companion with the kind of smarts and toughness and can-do, boot-strapping attitude that made iconoclasty possible. It was like she was in a secret club, just her and this cool, popular person. Together, they saw the rest of the world as trash. They themselves were singularly clean atop the rabble.

Gwami was something she could hold high and lord over the rest of the world. When they saw the empty seat beside her but chose one elsewhere, when they forgot her birthday again, when they had gatherings in her apartment but neglected to send an invite her way, it was okay, because she had Gwami. Because, though they didn't know it, they wanted her, craved her attention and affection and guidance. They lusted for her back, but could not recognize her face. And there's a kind of power in that.

But Gwami is gone, and Miranda isn't so strong with her power fractured.

Don't believe that? Look who she's dialing up.

"Thank you for calling *The Trier Group*, this is Alex Pepperidge's office, Diana speaking, how can I help you?"

"Diana?"

"Uhm, yes, who's calling?"

"This is Miranda. Swami? Calling for Caleb?"

"Oh, wow, Miranda, hi! Do you not, well, if you're calling, I suppose you must not, so yes, I guess I will be the first to tell you. Your brother hasn't worked here in months. *Months*."

"What? Really?"

"Oh, yes, it was all quite sudden. Mr. Pepperidge is Junior Vice President now."

"And bully for him. So, uh, do you know where my brother is?"

Diana makes a clicking noise with her tongue before saying, "Unfortunately not. The grapevine is unusually silent."

"Grapevines, yeah."

"Did you try his personal — "

"Yeah, I will, thanks," Miranda says, hanging up unceremoniously. Caleb not working for Trier? He had his head in that dickshit's lap for the better part of a decade, and now he's "moved on?" Weird. But also, who gives a shit? Caleb can do what he wants, and honestly, she's happy he's out of there. Maybe he's stopped being such a piece of shit without Trier's lead to follow. Who is she kidding? Of course, he's still a piece of shit. At his core, Caleb Swami is an asshole. Even if nobody around him has ever wanted to admit it, he's an asshole. She could write her Senior Thesis about it. There wouldn't be much in the way of substance, though she might get points for passion. And she has nobody else to call.

She has his personal number, but of course he prefers that line left clear. It's not really a personal number as much as it is a direct channel for important clients. *Was* a direct channel. Who knows what kinds of clients he's servicing now, or what kind of servicing he's doing for them. She dials anyways, bracing herself for the inevitable, 'Miranda, what the fuck? You don't call my personal number except in an emergency. *Are* you in an emergency, or *are* you just bored? Really, I'm busy. Can't you schedule something with Diana/Lizzy/Tawny/Bobbi' or any of the rotating secretaries he keeps out front?

The last thing she expects is for the line to be picked up after one ring, for Caleb's reservedly flamboyant voice to say, "Oh, Miri, hey.

Nobody calls her Miri anymore. Miri died long long long before Gwami was ever a twinkle in the proverbial eye.

"Caleb."

"How are you? How are you holding up? Are you okay?"

(Sometimes she forgets that he knows. That her grand secret, perhaps the biggest secret in the world right now, can be readily exposed by this man: a former low-level executive at a restaurant group and notoriously coke-addled bathhouse frequenter. This man, who also happens to be her only sibling.

It doesn't really even make sense that he knows. She never had a good reason for telling him, it was more just to have told someone at all. It never exactly excited him, probably made him jealous, and was responsible in large part for their most recent and most intense falling out.

That was at the beginning of this year, when Caleb was opening a new place in SoHo. It was a grimy little Korean taco joint meant to invoke some dark alley in Seoul where the knowledgeable traveler could find delicious, hidden eats *ala* Bourdain. All exposed brick, those amber Edison lights, the black countertops.

"It's so obvious, Caleb. You're better than this."

"It's not obvious, it's dated."

"It's kitschy."

"Kitsch is cool."

"Kitsch is kitsch. It's only cool if it's accidental."

"It's a pop-up, Miranda, the point is that it's on purpose. Take a *single* marketing class —"

"What do you want me to say? Do you want me to jerk you off, or do you want the truth?"

They shouted at each other from opposite sides of the space, Miranda facing the wall, disastrously glossy black brick. She was right, too. The hardwood floor was over-lacquered. The tables were going to be tragically close. The kitchen, open for all to peer into, was far too small to accommodate the shifting, meandering orders of 120 taco-happy, probably stoned, guests. And worst of all, people were going to come in fucking droves.

"This isn't the truth though, Miranda, this is you being difficult."

"I wouldn't come here."

"Of course, you wouldn't! You only go to cat cafes and cheap Vietnamese places. This isn't *for* you."

"Then why ask for my opinion? I was never going to be of any help to you."

"Miranda," he says slowly with his hands, too. "Let's not pretend that you thought I wanted you here to give your opinion on the — fuckin' — wainscoting. You're smarter than that."

"I'm leaving."

"Hey, come on!"

"Get off me."

"Miranda!"

"Get out of my way."

"It'll be a favor. Just do something in the corner for me. Something small. You don't even have to sign it. It just needs to *look* like Gwami. We'll say it was here when we opened the space."

"I'm not a fucking meal ticket for you, ass-hole."

"You can eat here for free whenever. Take whatever you want. Take lit-er-a-lee anything." He went so far as to drop to his knees, hands clasped before him in reverence…"Miranda, I really need this win. Badly. Really badly. Please. Please. Just put aside your pride and help me out, once."

He didn't ask for her opinion again. Didn't ask for her to scribble something on a wall again either. Conversation cooled completely. Not that they talked much before then, but, you know, they chatted occasionally. He invited her to stuff sometimes. Could he reasonably believe his restaurant's failure was her fault? Could that failure have been why Caleb left Trier? Her unwillingness to even slightly hemorrhage a fantasy character for the real-life success of her real-life brother, is that what she envisioned when she thought of Gwami affecting the world?

She remembers this all at once — it smacks her in the face, teleports her away, and brings her back panting — all before she can come up with a bullshit answer to his question.

Are you okay? If this were a phone call with any other person, the answer would be clear. "Yeah, fine, all good," she might say, or riff onto one of the million variations of the phrase, each one meaning, in essence, *don't worry about me, I am well-equipped to handle this life and all of its myriad challenges.* But this is Caleb, who knows firsthand that Miranda is, ahem, not exactly well-equipped to handle this life or its myriad challenges. A million ways to answer him, a million ways to lead Caleb towards the response she wants.

But what does she want?)

"Not really."

(Apparently, she just wants a friend.)

"Okay. Uhm, are you safe? Are you feeling, you know, okay?" Him, too, just like Lakshmi. Maybe that's just men, lacking the same nuance of thought and emotion that they do in action. And watch him fumble around with responses he is unequipped to wield.

"Yeah, I mean, I'm physically okay. I just…I could just use a friendly face right now."

"Then I hope mine will suffice."

"Clever. That's good. Keep that up, I want more of that out of you."

He promises she'll get more when they meet on Thursday.

"One of your places? Ahem, Trier's places? You'll have to tell me what happened."

"Yeah, uhm, my schedule is actually pretty tight, you can do dinner, I imagine?"

"I actually have to be at the gallery that night. Important critic coming at 7:30, big deal and all that jazz. Earlier, maybe? Please."

"Hmmm, I suppose I can swing something. Ah! But, well, are you okay with somewhere a bit less traditional?"

"I like it already."

So, they plan to meet. That's a big step forward. Despite herself, she's excited, genuinely excited to see her brother. She straightens her hair; she applies blush. She remembers to clean behind her ears. She wants good things reported back to Mother.

But Miranda's enthusiasm doesn't last long.

A youngish man with no hair holds out two robed arms to a crowd far too large for any Thursday afternoon afternoon.

"Look out and wonder, ye flock, on the state of your souls," he shouts. Someone cries "MMMMMMMM," and there are scattered sobs.

"Caleb, this is ridiculous."

"Miranda, shut up."

"He called us 'ye flock,' like this is the Old fucking Testament or something."

"Miranda, please."

"But, like, how pretentious do you have to be to use 'ye' or 'thine' or 'thou' in the 21st century?"

"If you're going to act like this just, please, wait for me outside."

"Whatever you say." How quickly their turgid peace is forgotten. The introductory wailing of the organ, one of those 270-pipe skeletal systems sometimes found in the more baroque New York City churches, saves her from more self-indulgent secularism. Life is too short and time too precious to waste any of it in a world of someone else's devising, and this is certainly not her world. When did it become her brother's? Miranda is all too eager to escape the cramped quarters, drawing the lolling perfunctory stares of adroit psalm-sayers.

When she gets outside the Church, she sits on the steps and runs her finger over her phone's glossy, black screen. How long does service last? Are you allowed to smoke within 50-feet of God's house? She feels bad leaving Caleb, for even if she can't understand his presence here, it's clearly important to him. Important enough to make him act so completely out of character.

He moved his mouth to the hymns, sure, knelt when he was asked to, stood when commanded, but why? Caleb has always detested this kind of thing. What could have possibly sparked such a change?

15 minutes later or so, Caleb emerges from the stone double-doors in a huff, his jacket half-on. A crowd of relieved post-churchgoers does not follow behind.

"Come on, let's go get a bite," he says smiling at her.

"It's over already?"

"Not exactly. But I'm sure God will understand."

"You could've stayed."

"Unnecessary, I saw what I needed to see."

"And what was that, exactly?"

"Just a few favorite hymns of mine."

"Caleb Swami, age 34, reformed, complete with a collection of favorite hymns."

"A lot can change in a year."

"More than I ever thought possible."

They hurry down the sidewalk, a sidewalk strangely bare for such a temperate day. Caleb sweats no matter the temperature, but something is clearly going on here; even his neck is damp. Perhaps he's anticipating the coming questions.

"Sooooo, what happened with Trier?" Miranda asks, some few steps behind Caleb, who's almost jogging.

"Why don't we talk when we get there?" Caleb suggests. "There" turns out to be a bifurcated French bistro-type-deal with a more casual café separated from a white tablecloth dining room by a row of potted, people-height ficuses.

"What do you think?" Caleb asks his sister as they sit.

"We just sat down. Haven't even looked at the menu yet."

"Yeah, but first impressions, of the space, of the vibe."

"Uhm, I don't know. It doesn't seem extraordinary. I feel like I've seen this exact place a dozen other times. Look at the tile," she says, eyeing down the alternating hexagonal pattern, black and white mosaic.

"It's supposed to be like a classic, French bistro."

"Clearly."

A silence. Eyes graze menus. Servers offer bread, they offer water, they offer suggestions. Caleb orders a salad, dressing on the side, and Miranda orders citron-marinated olives. She's not very hungry. On second thought, Caleb orders two Amaros. The server asks Miranda for her ID, and Miranda, without looking in her wallet says she, "Forgot it at home."

So, one Amaro. "Do you really not have your ID?" Caleb asks.

"Just didn't want a drink."

"Could've said so."

"I didn't say anything about a drink. That's the point. I can order for myself."

"Jesus, is this how it's going to be?"

"I don't know, Caleb, *is it*?"

"Fine, fine, I'm sorry. I'm a little on edge. Forgive me. I'm here for you. That's why we're here. For you. I just want to buy you things. You don't seem like you've been smiling much lately."

Miranda tucks her chin into her sweatshirt, biting the upturned hood. Her maw half-full of muffling cloth mumbles, "Not much to smile about."

"Yeah, tough times. How you holding up?"

"Poorly, Caleb, very, very poorly."

"To be expected. Thank you," Caleb says as the waitress returns with two Amaros, setting one down in front of each of her guests. She looks at Miranda and puts her index finger to her lips, quietly pirouetting away.

"Well she is delightful," Caleb exclaims. "And your type, maybe?"

"I'm practicing celibacy right now."

"Haven't you always?"

"Go to Hell."

"I'm sorry. *I am*. Couldn't resist. Cheers."

"To what?"

"New beginnings."

"Cliché. How about…to a couple of queers speaking French."

"*Ça aussi.*" *Clink.*

"You know it isn't over, right?" he continues.

"What?"

"Gwami. It'll just take time, everyone forgets everything eventually. Even Mel Gibson is making movies again, and —"

"Nah, I think it's done. I'm not going to be one of those people reviving all their past lives forever. It's over; it was great, now it's over, and I've got to move on. I think I want the stability of something more serious. I mean, I'm like five credits away from finishing my major, and Graphic Designers of my caliber have a really good starting salary. It's just, like, do I really want to keep *fighting* for the rest of my life? Would that make me happy? I don't think so."

"Wow, Miranda, I'm a little shocked. That's, uhm, very mature of you."

"I'm very mature for my age."

"Always have been."

"What happened with Trier?"

Caleb turns red. The salad comes. And the olives.

"*Bon Appetit.*"

"*Merci.*"

"So?"

"Creative differences. I saw myself as much more valuable to the company than he did."

"Pepperidge has your office now."

"So, you understand, then."

"What's the new gig?"

"Uhm, a food thing. A startup. Just working my way up, you know. Thought some more ladder-climbing would be good for me."

"Has it been?"

"Same as ever."

"Shocking."

Silence while the two eat. Miranda shuffles her feet.

"I really am sorry what happened," Caleb says between bites.

"I don't want to talk about it anymore."

"Have you talked about it at all?"

"That's the point."

"Maybe it would do you well to talk to, you know, *someone.*"

"I'm not fucking suicidal, okay? Why does everyone think I'm just going to fucking kill myself whenever *anything* bad happens."

"Hey, hey. *Hey.* Nobody's saying that. It's just, well, you know how you can get."

Oh no.

In another universe, perhaps Caleb took another moment to consider what exactly he was saying, to reevaluate his verbiage, to lighten his tone. But in this universe, he doesn't even lock eyes with her, nothing to communicate *Oh boy, that is SO not what I meant.* He says it, stuffs salad in his face, and seems utterly unprepared for Miranda to shoot back with:

"No, Caleb. Actually, I do not know how I 'get.' Care to enlighten me?"

"Don't do this, Miranda" he says, defensively. Too defensively. He's blowing it. "I was just saying —"

"I know what you were saying. You were saying that I can't handle any personal tragedy without completely flying off the rails. I know exactly what you were saying. God, why can't I just have a fucking conversation with *anyone* about something other than my fucking emotions? I *know* what happened before. I am well fucking aware, but this is not —"

"Miranda, I'm not —"

And, in truth, he might not be. But it doesn't matter. Sometimes, when too much pressure accumulates in a superheated vessel, the slightest structural deficiency can lead to an outsized explosion. And Miranda's "vessel" was never very strong in the first place. It's also never been so pressurized.

Crack, snap, kaboom!

"Caleb, if you brought me here so you can convince yourself that you're a really great fucking person, so concerned for your poor baby sister, then you shouldn't have fucking brought me here. There's not an altruistic bone in your body, we both know that. This was a mistake. A big mistake. You were always just going to posture and prance around and pretend you give a shit when you clearly don't. Fuck it, I'm going." Miranda tosses her napkin onto the table and jerks upright. Caleb grabs the armless sleeve of her sweatshirt.

"Sit down, Miranda. Jesus Christ, when did you get so sensitive?"

"Caleb! Fucking listen to yourself! You sound like a prick!" She's really yelling now, can't stop herself, can't control her pitch, and it's starting to attract the attention of the other diners. Their server takes a step towards the table but stops...not her problem. "You want to bring me here to make me feel, what? Like it's not the biggest fucking personal tragedy of *either* of our lives that I lost this thing? This was *ev-er-ree-thing* to me. You KNOW that. Don't sit here and feign sympathy when you and I both know you're only doing this because you still want to make a buck off whatever's left of her. She's *gone*. You've got to realize that the way I do."

"*You* called *me*!"

"Because I had nobody else to call! God, I'm so stupid," she says, muttering to herself as she walks.

"I'll *Venmo* you," Caleb says over his shoulder.

"PRICK," Miranda screeches, already halfway out the door.

Inside the restaurant, Caleb calmly motions to the waitress. "Check," he mouths, scribbling on his hand with a pantomimed pen.

Outside the restaurant, Miranda begins to break down. Or rather, things break down around her. She calls herself stupid, calls herself destructive, calls herself a monster. She thinks *he didn't deserve that*, then thinks *yes, he did*. She thinks she overreacted, then thinks he brought it on himself. She wishes she never called him, she knows she had nowhere else to turn. She wonders why she lied to him about wanting something serious, wonders whether she was really lying to herself, wonders whether repeated lies can influence the thereafter truth, like how people who smile more become happier over time. She feels alone. She feels apart from herself. She should smile more. Temporarily, she doesn't even know who she is.

Miranda Swami doesn't lie to avoid the judgmental stares of others. Miranda Swami doesn't lose her shit and storm out of restaurants. Miranda Swami has not and will not settle down for something more serious, will not let her accomplishments and her talent and the ideas in her head drain away in the hope that an ordinary, basic life of commuting and motherhood and peaceful death will bring her closer to some dead, dipshit ideal of happiness. She will not *fucking* smile more. Miranda Swami built an entity out of air, formed her aphysical ideas into semi-living flesh; she is a God, of sorts, and so why-oh-why does she feel all the weak parts of her person fraying even further? Why does she feel so torn?

She presses her shoulder against a block of brick wall, all alone in a city of eight-and-a-half million. She wants to smash her skull into eight-and-a-half million pieces. One for all her neighbors. She wants to scream as she does it, bludgeoning chips off her cranium again and again into the brick. She won't though, because she's strong, and also because it's exactly what everyone expects from her. She might be a lot of things — self-destructive and depressed, vile and unlovable, alone and exploitative, a murderer and euthanasia enthusiast — but she will not be obvious. Under no circumstance.

She enters a park she's never seen before and ducks into a shady corner, finding a nice bench set across from a eucalyptus thicket. Previously unknown feelings ooze uncontrollably from her pores. This is grief, this is rage, this is reactionary. This is so unlike her.

Her throat is full, so are her nostrils. Her phone shakes in her hand, and it's predictably devoid of remorseful texts from her brother. She considers reaching out to him, sending a long, meandering apology, because he'll probably understand. He must understand, right? How could he have known he'd set her off like that? He's a man, even the most feminine among them don't think about these things. They're so momentary, he couldn't possibly have known that his words would break down the door to something, that they were the jailer's key to a very vital cell. But she doesn't text him because apologies are pointless. She'd rather he disappear from her life, from the Earth, whatever. She never wants to see him again. Never wants to see anything again. Her cheeks are red and swollen from the tears, and she wipes them away with the butt of her sweater-covered palm.

But when her phone vibrates, she checks it immediately, thinking even if it's not Caleb, it might be someone else. An actual human. Even some words from Mother or Father, were one of them to reach out, would help stabilize her, bring her wayward spirit back from its far-away wanderings. But they don't even know anything's wrong. They have no idea who their daughter is, or was, or who she contained.

It is in fact from none of those people. It's a message from an unknown number, a number that's more *wing-ding* than digits, in a font that texts don't come in.

Miranda Swami, it reads, we know what's been done to you. We know who you are, who you were. Everything that's happened, it's all been a show. Everything. A conspiracy whirls around you, unbeknownst to you or anyone else. We have answers. About the suicide, about Cindi, about everything. Gwami is dead, but she doesn't have to be. Follow our directions, we have much to discuss…

Three dots. An ellipsis. A promise of more to come.

An insinuation.

Conspiracy.

Answers.

They know who she is.

If this is a veiled threat, it's an effective one. If it's a promise of information, it's an essential one. The "number" sends something else, a location pin, somewhere way far uptown. Miranda's feet begin to take her there before her brain can decide if it even wants them to. Her brain, to be fair, is plenty preoccupied. All it can think about, suddenly, is the revival of Gwami the Seer. "Gwami is dead, but she doesn't have to be."

All the flotsam floating in her skull, meandering and shifting shape-less in the shadowy dark, replaced by a single bright orb, and everything else is washed away by those words. Those words! So simple, so suggestive, so impossible, right? So impossible. But if there's a way…

Miranda would save Gwami's life over her own. She knows who she is, and she is *not* herself. Not in the traditional sense. *That's* who Miranda Swami is. She's more, she's expansive, she contains multitudes. Miranda Swami is a kosmos.

Looking up from those words, Miranda looks back into the world. The wind begins to blow hard, brushing up the green underbellies of the Elm leaves, sending the reflections of white clouds across the glossy building-side above her.

It must have drizzled. Miranda steps in a puddle. Water enters her shoes from the sides. She marches up town, unconcerned.

3

One thing about the City is it's different at night. The people are different, and so are the routines they engage in. Alternative businesses quietly open in the lacking light, peddling in obscene transactions that would shame a well-lit world. People move queerly, either more loosely or more self-aware — women in heels tip-toe along city sidewalks while the freshly drunk sway in search of something to lean against. In the daytime, it's a hive of commerce and interaction, but at night it's an oblivion of lost souls.

Night time is when they say the Demons come out, breathed from their subterranean lairs by the last gasp of the sun. In the deep night, those pitch-black hours when their power is greatest, they can take shape in this world, exploding into being from formerly spectral forms, able to stretch their legs (should they have legs) and unfurl their wings (should they have those as well). In the night, they take flight, seeking out sinners to punish and mischief to make. But you and I are reasonable folk, and we don't believe that drivel, do we? Sure, countless eye-witnesses have put their demonic testimonials on the internet for our pleasant consumption, but do you really believe in that garbage? In Sasquatch? Mothman?

More than most, especially at such a moment of erased rationality, Miranda does. Her parents, guided by a Professor-friend's truly terrible child-rearing book, used the threat of demon-snatching on their youngest to encourage good behavior (see *Kontrolling Kids: A Dialogue on Efficient Parenting*, chapter three, "The Implantation of Supernatural Phobia"). It could just as easily have been Krampus, or an eternity in Christian Hell, but, no, her parents wanted to use something both believable to a child (we've all heard the stories) but patently absurd to an adult, so when she grew up enough to begin questioning them, they could A) explain their actually-quite-effective reasoning, and B) easily debunk the fear of Demons in their now obedient daughter. Demon talk, after all, kept her safe in bed while her compatriots were sneaking out to beer busts and sleeping around in the senior's cars, kept her from speaking against her elders and coveting thine neighbor's goods.

Eventually, Miranda did grow old enough to question her parents, and they did successfully A) explain their reasoning and B) debunk the fear of Demons in their now obedient daughter.

Or so they assumed.

In truth, if you're anything like Miranda, you, or a part of you, will always despise your parents for the lies that got you to behave.Something about the parental willingness to fib makes obvious their weakness, their charlatan reliance upon parlor tricks. And even when they explained and debunked, they never did apologize, did they? Mother looked her daughter in the eyes and said, "It was for your own good." And she truly believed that. She'd believe anything to keep from seeing her own fault.

And if you're anything like Miranda, you *know* logically it's all ridiculous, all a lie, that the "eye-witness accounts" read aloud to you before bed were merely the psychotic ramblings of other grown kids with Mommy issues who were never quite able to quit fearing the Bogeyman in the closet. You might know this logically, yet you still feel goosepimples upon your spine at the whiff of something rank in the night air, in the sidestepping shadow you swore you saw duck into that alley, at the mere suggestion of Demons walking free amongst the drunkards and the nightwalkers and the dealers and thieves.

Enter Miranda into the world of deep night in New York City, where terrestrial forces give way, after straining all day against them, to others that defy comprehension yet walk on two legs like all else, masquerading as a part of the milieu.

Ipso facto, Miranda keeps her eyes away from alleys and stays breathing through her mouth. Adding supernatural panic into her already-bubbling emotional cauldron might lead to a psychotic break or murderous rage, both of which, of course, would be playing right into the Demons' hands. Or claws. Tentacles? General appendages*.

Whether demons are actually watching her from the shadows or not, she shouldn't be doing this. She should turn back home because this is stupid. She's staking her safety on spam, and more than likely, she's going to get hurt. A girl walks alone in the city, and a hundred thousand awful things wait to happen to her.

Somewhere inside her, this is known. Somewhere inside her, little voices scream and little arms are raising all available alarms. Her mind's safety centers are following protocol exactly, so if things do turn sour, it's not on them. They're going forward with all the requisite sweats and itchiness, with the dizziness and budding migraine headaches they're authorized to enact.

It's just too bad none of their best efforts will have any effect. We are now receiving confirmation that, yes, Miranda's lunch with Caleb was profound fuel for her already un-right mind. Caleb's latest slight was pointed enough to pierce right through some crucial myelin sheath and reroute a couple neuron firings. Before, all Miranda had wanted to do was sink into nothing. Now she wants to destroy something. Now she wants bloodshed. It'll be a rebirth for Gwami, and a baby Armageddon for everyone else. And *that's* why, at this very moment, Miranda hurriedly ignores her fears and sweats and teeny inner voices the entire trip up 'til 135th street, following the phantom instructions as they appear in the world before her.

In the same abrasive, abrupt font as the first text messages, more otherworldly directions plague her steps across the city. They rode uptown with her, replacing the blocky text on the MTA buses' foreheads (*Get on this Bus, Miranda*), drew her eye to the bottom of electronic billboards (*Turn left at 88th*), smuggled themselves into LED crawlers in the storefront windows (*Don't stop or make eye contact with anyone*), texted her the same message every few minutes, pinging and re-pinging the same location, some 24-hour video-game café in East Harlem. It's been conspiratorial messages and ads for Bananas (hopefully not from the same source) all the way uptown.

A block or two from her destination, it again begins to drizzle. Remember kids: in the city, even drizzles are dangerous. Because the drops fall at an angle, curving around umbrella edges, and accumulating power as they bounce off the skyscrapers, even the slightest rain feels rather like a choosy thunderstorm.

Ah, a Drizzle in Harlem! That might have been a Langston Hughes poem. Ah, Harlem!, you once were center of a world, site of a revolution! Ah, Harlem!, how you fell, fell into a vat of some fearsome acid, becoming sinister-sounding and bloated by your own dismal expectations. Ah, Harlem!, you stand rejuvenated by city-commissioned graffiti and day-cares and hair salons. O, Harlem!, you metamorphic Kaleidoscope; you have been everything there is to be, without rest. You have existed only in transition, impossible to amp down, observable only in superposition.

Two years ago, Miranda-cum-Gwami and, just before dawn, went to town on a bit of beige brick on 118th Street. If memory serves, the piece she did then was a mix of spray-paint and traditional brush-work, an allegorical mural where a half-dozen monkeys with billionaire faces clambered over puny skyscrapers as if they were Tarzan trees. The racial aspect of the metaphor was lost on most (probably for the best), but even still, the tiny spot sandwiched between a Baptist Church and an *Urban Outfitters* Pop-up became so highly-trafficked that the NYPD had to install an officer on round-the-clock guard duty. After a month behind hastily-erected bullet-proof glass, the city had the section of wall removed and replaced, the graffiti sold to the highest bidder and, thus, condemned it to collect dust in the basement of the Guggenheim, you know, as the artist intended.

Miranda considers a detour to scope out the former spot, but a talking traffic signal says, "Stop. Stop. Miranda. Don't get distracted. Stop. Walk, Walk, Walk." She takes its advice.

Besides the amber streetlights and a stale yellow glow coming from that third-story window, the only light on this block is the fluorescent, laundromat shine of the prophesied internet café, a rather austere, sterile kind of haven for some 30-odd Indian and Southeast Asian boys (do their parents know where they are?) *click-click-clicking* away. Miranda walks in slowly, trying to gauge which of the gamers — all too enveloped in their monitors to notice the intrusive female, which is actually kind of nice — could be her puppeteer. What a bizarre place this is: silent, all silent except for keyboard clacks and mouse clicks. I suppose you could call that Millennial Silence.

There are no open computers, so Miranda stands awkwardly for a moment, clutching her bag tight, awaiting an imminent ambush. Those aforementioned parts of her brain are straight-up freaking out right now. But a new text on her vibrating phone breaks the paranoia.

Enter the door. Close it behind you.

On cue, a door, silver and curt, is opened by invisible hand in the back of the café. No more pronounced than a janitor's closet, its sudden aperture draws nary a single eye away from its designated screen. Miranda looks around, not just to see if the door has gained another's attention, but to see if maybe someone will look at the door and then, puzzled, over at her waiting there, and shrug as if to say, "Hey girl, you do what you gotta do, we'll all understand." Even one regular client's slightest permission would provide her confidence. But alas... she's followed every instruction thus far, so why not one more? Miranda squeezes past a row of thin-lipped Bangladeshi boys and then slips through the door, closing it behind her.

Passing through is like passing into another world. Instead of fluorescent lights, everything is bathed in a UV Glow, all purple and neon green and everybody's grimacing white teeth vibrantly bioluminescent. "Everybody" in this context meaning the six or seven uncouth-looking characters who, unlike their compatriots out front, very, very much notice Miranda's intrusion into their space. They look up with their nose rings and their gauges, their glass eyes and face tattoos, their fingertip-less motorcycle gloves, staring poison, prison stares. It's a small hexagonal room, filled near to bursting with interlocking office cubicles, and it sure doesn't seem like outsider-sever venture in. Hence the stares.

But Miranda doesn't immediately announce herself as a cop or a narc or whoever busts internet criminals, so the gang returns to their presumably illicit activities while Miranda tries to act like she's been here before. Everyone is plugged into these ancient computers, blocky, tan monstrosities like you'd find in some early-90's government lab, computers that look like they'd eat her phone if she brought it too close. They're *beasts*, and only one is open, forcing Miranda's next move.

This terminal isn't welcoming and does not come with direct-ions. But two helpful clues exist for her viewing pleasure: a phone cord and a pair of VR Goggles both dangle from the desktop CPU. Some instructions don't require clarification. Her phone she plugs into the machine, bringing the brute machine to crackly, cranky life, and the goggles she wraps tight around her skull.

The goggle's screen sputters with long, green, digitized lines of swift-moving binary code. The lines form a dot matrix that thickens and thickens and coalesces, nay dissolves, nay explodes — somehow dissolves *and* explodes — into a long, mustard-brown hotel hallway flanked by red and orange doors. Most of the blocky doors are closed, but a few are cracked open, revealing opaque lights and shifty, silhouetted forms. There's a painting on the wall of a sad clown, and another opposite of a drab bowl of fruit. Miranda gets the shivers.

This is clearly a place for secrets and secret dealings. And she's clearly an intruder.

A little black box appears in the center of her vision, and the program automatically inputs into it what looks to be the local IP address. This, it seems, is some kind of key.

Stripped of agency, Miranda is whisked down the hallway, feverishly overtaking corners and twisting through a sequence of near-identical corridors. This is a Minotaur maze, though the beast has yet to show itself. If in control of her own movements, Miranda surely would end up traipsing through this place forever, but the Program's autopilot follows a precise plan. She's slowed, she'd placed in a straightaway, and an eye-catching door circumscribed with a shimmering whiteness opens at the end of this last long hallway. Into it she goes, overtaken by a blinding white light. She's stupefied for a second, but sight slowly returns, and when it does, Miranda finds herself in a room that can only be described as a shrine.

It's a shrine to Gwami the Seer.

All around her are relics of Gwami's life. Clips from her fame-making internet videos fade in and out like posters on the walls before dissolving completely. In their stead come private pictures of her and Lakshmi: she yelling at him, he on his knees before her, she sitting upon her famous gnarled throne (Lakshmi had it commissioned from a local craftsman who swore the roots around its base and back were bound in good swamp juju). Over there are her various profile pictures, arranged in chronological order. On the ceiling, all of her graffiti art muralized and transposed in hyper-realistic detail, a dramatically impressive little bit of coding. Even the floors are carpeted in her posts, comments and diatribes, all funny and funky and positively tickled to be trodden upon. It's Gwami's life made three-dimensional. Someone *had* archived everything she'd ever done, and laid it out like a leaf trap above a spike-filled pit. There would hardly be a circumstance where Miranda wouldn't willingly fall in.

Against the far wall is a table, small and black and Ikeanly unassuming. Sitting at it, less so, is a lecherous Carmen SanDiego, a tall, spindly woman's figure whose wild red hair falls to the hip of a gleaming, white trench coat. A very stylish cowboy hat drapes an impenetrable shadow over its wearer's face. Her face, quite literally, is being foreshadowed. Take that as you will.

A line of text slithers forth from the Woman's mouth, a beige backed text-bubble inflates around it. "You made it," the Woman says. "I wasn't sure you would."

"You underestimated me," Miranda types back. She doesn't need to think about it; speaking like this is as automatic to the Modern Millennial Woman as a heartbeat.

"In fact, Miranda Swami, we do exactly the opposite. We know your potential. Yours, not Gwami the Seer's."

A shudder emerges from Miranda's neck and slides down her spine. The woman says, "Do you like the room? As you can tell, we're big fans."

"Who's 'we?' *Big Banana*? Is this all some kind of —"

"Very blunt. Straight-forward, ignorant of possible consequences. No, Miranda Swami, we are not *Big Banana*. In fact, there is no *Big Banana*, at least not as you know them. And that is precisely the problem: nobody really knows them. They are a dark and cryptic organization, and yet, they have curried such favor in the wide world. But you, Miranda Swami, you came the closest of anyone to the truth. And you have been punished for your discovery. As expected, they couldn't allow you to continue."

"What do you mean?"

"You were right, Miranda Swami. About so much. This 'company' is not as altruistic as they would have you believe. Nor are they just some environmentally-destructive, socially-manipulative alpha corporation as you believe they are. No. They are something much worse."

"And what's that then?"

The woman stands suddenly, her avatar running its finger along the nearby stretch of wall. How does she have such body control here?

"Miranda Swami, do you like this room? We wanted you to feel at home here. Do you feel at home? Do you feel safe? We wanted you to recover a little of what was taken from you."

Miranda pauses. "Yeah, it's nice, I suppose."

"We've been collecting these, watching you, waiting until the time was right. The time is finally right, Miranda Swami."

Chills run down Miranda's back. A charged energy travels through the goggles into her skull, and every small hair on her arms and shoulders stands at attention.

"Miranda Swami, Gwami the Seer, whoever you believe you are, you must know this: Cindi Lapenschtall did not jump off of a building. It was a hoax, all chicanery. And all those important voices calling for your death? Manipulated, paid-off, bribed, 'negotiated with.' You wonder why there were no voices coming to your defense? It was not financially feasible for them to do so. The culture has been bought, Miranda. This entire saga, Gwami's entire downfall, it is a vast and insidious marketing stunt intended to destroy you, intended to draw sympathy towards their brand."

"Oh, yeah, I'm *sure*. A hoax. *Totally.* Then where is Cindi now? Then who did they throw off that building if not her? Making all of these claims...why don't you prove it? Enough talk, I want something concrete!" Miranda's getting flustered underneath her goggles, her face turning a thankfully-unseen scarlet.

"'Prove it,' she says. 'We shall,' says I. Have no fear. But not yet. Prove yourself first. Come find me again. Do not be vexed. Those who live truly enough in this world will learn to navigate it. I do believe we will meet again."

"Wait I —"

But that's all there is. A gargantuan power-surge knocks the electricity out of the entire room, and, apparently, the entire block. Miranda rips the defunct goggles off, plunged into a world of similar darkness as the one she so suddenly exited the moment prior. For a second, she thinks she may have died. But in the afterlife, would there be this many outraged Pan-Asian expletives being thrown around? It's a regular Babel, a certain madness pervasive in every screamed word. Miranda doesn't wait for answers. She grabs her stuff and bolts in the direction of the door. There's a lot of flailing, and at some point, a door, and then a larger scrum. The outer sanctum has devolved into monkey cage chaos, meandering moonlight offering the only slight visibility. Somewhere, a hand lunges for Miranda's breast, grazing it. Miranda, always half-expecting something like this, swings her bag halfway around her, connecting noisily with someone's face. If it was her assaulter, great. If it wasn't, well this is a blow against all men on behalf of all women. She escapes with herself mostly intact, her heart beating like a kick drum.

It doesn't dawn on her until she's halfway home on the 1-train that she's shoulder-deep in the plot of a spy novel. Conspiracy? Underground organization? Dark web secrets and mystery abounding?

Which scares her more: the more-poignant threat of *Big Banana's* insidiousness, or that some shadow organization has been watching her every move for God-knows-how-long, collecting every artifact she carelessly left lying around the internet? Talk about Macro and Micro issues. Anyone on this train could be an agent of either sleeper cell, watching her for clues as to whether she really is who they think she is.

A lesser woman might be crippled with the responsibilities entrusted to her, paralyzed by the importance of every decision she'll soon make. But this is Miranda-fucking-Swami here, and even with all the depression, all the pain Gwami's death caused her, she can just as easily tap out of whatever plot pulls her along, ditch her phone, forget this ever happened, and return to the simple life of a struggling artist. Or, maybe, just maybe, if she can charm Judith LeMeur tonight…

Wait. What time is it?

Oh shit.

Oh no, the gallery.

She jumps off the train at Harold Square, her heart trying its best to break through her breastplate. When signal returns at street-level, she sees that aforementioned escape route has vanished, Gwami-like, before her eyes.

You might have thought he'd have given up after four, maybe even five missed calls. But no, it's a whopping twelve. *Twelve* times this poor professor dialed Miranda, probably pacing, probably praying that she would show and spare him the embarrassment, the embarrassment that grew with each failed attempt. She can almost see him, bedecked in tweed, glasses low on his nose. "No, I don't know where she is, really, I was very clear, 7:30 I told her. I just hope she's okay!" Low, doofy voice, Gerry-curls; poor guy, he needs a win.

"Professor, hey," she says into the receiver, "I fucked up, didn't I?"

"Are you all right?"

"Yeah, yeah, I am."

"Okay, maybe meet me down here. We should, uhm, talk."

Everyone always wanting to "talk," wanting to "chat," beat around the bush, dilute the full brunt of a negative situation. If she were a little bit bolder, or a little less distracted, she'd spare herself the extra $2.75 subway ride to the gallery and just call the guy back up, demanding to do this dance ASAP and over the phone. But the $2.75 is soon gone, and she's outside the gallery working up the courage to go inside, and in time she does, flashing her student ID to the security guard as she hurries past, but he calls her —"Hey, young lady! Yes you!"— back because she needs to sign-in and she says but I go here what do I need to sign-in for and he shrugs and says not my call, policy, and she says but it's *my* gallery and that's *my* name on that brochure *right* there and he says, well it's my detail, so sign the form, the form he actually literally physically throws at her. She scribbles something down and slides it back to the guy, going on her merry way with a fat, satisfied smile. A few minutes from now, he'll look down and see that the snotnose girl wrote "DICKHEAD" in big, blocky letters across the entirety of the paper. She didn't even sign her name.

"It's just that…Miranda you have to understand —"

"Professor, with all due respect, I have a lot to do, a lot on my mind, can we just get to the point?"

"It was just an opportunity, Miranda. A big one. And you kind of blew it."

"Did she say anything about the pieces?"

The Professor stalls, not wanting to be driven off-topic. "She said they were fine, that they showed real potential, but —"

"But what? She liked them! Isn't that enough for now? Why did I even have to be here?"

"Because she wanted to meet the *artist*, Miranda. Ask you about intention, experience, have you walk her through everything, piece by piece."

Miranda's forefinger and thumb go to massage to her nose, desperate for something to do. "She's an art critic, can't she just critique the *art*?"

"It's not *about* the art, Swami. Don't be naïve. It's about the artist. It's about the queer daughter of a former Congressman creating a series of high-concept pieces in her dorm-room well outside the bounds of her Graphic Design degree. Art is only compelling because of the artist; you understand that, right?"

"But this is bullshit!" Miranda shrieks. "She stood me up, and she was all '*I'm soooooo sorrrrrrry,*' and 'can't we just rescheule?' But if I do it to her, that's just it? Everything I worked for is just disregarded?"

"Judith LeMeur isn't the only critic that matters, you know."

"You're actually serious? She actually won't see me?"

"Well, I —" But he trails off.

"What?"

"Miranda let's not —"

"What!?"

Sighing, Gillibrand shuffles through his phone, pulling up a voice-mail, and holds the device horizontally, speakers facing Miranda.

"*Charles,*" an elderly woman's curt, sharp voice says through static, "I don't think I have to tell you how *disappointed* I am in today's events, and in you. This was a *very* embarrassing ordeal for me. As you know, I am *extremely* busy, and I do not have the time nor the energy to wait around for another of your self-important pseudo-artists to work *me* into their schedule. You can tell this 'Miranda Swami' when you see her that there are *rules* in the art world, and respecting those responsible for your *future* success is the first. The next time you want to peddle one of your little, ahem, social projects around me, please have the decency to ensure they aren't a truant. Good day."

"How's that for context." Gillibrand says. Don't let the sentence structure fool you, it most certainly was not a question.

Miranda's bag feels supermassive on her shoulder all the way home. She's sore in her side, and every foot falls heavy underneath her. She nearly trips over a package left on her doorstep, and, angry at the cause of her near faceplant, she kicks it over the threshold into the kitchen.

The place is dark, meaning the Twins are at some work *thing* (they sleep with their light on). Miranda is thus spared any eavesdropped gossip. Turning on the kitchen lights illuminate a couple of things. First, two identical letters, sliced open at the top, in tinted yellow envelopes lay on the counter. Miranda can see the B's through the paper, the *Twin B's*, the sign of the devil, the number of the beast. An urge to pry takes hold of the girl, and she listens in perfect stillness for a moment, applying the scientific method to her Hypothesis on the Absent Roommates. It certainly seeming to be correct, Miranda takes hold of one of the letters, catching a whiff of the synthetic banana fragrance spilling out its decapitated neck. Just like those fuckers to do a scratch-and-sniff type deal.

The letter is made of heavy card stock and is filled with praise, praise that's typed out in Courier, discussing what a wonderful first month it's been having the recipient, in this case Kathy, on board.

The letters firmly make plain the fact that her great enemy has invaded her home, unsatisfied with taunting her from afar. She tosses the envelopes aside, and if the Twins wonder why she was going through their stuff, hang 'em.

The *second* is the just-kicked box, not the *Amazon* order of impulsively-purchased blouses or makeup remover usually piled up by the door, but a naked wooden crate marked only by a fuzzy postcard on its upward face, a postcard with the word "PROOF" scrawled on it in *Sharpie*. The 6"x 8" picture on the inverse side is blurry, sure, but all surveillance-camera footage is. Nothing is in the frame but a figure, a figure in dark glasses and a heavy shawl, but tall, tall and long in both chin and tooth. It is absolutely the aforementioned proof.

The figure in the frame is unmistakably Cindi Lapenschtall, and the date on the photo is three days prior. Cindi looks great for a dead woman, hardly any rot on her, but, Hell, she'd look great in any state.

The fact that they know where she lives, that they have clear proof that Cindi Lapenschtall is alive, that fighting against them seems right now more unwise than going off on this mini-adventure at their behest, all of these are reasons enough to tear open the package, remove the familiar VR goggles inside, pry off and crumple the post-it tagged onto them that reads, *Join Us, Miranda Swami, Become Yourself,* and march the whole thing into her room. Everything other than the goggles she throws in a pile onto the bed while the goggles she lays out beside her, contemplating not just one, but the *two* lives she lost in a span of just a couple weeks.

What an awful day it's been. An awful day in an awful world. She wishes to escape this one into another: a trip to the shore house might be in her future. If only she weren't so damn exhausted. But fortunately, a much-less committal escape is dangling a carrot beside her. An escape that doesn't even require her to leave the East Village. Hell, she won't even have to leave her room.

Phone aside. Phone silenced and off in the corner so she won't be bothered by classmates asking for homework help or delivery service ads. She has some exploring to do. She applies the goggles to her dome, plugs them into her computer, and waits for a dot matrix to appear. She waits to be taken away. To there. To Gwami. To something else entirely.

BANANAS!

In most conceivable universes, Miranda, sans hints or help, stumbles endlessly around the Program for some small eternity, ending a nevertheless-valiant search in eventual defeat.

In those universes, she is never truly able to ground herself in The Program; no friendly hands reach out to guide her. She becomes frustrated over the course of weeks and eventually throws the goggles in the trash. She is driven out of The Program altogether, ending her quest, cutting her off from Gwami forevermore.

Those Other Mirandas settle in to watch *Big Banana* distantly rise and fall, brought down in due time by either their own Caligula hubris or the general wavering of the market. Her actions are unrelated to the company's eventual extinction. Those Mirandas live lives peppered with regret, but that regret is tempered with the eventual understanding that all their struggles, so seemingly important at the time, were ultimately insignificant, "in the grand scheme of things." There are just so many stars in the cosmos. Those Mirandas meet conceivable and ordinary ends punctuating conceivable and ordinary lives, and hardly anybody in any universe bothers to tell their stories.

But in this world, almost entirely *inconceivably* and totally *extra-or-dinarily*, two frogs in a yellow wood need help defining soup, and that makes all the difference.

Let me explain. Miranda right now stands, just like her co-dimensional compadres, in the center of an endless, snaking hotel hallway.

Flanking her are these unmarked and aforementioned faded-sienna doors, another pair a few yards away, another after that and after that. Underneath her feet, a red shag carpet like from some 70's porn-producer's fuck den stretches out endlessly, the dirty fibers clumped and looking damp.

No bananas, though. Nowhere in sight. Clean walls with clean, purely decorative art untouched by *Big Banana's* graffiti or subliminal marketing messages. The painted fruit bowls opt instead for Rosaceae. That's a plus. A massive plus. That means either this place or its denizens or its creators are immune to *Big Banana's* dastardly charms. Good looks, Program. That's a point on the board for the Woman with the Red Hair. That goes a long way.

Remember in Harlem, when that bulky computer's IP address entered itself into the Program? Miranda was brought through these hallways automatically, the Program taking her directly to where the Woman with the Red Hair waited.

But when her home IP mimics its uptown sibling, those wonderful, troublesome auto-navigational properties vanish. She can move around with full autonomy, which is great! She can walk back and forth, press herself right up against the wall, spin and spin and spin with alarming speed, even jump in the air if she taps the space bar. But what's it all worth anyways since she can't understand how to open any of the doors in this damned, inoperable place?

All the nearby doors are protected by esoteric passwords with weird hints ("Satan's rope is made of black licorice") or the kind of arithmetic, blockchain lock you'd need a seriously epic mining rig to bust through. Behind these doors are people's secrets, their secret lives. The infrastructure surely aims to keep them that way. Further down the hall, around the corner, further down *that* hall, it's the same everywhere. She's totally locked out. Figures: freedom, and not so much at all.

Each subsequent failure at another optimistically-approached door strengthens in our Miranda the same desire that eventually conquered the others: a desire to cease this stupid endeavor altogether. Those Mirandas also came unsuccessfully to the end of corridors, having taken maddeningly logical movements — turns and backtracks and loop-de-loops and diggysteps — and found the same inaccessibility at every one. They were driven mad by the myriad impasses placed before them, and by their own inability to brainstorm a successful solution. They spent all night and all the next night and all the nights after that backtracking, retracing their steps, trying to outsmart and outthink their way from a spider's web. They never ended up going anywhere.

And that kind of successive failure really chips at someone's spirit, no matter how inspired or intrepid it might be.

And maybe our Miranda would wind up sharing the same fate as those others if not for the loud *knock* on her bedroom door, so sudden and forceful it sends her jumping up out of her seat and onto her feet. In a moment of careless unthinking panic, she flings her headset down onto her keyboard. It lands with a sickening *crunch*. Internally a mess, certain she's just destroyed her keyboard and goggles both, Miranda nevertheless makes an attempt at looking chill before moving to the door, smoothing her hair and, you know, relaxing her shoulders and such, trying to hide her jitters.

"Yeah?" Miranda says, opening the door slightly for her roommate, a rarely-seen version of Katie, one with under-eyes black and beautiful hair all disheveled and the faint air of stale vodka leaking from her mouth.

"Hey, uhm, so sorry to do this," she says, her voice coarse as sand between your molars, "but your light was on, and, god, sorry I just could really use some Advil if you have any."

"Oh, yeah, *haha*, sure. Come on in."

Katie, exaggerating for effect, takes a few wobbly steps into Miranda's room before half-falling/half-sitting down onto the bed. She lays back amongst bubble-wrap and cardboard, groaning as she does so. Praying that the rubble on her bed won't be fodder for discussion,

Miranda rummages quick as she can through some desk drawers look-ing for medicine. Katie says, "Making an unboxing video, hon?" hic-cups loudly and continues on, "Are those VR goggles?"

Damn it all.

Though Miranda in that same moment finds what she's looking for, which means she can convincingly cast Katie from her cave, her heart goes cold. "Yeah, they are," she says, standing. "I won a contest, but they don't seem to work. I think something broke during shipping."

"Sucks," Katie says, gratefully and gracefully accepting the pill bottle. "Let me just —"

"Take them all, no worries. I like never use them," Miranda says. She knocks her knuckles against her skull and says, "They always said I was hard-headed." The joke does not land.

"Oh, uhm, okay," Katie says, standing, teetering, catching herself, standing, moving to the door, saying, "Are you like *hiccup* genetically predisposed or something — ?", thanking Miranda, slamming her own door down the hall a bit too forcefully.

Kathy, woken by the noise, groans, "Why are you always so *freakin'* loud?"

Miranda's heartbeat only settles once she again locks her door, hides the cardboard evidence under her bed, and sits back down in front of her computer. And there, she pauses.

If she doesn't lift the goggles to her face, never attempts to use them again or, in fact, never even removes them from her keyboard, she'll never discover the fact that she's broken them beyond repair. Schrodinger's Headset will remain uncertainly operational for the rest of time. She can live the remains of her life knowing that she *chose* to end this endeavor, that she was not simply subject to an act of neglect she'd wish undone for all her days.

Maybe she feels herself jockeying with these same thoughts in other, adjacent universes, other universes where Miranda's story here ends. The shame and guilt from discovering that, yes, she's destroyed beyond repair her goggles, will prove too intense to recover from. In those universes, she never again receives strange texts or sees coded messages in billboard pixels. Therein she waits for some redux, some second chance, and waits, and waits, and waits, and eventually gives up, not only on the Woman and the Program and Gwami, but on herself.

Knowing painfully how profound the effects of a momentary slip-up can be on a whole life, well, that realization cripples the girl, making existence even more difficult. Her anxiety gets worse. Simple decisions greatly unnerve her. She's too careful with how she crosses the street, so she's frequently late. Her existing relationships fracture further, and new ones form with even less frequency than they do now, if you can believe that. If our Miranda is to avoid that fate, it will be by only divine intervention. Hopefully, something omniscient is looking out for her. Something wordy and earnest beyond her wildest dreams.

But Miranda's always had a strong will, and wields it now, flexes what she's got, putting on the goggles with gritted teeth and finding that, somehow, Oh God somehow, she hasn't broken her keyboard or the goggles. Everything is patently, extraordinarily *fine*. Divinity, *finally* doing Miranda a favor. Still, she and they aren't even close to being even. This she knows. This she tacitly reminds them from time to time.

While she hasn't done any lingering damage to the technology, she finds that the weight of the goggles upon the arrow keys has directed her avatar to take a sequence of turns she *never* would have consciously made. None of Miranda's rational, intentional actions would have brought her here, to this specific segment of the Program, to this stretch of hallway.

Which is pretty all-important because, well lookie here, something encouraging: a soft light puddling on the floor ahead, coming through an ingress ajar. Upon the open door hangs a sign drawn crudely in Microsoft Paint: *Help Wanted* ☺. Miranda, hoping her avatar is of the friendly-looking sort, heads inside, transparently here to help.

The virtual air shimmers slightly as she steps over a doormat of toadstools into her first new world. She is one of only a handful of Mirandas to take this step. Bully for her.

Walking inside, a bright white light overtakes her vision, a sensation she'll come to learn is a kind of universal loading screen, analogous to waking up in a sunlit room after a deep nap. Her sight returns in fashion, slowly revealing an endless mid-forest marsh around her, a woodland stretching on in every direction, this either the traversable landscape of a huge open-world or a startlingly photo-realistic wallpaper.

Immediately before her is a lazy little section of pond slowly giving itself over to the cattails and reeds growing fat and morose at its banks. Rippling lily pads on the surface roil around with an unfelt breeze.

Miranda turns back to the doorway, not fully expecting it to be standing upright and tawny right where she left it, like a glitch in the universe, a piece of erect trash left out in the wilderness. The swampland world stretches on behind it, disregarding that the door contains within it an entire, somehow *larger*, universe. Ah gather and observe, ye physicists: a truly Whovian object larger on the inside than the out.

Turning back to the pond, Miranda is touched by a poetic sight: three young lotus flowers, pink as cartoon bubblegum, floating languidly at the pond's edge, their glitzy leaves unbothered by the pond muck. Then there's a *ribbit*, and from out behind the flowers hop two stately male bullfrogs of yellow and green, their necks puffing and receding rancorously. Uncertain of her literal and metaphoric next steps, Miranda wades further into the water.

"Hello?" she types, wondering if this world has a host, and if so, whether they'll arrive with any prudence. She wipes her IRL forehead and finds her IRL palms have become quite IRL sweaty. Fortunately for her, it's easier to seem calm when you can type, edit, and revise all your responses, when your bumbling heart-beat and strained eyes and leaking hands don't immediately give away your anxiety.

The strained hum of her computer, nearing its technological limitation, emulates well the buzzing of the blowflies which hang about in the air.

But it appears her hosts are already here. The first of the two bullfrogs, Heavier than its companion, hops forward, saying "Well well well, welcome, welcome! We're so happy to have you!"

"Yes, yes, a great pleasure," the other frog, Grassier in color, notes.

"So, you noticed the sign on our door, I presume, and have come to help?" Heavier asks.

In her head, Miranda hears some of Father's old advice: *Act like you've been here before. Act like you've been here before. Talk to the frogs, it's cool* (that last bit was a paraphrase). Methodically, careful of typos and colloquialisms, she types "Yes, hello! What is it you need help with? I'm not much of a programmer, but —"

"Oh, my dear, you need have nothing but a functioning brain and a discerning ear to lend us assistance. You see, we are — How should I put this? — old friends engaged once more in a theoretical argument that has plagued us for years. Like a carousel, our conversations go forever on, circling and circling this one basic question, one that, having dogged us one time too many, we've thought to open up to the inquisitive outside perspectives of this strange Program's denizens."

"I'm sorry," Miranda interrupts, "but just for, you know, posterity's sake, this doesn't have anything to do with Bananas, right?"

There's an empty moment. An internet silence. And then:

"Oh, *ho ho ho*, my dear, worry not. Our ponderance peddles in a far more philosophical food. We trifle not with that Banana drivel. Nay, we are at yet another impasse, you see, in defining the concept of '*soup.*' Now, now. I know how trivial that must sound, but please, don't be dulled, and do not run off just yet. Listen. It will be worth your while."

"Okay."

"All my colleague and I can ever agree upon is that soup's most crucial characteristic is its being *perceived* to be soup, for otherwise any definition would run rampant with coulis and salsas, dashi and other simple broths. Beyond that, we find ourselves at dead-end after dead-end. Think for a moment, for this we truly believe: our question is one of the great philosophical dilemmas of our time."

"To be earnest, we are running out of great philosophical dilemmas."

"I'm not so sure about that," Miranda starts saying, but trails off.

"Many years ago, after a dinner party at a mutual friend's, I posed the question to Sartre, just as we're posing it to you now. After a few minutes of intense thinking, he said, 'I don't believe I'll be able to enjoy this next course,' and excused himself for a cigarette. He never did come back into the party, and in fact, was dead within the year. Suffice to say, this particular question has quite an illustrious history."

"What do you two do for a living?" Miranda asks. "I'm sorry if that's quite forward."

"Oh nonsense, you doll. Isn't she a doll? Please, we are all friends here. I'm a Professor of Economic Theory at Yale. My esteemed colleague here is the Regional Director of Operations for all *Southwest* flights operating out of O'Hare."

"And you two are just hanging out here? Discussing soup? Pardon me, but don't you have, like, actual work to be doing?"

"Let's not quarrel over details, dearest. Not to sound rude, but we won't question the circumstances of your life if you allow us the same courtesy."

"Uhm, okay," Miranda says, wondering if she's blowing this, feeling the sudden bubble of self-hate rising up from her gall-bladder, threatening to pop in her throat. She pushes it back down and asks "So, uhm, why don't we start at the beginning?"

"At the very beginning. Good idea. Deconstruct to then reconstruct. Perhaps a *Google* search is in order."

And off they go, googling and talking over each other and bickering, cursing themselves and cursing the brains in their heads that have led them to this immovable object. Miranda, soon intrigued by the subject herself, plays with them, engages in their little game for how long she cannot say.

"Well, what if it *has* to come from a larger container?" Miranda posits, "A large receptacle of soup is the norm, yeah? Like if you order chowder in a restaurant, it comes from a big pot of it."

"Then you are damning Andy Warhol's dearest and giving new life to Aramark's Middle School Cafeteria Nacho Cheese, when served in its drippiest, ooziest form."

The Swami body behind the goggles is made more and more exhausted as it is kept up later and later, its hold on language and its ability to follow long logical labyrinths becoming compromised. It gets snippy and uncooperative.

"No! Of course not!" Heavier says. "Salad dressing *cannot* be soup! Under no pretense, no matter how it is served, thickened, thinned, or perceived. I will not hear it."

"But you're coming at this from a point of privilege!" Miranda hits back. "You don't have the right to litigate foods that *others* might consider soup!"

"I simply will not hear it!" retorts Heavier. "We are missing that ineffable soupiness which evades our dear dressing but is imbued within our bisques. Damn it. Damn it all."

"Uhm…I…well…soup has a certain thickness, right? As you mentioned, bisques and such. That seems like a good place to — But, no, God damn it! That discounts —"

At once, all concerned parties voice the same correction:

"Hot Broth!"

"Hot Broth!"

"Hot Broth!"

The Frogs, as if sensing weakness, confound her poor brain with ethical parameters and obscure philosophical frameworks they apply in their further responses. As the conversation spikes further up over her head, Miranda gets ornery. Still, they don't make it any easier on her.

"Not falling asleep on us, are you dearest? Are we boring you?"

"I just don't understand what Hume or Spinoza have to do with this."

"It's important, you understand, that we have ethical and moral structures underneath any attempt at definition. Otherwise this would never hold up under any scrutiny!"

"Why do you need it to hold up to scrutiny? What kind of cynical person is going to pick apart your definition of soup?"

The Frogs involve each other in some new turn of the discussion as a kind of baby realization impresses itself upon Miranda's mental uterus.

"You're looking at this too cynically," she interrupts.

"What?"

"How dare you!"

"No, no, listen! You had it all along. At the beginning. We *had* it. We're getting further away from the answer. Occam's razor. The *only* definition of soup is something that's perceived to be soup, because —"

"Darling, we've been through this…what about Caesar dress —"

"— because *everything* is only what it is perceived to be."

"Hmm?"

"Listen. You want a framework for the world, here it is. Soup is soup because we as a society, as a collection of individuals, have decided that only certain things can be identified as such. Ditto anything. Men and women, economic structures, plant species, personality traits. They're only accepted as what they are because we agree on our perception of them. Sartre said 'Essence preceded Existence,' at least as it relates to objects, right? But the collective *we* control that essence. *We* imbue the thing with itself! I'm not sure if he said that somewhere, but but but that doesn't necessarily matter. 'First man exists: he materializes into the world, encounters himself, and only afterward defines himself.' I'm pretty sure that's a direct quote.

"But soup is different. We define soup before it exists, and then we encounter something. But that thing doesn't exist as soup, unless it materializes into the world matching that essence! We don't collectively agree that salad dressing is soup, and so it isn't. We haven't made that a part of its essence. We look at it, but soup it never becomes. We we we collectively agree that pizza is a certain subspecies of dough with sauce and cheese, but if we slather tomato sauce and shredded cheddar on a cracker, that isn't the same, even if the dictionary "definition" might say so. The essence is ineffable but easy, as ineffable as the human soul, yet we all know what it feels like to be alive, what having a soul entails. Here's what I posit. Definitions are capricious, they must be! As capricious as human whim. Soup is what we accept to be soup. Soup requires humanity as much as humanity requires itself. All things require an imbuer. The unimbued imbuer…

"Or maybe I'm rambling, I don't know."

Only a prolonged silence offers itself in the place Miranda expected cheers and celebration to be. She waits awkwardly, kind of surprised at her own ingenuity, hoping the frogs don't chide her for the unintentionally-pilfered philosophy.

Heavier clears his throat. "Oh, goodness, I'm so sorry dear. I didn't realize you were so very new here."

"What?"

"What?"

"Oh, it's just that's pretty *presumptuous*. How would you possibly know I'm new here?" She snaps back.

The Frogs puff and retract their throats as if in laughter. "Well, my dear, you don't even have headphones in."

"And how could you possibly know *that*?"

"Because we brought this up earlier, and when you didn't respond, we thought, well, we thought you weren't going to dignify such an absurd point of view with a response."

"But now, of course, we recognize that you just didn't hear us."

And in an East Village apartment, much past her bedtime, a girl's cheeks glow bright red. To be embarrassed in so many worlds, in one day, what a unique gift, a unique humiliation.

Mortified, and with her guard down, Miranda spills the off-topic truth in long, unbroken fashion: that she doesn't know where she is, that she's scared and in over her head, that she's looking for a person whose face she's never seen, that she's metaphorically adrift in a faraway sea, and that she fears no number of friendly buoys or lucky life rafts will likely lead her where she needs to go.

"See, she *is* completely lost," the Heavier frog says. "I was right." The self-satisfied, smug little *Salientia* sits smiling stupidly. Miranda's semi-miffed at the sentiment.

"Sweetheart, look," Grassier interjects. "Forget this silly conversation and listen to me. This Program is a dark and majestic place, full of contradictions. Forget the effect of our silly conversation, or any silly conversations you may encounter, and just enjoy the being here. Whether you find your mate or not, just enjoy the being here. It's a special honor. My advice to you is to assume that everything you see is normal. And maybe be a bit more selective with who you speak to, and what you decide to hear. A pair of headphones is *vital*. You don't ever want to appear very out of your wits. Besides, some knowledge can only be safely transmitted in audio. Never know who's reading along and such."

"Thank you, really," Miranda says. "You're too kind. Why are you being so kind?"

"Well, darling, you helped us without goading, simply because you cared enough to care. Shouldn't we afford you the same courtesy?"

Stupid solitary tears, just a few, fall off Miranda's face and hang off the edge of her eyelashes, collecting in a little pool within her goggles. "I'm sorry for burdening you with all this. This isn't at all what I came here to do. So embarrassing. But well, uhm, do you have any idea where I should go next? I haven't seen any other door open like yours was. I have no other ideas."

The Frogs, during a brief pause, might be conversing, figuring the consequences of what they're about to divulge. Heavier says "Well, frankly, I'm not surprised. Not many in this program are as welcoming as we are. In fact, a great number of those you meet will likely be some shade of paranoid, aggressive, gruff. Not their fault, this is a place designed for only two kinds of people: the ridiculous and the secretive."

"You know what she needs? If she can find one, a skeleton key," Grassier posits to his froggy friend.

"Well yes, old chap, of course that would help her, and certainly we would all love a skeleton key, go traipsing from here to there without a care in the world, but where the hell is she going to get one?"

"Is a 'skeleton key' what I think it is?" Miranda asks.

"Well it's not an actual key hanging around someone's neck — well perhaps it is in somebody's strange world — but for your purposes, it's just a password, a string of numbers that'll get you through most any one of those doors out there. Those who have one are pretty keen on keeping it to themselves, however. Or else they command a high price. I'm regretfully not sure what more help we can be. Perhaps you will meet a generous soul who empathizes with your plight. There are so many intertwisting plots in this place, I wouldn't be surprised if you're involved in one or more yourself. Unwittingly, of course. But those are the best kinds of stories, the ones you don't even know you're in."

"Or a drunkard in a gutter might spill suspicious integers from his mug onto the pavement below him, hoping subversively you'll take note. And, indeed I implore you, take note of such things."

"We can at least point you towards a more populated place. Perhaps someone there can help you continue your search. After all, we two are relatively stationary creatures. We don't much get along with the others who frequent these rooms, nor do we know many of them at all."

"What is it? Four doors down?" Heavier tries to remember.

"Four, indeed," Grassier confirms.

"Four doors down, then, and on this side of the hallway. 7-digit-password, it's *Ferengi*, you know, because we're all real nerds of a feather here, and maybe someone within can help you. All the best. And please, you've been such a good sport, sweat-pea. Don't be a stranger."

"Unless it's demanded of you."

Our Miranda thanks the Frogs and leaves the swamp, the door left open a smidge behind her. Maybe the next passerby will be of more assistance.

Smiling for no good reason other than she's a part of something, even if she knows not what it is, just a character in a story with a real plot, a plot just chugging right along, Miranda goes searching for this so-called "next world," wondering just how many such worlds she'll see after all is done, and whether she'll seem new and unaware in each one.

Millennials are, like, concerningly on board with getting an addiction, and to anything. We got hardcore addicted to fucking *Farmville, for Christ's sake. And not just like oh, maybe I'll log on and tend the crops everyday addicted, I'm talking, oh, I'm going to pump an astonishing amount of real human dollars into the growth and care of this, my virtual farm, think about ways to increase my crop yield and constantly patrol the property looking for coyotes and treasure, watching this little farmer o'mine hoe new plots for sweet potato seeds, mindlessly invite all my 1600 other friends to "Join Me" because if they use my referral code I'll get six extra bottles of milk or some shit for the merino sheep I paid $25 of actual, interpersonal currency for. Farmville, Candy Crush, World of Warcraft, Fortnite, Instagram...* it's easier than ever to cultivate an addiction. And sexier. All the cool kids are doing it. I bet you have a pretty sizeable collection yourself. Do you like to take 'em out and show your friends?

Now here's Miranda Swami exploring a computer program more sprawling than the grandest MMO, using as immersive a technology as anything in existence, walking along the bleeding edge, spurred on by a quest so personal but oh so grandiose in its origins and in its potential outcomes that the sheer totality of it has infected all parts of her thinking and all parts of her life. Now, tell me truly: if you were in that position, or one with far lesser stakes even, wouldn't you get addicted, too?

Hell, I'm jonesing just describing it.

She follows the Frogs' instructions and heads down the hallway to the fourth door on her left, carefully inputs the password, and lets the fresh light from the opened door wash over her skin, effectively sealing her fate. Nobody but nobody, I say, could resist the promise of what she finds within.

What she finds is this: a lavishly-detailed and very VERY LOUD, and surprisingly well-populated, city set atop a helicraft's sextet of enormous, continuously-*whirring* propellers. You can see them, big as kraken's eyes, from your peripherals as soon as you step through the door. If you close it behind you and turn around to face your surroundings, you might justify your entire quest on the merits of the landscape alone: an entire Earth sprawls below, a geographically breathtaking array of high-mountain peaks and endless, wide-open seas, of ancient fissures splitting the soil, and mammoth poplar forests so tall their bristles threaten to brush the underside of the airship city.

Being that every on-boarder into this world starts in this very spot, it makes sense that, when turning to the city proper, Miranda finds herself amidst the virtual bazaar designed to accost the freshly arrived, to take advantage of their infant excitement. All manner of cosmic creatures, hocking slapdash items tagged with cryptocurrency price demands, are gathered here opposite others of their ilk across the way, forming a kind of main street for newcomers to pass through and peruse should they have business further into the city.

"I got all seven seasons of *The Sopranos* here! All seven seasons of your favorite hit-crime show, for just 36 XRP. That's right, Sir or Madame or whatever you are with the tentacles there, you heard me correctly! 36 XRP is all you need to own the show that kickstarted the Golden Age of Television! You, sir! Yes you! Have you seen the inimitable work of the late-great James Gandolfini? Don't miss your best and cheapest chance! What about you, Miss? 30 XRP, a great discount for such a lovely creature!"

"High-pitched frequencies to make a mosquito gag! Cast them out of any nearby device, cast them out of your dad's new TV! Do it all for the low-low price of three Litecoin. Prank your friends! Freak out your boss! Punish anyone still using those horrible Bluetooth headsets! Eight intensities range from 'bothersome' to 'histrionic.' Don't miss out on the hot new technology *all* your friends are going to hate you for!"

Miranda stumbles through the market, ignoring the merchants' cries and the small, tan-faced children who surround her with cupped hands, hoping for just a slim shard of *Iota*, if she has any, or some *DogeCoin* will even do for supper tonight. Pushing them away with not so little guilt, Miranda must remember that they are not real children, that they will not starve, that they are pixels and algorithms and, quite possibly, straight, white men looking for workless income, a last legal gasp before tax evasion proper. But then she stops. Stops moving, stops pushing. She lets the hands swarm around her, lets their fingers enter her pockets (empty anyways) because she's suddenly distracted by something very, very important in the world around her, or, I suppose, the lack of something.

Look around, y'all: this place is pristine. Ignore the dusty street sign posts, the grime and cobwebs hung up like decorations in the musty corners of the sellers' stalls. Disregard the ugly, uneven weeds emerging into open air from between the mud-caked metal panels underfoot. Yes, the tattered tarp tents over some of the merchants are wispy from overuse, turned colorless from all the sunshine. Yes, this is an ugly, low-born market full of swindlers and scoundrels certainly, but to Miranda Swami, it's the most beautiful thing she's seen.

No Bananas.

Nowhere.

None at all.

Weird, passing lifeforms dress in awkward, odd ways, but there are no bananas adorning their hats or ass-less chaps or jingling jester-wear. The alley walls are plastered in graffiti, sure, but it's all clan tags and Twitter handles, just normal people looking for attention through virtual spray-paint. No half-ironic, pandering street art of Bananas here. No Bananas doing kung-fu, Bananas holding tiny humans to their ears like telephones, Bananas driving cars or dressed in military regalia with their fingers hesitating over a big, red, missile-launching button, Bananas painted into the Yellow Submarine album cover (as the Beatles *and* the Meanies), Bananas as the cast of *Seinfeld*. None of it. Just normal, innocuous, maybe half-threatening but still generally familiar, graffiti…you know, like from the time before.

Miranda grins widely, exploring with her eyes the fruitless facets of this fresh place. It doesn't take any more conversation or contact for her to know she's among friends. Even the attempted pickpocketers she, removing their fingers in defeat, seem newly sincere. Whether the responsibility lies with whoever designed the place or whoever populates it, at least one party agrees: Bananas are Bad, and will not be represented in this wholly pure place.

Our Miranda, we can say now with confidence, is all in on the Program! It has already, even this early, captured part of her soul.

Further on and past some stagnant cirrus clouds hanging about head-high, Miranda is a moth, attracted forward by a neon beer-stein sign, fluttering through a red curtain into an old-timey steampunk saloon.

Inside, she's immediately unsettled. Sudden stares are tossed her way by the shadow-bathed patrons in their booths and dim corners, and even those playing pool in the far room take time from the game to unwelcome the fresh meat. Steeling herself, she sidles up to the bar, meeting the glares of the other bar guests — three racially-insensitive African pygmies and an anthropomorphic mushroom — with kind words, offering to buy them drinks, attempting to start this local life off with a laugh.

"You can't actually buy anything here," the Bartender, a bumbling Easter Island Head, says to her in monotone.

"I know," she says back, "I was just being funny."

"There's no being funny in here either."

"Oh, I'm sorry. I'll suppress my natural hilarity." She turns to the Pygmies beside her and deadpans, "It literally explodes out of me."

Rising after a pointless and silent few minutes at the bar, Miranda walks into the center of the room, looking around in ashamed boredom before locking eyes with a creature in a corner booth. The thing, a blindfolded beetle with thirty boat-shoe bedecked arms, waves her over with a dozen limbs at once.

"New here, huh?"

"Everyone's been saying that."

"No wonder why."

"What do you want?" Miranda asks, already fed up.

A message pops up on her screen, a little red speech bubble asking her to join a private voice channel. No way this could go wrong, right? Anyways, what the hell? Still feeling the high of a banana-less life, she figures nothing can much hurt her in here. Not while she feels like *this*. Miranda accepts the invite. Her ears fill with the ambient sound from someone's faraway room.

Expecting a deep, unsettling robot voice, like of some anonymous interviewee on *60 Minutes*, Miranda is pleased to find her conversational companion has a bouncing British lilt, a voice like a Rudyard Kipling book come to pretty, flitty life.

"So, you're rather new here, and you're trying to orient yourself, yes? I dared imagine this was the case. Something rather...*uninformed* about you. Well, fortunately, you have stumbled into the most fortuitous of bar rooms. Like those rogues out in the alley, I too am a salesman of sorts. But where they peddle torrents and jailbroken apps, I deal in information. In fact, I was one of the first occupants of this Program, back when the developer kits were invite-only. Now that they're open-source, it's altogether too easy to wander endlessly here, lost among so many competing imaginations. As it happens, I meet a great many adventurous souls like you: so brazen, so naïve, walking into a bar like this expecting open arms and easy answers. Am I correct?"

"Keep talking," Miranda says into her microphone, bringing her lips close, hoping the spittle and friction obscure her voice.

"My trade is information. And, for many items, I am the sole merchant. Of all the gin joints in all the towns in all the worlds, you walk-ed into mine, so play it Sam…take advantage of your good fortune. You tell me what you want to know, and I will charge you modestly per answer."

"Charge me what?"

"Well, that's entirely up to you, Madame: what's in your wallet?"

Miranda, like so many of her contemporaries, had experimented with cryptocurrency speculation during the brief Bitcoin boom, buy-ing a quarter-token when the getting was good, just before it got great, and not long before it got godawful. While she wasn't as vocal in her crypto-support as those rich tech guys I'm sure you've had the mis-fortune of overhearing — the ones who spouted off about their *really exciting, totally cutting-edge* new investments at every BBQ, work party or bar-room they afflicted with their personage — she was nonetheless excited by the prospect of centralized, post-national currency, of gains on gains on gains *ad infinitum.*

Then, as you know, the boom busted and Bitcoin bottomed, but Miranda preferred to hang on to her investment rather than purge herself of it for a loss. Convinced bullishly all this time that the "cur-rency of The Dark Web" will any-day-now become the currency of the world (owing to either global unity, or outright apocalypse), she's nevertheless been hopeful about finding a consistent outlet that'll accept her made-up money. Enter the beetle.

When she's done linking her wallet and the creature says, "Okay, my new friend, ask away," Miranda goes right for it. She asks him directly about the Woman with the Red Hair (as if tempting fate's architect to intervene), and he proceeds to rant on, like he's been waiting ages for a question like this, blathering about the shadowy syndicate that designed this Program's infrastructure, about how this virtual world, while heavily populated for such an off-beat experiment, arose out of literal nothingness some nine-months earlier, with a coding schema that allowed incredible innovation in no-time if you had that kind of know-how, that it was confoundingly fully-functional and completely debugged by the time most settlers laid eyes on the land, that any concrete information about this syndicate was obviously hearsay, hearsay even to one as experienced as he, but *yes*, he *had* heard vague whispers about a Woman with fiery Red Hair, a developer with unlimited terraforming access to every room in the Program, who could build worlds out of nowhere and destroy them outright should it fit her fancy, this Woman perpetually traversing the realms like a bounty hunter or protective deity, how nevertheless he had never actually encountered such a Woman in all his time here and couldn't imagine that such a someone could exist, how he's heard her sometimes referred to as Cypher, other times Athene, and once or twice, Abaddon. Most importantly, while he's met a handful of travelers who've supposedly met the Woman themselves, he tells her that there's been no obvious connecting-tissue between them, but ain't that the rub? It's a universe built for discovery and disorientation, he tells her, so go out, discover, and be disoriented.

She says she wants to do that, only she doesn't know how. She says she's heard that some people here have skeleton keys, that those keys are the only way she'll be able to get from place to place quick enough to track her target in even the most liberal of timelines.

And the Blind Beetle says, in essence, well little girl, I think our chat here is over. You seem to be out of funds.

And son of a gun, he's right. Freewheeling cretin he is. That's almost $1500 dollars he's drained from her, silently, in the span of no more than a half-hour.

"Wait, what? Dude, are you kidding me?! That was *a ton of money.*"

"Answers are expensive. Consider yourself lucky I'm leaving only with this meagre sum."

If Miranda could jump through the computer and strangle to death the faceless thief on the other side, oh God would she. Her brain rummages through itself looking for any way to extract vengeance on this thing that's just robbed her, to justify her quixotism, and around such a treasonous creature. She'll find neither.

"But I'll leave you with this," the Beetle says standing. "Take a long walk outside. Maybe visit the plaza down the way. You never know what people are peddling out there, and what they will ask for in return. Here, because I'm not such a bad guy. Go buy yourself a cheeseburger, kid."

Ten dollars he deposits back into her wallet, and the Beetle, without another word, logs out of the chat, then out of the program altogether apparently, dissolving into the very air, leaving Miranda alone in the seedy, virtual bar, penniless for all intents and purposes, with answers she'll never get to capitalize on and an appetite for destruction.

Outside in the bazaar, our furious Miranda looks at all the things she could've bought instead of shitty information from an exploitative salesman. Every Kevin James movie, *with* director's commentary. Practically giving it away. 6-month subscription to *Tidal*, which they actually are giving away. A small drone shaped like a bird with "talons that *really grab*" could have been delivered to her nearest Amazon Locker for a fraction of the cost.

Pointless garbage all of it, but Miranda takes another few trips up and down the lane, hoping to catch a glimpse of some wizened old merchant she missed the first few times, someone reluctantly selling the Dark Web equivalent of a Mogwai.

Finding nothing of note but needing to walk off her rage, Miranda passes through the market further into the city, the lane eventually opening up into a town square of sorts, a sterile, metal-plated plaza surrounded by faceless office buildings, but empty except for a few souls gathered around a folding table.

It's time to find her way to a new world, she decides. This place has given all it's going to give, and taken all it's going to take. And it's taken so much already (not that a loss of $1500 is going to leave her destitute, but whatever confidence she had gained in this place was sucked away in the transaction, sucked away *along* with $1500. Losing either one by itself? Not so bad. But both together: *yikes*).

Her attention soon turns to the flimsy table across the square, around which a small group of Wild-Wild-West-types hang around, like they're setting up for a bake sale. A sign on the stand reads, "Step right up, and test your mettle. Win a fortune, live like an outlaw."

Miranda approaches the cowboys, none of whom notice her except the one manning the table, a stick-thin man with a bandana covering most of his face, whose eyes wildly jump around the square, as if on the lookout for something silently hunting him.

"What's this then?" Miranda asks.

"Accepting applications for a game, little lady. Of gunslinger and murder and *outlawis extremis*. Fancy yourself a five-shooter?"

"Don't think I have anything better to do at the moment," Miranda says, recognizing an opportunity to get off-world. And isn't that what this is about? Hopping from place to place until picked-up pieces fit themselves together? She'll invent her own skeleton key. She has her wits. "What's your pitch?"

"Look here: me and some others are putting together a team, going to join a little game of Search-and-Destroy some E-sports folks are playing a few rooms over. Last team standing gets 20k, and, well, we're going to be the last team standing. The others won't even see us coming."

"And you're just accepting random applications?"

"Warm bodies are good bodies. Either you'll hold your own, or you'll be a serviceable bullet sponge. No real risk on our part."

"This doesn't seem so couth."

"Then don't ask any questions."

"How do you plan on getting me or anyone else into a locked room?"

"Well, let's just say our fearless leader has a way of getting around. One she's happy to share with her friends and followers. Very lucrative possibilities for those looking to head into harm's way."

"A way of getting around?"

"Yes'm. She's one a kind."

Light bulb.

"I'd like to meet her."

"You can sign right here, then."

A pop-up appears on her screen, requesting her signature and initials on an electronic form riddled with x's and long, empty underscores.

Ah, these Swami siblings. Can't resist the temptation of the dotted line.

"God it's bright. Can you, like, dim the brightness or is that just going to be part of it?"

"Shut up, new meat."

"Really with that shit? Fuck you, dude."

"*Everyone* quiet. You'll give us away."

Quashing this confrontation between Miranda and a facsimile David Hasselhoff is the Bandana Man from the table, who made it seem as if he was taking everyone into his confidence when he requested they call him "Druid."

David Hasselhoff continues saying something quietly disparaging into his mic, drawing Druid's ire, who stops to scold him privately, four red macaroni squiggles of anime anger launched from his forehead.

They, the Druid and Hasselhoff and Miranda, are accompanied through this Wild West ghost town by a green-haired Pixie floating a few inches off the ground, and four slender, silent Medieval Doctors, like with the creepy bird beak masks and the black, ankle length robes. They're all keeping quite still, the lot of them, hiding in a thin back-alley, one sandwiched between two rows of red and brown and sandalwood boarding-houses. Though the plan was to move through this town as quickly as possible and get to their outlaw camp in the boonies without drawing any attention, Druid has demanded they stop, thinking perhaps they're being surveilled. A dust devil down the lane whips itself up into a playtime tornado, threatening to grow angrier, but only ever threatening.

Right about *then*, there are eight too-audible footsteps from a ledge above, and Miranda turns just in time to see a figure running into a door on the second-floor of that barrio over there. She starts saying "Did you guys see —" but her words are cut off by the slow-moving bullet smashing into her cranium, sending her screen to black and darker black and darker black still. Though there's no more to see other than the black of unforeseen death, wartime sounds of panic still bounce around inside her stunned ears: the gunshots and bootsteps, - the screams and Hasselhoff cursing himself and cursing God and cursing his mother and cursing "this fucking bitch to the right of me," and finally this "whole bitch of an MMO." Some confounding soul says, very clearly, the words "Don't be a rage-quitting proto-twink," and then everything goes quiet.

And Miranda takes off her goggles.

And the early morning daylight stings her eyes so bad they feel like eggs *popping* on a hot skillet.

And she falls back on her bed, defeated and exhausted and absolutely clueless as to what she's going to do next. This isn't the first time she's died this month, but you know what they say: it never gets any easier.

She's had it for the night. Or what remains of the night. It's objectively turned morning.

And oh, shit. She *completely* forgot. She has a paper due today. Isn't that sweet? Miranda, for the moment, stillest least pretends to care about school. We'll see how long that lasts.

Better get working, Miranda! Gotta get that A+ if you want a good job with a good salary aaaaaaand ben-e-fits! Sleep, we now helpfully remind her, will be provided for her in plenty quantity after her proper, perhaps approaching, death.

But, honestly, how can she even pretend to be interested in the drivel of her Art History professors? Once vaunted, their ideas fall from mouth to ground, words without wings but with plenty of weight, gathering like attic clutter around her feet. And the other students drink it in. Pens go to notebook. Thoughts go to whiteboard scribbling. Once, Miranda was like them. Once, she was more them than they themselves are now.

But to Miranda, all these theories seem suddenly so hypothetical, the assertions so far-flung and philosophical, the assignments utterly unnecessary and, mind you, impractical. She can see that the professorial words, if taken to heart, will not help the aspiring artist, but instead entrap them in pedagogical sludge. All of this information, the criticism and hyper-examination, why it'll scare off all but the most dauntless among their rank. *Here is what art is truly about, they seem to say, and it should hardly keep you awake.*

Yet it is here Miranda sits, feigning attention, a 3200-word run-on sentence in her lap chronicling Botticelli's influence on Marc Chagall, amongst perhaps the most qualified group of pre-museum-curators in the Western Hemisphere.

The unruly pointlessness of it all, to a girl fresh from a gunfight. To a girl who'd just died. Again. So how could anyone expect her to pop over with any real pizzazz from her 10AM to the dining hall, to the vegan station where they're serving crusty tempeh again, and from there to the school-mandated therapist, whom she won't say anything of value to anyways (this her way of protesting against the idea that an institution of higher learning should have any say over the decisions a student makes with their own body, or lack thereof) (the withered, fully-grey therapist likes to ask questions such as "Are we having those *hmmmmm* feelings again?" and "Don't you want to *hmmmm* expand on the subject?") and from there, right to her 2PM, an exploration of astronomical principles via Van Gogh, and from there right to her 3:30, a *Photoshop* crash course? Everyone in that last class was asked to come in today with a full-length picture of themselves on a USB drive, which they would then be editingfreehand over the first half of the semester, a completely ridiculous request Miranda protests by producing a picture of a howling baboon, rather condescendingly telling the professor through a yawn that she'd make it look like Princess Jasmine by the end of the term. Or the end of class…whichever he'd prefer.

And from there thankfully, mercifully, back home. Where, right on her bed as she left them, the goggles sit somehow fully operational, the yellow-and-blue images — images of life — on their screens distorted by nothing other than distance, begging the girl-arrived to come take a peek at what they've done in her absence.

Now, *this* is a development worthy of melodrama.

With great recklessness, she throws her bookbag to the floor, at once forgetting its contents and the life it symbolizes. The girl moves in a trance towards the goggles, led by her head and her eyes and a crushing desire to again leave this old, blasted world of hers that has, through the course of the day, confirmed its commitment to remaining soul-crushingly dull.

"She's moving," says a voice through her headphones, and as Miranda comes to in that other world, it's with a pair of faces up close to hers, as if inspecting her for tooth decay.

"I ain't understand how this is even possible," says the first face.

"Shit. Johnny, you sure you really up'n shot her?" asks the second.

"Shot was clear as day. Checked the entry wound and everything. Girl just didn't blink out, what can I say?"

"Annnd, now she's moving. No problem, right? 'Shot was clear as day' my ass. 'Checked the entry wound?' I reckon."

"Ey, little girl: you can hear us, yeah?"

"What are you talking about?" Miranda says quietly, very disoriented and trying to gain her bearings. Trying, trying to see straight, but beyond the immediate faces — which, though finely-featured, blur together into a strand of thin, mustachioed visages and clumps of brown hair — the world she sees is a blur. Vague tannish hues and a dirty, auburn-tinged yellow light cast down upon everything. The spot over there where that bright white is shining through, that must be a window, and the movement back by it must be from other people.

Her inspection of the landscape is interrupted when the first voice barks, "Why ain't you dead, girl? Where you come from?" It's a voice that rustles under a mustache; a keen, high-pitched voice like a lascivious whistle, a certain twang of Ye Olde West inherent in its slight rasp, a kind of atmospheric gruffness belaying a violent side below the exterior. It's a strained voice that shouts again with less patience, "Where you come from, huh? Why you here?!"

"I'm sorry! I don't have any answers for you. I was roped into this whole thing, I swear. I have literally no idea what's happening."

"Well, shit," Mustache says, throwing his cowboy hat down onto the floor. Her vision appears to clear some, and as it does, Miranda makes out the rest of the room's details: two women in hoop dresses sitting wistfully by the window, through which a pair of horses drink out of a trough, a man sitting at an old-timey piano by the far wall, an overweight and monocled gentleman in a suit and paisley tie pacing around the room, and a toddler with a single big tooth dismantling a gun over on the floor by the stairs. Some party.

The Piano Man, tapping his foot, begins to play something by Randy Newman.

"So how do you all know each other?" Miranda says coyly.

"Do you know how much trouble you're in, Missy?" the man with the Paisley tie says suddenly, enraged, he being the Second Face from before, it's clear. "And you're here making jokes. The nerve. The blasted nerve!"

"Calm down, Josephine," one of the girls calls out mockingly, "you ain't scaring her, nor none of us."

Paisley checks his watch. "We have to go," he says. "They're going to come after us if we stay here too long."

"Hey girl, look at me," Mustache calls from the barstool he's slouched down in, his legs out and crossed in front of him, revealing the intricately hexagonal underside of his boot. "Watchu know about all them folk you come here with? You know their names? Who they working for? Things like that? Anything?"

"And why should I tell you what I may or may not know?"

"Well, you're here for the prize money I imagine, and for that, you gotta be alive. But if we keep you locked up good and nice, like you are now, and have that little Baby on the floor o'er yonder spend an hour or two exploring your source code, we could get all the answers we need *and* have you out on your ass in no time. Right, Baby? We can do that, yeah?"

The Baby calls back, in a baritone deep as the movement of tectonic plates, "You bet, Johnny."

"Yeah, we can do that."

"But you haven't yet."

"But we haven't yet. That's true."

"Why?"

"Hmmm. Because I'm a gentleman —"

"Or a blasted fool!" Paisley interrupts.

Ignoring him, Mustache Johnny continues, "or cuz you might be useful yet. We just want answers, girl, assistance, nothing more. And in return for your assistance, we'll keep you alive long enough to get a share of the cut, if you don't screw us something fierce."

"How do I know you aren't going to kill me? Why would you even keep me alive?"

"Good questions, Miss. Weeeeeellllll, Johnny? How does she know… you aren't going to off her? Why *are* you keeping her alive?" Paisley seems legitimately curious.

"Gotta trust me. Come now, look at me. This is a face you can trust. As for the latter question? Well, put it plainly, we're all gon' die unless we get some answers and get 'em quick. A bit less money's better'n no money."

"Well, uhm, what do you want to know?" Miranda says, feeling herself jerk suddenly into survival mode. It becomes vitally important she does not get booted from this world. She'll jump ship to a new one as soon as she can, but if she gets kicked out, killed, or otherwise cancelled, who knows where she'd end up? Who knows if she'd be able to find her way back? And to where?

"I told you she doesn't know anything," the girl by the window cries out, obviously bored. "We really should go." Panic, uncovered, stains her sentiment.

"Baby, how's that project coming?"

Mustache Johnny, ignoring Window Lady, turns to Baby on the floor, who's assembling the disparate metal parts around him into a gun bigger than he is, with a barrel that could eat an orange and a long, blunderbussian tail behind it. Baby says, "Yeah, one sec, Boss. Just a minute more."

"*He* is not your boss. *I* am your boss," Paisley shouts at him. "This man," he says, pointing a long, grubby finger at Mustache Johnny, "is on *my* payroll. You can do what he says *only* if I allow it."

"Please, Mayor, no need for such fighting."

"Then listen to me, God damn it! We have to go. They are going to come for us, and regardless what it is *he's* building on the floor over there, we ain't got the men, *and* we ain't got the firepower. Now, *I'm* paying you all, so we do what I say, is that clear?"

"Sure thing, Mayor, sir." Mustache Johnny says this with such sweeping servitude, it'd be foolish not to believe him. "But if you're in charge…" he starts saying over his shoulder, crouching down in front of Miranda. A moment staring at this full frontal of his yellow, morbidly corroded teeth reveals holes big as bullets and caked dirt black as burnt oven trimmings. "…you gotta decide what we do with the girl."

And that's how Miranda ends up, still tied and immobile, in a saferoom underneath the saloon, a location assumedly more secure from an ambush, which seems to be everyone's main fear right about now: a sudden onslaught from a group of outlaws, retaliation for a previous skirmish.

Well, Miranda's here, in the cramp and dim light, while the Mayor slouches over in a corner biting his lip. They all continue their quiet conversation amongst themselves; Mustache Johnny paces back in forth in front of Miranda, and Gun Baby is back to his construction work.

"So, you going to give us some answers, girl? Or we gonna haveta keep you here some time longer? You have places to be, don't'cha? You don't wanna stay here with us so long, now do ya?"

"How do you know I'm not currently coding my way out of here?"

"Go right ahead missy, if you can, it won't hurt us much. We're bored as sin besides; we ain't got nothing else to do but watch."

"Who are you even hiding from? The people I was with? Why not just go out and face them? You all seem prepared. They didn't look that scary to me."

"Well, seeing as you have some questions of your own, how about we go answer for answer? Or, you know, you can just keep on askin' into the oblivion…your choice."

"Not much of a choice."

"Ain't that a stinker?" Mustache lights a match, brings it real close to his eyes, like he's looking for something in the flame.

"Fine. I'll tell you whatever I know. Fuck those guys anyways, leaving me here with you clowns."

"Well, I'll start then," Mustache Johnny says. "Where you come from?"

"Like where I was born? Or where I met up with that lot? Because I sure as shit am not telling you anything about anything outside of this stupid computer game."

"How 'bout the latter then?"

"I don't know what it's called, but it was a city on a giant helipad. Does that narrow things down for you at all? Signed up to come here because this guy with a Bandana told me his 'leader' might have something I'm looking for."

"And what's that you're looking for?"

"Nah, man. My turn to ask. Why are you hiding from those people I came in with?"

"Cuz they ain't supposed to be here," Mustache says, sitting up, putting his elbows on his knees, looking mean. "Not supposed to be here, sabotaging everything, we have no idea what kinds of rules they're playing by. We's lucky we got out as we did. The other team, not so lucky. Decimated, each and every one of them. Don't you know that? Or were you already blown to bits by then? Wanna know why we're hiding? We're scared, and we don't want to lose 20k acting like dipshits if we can do it being smart-like. Happy? Now, whatchu looking for with that lot?"

"You're going to think I'm stupid."

"But?"

"But, uhm, I think they have this, uhm, this skeleton key. At least, that's what I heard, you know? I'm an, ahem, traveler of sorts, but finding it rather difficult to travel the way I need through these rooms. So, if I can get what their leader got, well, that'd make my life a lot easier."

"Ah, yeah. That actually makes some sense. We was wondering how ya'll could get in here. You know, we randomize our locks when we host games like this, so you gotta be hella crafty or hella mean or hella hooked up to be getting in here unannounced, and I'm judging she's the latter, otherwise the money'd've just been stolen from right under us. It's happened before. But your leader's *playing* for some reason, which means they either can't take the money, or are here for something else. Odd."

"What do you want with me?" Miranda asks suddenly. "And I know I'm out of turn, but that's a most important question, seeing as I have that pretty important business to attend to. Elsewhere. Now-ish. I expect a full answer, by the way."

Mustache turns back to the Paisley Mayor, who's engaged with the ladies in some kind of heated conversation, all animated and such but totally silent to Miranda's ear, so they must be in a private chat, a fact that alternately relieves and scares the heck outta her. Well, Johnny is looking over at him for some kind of sign he's listening to their conversation, or perhaps he just needs input, but Paisley isn't paying any attention at all, so Johnny turns back to Miranda, all suddenly relaxed-like.

"To tell you the God's-honest truth, kid, I'm not totally sure. Never was a real agreement on all that. I mean we definitely want some specifics, you know, like how many o'them there are, what're their names if they have 'em, where they hail from and what they want, but from there we can't agree. I think we should use you as bait and lure them into a trap. Some of them want to keep you here indefinitely, and some want to keep testing out this power of yours."

"What power?"

"'What power,' she says. What power? What power!? Kid, you should be dead right now. What I mean is that, well, I shot you in the head, watched you die. Most times that happens — correction: every time — body disappears, Program deems the player a loser and kicks 'em from the game. But you stayed solid. Outlaws out there left you to die, of course: they ain't know the rules of the game 'well as we do. But we knew that was weird. Picked you up, brought you here thinking you might come on back to us, and lo and behold, that's exactly what you did. You're a survivor, my friend. And as far as I'm concerned, that makes you real valuable to all parties involved. You got a wallet hooked up to this here Program?"

"Yes."

"Then you're worth a pretty penny, too. If you're the last one standing, you're worth 20k. A powerful bargaining chip you are."

"Yeah, but I'm worthless to you," Miranda shouts. "The only way I get that money is if all of you *and* all of them go down before me, and being that I'm unarmed, that seems unlikely, huh?"

"Go on."

"Why don't we make a deal? We both want something from our friends out there. I want that key, you want them all dead. And I can't die. So, let's say I walk in there and start shooting, take out everyone but the one I want. You all come in on my tail, clean up the bastards, and we both get what we want. I get that key from that outlaw's cold, dead hands, and you get to split up 20,000."

"You're making a deal with her?" The Mayor shouts suddenly, coming up behind Mustache. "You're going to get us all killed! I will not allow it."

But despite Paisley's urging, it's clear who the real boss of these here parts is.

And that's how Miranda ends up on the back of a horse at the edge of the city, looking out into the wild wild country, a small army of fortune fighters ready to pick up her trail, tracking her heavy footsteps from a great, great distance.

Her gaze facing outward onto the playa, she waits, and waits, and she waits for a sign of *something*. But here the thing about going looking for trouble…eventually, you're going to find it.

Looking nonchalant, a silhouetted figure appears up on that crest over yonder and lifts something to its eyes before sidewinding back over the ridge. While unseen crows caw and hidden desert crickets continue their maniac chirping, Miranda hops from her horse, sets it running in the opposite direction as a sign to the others, and after a short wait, treks up to the ridge's scalp, hot on the trail of the trouble she saw waiting for her.

From up top, she can see the figure some distance off. It's the only thing with any height in the other flat, listless distance. Other than it walking, there's only sand, only dust-devils, only the passing black of flying insects appearing, by way of their speed, to be glitched pixels against so many otherwise uniform.

There's following and there's speeding up and of course there's slowing down, but when our faraway figure dashes into a rocky outcropping, and though Miranda runs violently after it, the trail goes cold. It takes quite a while for her to emerge on the other side of the red stone maze within the rock, but when she does, when she looks out over this fresh, new patch of wasteland, there's *nothing* out of place. A few saguaros with carved faces stand singly stolid a ways away, their green hides the only welcome change from the orange and sandstone and beige rest of the world.

Miranda treks out to the Saguaro shade, where she decides to wait for the rest of her raiding party to catch up with her.

Off in the distance, she sees flat movement on the sand. If she squints her eyes, she can see the flitty forms of two lizards crawling all over and around each other. She watches the bearded dragons with interest, wondering if their movements have been coded with real

David Attenborough accuracy. They stop, one mounts the other, and Miranda averts her eyes, not wanting any eavesdropping eyes to think she's some kind of creep.

"You're in the wrong place," comes a voice from above. Miranda looks up, and the tall Cactus looks back down at her.

"Pardon?"

"He never came out the way you did. I would've seen."

"Well, thanks a lot. That's very helpful. How did you know I was looking for someone, though?"

The Cactus shrugs its prickled shoulders. "We all are connected by the same root system. Consider us watchful observers. Friends."

Miranda thanks the cactus and trudges back to the canyon, seeing from this new angle, in the final antechamber of the crag, a small, human-sized crack in the rock that's just large enough for her to shimmy through.

Like watching a character in a movie suffocate or drown on screen, when Miranda squeezes into the virtual crack in the canyon, she finds herself short of breath. It's hard to distance your body from what your senses are experiencing. In Miranda's claustrophobic momentary delirium, she can almost feel her own hot breath coagulating back around her face, as if there really were red stone just inches from her nose.

Shortly, mercifully, she comes to a clearing at the end of the fissure. When her last boot is pulled through, she turns to look upon a campsite not far off, dotted with tents and smoldering fires, the only thing standing in this open bowl carved from the rock.

"You'll forgive me for this, I suspect," says Druid, the figure, sly as a bobcat and quick as a lynx and already pressed close behind her. She can't turn to face him and in fact sees only the slightest glint of his knife before the screen goes black. He offers neither grunt nor grimace in the way of being affected by this murder.

Miranda resists the urge to give up on the game entirely this time, using this moment of inactivity to use the restroom, get a snack, check

Big Banana's stock ticker and become furious at yet another day of big gains. Somewhere, Jim Cramer goes crazy with the buy button. The Twins aren't home, she sees, and also, it's just after midnight. She'll have to decide soon about further ignoring the real world. But not yet. In the kitchen, she wolfs down a hard-boiled egg. In the bathroom, she pops a pimple on her chin. In the living room, she's drawn towards the window. She leans her forehead against it, until the hot air from her nose fogs up the glass below her eyes.

In her room, she finds the brief death has ended, the story continues to plow ahead.

"Told you ma'am," she hears as she reenters the Program, "Girl can't be killed."

The room she awakes into is a luscious octagon encircled by furs of all kinds — Kodiak and jaguar, fur seal and orangutan — lit by lava lamps. Some splintered sunlight shines in through the open tent flap, too. An oaky, big-important-oh-look-at-me-and-all-my-money-business-man-type table stretches the length of the space over there, and all sorts of obsolete explorer gew-gaw plaster the walls and shelves like this is Francisco De Gama's fuck dungeon or something. Talk about a sextant, huh?

In the center of the room, practicing her mini-golf swing with a ball and a club and a red solo cup, is a Japanese Woman in a very-appropriative Native American headdress.

"You really shouldn't be wearing that," Miranda says.

"My grandfather was a quarter-Cherokee," the woman responds in an androgynous, authoritative voice.

"Okay, well…Not really sure the politics of that but, you know, I shouldn't really be —"

"Leave us," the Woman says to Druid, who'd been standing silent in that corner, wrapped in tiger fur, this whole time.

"Yes, Ma'am," he responds, this pathetic thing, slinking out of the tent. Miranda is unsure whether that sound she just heard was general machine static or Druid hissing at her. Men, man.

After sinking another putt in the red cup, the Woman turns to Miranda. "So, how did you find out who I was?"

"What do you mean?" Miranda asks. "Who are you?"

"Don't play dumb," the Woman says, looking at her now. "What with that obvious getup of yours, you're clearly here to fuck with me. How'd you find out?"

"What getup? What are you talking about?" Miranda says, suddenly aware, strangely aware, that she was no idea what she looks like. It's never mattered, never been a point of question. She's never imagined her appearance because there's been so little of her own imagination needed in this already so expansive place.

"The face-paint, the horns, the ridiculous robe…it's a great imitation, I'll give you that, but you're no Gwami the Seer."

"I'm Gwami the Seer?" Miranda asks, dumb-sounding and slow.

"I don't know, you tell me? It's *your* avatar." The Woman is getting impatient, obviously perturbed by Miranda's ignorance, which she must believe is a feigned one. "Well, I don't know what you want, but since you found your way to me here, you're obviously looking for me, and, well, you found me. What do you want? An autograph? A personal AMA? You want to know who the real Gwami the Seer is? You and everyone else. Keep moving, dude, this is me obviously not wanting to be bothered."

"Wait," Miranda hears herself saying. The gears in her brain turn and make an awful grinding sound, like they can't figure out how to spin in unison. And then they unclick and the gears go, and up through the pully they engender comes a word she never would've thought she'd need to utter in here.

"Lakshmi?"

Lakshmi.

Plot twist! (Oh, god, really? A plot twist? Millennials always semi-expect a cliffhanger, a startling revelation at a crucial moment. Blame all the post-credit scenes. We're tired of twists, spent by surprises. So is Miranda. Or, well, she *would* be, if it weren't she the plot were twisting.)

"What are you doing here?" Miranda says, half-stupefied.

"Well, I'm kind of in the middle of a game. How did you track me down? This place is supposed to be all-the-way encrypted?"

"Lakshmi…it's me…it's Miranda. Miranda Swami!" She knew that was a bad idea before she typed it, knew putting this information into written existence could be trouble, but she didn't and doesn't care. "Where have you been? Why haven't you called?"

"Miranda?"

"Yes!"

"Miranda…Swami?"

"Yes, dude, yes!"

"How did *you* know I was here?"

"I didn't! This is a ridiculous ridiculous coincidence I think."

"No no. This doesn't make sense." Lakshmi says this and begins pacing, dropping the golf club and moving around to the other side of the table, sitting himself atop it. "I was *brought* here. I got these texts and on the busses, there were —"

"Me too. Are you saying…"

And there it is. Confirmation: this *is* a larger plot, and everyone's in on it. Her and Lakshmi, someone has been watching them both, has brought them both in on some crazy quest, has tested their forces of will and brought them together. Insert something about Wonder Twin powers here.

"I met with this Woman —"

"— with Red Hair?"

"Yeah."

"Yeah. Holy shit."

"My brain hurts."

"Well, what are you doing *here*?" Miranda says. "How did you end up leading these people?"

Lakshmi shrugs. "I've been, for lack of anything else to do, just accumulating wealth, you know? Seemed like a safe thing to do. I've been waiting for something to happen, had a feeling something would, and, well, now it's happened."

"I'm so happy you're here," Miranda says. And it's true, Miranda is frantically overjoyed. It's that kind of happiness that floods up and out of you, that puddles around your eyes, that makes your face hot and your toes start tapping, too. Lakshmi! Lakshmi is here! Everything is going to be okay because Lakshmi is here! Finally, she's anchored in place, after so long spent adrift.

"You too," he says.

There's a long, awkward silence. Miranda searches her mind for something to say, but comes up short.

"So, I hear you can jump from room to room," she says finally. "That's actually why I came here. I'm looking for the Woman obviously. She told me all these insane things and — well, I don't know if she told you, too, but I've got to find her. It's very important. And then I heard about this skeleton key thing, and that you — well I didn't know it was you you — but that you had one, and so I came looking."

"I hear you can't die."

"It seems that way. You're going to give me your password thing, right? You're going to share it with me and we're going to go on this quest together, huh?"

"Don't you have schoolwork to get to?"

"Shut up, dude."

"Yeah, I'll help you."

Miranda stands up from her chair, stands up and begins shaking her limbs out, like she really can't believe what's happening, and a part of her really can't.

"So, you give me the code, and then you fly out to the City — you can stay with me of course — and we'll get together and do this whole thing together, and we'll find the Woman and get Gwami back, oh oh oh, and we'll fucking *destroy Big Banana*. We'll be heroes, Lakshmi. Absolute heroes. This is so big, so much bigger than us. That's what *she* told me. We can have a real effect, make real change. That's what you wanted, right? To *matter*?"

Some rocks fall in the distance, someone shouts, and Lakshmi stands up from the table, bending over to look inside a drawer. Within it, after some rummaging, he produces a silver key, oversized like a fist, with a skull carved in its head. "Wow, that's like *really really* on the nose," Miranda says.

"You need to get going," he says. There's some more vague shouting from outside, and Lakshmi brings the key to Miranda. "But yeah, I know. Not very subtle."

She takes the key from him and, at once, a transparent blue door, shimmering and wavy like the Mexican coastline, appears beside her. It tells her to hit the F1 key to exit the room. Miranda motions towards it. "Is this going to follow me around now?"

"Good luck, Miranda Swami, my friend. Keep going." he says. A white light emerges from the door and begins enveloping the world.

As it spreads, so does all this maniac screaming, the boulders falling faster and harder and the shouts, the gunshots, the boulders which are really hoofbeats trodding upon hard rock and then the tent is coming down, coming apart at its seams as a horse without a rider flies through the structure (though God knows how they fit a wholeass horse through the canyon), and the light gets larger and brighter and she feels her skin get actually hotter and then it's all gone.

She's back in the hallway.

Burnt doors and the key still in her hand. There's a little text box just nearly faded sitting in the center of her vision. "Don't lose that," it reads, "some people would kill for it."

Then *poof*, it disappears, the signpost gone from her world for good. There's no sound, no desert sky, no texts and no Lakshmi. All remnants of that little life are gone. Everything but the key in her hand.

Briefly, she walks down the hallway, stopping at the next door on her left, which she approaches and, following another easy-peasy button command, opens.

Without stepping through, she sees inside a grand ballroom filled with turning, twisting couples — the men in tailcoats, the women in hoop dresses — all of them performing a synchronized waltz. A pair of gentlemen wearing gold top hats sit and watch it all from a high dais. One looks towards the door, locks eyes with Miranda, and appears mightily disturbed. He nudges his partner, who looks that way too, but by then Miranda has closed the door, retreated back into solitude.

Being an intruder, she thinks, is a feeling she must get used to.

She must get used to that, and also, she must call Lakshmi.

But tomorrow, maybe.

She sends him a text. *Thanks for all your help, tonight. I'll call you in the morning.*

He doesn't immediately respond. That's probably for the best; they could both use a break from their new, shared reality. She shakes the other world out of her eyes, sets the goggles down on her desk, and realizes that she's tired as sin.

Which makes sense; being two people again after so much time spent being one, well that's liable to sap the life right outchea.

Miranda, I have literally no idea what you're talking about.

Imagine waking up to a text like that. You've collapsed finally into bed, shed the Apollo weight upon your shoulders for just a moment, and slept a deep, dreamless sleep. But when you awake, instead of finding a message of camaraderie and brotherly understanding upon your phone, you find one of confusion, a denial, a distance.

But…but the plot twist?

She reads the text over and over again, thinking maybe this is like what Lakshmi said weeks ago, not wanting to put anything down on paper that could be incriminating. She wishes she thought of that before. She knows calling him would put this confusion to rest but can't quite bring herself to do it. Can't quite bring herself to make any words at all.

Instead she writes, *Last night? You don't remember us, uhm, chatting yesterday? Exchanging things *wink wink*?*

Three little dots appear on her screen, and then they sink back down. Like a sin wave she can only see the crest of, the dots rise and fall, remaining invisible under the x axis of her screen, rising and falling again.

Finally, she gets a response. *Idk dude (sic). Hope you're okay, you're making me nervous lol.*

Three dots that just can't make up their minds. Up and down, up and down, and then:

Want me to call someone for you?

Almost against her wishes, the events of the previous night replay themselves. She met Lakshmi in the desert, and though it said it was Lakshmi, it doesn't seem like it *was* Lakshmi, and she told it she was Miranda Swami, she was baited in by it and told it who she was. She admitted to being Miranda and admitted to being Gwami the Seer, to some unknown entity that sucked her in with the promise of friendship, someone who knew exactly the kind of weakness best exploited. Someone in that Program knows who she is, knows that Miranda Swami and Gwami the Seer are the same entity. That brings the total count in-the-know to four: Caleb, Real Lakshmi, Fake Lakshmi, and presumably the Woman with the Red Hair. She has no idea in whose clutches that knowledge is the most dangerous.

Finding the Woman with the Red Hair is now mandatory. Not that the task didn't have urgency under it before, but now, with some lunatic running around knowing who she is, spewing that knowledge to the rest of the world potentially, a need to clear her name and retcon her image is more important than ever. She needs subscribers, she needs advertisers, she needs the security that comes with presence.

Wiping the tired from her eyes, she trudges into the kitchen, left amok apparently after the Twins came home last night, though she heard them not. She finds someone's energy drink in the fridge and gulps it down quick, feeling her heart beating strong against her chest, a reminder of what world she truly exists in.

But that uncomfortable heartbeat and a quick curbside cigarette are going to be enough of the real world for the day. She goes back into her room, hits the lights and locks the door, ready to go back into that place for the final sequence, ready to destroy anything that stands in her path, ready to become death, if need be, before death can motherfuckin' become her.

BANANAS!

5

When they talk about her, it's in hushed tones, in private chats and secure spaces, always looking over their shoulders before they do so, ensuring that she isn't going to *be there* — Where? There! — in that shadow-darkened corner, having silently entered while their backs were turned. They discuss what they would even do if they saw her, this thing that can appear and vanish at will, that can infect their private spaces, listen to their private thoughts, that will follow them tirelessly, destroying everything nearby until she's given what she wants. She'll rip you in two if the programming allows it, or so they say.

And boy, do they love saying. Maybe their general inability to keep quiet is why Miranda trails a lengthening legend behind her as she jumps from world to world. I mean, yeah, she's appeared in shadowy corners before, has eavesdropped on some conversations perhaps she wasn't meant to be privy to, but this isn't a killer witch or soul-stealing hacker or anything like that! It's just a girl — just Miranda Swami! You *know* her! Just a girl with hair like a dragon's horns and dingy, initiate robes and warped, pallid skin like underneath a wet fingernail.

Yet the legend grows. If it isn't she herself who is haunting them, it's her watchful spirit, for who's to say where the limits of her power lie? Could she be invisible, hugged tight to the walls? Could she have taken the form of an inanimate object? That coffee table over there, yeah that one, doesn't it look kind of funny? You don't think...no, couldn't be...but what if?

But what if?

To make the most of the little time she thinks she has, Miranda cuts out all the distractors from her life, anything that will get in the way of her (con)quest. Her university, believing she's on some sort of medically-mandated mental-sabbatical, has, after some tense negotiation, generously frozen her credits. Meanwhile, Miranda now gets her nutrients from bottled meals, ones with pseudo-medicinal names like *Vivi* and *RegenX* and *Sate*. Anything else her body needs she absorbs in vitamin form, ingesting handfuls of cloyingly sweet grape-and-orange-flavored chewy tablets at a time, figuring that more vitamins cannot possible be worse. She gives a delivery service her building code and has them leave at her doorstep whatever her whims wish for: *Soylent* and *Flintstone's Gummies* and *Hot Cheetos* and Tampons, *Advil* and *Milk Duds*, *Breathrite Strips* and Coconut Water. A basic kind of life support for our inter-dimensional heroine.

After a while, these days spent hooked into the Program, spent hunting, days with a singular purpose, each one so like the last, they begin blending into one another. It was always Miranda's tacit intention that she stop realizing just how much of her life she's passing within the walls of the Program. Easier that way.

Easier still because time doesn't appear to pass in the Program the way it passes outside. Time, as we understand it, cannot be measured in the Program on account of there being no windows. In other words, without the way windows (and the light that floods in through them) help us absentmindedly catalogue its every movement, time ceases to adhere to a circadian cycle, becoming instead of a measurement device of days and moments and meetings, merely a force that links events together, that carries action over from second to second. Without windows or clocks, without anything to ground it in a routine, time becomes the easiest, basest version of itself: chronology condensed.

How simple, how natural it is to cease her studies and her pesky relationships, to lose uncountable hours within the machine, to eat only when necessary, to answer nature only when it calls, to sleep in short unpredictable bursts with the goggles still on her face, to keep her stalking subconscious at bay with energy drinks and Adderall tablets, to feel fully the torsion between two disparate worlds, as the rhythms that define one world try to cope with the indefatigability that governs the other.

And what is it she's actually *doing* in that other world? Besides inspiring fear, of course? Exploring. Intimidating. Spying. Behind those goggles, she's a pirate, traversing worlds and raiding communities with Vespucci swagger and De Gama torque. She is Francis Drake if he weren't a slave trader, didn't wage a scared white man's war on any native populations he found, and didn't die of sad, trivial dysentery in the shit-smelling captain's quarters of the same boat just weeks earlier torn apart by a better sailor's cannonballs outside of San Juan. She does, however, adopt his solipsism and slight Jesus complex.

She fancies herself the seaman's child, who looks out at the sun, setting against a pink and red and gold-twanged ocean, seeing nothing of man's devising out on the horizon and wondering, with a sudden and desperate and vital fervor, *What is out there? What might I find? And could it ever be as lovely as it is in my longing?*

But to her yearning is attached something more sinister: a dark kind of apotheosis. The kind of thing that happens when you believe you have met God, and thereafter have been guided by one of her archangels. For in some hardened part of her heart, rests a belief that this entire world might very well exist for her, and her alone. The machinations she observes and the people she meets, the strange and false claims they make, they might've been placed deliberately for her whimsy, for her to bribe and chide and torment with her presence. The processes and protocols in this place are nothing more than gentle hands pushing her forward, friendly, windswept waves lapping against the side of her vessel. No matter how you struggle, you'll never even hardly disrupt the current.

She comes to see her computational compatriots less as people and more as obstacles. And this causes her, at times, to behave rather egregiously.

Thus, we see her adopting her first pose: *The Monster*.

For example: in one of her first attempts at inter-Program travel, she opens a random door and enters into a purely pitch-dark world. Some voice says, "Who is that? What's that glow? Did someone just leave? Is someone *here*? Dammit, you're going to give us away, close that damn door!"

And another, so-so-similar voice: "Why is that door blue?"

The door closes, dissolving into the shadow just in time. There's a collective sigh of relief, but it's a false one. A thin sliver of light scars the darkness, further illuminating the world around Miranda as the bright wound opens wider. Mountainous shakers of salt and pepper high as a flag-pole tower over her head. She couldn't see their caps even on tippy-toes. Beside her is a container of old bay seasoning wide as the back of an eighteen-wheeler. A silo of cooking spray, house-high vials of honey and vanilla extract; an Everest of white flour, the writing on the bag made illegible by its size. Unseen bodies tense. Someone's teeth chatter fiercely.

"Get down! Now!" comes the voice, and Miranda is pulled forward onto her belly, joining a small platoon of diminutive Green Army Men, of the classic gumball machine variety, lying prone behind a Balsamic Vinegar rocket-ship.

Light, a rapturous light enveloping everything, and a gargantuan woman's face comes peering into the spice cabinet, her Galactus hands searching slowly for something among the jars, each accidental tap on the cabinet floor or brushing of something aside causing earthquake rumblings that threaten to knock the regiment's cover clean over.

"What's happening?" Miranda whispers to the nearest Army Man Ear.

"Please be quiet, wait until she's done."

"Who?" Miranda says, peering out at the giant blue-eyed, red-haired face out there in the light. Red hair? Miranda, feeling deific, ignores the warnings, asks "Who is that? Is she...? Wait, who are you?"

"*Shhhhh.*"

"Do you know that woman? I think I'm supposed to be looking for her. I'm Miranda Swami. Did you hear me? Miranda Swami? Aren't you going to say anything?"

"Dude, what the fuck are you even doing here?" another of the Army Men interjects. "Just go away if you're gonna ruin this for us."

"Okay, cool. Yeah, fine, totally...totes, I'll just 'go away'" Miranda says, stepping out from behind the vinegar, hopping up and down, waving her arms around. "Hey! Hey, over here! Yeah, right here! It's me! I found you!"

Because all the Army Men start screaming insults at her, Miranda turns, which means she does not see how the giant woman's face grows scarlet or how her teeth grow monstrous or how each strand of the Woman's red hair cracks like an eggshell, birthing onto her skull a mound of purple-gray snakes with yellow, glaring eyes, how she begins changing from housewife into some virtual goddamn devil. When she does turn to see how the Gigantress has changed, it's because The Beast's big ol' hand has turned into a fist and is flying slowly towards Miranda's location. But that's okay, Miranda just calls herself a door and passes through. She does not hear the cries of those she left behind, or the *womp-womp-wooooomp* of the *Game Over* screen.

It's little things like that — annoying and selfish if not exactly dastardly — which prompt players like those Army Men to gather in a nearby city, sit at a virtual gambling hall, blow Bitcoin playing Blackjack and talk about the Dragon Woman who ruined a *very fucking important* speed run they had been, until then, cruising through, looking fit to approach a world record. But then, she happened. And now they have to debrief. In passing, someone might overhear their words and join in the discussion with their own anecdote of a suspiciously similar character. The sympathy will flow like cheap cognac. Or perhaps it's the Dealer who says, "Ya'll talkin' about a girl with dragon horns for hair, real pale white skin?"

And one of the Army Men will say, "Yeah, you know her?"

And the Dealer might sigh and say, "She was here not too long ago, actually, going to every table, interrupting every player to ask if they'd seen some lady, knew anything about this random broad. She was talkin' crazy from the start. We're quiet people, you know, stayin' to ourselves, so of course we've got no idea what she's on about, but everyone's tryin' to be friendly, right? Sayin' 'Naw, ma'am, awful sorry but we ain't seen anyone with such a description.'

"So, she starts stomping 'round, starts screaming everyone's cards out, ruining everyone's fun, and even when people are muting her, she's still up in their faces, typing on and on and on in all caps about what chumps we are. When people start logging off, leaving 'cuz why deal with some crazy boppin' about, my boss comes out to see about all the hub-bub. Well, she's ranting on about how we're all machines, how we ain't mean nothin', and by this point she's just actin' up for kicks, knocking over tables and breaking bottles behind the bar. I mean, they're just for show, the bottles — for ambience, but still, someone's gotta put 'em back. So, we try to kick her out and she's yelling, 'What aren't you telling me? I want some answers!' And there's all this hullaballoo, goes on and on and on, and before you know it, the place is clean empty. The girl starts sighing and a door, I swear to Christ, a blue door like I ain't ever seen before, appears from nowhere right behind her, and out she goes, never to be heard from again. We didn't have a single customer for a week. I got a son at home, man. I gotta feed my boy."

For Miranda, these rooms ransacked and forsaken are mere minor casualties to be searched, forgotten about and moved on from, small stones turned over and nothing more. The momentary inconvenience in another's group hangout or weird indie IP or virtual gambling hall is a small price considering the stakes of the game she, and only she, is playing.

So, doorways and rooms within the Program are entered and experienced and, by virtue of their ultimate disappointment, clumped together with all the other failures, the sheer glut of all their unnecessary information quickly supersaturating Miranda's meager short-term memory.

Questions are asked to locals; private chats are set up, and in a few instances, she exchanges more cryptocurrency for answers. She receives many more answers than she expected, she just wishes they were all the same. Time after time she juts into a room, having followed specific directions to get there, only to find herself in some random simulation without a trace of the Woman she's looking for. In many of these, yes, she acts a monster, but be kind to the girl, she's frustrated, like she's been running down a hallway that stretches a little longer with each of her steps.

But with time, the aggressiveness wanes. She begins to understand that, in all likelihood, she won't get where she needs to go on the advice of others. Her exploration might include the people around her, but it can't rely on them. There's a freedom in this, a liberation unto place. She feels settling into herself the traveler's life, the observing and conversing, and the explosive ease of simply being there.

Thus, she strikes her second pose: *The Wanderer.*

On the cusp of an eruptive volcano live-broadcasted from Bali, she sits with a troupe of Pan-Asian Boy Scouts, regaling them with stories of New York City's grandeur. She hyperbolizes her world. They in return, tell of fishing the rivers in south Cambodia, of their school in Hong Kong, all in convoluted but sincere attempts at English. They euphemize theirs. They display a nasty habit of speaking at the same time, with the same voice.

"What is it like being so many people at once?" she asks them.

"Like being one," they say in unison, "but with more surface area.

Miranda finds a door which, upon entering, sends her skydiving down towards Earth, her and a gaggle of bald, Buddhist monks seated lotus-style in the air. Engaged in some kind of circular meditation, they sit silent but eerily wide-eyed as great envelopes of yellow and green farmland open below the clouds. Miranda, curious what will happen once they hit the ground, stays in their midst as the incoming Earth grows larger and larger still. Unperturbed at their coming plight, the monks fall and fall and fall, and no wonder their calm: instead of smacking into the Earth and engaging *samsara* in a hundred-million shattered pieces, they instead phase right through it, rising steadily upward now through an infinite world of bent starlight; hanging, chandelier-shine crystals litter the otherwise errant black void around them. When, somewhere way far up near the very top of this world, they all slow and then stop and then begin falling back down, Miranda realizes what this is: a swinging pendulum of Buddhist bodies. Maybe someone's using it as a clock. Maybe at midnight, the Buddhists self-immolate. Through the Earth they all go again, and then up through a familiar sky. Somewhere along the heave, Miranda leaves the same way she came in.

Elsewhere are two houseflies in a hut engaged in a lover's quarrel, and though they were at first startled by Miranda's unceremonious entrance into their abode, they turn out, most conveniently, to be huge Gwami the Seer fans.

"Yeah, me too, as you can tell," Miranda sputters.

"Oh, this is so funny. Marc come here — now don't for a second believe I'm not still furious at you — but come take a picture of me and Gwami. Okay, okay what should we say?"

"Uhm, Gwam–ee?"

"Okay, on three! One, two, three, Gwam-eeeeeee!"

Flash. Immortalized forever, she becomes an angry insect's pre-divorce mantelpiece.

On a ring of Saturn, she meets a trio of would-be astronauts lamenting their thyroid issues, cursing their mothers for providing them the gene that would forever keep them landlocked. But this place, they say, is a worthy second-option.

"Want to see something cool?" one of them asks. "Got your headset on real tight? All right! Remember to breathe."

He gives Miranda a running push that sends her spinning flipping rotating gently through all those rings and then straight into the stars, moving with constant force and soothing centripetal motion, until the whole of Saturn appears like an apple, graspable within her palm; until Jupiter rises up like a giant's eye from the otherwise nothingness. The planet's swirling storm clouds appear like red velvet batter, until, of course, she passes it completely by, due for Mars in a few minutes more.

Who would have thunk that an entire universe — traversable, expansive, and nuanced — could exist with such furious detail behind a 15-inch screen? Roiling through space in just this slightest segment of the Program, this world-within-a-world-within-a-world alone offers a bounty as rich and thickly enveloping as the one she can touch with her fingers. And what this world lacks in sensual pleasure, in tactility, it more than contains in possibility, in exploratortality.

This new world stretches outward *ad infinitum*, its fingers continuously reaching just further than the day before, than the moment before, ever closer to some glorious wash of sunlight, to some impossible ideal of endlessness, but reaching, reaching always. For when we strip away our stories, our plots, the machinations of man and mind within the machine, we have only that which this world mimics: a stretching of the human spirit, as it moves towards something even it knows not what, just towards, just forwards, just on.

Dizzy, Miranda exits into the hallway, wondering if there's a button command for kissing with relief the flat, constant floor below her.

What the programmer does within these walls and halls is one-part architecture, sure, and several-parts engineering, of course. But this kind of peak programming semi-regularly approaches magic. And at times (dare I say it?) even art itself.

From where comes our exclusionary list of what acceptably constitutes *art*? Film and poetry and cooking in the fine French style, dancing and painting and sculpting, playing the guitar and the cello and singing in a high tenor, and, honestly, not much else. But, I ask you, what is a novel but a writer's fantasy world? What is a transcendent painting, a dance, a film but a causeway to another realm, an analogue locale? The places within this Program, these madman works by virulently obsessive programmers, do they not rival in intensity and compulsion and creativity anything crafted at Yaddo? Imagine the wonder we might wake within us should we elevate all simple acts to art. Tooth brushing and the hard-boiling of an egg.

Whatever you do, make it an offering to me.

Art is too sly for us; all it requires is invocation, and dutifully, it appears, already imbued, already full.

Time duckwalks onward, and Miranda is nowhere nearer to the Woman with the Red Hair. Her trails have all run cold, and neither intimidation nor charm, neither gall nor cunning nor so much passing time thaw them out. Miranda is left with only the fruits of this world to soothe her. Her higher purpose has retreated further and further from both her grasp and understanding. With that purpose fading, too, she has only this world, and the treasures it can sometimes be induced to show.

With this acquiescence, Miranda eases into her third pose: *The Observer.*

The more time she spends in the Program, the more she re-enters rooms she's been to before, the more people she apologizes to for her ghastly past behavior, the more "You again?"'s and "What are you doing here?"'s said to her incredulously, the more distant the whole point of this becomes. She's simply here, with nowhere to go, content to watch leaves change, to watch faces wrinkle, to watch construction, and paint dry.

The seasons change fully: cold sweeps into the city with a long, unsubtle sigh. Three of *Big Banana's* Board Members have written best-selling, book-length retrospectives on Cindi Lapenschtall's life, and Miranda further forgets why it is she's searching this other world, and who for?

Each passed day takes from her more of Gwami's memory, too. Here, it's the title of an early Gwami video she has trouble recalling. There, it's a ghastly mention of Gwami on some blog, a throwaway line filled with hate, that fails to elicit any of the usual brutal, emotions from Miranda's idling mind. She becomes more Miranda Swami as each hour falls into the next, but a new Miranda Swami, one with no illusions or delusions about what has happened to her.

What's happened is this: Gwami is dead. The Artist Formerly Known as Miranda Swami, she's dead too. In their place is a new Miranda, a paler and less convivial Miranda. A forgetful and foggy Miranda. This Miranda escapes for further hours into the Program less and less to right a wrong, less and less spurred by a vague vengeance, and more and more because, well, she has nowhere else to go. Even sitting silently in some dark, half-public place of that online realm is nicer than any activity in ours. In there, she can be among others, a silent and smelly and solitary mess, without being *othered*. Nobody looking at her, judging her, placing her in a phony context of their own devising, falsely exposing her imagined innards, making her a statistic.

The Twins think she has some kind of sickness, is why she's always "in bed." She told them it's "a really aggressive Sickle Cell Anemia." They leave her alone for the most part. Actually, they're quite nice to her, you know, when they remember her at all. Sometimes they bring home extra pizza, or invite her to the movies when they're out of work early. These acts, in a younger, stauncher Miranda, would have gone unnoticed altogether. Though noticed, they're now actively ignored. Miranda, all too aware of herself, demands to be alone and untouchable, damn any outside effort to the contrary.

She turns on her clock radio and *Z100* is talking about some cryptic countdown clock *Big Banana* has begun projecting onto the Statler Building. They're talking to "experts" about what it could mean.

Tuning to the classic rock station is no better: apparently *Big Banana* is sponsoring a high-end music festival in the Florida Keys, and *only Q104.3 has the tickets. So be caller number 14 right now and...*

It's raining, so Miranda looks out the thin window by her bed. Through the distorting drops she sees New York's forest floor below her, enveloped in neon-yellow like it's riddled with fungus, like the banana billboards are a hot rash. Yellow umbrellas and yellow taxicabs unwittingly advertising, and somewhere among them all is a being that shares her blood. Caleb Swami, out for a stroll probably (he's always liked the city in the rain), at peace with a consumerist world finally being consumed, probably making a buck off of it, honestly.

Why hasn't he called?

To spite the questions that come with such real-world window-gazing, she returns to the Program. She needs refuge from what our world makes her think, and she finds it in a quiet place, a seaside realm as elegantly designed as any Renaissance painting, where she sits at a bus stop watching old-timey cars pass by on a loop. Three Eastern European geriatrics keep to themselves just down the street, every now and then stealing odd looks at her but otherwise making no fuss.

It's her first time in this room, so it must be a new one. New rooms, and the discovering of them, have stolen Miranda's heart, make her feel like a pioneer. Make her feel like a young girl who sees something shining in the soft, mossy loam beside the redwood in the backyard, and, digging down, removes from the Earth a tiny heart shaped box within which she finds an empty locket, it having been placed there 80 years before by some young, strapping, thoughtful gentleman before a great tragedy took either he or his beloved's life, a tragedy that would have cursed the box to the bowels of the Earth for all eternity if not for her brief glance at the glinting thing and her taste for adventure; this she knows…she knows.

The room is cast in an intentionally-stylistic, sepia-toned hue, lending the passing automobiles, fat Plymouths and Studebakers and Packards with gaudy white wheels and open compartments, a great historical nostalgia. Whoever designed this place coded love into every pixel. Miranda feels safe in a place of such care, safe like a cozy, well-insulated home, one with a fire and a comfy chair beside it, one with music and the smell of spices settling over a roast in the other room; and someone softly singing.

But for all the beauty of this painstaking portrait, does it not seem somewhat, I don't know, bland? Pointless even? I mean, why would someone possessing such deific programming power be contented spending themselves on something so vapid? A virtual bus-stop in an automated rendering of some Lithuanian seaside village…where is the intrigue? What's the rub? Weird, frivolous even, but she knows not impossible. After all, human beings can be weird, frivolous sorts of creatures.

In about five minutes, though, Miranda's general restlessness, combined with the growing hostility of the Europeans, who've ratcheted up the agitation and volume of their heavy, Slavic speaking, might force her to abandon this place and its weird, frivolous sort of creator both.

But she likes it here, or rather *wants* to like it here. All the Adderall has left her blood jumpy, so she really has to *will* herself to ease. She tries focusing on the audio playing on loop in her headphones. Such a sonic addendum is a rarity in these rooms — it's far more labor-intensive to record and code sounds than simply design objects — especially one as detailed as this, one that seems to have actually been recorded in such a seaside town (with impressive specificity and realistic timbre come the lolling car tires of the passing vehicles, the distant lapping of waves upon concrete sea buttresses, the ecstasy of gulls setting upon bread crumbs, opened shop doors with their jingle-bell trip wires).

In this small sector of secret peace, she thinks how nice it is that at least *some* of the Dark Web frequenters aren't looking for profit or excitement or advantage, but just this: a quiet place to sit and ponder, a place to sate a certain pang.

But the found peace doesn't last long, as the Europeans take to truly shouting at one another, in phrases that, to Miranda's unlearned brain, sound the same as the last and the one thereafter. Like many Americans, Miranda somewhat subconsciously believes that any non-English speakers around her inevitably use their multi-linguality as a slandering device. Even as she reminds herself how ridiculous this thought is, she feels herself becoming suspicious, paranoid, bothered, the denial counterintuitively convincing her more fully that they're discussing her, insulting her, trivializing her. Then one of the Europeans clearly gestures her way, and Miranda takes matters into her own hands.

She drops an earbud out of her ear and lays it flat across her phone's microphone, which has been tasked with recording all spoken speech for the CPU to translate into English. It's vital that she knows what they're saying, that she dispel the ridiculous thoughts of her anxious mind. This was a trick she was taught in an early-on therapy session, to recognize and debunk thoughts that seem out-of-place, somehow un-hers, ones too paranoid and far-fetched for her most disastrous logic center to have produced. She was taught to parse out the thoughts that were her's and the ones that were her illness', and in thwarting that *nega*-Miranda's thoughts, she could depower them. So that's exactly what she does. She really would like to stay here longer.

Confirming her suspicion, the men are indeed not talking about her. She has exposed her mind in its attempt to dupe her. Strangely, though, the men don't appear to be saying sentences at all. That, or her translation app is bugged to all hell. It shows that the men are repeating — despite their gestures and wavering tones and conversational asides — a sequence of numbers: *24 – 60 – 255 – 130. 24 – 60 – 255 – 130. 24 – 60 – 255 – 130.*

Miranda has a *no duh* realization: these aren't men at all, but set-pieces. Objects. NPC's. They've been placed here for realism's sake, but they're as obtusely unreal as those billowing trees in that park or the squeaky wheels of that Studebaker going by. They sit here on as much a loop as the audio, until always and forever, motioning to the bus stop, screaming and yelling, and then, before long, they'll go back to their initial, quiet conversation, back to following the algorithmic machine function they carried out when Miranda first came to this place. With that in mind and her consciousness calmed, Miranda tries to incorporate their ramblings into the milieu.

Feeling the pangs of hungry sleep nipping at her planted feet, Miranda ingests another Adderall, her third in as many hours. At this point, they're like caffeinated taffy's, like candy, like crack. As her senses stretch themselves further, as colors become strained and oversaturated, as her nerves thin and fray at their edges and little jolts of electricity send Miranda's tired shoulders careening into the crook of her neck, she has a thought. It's a thought that starts small but increases in power and unavoidability with sudden, spiraling commitment: *Hey, this lifestyle isn't good for me. I'm hurting myself.*

She repeats her thought out loud, as if to make it real: "This lifestyle isn't good for me. I'm hurting myself. I'm hurting myself."

It's a profound moment. A moment of realization in her fingernails and soul alike.

It's just this kind of soulful, strong conviction come-from-above that holier folk might call a 'divine realization,' what alcoholics refer to as a 'moment of clarity.' And poor girl, it's just about to hit her fully, just about to convince her to rip off those goggles for good, when, abrupt as a heart attack, a *screech* blasts outward from the center of the program, and with it, a virtual wind so strong it sends the Europeans clutching at their derby hats, so stentorian it stops Miranda's thoughts of self-help at their larval stage. Her virtual hair blows up into her eyes. Ah! What inspired programming! This world has not unclutched her yet. It fights for her affection.

Two of the European trio crane their necks towards the street with fresh interest, but the third stays staring at Miranda. A proverbial parade of Cyrillic marches forth from his mouth, the characters matching the ones she'd been recording. But when he suddenly ceases speaking altogether, the two others turn to look in Miranda's direction, too. It's eerily quiet without their ramblings, and Miranda is overcome with the strangest feeling: that they're looking past her avatar, somehow, at her directly. She begins to shiver.

Then the audio cuts out. All of it: Slavic shouting and simulated beach sounds no more. All of it is swapped out for silence, a silence which lasts only a brief moment before giving way to a distant rumbling, rumbling like thunder, but a like from a diseased, hack thundercloud, one that's less rumbling and more chugging, like the very act of thundering is taking a lot out of it, like this is the whooping cough equivalent of a thunderclap. As it becomes louder, Miranda recognizes it as the unmistakable *chugging* of a city bus, followed by its painful braking *squeals*, all of it in the generally-unwell timbre of a vehicle thirty-years past its expiration date.

The air over there glistens and then cracks completely as a black hole appears in the program's fabric itself, heralding the arrival of a fully-rendered *NJ Transit* Bus — striped with wavy purple-and-orange lines — that crawls like a centipede from the gap, growing in size and approaching and stopping, finally, with a gaseous exhale in front of the bus stop. The rip in the program closes behind it. This is something Miranda has never seen before. A glint catches her eye from beside the Redwood.

Because the Europeans immediately scramble forward toward the slowing, *fwooooosh*, idling bus, it's safe to assume that any extended dawdling might prevent getting onboard, and that getting onboard is the goal. Miranda, not in the business of being left out, wants on too, obviously. And being that she's no slouch, as soon as the bus even nears, she leaps forward, eager to interrupt the proto-Soviet powwow and join the three curmudgeons on their voyage wherever.

But, *ahah-hah*, her controls are somehow *sticking*.

Despite her best maniac efforts, her twitchy trigger-fingers pounding on the arrow keys, she remains glued to her seat, a pox upon her that does not lift no matter how many times she types her Skeleton Code into her keyboard. Nary a single blue door comes to her rescue neither. *Ipso facto*, she can neither run to catch the bus nor throw up an angry exclamation as it fills its belly with European meat. Miranda resigns herself to her fate. The bus pulls away from the station, leaving its last prospective passenger to await another ride to the end of the line.

This is a whole day of firsts, apparently. She hasn't been immobilized like this since before she met Fake-Lakshmi, hasn't been so obviously flouted by the Program since before she began traversing it in wide swaths. Such strange happenings, such suspicious people, such oddities the likes of which she has never seen, and has never heard of anyone seeing before.

If she were in a different pose, she might, with avenged purpose, throw herself into solving this fresh mystery.

But this is *The Observer*. And the Observer is done for the day.

She takes the goggles from off her head and, thank the lord, it's late evening. No errant sunlight to singe the inside of her eyes, and no footsteps from outside her room. Sleep rushes at her from all angles; Miranda is bone-exhausted. It's an exhaustion that emanates from within her blood, and is, as such, afflicting her every capillary, vein and artery, that spreads itself into every small segment of her being.

She does not brush her teeth, she does not use the bathroom a final time. She does not feel the effects of that freshest Adderall as she lay back in bed. Her mind does not take her to any wonky places, it does not dwell on the happenings of the day. Her phone, still trying to translate the nonsense in her headphones, will gently kill itself, percentage by percentage, so that, when Miranda awakens, she will be unconnected and untethered for the first time in recent memory. It will be a very un-Miranda way to wake.

Sleep feasts on her slowly for nearly 14 hours. She wakes groggy, in a world just as dimly lit as one she could swear she just left. She looks around her room, at the grey dismal room, and then over to the phone on her desk. If she had awoken a few moments later, she might have missed it. The phone is on one percent, after all, and the good ol' thing is really stretching that battery as far as it'll go. Miranda looks over at the bright screen, at some digits she might otherwise have never thought about again — *24 – 60 – 255 – 130* — numbers that catalyze a chain reaction in her brain, a reaction that wakes her up fully, that unleashes a dormant energy, numbers that prove key to some spinning Rubik's Cube of thought within her.

"24 – 60 – 255 – 130," she says out loud with realized immediacy, repeating herself again and again until she can find a not pad and pen. Stumbling around with hair sweat-caked to her face, her bare feet nearly sticking frozen to the cold hardwood floor, she searches. Though there's only a baggy white t-shirt and underwear covering her scant form, she still manages to get all twisted up and stuck in them, floundering around the room, nearly tumbling head over feet. Miranda is not the most graceful of girls. Her phone finally gasps and dies, swallowing its words, but Miranda continues to speak for it. "24 – 60 – 255 – 130."

"24 – 60 – 255 – 130."

Finally she finds what she needs, hiding in a pile of scarcely-used textbooks she's still hoping to return for profit. Paper…and…and… pen! She writes it down and then writes it again on a different sheet in the event of sudden conflagration, takes a breath, plugs her phone in and begins bouncing around her room with excitement.

She didn't understand until it was written down in front of her, until she could look at the digits in a clean, crisp column. It's a *phone number*, god damn it.

They were feeding *her* a phone number.

246-025-5130. That's a Barbados area code, apparently. Might there be some Pina Coladas in her freaky, funky future?

As soon as her phone comes back to life, she's got a call to make.

In the meantime, she brushes her teeth. It was very uncharacteristic of her to forget such a vital hygienic task last night. On second thought, she could use a shower, too.

What a lovely day to be alive. What a way to return to this old, tired world. And with new eyes, the world is brighter, fresher, more inviting. Miranda turns the water up all the way hot. She wants it to burn. She wants to re-feel life.

BANANAS!

It's a disaster, the likes of which she hasn't seen since Gwami's death. It's a fireball sent from the heavens to blow her entire life to smithereens. It's *that* big and *that* raw, and if the metaphorical dinosaurs metaphorically die out, it will be a tragic but consistent course of events. After all, that meteor set off a chain-reaction which their food supply. Miranda and the dinosaurs, sans their usual nourishment, condemned to die.

And she's not even being *that* melodramatic about it. IT: this happening, this latent in a sequence of happenings, the first being that the phone number was a fraud, and this being the second. The phone number worked no better on the forty-seventh attempt than the first, always ringing thrice and then being answered by a shrill, uncommonly-welcoming computer matriarch speaking for all of us when she said, "We're sorry, but the number you're trying to reach has been changed, disconnected, or taken out of service. If you'd —" but Miranda never made it further than that. If she had, her boiling blood surely would have entered her brain and caused a stroke of some sort. She has better survival instincts than you'd think.

And if that weren't enough, as if the shock and pain from that dead end weren't enough, as if a tragedy that sent her chain-smoking on the yellow-lit steps of her apartment building (the closest convenience store has, in Miranda's absconding to another world, been taken over by some *Big Banana* sympathizer/try-hard, which, as such, sells only

Banana-related items. This includes, apparently, *Big Banana's* foray into the tobacco game: *Banana Jacks*, the smoking of which make Miranda hate herself even more than fruitless cigarettes) weren't enough, there was this second, more-horrible thing.

She's been locked out.

The Program that has been her haven, her adventure, her cocoon and her world, her bosom and her beating heart, the totality and the singularity for her entire post-Gwami life, the only thing she's had since and all she had wanted or needed, it's reared back like a thunderstruck horse and kicked her square in the jaw. *Miranda*, it's apparently said, *your time here is up.*

And there goes the other half-a-pack.

There are only two reasons Miranda would be locked out: 1) she's failed in her mission, missed over and again all the secret, esoteric clues to the Woman's whereabouts, meaning obviously the developer has moved on to frying bigger fish; or 2) Miranda already has everything she needs, and further time in the Program would only hinder her. Because her entire life will lose its purpose if her brain allows itself to believe option-1, it throws its full weight behind option-2.

She has everything she needs, and it probably has to do with that number. Maybe she needs to track down its owner. Maybe she needs to call at a specific time of day. Maybe she needs to go to Barbados. Maybe this has something to do with Rihanna.

Defeated and tobacco-fried and feeling the first of what will be many pangs of nostalgia for a world so suddenly far away, Miranda tries the goggles again. She just wants to sit in the hallway, among those doors and think; even if she can't enter, even if her IP address continues to obstruct her, she has to be there.

Maybe her exile was the result of some bug. Maybe she'll be welcomed in, no problem. Maybe she's been freaking out over nothing.

But again and again and again and again, and I could fill an entire page with agains, the Program remains out of her reach. At least it's concise and clear with its criticism of her IP. Underneath her broken entrance code, a little message reads *Account Locked. Please Input Correct IP*. Of course, her skeleton key has no effect. It seems she has a 10-digit number to track down if she even wants to continue with this ridiculous, babbling ques —

10-digit number.

24 – 60 – 255 – 130.

It's not a phone number. Not 246-025-5130.

It's a motherfucking IP address! 24.60.255.130! She overthought it! She has all the answers! She has a way forward! She chained all those cigarettes for nothing! Invested a foolish $11.30 in *Big Banana's* bottom line for nothing! All she had to do was take a step back and see the banana plantation for the banana plants!

Now, it can't be that hard to trace an IP address, can it? Can it?

…

…

Yeah, turns out it's pretty hard.

Let's not mince words: it takes either serious knowhow or buying power to do a thing like trace an IP address, and, since there's no app for this, and since the dollars aren't exactly overflowing into her accounts right now, Miranda needs help. Not too tall an order, she's just got to find someone with a delicate enough touch to not arouse suspicion as they sneak past the thousand-and-one firewalls that guard the big Internet Service Providers — the keepers of such information —, with enough experience to know where amongst thousands of unimaginably dense folders and servers and filetypes the necessary information would be, to unzip and access the correct information, and, of course, with staunch-enough morality that they won't be spurred to abuse their power and shut down internet access to everyone in St. Louis. Simple.

If she hadn't been locked out of the Program, she might post-up in some seedy, steampunk place and advertise her needs to the nearest bidder. Funky people do freaky things in that place; it wouldn't be too difficult to coax someone into obediently fucking around with some ISPs, especially if there's a whole big chunk of change waiting for them on the other end of the engagement.

But that's not really an option, obviously. She ain't have the cash nor the access. And if Miranda were to, say, zip around the proper internet in a tizzy, trying to summon a hacker of the caliber she'd need, it would end in her arrest or otherwise total excommunication from polite society. Besides, those that publicly identify as "hackers" aren't *really* the kind she's after.

She doesn't want to take control of someone's Facebook or steal some poor sucker's credit card information. Any two-bit hackjob with a bot could pull that off. No, the hackers she needs are quiet cats, subterranean detective-caliber-homies who don't advertise their wares because they're not up for sale, anyways. Their brethren in qualification are the ones all the terrorist cells and foreign governments use, paying them a pretty penny to do so.

But the ones we're after are a less ambitious strain of the breed. The black hat badasses working for China are like Orcas, pouncing quick and leaving no flesh on the bone, swallowing and crunching and chewing and moving on to the next meal, marking their territory. They're in this line of work because they're after immortality, like any good artist, or because breaking through walls, and feasting on whatever sweet meat lies behind them, gets 'em off real good. They're too dangerous for Miranda to wrangle.

Their brethren, however, are quieter leviathans. Meandering slowly just underneath the internet's crust, they take up mucho space but move in slow berths, awaiting a strong current or the scent of krill to stir them from their floating minutia into action. Nothing less than a ruling from the bonafide court of public opinion is like to catch their attention. They're the ones responsible for the reprehensible audio leaks of nutjob politicians, Top-Secret government drone-strike statistics mysteriously extracted from their secure-but-not-enough servers. And they don't leave a trace because they never act as individuals. They do what they do because it's where the internet is going, because it's what the culture wants. They're just fists. They're slaves to mass marches, lone members of the throng blessed with specialized skillsets. And if it's one of these behemoths Miranda wants to exploit, she'll have to find not only the beast of burden, but the trail they're traveling upon.

Fortunately, Miranda knows a certain cause that, even now, even weeks later, so many would-be crusaders in the internet militia still wave banners for. Even for our recently detached, galactically-minded Miranda, this takes some steeling. Like jumping into an ice bath, it's not so bad once you're submerged, but it takes a certain gall in getting there. Miranda takes three swigs of tequila from the Twins' birthday bottles above the fridge (they'll never notice), and turns to her task, braces herself, plugs her nose, jumps.

Miranda seeks out and submerges herself into the underground forums wherein the calls to *#UnmaskGwami*, and far worse, first emanated. These are the sprouting sites of the ever-enraged *Big Banana* loyalists, wild motherfuckers with a bloodthirsty passion for fads and serous internet intelligence to boot. A veritable feeding frenzy, wherein she hopes to hook the big one, boys.

Now, of course you remember Lakshmi's warnings? About those people who would and *could* actually unmask Gwami, who *could* find Miranda, who had sufficient free time and psychotic leanings to, say, lead a mass mob march on Miranda's apartment were they to find even fleeting information about her real identity? Yeah, these are they. They all have infantile usernames like @shadowlordhexxx and @sycosycosis, but don't let that fool you, these are a terrifying breed of upper-middle-class white male, pimple-faced and woman-hating. Though worried by its juvenility at first, Miranda's moniker, lifted from her adolescent social media habits, mollifyingly melds her into the milieu. @MSGoth-Kid666 joins the fray.

So, she heads brashly into the belly of the beast that broke her, planning to divert its vengefulness for her own gains. Although these are tight-knit communities, in their forage for fresh flesh the individuals within sometimes take big bites out of their own kind.

Take, for example, this poor sucker right here in "/justice" who has very thoughtfully posited for public comment "Do you guys think Gwami is like, IRL hot? Or nah, is she like a hag lol?"

As if his 380 downvotes weren't enough to let you know how the Gwami-hating public felt about his message, perhaps this response from a moderator named @JorgenVonDangle will clue you in:

@SweatyHairy6969 [that's OP's handle] *we've been over this, you misogynistic piece of shit. Why don't you go to/fuckable if you're going to keep at it with this tired, beta-male, has-been shit. Another one of these and you're banned, you Roger Ailes-ass-motherfucker.*

Bloodthirsty, they'll devour what they can get, even one of their own. Our moderator, only caring about marginalized communities in the most basic and transparently self-serving of ways, reminds everyone why they're *here*, and not on/*fuckable* presumably, with a newly pinned post.

Hello all. /Justice is a place to discuss and share all the ways we think Gwami the Seer could and should be punished, whether through the U.S. penal system or other avenues. Threats of violence will not be tolerated unless OP could actually make good on them. Any information relating to the #UnmaskGwami initiative should be posted under /Unmask. General Gwami bashing can be found at /GetGwami. Thanks to all for abiding.

What this means is that Miranda must be extremely careful with what she posts, commenting on the general Gwami restlessness with intentional sloth, upvoting with major discretion, but most importantly, legitimizing her presence here with just the kind of obscure

Gwami knowledge that only a zealot or a 1st-degree murderer would know.

As the days go on, she gains their trust through sheer volume, masquerading as a kind of hacker herself, one who's found some underground archive of Gwami's work and so posts private musings, time-stamped photos from those first videos, on-set and extremely private. Through deliberate mimicry of their ideas, no matter how horrifying or destructive they are, she comes to earn a tenuous respect. Sometimes she's spoken about in threads she's never even visited. @MSGoth-Kid666 is the one with the scoop; soon everyone knows that.

With what other time she has, she scrolls. She reintroduces herself to a land she was once Queen of. She picks up on what her classmates are doing, spends hours watching cooking videos for dishes she won't actually ever make. When the quiet echoes of her empty apartment make her feel especially alone, she finds solace in the few places impervious to the Banana rash. The public library branches are strong hold-outs, and within their coziest corners, she inhales communist manifestos and conflicting timelines of Modernism.

But only between the hours of 9 and 5. If the Twins could even possibly be home, Miranda needs to be, too. She needs them to believe fully in the crippling nature of her illness, afraid that they will find her traipsing out around town, see through her ruse, and obliviously report such a sighting back to concerned professors and administrators. Equally unconscionable is the idea of the two doing *Big Banana's* private bidding, unobserved within their shared walls. Somehow Miranda feels that if she can be in the Twins' presence, she'll be able to stay up-to-date on any attempts to find or destroy her.

cough…cough "Hey, what are you guys doing?"

"Oh, hey Miranda! Nothing much, new assignment. Trying to figure out who Gwami is from these bugged phone recordings," or maybe "Oh, Miranda, hey! Yeah just work. Work work work work work, you know how it goes. We have proof that Gwami has Neo-Nazi ties, so we're just trying to figure out the best way to tweet that, nothing too interesting."

Suffice to say that Miranda would rather be bored than paranoid, so she stays mostly holed up in her room, her ear to the wall, her eye pressed to the crack under her door, on the lookout for stylish boots and the tracks they leave.

Finally, 13 long, repetitive, soul-sucking, deceptive, crude, dubious, slooooooooooow-moving days from when she started this crusade, Miranda finally cuts into the usual anti-Gwami banter with promises of *something big, something she's working on*, whetting the general appetite. All this so that later, when she logs on in the dead of night and opens a big ol' wound, saying "Hey guys, I did it, I found her IP address. If someone can get me a location on this, I can go check it out, but I'm pretty sure this is from Gwami the Seer's computer," the masses even way out in the open ocean will get a feverish whiff of sweet, sweet blood. Line in the water, she waits.

And by morning, some housebound dreg, a casual anti-Semite with invasive knowledge of some fat-cat ISP's private directory, pops back in a (mercifully) private comment and says, "Just for you, @MSgothkid666. The address is 49 West 70th St. Hope the stupid, Jew bitch pisses herself when she sees you."

Just like that, her work there is done. Affirming her longtime hypothesis, the overly outraged are an easily manipulatable sort, especially in the "safety" of such numbers as these. *Big Banana* proved quite keen selecting them as their secret soldiers.

Miranda leaves the site at once, rewarding herself for her days of dirty work with a long, positively scalding shower, so as to get the message board grime off her skin. Then it's uptown without delay. An end to the saga is nearly at hand: The Woman with the Red Hair must be waiting for her there.

The only tiny, teensy, itty-bitty little issue here is that Miranda, her memory as shallow as the internet's, forgets again that all these worlds don't just shut down when she leaves them. She forgets that this specific site has users with motivated minds and long lives at which they are the center. She's absentmindedly left an already rotted corner of the internet an incentive to fester further, and this time with a possible path to its own self-perceived salvation. You see, there are other stories, adjacent stories to ours, told by terrible tellers and full of harrowing heroes, and those stories lurch forward, too. In them, Miranda Swami is but a bit player, a plot mover, her real name unimportant, her manipulation unknown and unnoticed.

In other words, things are happening. Bad news bears.

But of course, that isn't on Miranda's mind. What *is* on our heroine's mind is the shadow-hidden face of the Woman with the Red Hair. Will she in reality be beautiful, a seductress? Will be she an old, ragged crone? Or will this be another dead-end? Another overthought nugget of information that will lead her to a very confused doorstep, and thus, after much apology and embarrassment, end this stupid squabbling horse-and-pony show for good?

Because, for real this time everyone, this is it. If this is a dud, then this thing and Gwami and Miranda, all of them are *kaput.* She'll drop out of school and steal some money from her folks to go traipsing the world, fucking French girls and drinking absinthe and getting into lightly-European drug trouble like any other confused, twenty-something, rich girl, kid-of-a-congressman would do in a time of crisis. She'll chalk all of her interdimensional travel thus far up to an elaborate but loosely-controlled practical joke. She'll start calling herself Wanda.

With all her might, she pushes such thoughts from her mind, assisted in her task by the suffocating subway gaggle amassing around her and the horrible squeals of her stopping, sputtering train.

Lincoln Center, when she emerges into it, is a rodeo of tuxedos and ballroom gowns, long inhalations and expensive doublets and the orgiastic, ephemeral blowings of faraway flutes, oboes, bassoons.

It is not a world Miranda has ever felt comfortable in, especially a Miranda who looks like this: eyes veiny and cheeks blotched, teeth crawling with resilient, fuzzy plaque. She should've brushed her teeth again before she came here. Oh God, and she should have put on makeup. Miranda ducks into a *Duane Reade,* where our closeted kleptomaniac steals some product from aisle three, ducking into the unguarded employee bathroom to use it. The toothpaste goes into her mouth blue and comes out yellow. She brushes again. When she emerges, her eyelashes are twice their usual length, her cheeks rosy as can be.

With a cleaner mouth and a clearer head (though a somewhat cloudier moral record), she walks slowly uptown, passing brownstone after brownstone, ducking under untrimmed tree branches, wondering what types of trees these even are and how many New Yorkers would know that answer.

Miranda is running her fingers across tree bark when it appears, *eureka!,* like a mirage on the other side of the street: 49 West 70th Street, the white, varnished duplex that contains all her intrigue. If this is where the Woman lives, it's a far cry from the hovel Miranda once imagined. In her head there was a dingy basement, dilapidated ceilings and old Chinese food cartons strewn about like asteroid debris around a crater; a Lisbeth Salander-type in a room glowing green from the ambient computer screen. Would've been weirdly situated in this part of town, but even in her wildest dreams she'd never have expected this. Spiral staircase swank? Resilient petunias growing on the windowsills. An expensive crystalline chandelier hanging visibly through the many wide windows, easily seen even from out on the street. Good for her, this Woman with Red Hair, but seems against type.

Unperturbed, Miranda climbs the stairs, rings the bell and puts her premature judgments aside, holding her breath until a shape shambles to the door. Miranda's left hand reaches into her bag, grabbing tightly the goggles inside. She's brought them as proof that she is indeed the requested savior, Miranda Swami. Not that there could be much confusion. She's one of a kind.

An elderly smell of lilac and lemongrass rushes forth from the opening door like an excited dog, catching Miranda off-guard. Behind it, thin, poofy blonde curls and emerald eyes, an aged frailty in the face around them. A confoundingly familiar face, and a neck encircled by a black, wrought-iron key on a necklace.

Where has she seen this person before?

Why does she know this face?

Back just before her *Eldred L. Apple* exhibition opened, when there were Professorial rumblings of a certain powerful art critic's desire to come christen her exhibition, Miranda, preparing for a chance encounter on a sunny side-street, memorized this face, knowing that with socialites of a certain sort, flattery and recognition are as compelling a currency as cash.

Judith LeMeur smells like you'd expect, like she sleeps among dried flowers and plays bridge on the promenade. She looks Miranda up and down and groans "This better be good."

"Ju-dith Le-Meur?" Miranda chokes out. She should have known.

The lady looks at her incredulously, almost concerned. "......... Why?"

"I should have known. I should have known." Miranda says smiling, taking a step forward.

"Young lady, I do not know who you are or what you want, but if you take another step towards this door, I *will* call the police."

"No, no no no. You don't understand. It's *me*. Miranda Swami!" She takes the goggles from her bag, holding them up as proof.

Judith LeMeur raises an eyebrow, but still this strange girl stays smiling, holding a piece of shabby grey plastic up to her as if as an offering. Then she begins closing the door.

"Miranda *Swami*! Ma'am. You know me!"

The door hesitates, three-quarters closed. Behind it, LeMeur says to herself "Swami…Swami. Swami. Wait, yes, yes, I know *you*. You're the girl who stood me up at the *Apple* exhibit, aren't you?"

Is this a test? "Oh, uhm, unfortunately yes, Ma'am. Completely on accident, though, for what it's worth."

"Well, I don't know what you're doing here…" LeMeur says, trailing off. She rolls her eyes and sighs, internally acquiescing to something. After a long moment, the door opens fully for Miranda to step through.

"You may hang your coat there beside the umbrellas."

In the hall, LeMeur says something about tea before coaxing Miranda into a broad, eccentric parlor (at least that's what a more learned socialite might call the room) directing her to a seat nestled at the intersection of two sienna walls. LeMeur leaves her for the kitchen, giving Miranda ample time to appreciate what appears to be a deliberate collection of post-modern finger-paintings and taxidermic animal skulls in glass cases. Miranda fidgets in place, somewhat shaken at being the only living thing in a room full of just-abouts. The chandelier, giving off rich, luscious light, sways slightly overhead, as if taunting poor Miranda, a creature so low to the ground.

Unsure whether her patience or her tenacity is being tested, Miranda waits, and waits, and waits for LeMeur to return, until destiny demands to be taken in her own hands. The rest of the house, as she peeks around the corner, is dark except for an amber glow coming from down the hall, which is where Miranda finds LeMeur halfway done with a mug of amber tea, the kitchen reeking of *potpourri*.

"So, young lady," LeMeur says without looking up, "you stood me up at your gallery, and now you've stalked me to my home. Why is it that you and your generation all believe you're at the center of the universe? In my day, if we had a meeting with someone we *needed* to impress, we arrived twenty-minutes early with a new suit and new haircut. And if we were late or, say, forgot to show up altog-ether, and if, say, someone felt strongly put off by us thereafter, we took *res-ponsi-bility* for our actions. We did not show up unannounced, looking half-murderous on their doorsteps."

"But, Ma'am, didn't you —"

"Hush. However you got this address I do not care to discuss. Charles — Professor Gillibrand — knows I would have him killed if he told a student where I lived, so I can only assume it was through the uncouth means available to your kind. You 'millennials.' But, Miranda Swami, you are here and since you did not take the ample opportunity I gave you in the parlor to more seriously consider leaving, you obviously have something to say, so please, out with it."

"May I sit?" Miranda asks cordially.

"I'd rather you not."

Miranda isn't sure whether to snicker or sob. "Ma'am, maybe I got the wrong impression, but I thought that you *invited* me here."

There's no sound worse than the kind of mocking chuckle LeMeur mockingly chuckles just then, between sips. "And what on God's green Earth would have given you that idea, girl?"

And that's a wrap folks. That last comment is going to just about do it for our fair Miranda Swami. She's had a good run, but Option A: that the resident of this apartment is the Woman with the Red Hair, officially *rejected*.

Though Option B: use Judith LeMeur's IP address to try and regain access to the Program, officially *still possible*.

And don't sleep on Option C: forget this ever happened and beg Father for a ticket to Europe, officially *pretty appealing*. Whatever option she will eventually choose, its first step will involve getting out of this continuously-more-embarrassing conversation as soon as possible.

"Ma'am, I'm so sorry, I must have misunderstood something." Miranda applies her phoniest, most sycophantic smile. "Didn't mean to waste your time, so I just…I'll be going now."

Promptly, she turns on her heels as if to walk out of the apartment. But LeMeur, the lilt in her voice perhaps a bit *too* sardonic, calls out,

"Oh, is that *it*, Ms. Swami? Just going to run away? Scared out of your wits by an old woman and her jasmine tea? I thought you would have more fight in you. Truly, I did. But no, that's fine, you took a chance coming here and obviously it's not going your way, so just flee the premises. Isn't that what you Millennials do? When the going gets tough, you just vanish, *poof*, right? Better things to do and all that jazz, hmm?"

Honestly, there's only two things LeMeur could've gone after just now that would demand Miranda Swami's retaliation, and one is making an affront to her Millennialism. Curmudgeonly old bitch. So, Miranda does what any good Millennial would do when some septuagenarian, thinking they're unique or revelatory in their disdain for the youngers and not just unwitting prey to the same recurrent generational opinions that have plagued the aged since there first was an aged: she turns right around and claps back.

Okay, boomer.

"I don't think that's fair at all," Miranda says.

"I figured you'd think that," LeMeur replies.

"Do you think you know me? Know us?"

Oh no. Oh no no no. Miranda doesn't realize what's happening. She doesn't understand that LeMeur hasn't really been drinking tea, but has actually been digging a hole, filling it with spikes, and carefully laying it over with an underbrush disguise. This is a trap, and Miranda's about to step right in. And she knows it, too, can sense it. But, sweet thing, she can't resist.

"Sweet Pea," LeMeur says, smiling so wide you can see each one of her 32 pristine, ghostly-white teeth. "I know you better than you know yourself."

"Do you really believe that?"

Metaphorical knuckles set about cracking. "Do *you* really believe you're *that* unique? Here's what I believe you are: habitually late, unkempt, white…like so many of your generation's 'artists.' I can tell by your hair that you're queer, by your eyebrows that you're angry and since you can't stand still for a moment, I assume you're probably off abusing a well-intentioned Adderall prescription. So yes, Ms. Swami, I do feel I know you."

"*Ms.* LeMeur, saying you can tell I'm *queer* by my hair is, pardon my language, fucked up. What the Hell is wrong with you?" Miranda's getting righteously, and rightly, angry. Enlivened hair jumps off her head and sticks to her sweaty forehead. She's beginning to itch. All these extraneous variables just make her angrier.

"Oh, I'm *so* sorry, are you very offended? Spare me a lesson in civility, dear. I'm well aware when I'm being incendiary, I've been doing it a long while now."

"Ms. LeMeur, I don't know if your *arthritis* has kept you from getting on a computer anytime in the last ten years, but that kind of demeaning, belittling, *marginalizing* attitude isn't really acceptable any more. Like you're *so* important. Like your opinion matters so much. You're just an art critic. What do you know about anything else? About us? About me?"

Easy, Miranda. See what's going on here, girl. Through Miranda's entire red-faced tirade, LeMeur sits stoic, taking quiet, polite sips of her tea, exhaling the steam through her nose.

"God damn it!" Miranda continues. "Every angry, unkempt, imprudent queer has a *different* and equally valid story to tell. Get the message?" Miranda has to catch her breath. She is at the mercy of something stronger than her restraint. "And-and-and and, but you're *famously gay*, for Christ's sake! That was like *your thing*! And now what? You're going to adopt this patronizing attitude because…because why? Because my sexuality isn't the thesis statement of my life? Because I'm not going to let you define me by it? What are you? Bitter? Don't you see what you're doing?"

LeMeur takes a very, very, very, fucking excruciatingly long sip of her tea. Very long and very loud and positively slurpy, followed by a nice, proud lip-smack. And she looks up at Miranda, smiling.

"Miranda Swami, listen to *me* carefully. First of all, do not deign to tell me what it was like to be a homosexual in this industry these past decades. You have *no* idea. *None* of you have *any* idea. You know, maybe I am angry. Because in a lot of ways, I envy you desperately. Desperately.

"I never wanted to be a critic, you know. My initial foray was into artistry, in fact. That was vital, for what it's worth. Investing myself into art helped me greatly in time, for I believe all great critics have to have a background in the art they critique, otherwise how would they know? How would they know what it's like to throw your soul into something, your very being, to try and coax people to *listen* through your work? How would they know? The greatest critics have an understanding of that, an empathy that is absolutely vital to truly understanding a work, be it of value or not.

"I was an artist and it was the 60's and suddenly there was this wave of acceptance for everything. You could sleep with who you wanted and think what you wanted and decry the government or God, and it was all okay. There was freedom for everyone. The blacks had leaders making real change while the long-haired hippies had their, you know, Woodstock music. Bully for all of them. But no matter what I did, no matter what I tried, my art, my career, my life was always trapped in the shadow of my sexuality. I didn't have a choice. I was a queer artist, and all of my art, my criticism, my trips to the corner store reflected that.

"Look at you. You call me a 'famously gay' critic. Why in God's name does that have anything to do with my work? With my criticism? Why is that the factoid about me you can pull from your subconscious? Imagine that. Try to imagine. I did not shy away from my sexuality, I leaned into its totality. For the greater good. So that one day, *you and your generation could live a life freed from that bondage.* I did all of this for you! My sexuality was a sacrifice. For you! What you are, what you *get to be*, I did that for you. Me! And yet you come here so self-important, nursing your sexuality like it's a war wound, holding it tight as if someone is trying to take it from you. I gave up *my* freedom, *my* choice, for you. And you squander what I gave you. You squander it and scream bloody murder when I do not conform to your strange little understanding of what it means to be gay. It means something different to me, young lady. You exploit this thing of yours. It becomes you. And you suck what you can from it because, and this I tell you true, because you can shrug it free at any point. But you choose to look like that, to make art the way you do, to bathe in it and decry your marginalization."

She says this all in one almost-uninterrupted thought. So many times does Miranda want to interject, but the words can't be cajoled out from her throat. They hide fearful under her tongue. Her brain is mush, and no matter how she plumbs its depths, she is not able to find any sufficient words of retaliation. They will not come to her for weeks, until she is standing in the shower, thinking about what she'll have for lunch, when the full experience of this moment will erupt from underneath her cerebral cortex in full, flashy detail. It will come over her like nausea, and she will vomit up all possible responses, the obvious and the witty and everything she should've said that she'll never get the chance to. But for now, She stands stri-cken and silent, knowing, *knowing*, that she did this to herself. She poked the bear.

"And on top of it all," Judith LeMeur continues, "you were late. So, let us recap, yes? Trite of skin, *exploitative* of sexual orientation, lacking in experience, talented but entitled. A *statistic*. Why is it *really* that you have stalked me to my home today? Murdering me here would be a *highly* cliché act."

And Judith LeMeur, bitch extraordinaire, *smirks*. Her smirk has a sound, like a whip being cracked, like lightning rending open the sky, a far, faraway sky. It's not even clear if she believes what she's saying. Whether she's right or wrong is beyond the scope of either woman. It's not about homosexuality, about exploitation, about imprudence. No. This is a generational argument beyond morality, beyond correctness, beyond themselves. This is a spokesman battle of souls, and whose is stronger, and who has earned theirs more.

Miranda says, "There is so much more to me that you don't know," in a voice strong but quiet, like timber.

"Yes, I'm sure, my dear. I'm sure. And what *is* that exactly?"

A cloud descends upon Miranda. A cloud of fear and angst descends upon her shoulders, a tight scarf that constricts around her throat. It's a familiar scarf, one she wears often, always enjoying its automatic adornment. But a tiny, ardent light from her cerebellum fires itself through the cloud, and Miranda finally blurts it out, without any of the conviction or grandeur with which she always imagined she would.

It comes into the world squirming, a meager whimper is all it is.

"I'm Gwami the Seer," she putters quietly.

As LeMeur takes a deep breath in, the kind of breath that precedes a speech, Miranda repeats the words in her head. *I'm Gwami the Seer, I'm Gwami the Seer.*

She's never said those words aloud.

As LeMeur embarks on a fresh soliloquy, Miranda meanwhile feels the pressure in the room change. There's a minute shift in the air and also in her skin; everything becomes sharper, clearer; she can hear individual bird calls. It's obvious she's set something in motion just now, revealed something not only to LeMeur but to the random, eavesdropping universe.

Miranda, who has been staring off into the middle-distance for who knows how long, looks back at LeMeur, who appears to have been talking this entire time.

"...and it doesn't *really* matter who you are, Ms. Swami. You could be Henry-bloody-Kissinger made youthful by secret serum, and you *still* wouldn't play to anybody but the coffee-shop crowd over on Astor. And do you want to know why?

"Because no matter who you are or how you say what you say, you're still saying the same boring, trite, tired things everyone's always said.

You *are* a statistic. So, why don't you kill me now or come back when you've got something new to say, if I'm not long dead and buried by then?"

The rage drains from Miranda, as does every other emotion. There's been a sea-change, a cooling, a chilling out of everything. She has to concentrate carefully on her next movements, for they must be perfect.

Okay, Miranda. Easy now. Act angry, yes. Storm out without a word, like she's broken you. Great job. Get out of this room before her old, weak legs can lift themselves up from the table. Let her shout after you, let her make all the noise she can. Grab your coat and be noisy about it, take your shoes in your hands and give the door a nice, firm slam.

LeMeur's old, weak legs do eventually get her up, get her down the hall, and get her to the door. Her old, weak hands ensure the door is securely shut, lock the deadbolts and mortises and fumble with the final fat black lock that requires the key around her neck. Those hands arm an alarm system, adjust the security camera angles, basically do everything but let the Doberman out of the cage, and that's only because Judith doesn't own a Doberman. She's terrified of the beasts. She does spend a not-insignificant amount of time checking her security cameras before bed, staring at her patio and front porch both, feeling somewhat scurvy about that girl who accosted her earlier, though she can't quite remember the details of what they discussed, only that it was engaging and infuriating in equal measure. This hazing over of memory is normal when confrontation works her up. The cameras are somehow less enthralling than you might think, and even LeMeur eventually gets bored. It's with her alarm-clock reading 9:58 in the PM that sleep swallows Judith LeMeur, her favorite 24-hour shopping network tuned into, her ever-weakening body protected by three layers of heavily-locked doors, and the windows are barred.

But none of that matters, because Miranda Swami, all this time, was hiding in the front hall closet. Ain't no camera in *there*. Although hiding is perhaps too confident a word. She was quaking, hyperventilating, making herself small within the space. Holding in her breaths and her urine and waiting for the mumbling, light-footed old woman outside to climb the stairs and head off to bed. She was too scared to even use her phone, terrified that an errant Instagram video might loudly give her away.

If LeMeur had found her in here, she would have had to have made a quick choice between failure and felony. That wouldn't suit anyone.

After much quaking and shaking, waiting and hyperventilating, she exits the closet into the darkened house. With each step through the halls, no matter how careful they are, the nearby frames on the nearby paintings shake lightly, as if not completely secured to the wall. Miranda wonders if LeMeur ever lets outside help into her house… She can't possibly have done all this decoration herself.

Miranda steals an aerosol can from the bathroom and sprays it down the hall in case of crisscrossing lasers.

But there are no lasers, nor guard dogs. Anyways, LeMeur's paranoia is a rampant but fundamentally ignorant one, one that believes locks will save the soul, that believes safety in the home is the only safety necessary. Poor Judith LeMeur, investing in fresh locks every week, unlisted in the yellow pages. Yet Miranda Swami needed just a few days of impersonation to pull her address out of a string of digits she got from a man in a computer game. Safety is relative.

Safety *is* relative, and Miranda pokes her head around corners and carefully opens doors, all in an effort to find that elusive space ubiquitous in the homes of Boomers-and-above: The Computer Room. There's the kitchen and a pair of seashell-themed bathrooms that really don't belong in a house like this. There's a thick door letting in a slight draft which must lead to a garage, and a laundry room/pantry stocked with all kinds of dog and cat food, though Miranda has not seen or heard a living animal in her time here. And there are plenty of locked doors, too. Like, an aggressive amount of locked doors. Should

Miranda flounder in her initial search, there might be secondary heists to consider.

The "computer room" is all the way at the end of the thin hall past another first-floor bathroom. Somewhat ironically, *this* door remains unlocked. Fully open, in fact. Miranda can't help but feel bad for the critic: a key worn around her neck for safekeeping, and still not quite cunning enough to keep out intruders.

Inside the room, which Miranda carefully closes and locks, she discovers that LeMeur is one of the much-mythicized last people in the city with a desktop computer, and a serious clunker at that. It's a *beast*, a blocky, tan monstrosity you'd find in some early-90's government lab, a computer that looks like it'd eat her phone if she brought it too close.

Wait, she's seen something like this before.

Oh, shit. She *is* in the right place.

Chills, the shivers. Butterflies in her stomach. This is happening. This is actually happening. She, Miranda Swami, has trespassed into the house of one of New York's most influential art critics, has set up shop in her computer room, has ensured that the door behind her is locked, and that the window there is an *un*locked and practical emergency escape route, is preparing to use her Neolithic computer as a portal to another world. Conveniently but confusingly, that computer's startup is a fully silent process. These old computers, the proto-desktops, some of their settings don't just defy convention, they defy logic itself.

A password prompt causes a mini-panic, but remember: LeMeur is a woman in her early-seventies, so the password is inevitably written on a post-it stuck on the screen's southwest corner. It's almost like she's inviting strange folks to peruse around her online life. Anyways, Miranda's in, and there's nothing left to do but what she must. The goggles wrapped around her face, the heartbeat in her chest thumping as powerfully as it ever has, Miranda connects a cord and falls through a familiar rabbit hole.

There's the familiar dot matrix, and the familiar dissolve of blackness to color, and finally the familiar hallway. A familiar black box in the center of her vision, and into it, a recently-memorized and now-confirmed IP address enters itself. The black box disappears, the code accepted. Miranda didn't realize she was holding her breath, but lets it go. It *was* the key, after all. The IP, that is, not her, uhm, her breath.

Instead of moving under her own power, Miranda is nostalgically whisked around a corner and another and then, down a twisted, monstrous corridor. This is just like the first time she was here, except that, woah, whatever turn the Program has her take, it's one she's never taken before.

The walls become bare and then haggard; stripped of their wallpaper and ornaments, once-covered cracks breathe digital air for perhaps the first time. Picture frames lie shattered and empty in the crease between floor and wall. The Program itself looks to be falling apart. Splintered floorboards reveal holes to nowhere opened beneath her, and there are no more doors flanking her either, just the walls with their black cracks, an empty nothingness behind them nothing programmed, nothing existing. This, a walkway at the center of a void.

And at the end, a literal light at the end of the tunnel, a whiteness needing neither password nor button command to enter, just an open door-sized rectangle leaking straight-up starlight. Miranda is pulled through. The path forward, open and awaiting her inevitable steps. Calvinism proves alive and well within the Program's tangle.

Miranda expected to find Her seated upon a throne. Something gaudy, grand, baroque. I mean, wouldn't you? But it seems like the Woman is going for a more Nativity-Scene-type-thing, which explains all the hay bales and the barnyard sunlight throwing smattered stripes across the floor. Christ himself would have felt right at home in the early-morning glaze, encircled by Three Wise Men, like the Woman with the Red Hair, her face still cloaked by shadow, is by the European Men from the bus stop.

The photo-realism of other worlds is ignored here: the details fuzzy, the frame-rate choppy. Look hard enough and you can even see the pixels; amateur work. The light doesn't' reflect correctly, there isn't any floating dust, nor even a trace of varnish on the barn columns, and behind the slats in the windows is only this lazy, abject brightness. It's exactly the kind of unfinished place that would drive away any too-lucky soul who happened to stumble in. In that way, it's a fitting safehouse: devoid of detail, just barely functional, and only just.

One of the Europeans tongues an extensively ashy cigarette, the smoke rising up in ambient ripples before surrendering to the same low-res crappiness as the room around it.

"Hello," The Woman with the Red Hair says, as the men disperse to the corners of the room and then into thin air. "Can you hear me all right?" Her voice is like balsamic, so sharp and tart and syrup-thick. It's one of those familiar voices, a voice like you hear in dreams, one that seems to be all voices at once.

"I can," Miranda types back. Her heart is beating so hard she can feel it in her tongue.

The Woman sighs. "You've made it."

"I have."

"You've finally made it."

A pause.

"You didn't make it easy for me," Miranda says.

A *long* pause.

"I couldn't have. I wouldn't have known it was really you."

There's a real tension. Something isn't being said.

"Well I'm here."

Miranda wants to say more, has so many sentences to speak and questions to ask, but the words for them have gone. Some after-effect from her conversation with LeMeur, must be. But really, what should she even say? What could she? It's the Woman's *turn* to speak, and there's nothing more desperate than texting out of turn.

"Yes, you're here," the Woman says, *finally*. "You're really here."

And then, it's as if a divine knife falls to slice the tension. *Sliiiiiiice.* The Woman careens herself onto the floor, letting forth the wild squealing of a trapped animal. "Oh, thank God!" she screams (Miranda has to readjust her headphones). "Oh, thank heavens, you're here! You're real and you're here to save me! You, Miranda Swami — Gwami the Seer — are here to save me! To save us!"

There are weeps, true, trembling weeps coming from the Woman's prone body, but they soon become quiet or far off, like their producer has moved away from her microphone.

"Are — are you okay?" Miranda asks, suddenly sheepish…suddenly *scared*. Imagine God appearing to you, inconsolable and in tears. You too might feel a certain shiver.

"Yes, yes, oh yes," the Woman finally says, "I've just, just been so nervous and afraid, oh so, so afraid, for so long. And and and it all depended upon you. But now you're here, and they said it couldn't be done, they said it wouldn't work, but *finally*, because you're here, I see a path forward from out of this Hell."

"Wait, what's going on here? You said you had information on *Big Banana*, you said Cindi Lapenschtall was…this was all about…aren't you going to help me save Gwami? I'm not here to save *you*."

"But but but, Miranda Swami, you already have, just by coming here! Nobody else would have done all that, persevered so long, searched and searched, out there and in here, disregarded so much else in their search for answers. So clever, so cunning. I thought it was you, was 99.999% sure but needed definitive proof. I knew it. I knew you'd be just like I imagined. In my dreams, you always were. Strong, smart, so sharp-witted. I've been watching you of course. Not the whole time, but, well, a lot of it. And you were willing to sacrifice yourself for *her*. Every impasse, every near abandonment of this whole escapade…you always came back for her. For me. For us. And I-I-I had to be sure it was you. It could only have been you. It could *only* have been you. I had to be sure. I had to make sure you were *committed*."

"I'm so confused. Did you design this whole place *for* me?"

"Miranda. What happened to you, to Gwami, it *was* all a stunt. What happened to Cindi, it was a stunt, too. A devilish trick, I *swear*. It was all marketing!"

"And?"

"And? *And?* And what!? This is it, Miranda Swami, finally you and I are together, working towards a common goal. Can you imagine what people would've said about this, like, two months ago? It would've set them on fire! The entire world has been preparing for our partnership and now —"

"'Our?' Who are you?"

The perpetual shadow over the Woman's face begins to lift, and a Cheshire Cat smile opens along her jawline. A prearranged swelling of orchestral strings starts low and rises up, reaching a crescendo as the Woman says, "Miranda Swami, don't you see? Don't you know, can't you tell? I'm Cindi Lapenschtall."

But you probably knew that already, didn't you? Something about twists.

"Well," Miranda says finally, trying not to offend Cindi (whose famed beauty is much diminished with all these blocky-ass pixels) with too quick a response, with too inexuberant a heartbeat, but her capacity for awe has been diminished in all the hubbub. "What now?" she asks, genuinely uncertain.

"What *now*?! It's *me*: Cindi Lapenschtall! Former CEO of *Big Banana*! And you're Gwami the Seer! Fallen Queen of the Internet! Digital Lucifer! Maybe that's not the best metaphor. What now? Now we work together! To bring down the company that wronged us! The both of us!" The music slowly fades, eventually settling into its place as soothing, quiet ambience.

"I don't understand…" Miranda starts to say.

"What's not to understand? They framed us! They *faked* my death. It was probably some intern they threw off that building in my stead. I honestly don't know. But I was wise to them, some friends helped me escape their clutches, thankfully, but if I showed my face after that, I would've been killed. And I *thought* about going public — I think every day about going to the police or the FBI — but they have everyone in their pockets, you know, *EVERYONE*, the heads of so many companies and all the authorities. It'd be actual suicide. I've had to be so so so careful. And if I were to suddenly reappear in the wrong way or without enough attention on me — I mean they can change the news cycle like *that*, so I've had to be careful, and that's why I've invested so much on the infrastructure here, cuz it's very invite-only and I'm the only person — well not the *only* person who can invite people on, but you see it was about creating a network totally outside of *them*, you know, and that's why it had to be *here* I brought you, somewhere safe and away from them, but getting there, here, away from them, was so much harder than I thought which is crazy, CRAZY, because I was their CEO, right? But I was always just a face and there's no way —"

"Wait. Please. Please slow down." Miranda's in a tizzy, tossed topsy-turvy by the tsunami of talk the trembling teller touts. "What are you saying? That there's like a shadow company within *Big Banana*? That you, *Cindi Lapenschtall*, built this place to escape them?"

"Oh. Yes. Of course. You don't know? Well, you couldn't possibly know, I suppose. Oh, this is so overreaching of me, so characteristic — Easy, Cindi. One thing at a time. — so yeah, okay, let me start over. Or, you know what? We'll skip to the end and double back. A classic trope. Watch this."

Behind Cindi, the barn wall disintegrates into dust, swept away by a supernatural broom, leaving a black screen where it once stood. A flickering video appears atop the blackness, old-timey-like with the countdown reels: *5, 4, 3, 2, 1.*

In the grainy, security-camera video that plays thereafter, eight hooded figures encircle a flaming trash drum in a warehouse, and Miranda feels the hair stand on the back of her neck. Even the crappy surveillance footage, tinged blue by tungsten light, eclipses the most hyper-realistic CGI in quality. The video has an ostentatious *realness* to it.

"Bring it out," Cindi says to the screen. Then to Miranda, "You better pay attention; we can only show you this once."

A moment, then the slow-approaching sound of rollicking chains, and with it, the snarls of a livid, lashed animal. There's a guttural note in the animal's raving, a hollowness if you will, just like you heard that one time when you were a kid, remember? You brought your ear up to the hole in the trunk of that old Oak behind the abandoned McGillicuddy place and you heard something, yes, you heard some*thing*, but it was way down the hole and though you were only hearing the reverberations against the grain of the bark, it was still so terrifying, so chilling to your very essence, it made you run, nay sprint, right home… and you've never really stopped thinking about it.

At first, stillness on-screen, then a pair of robed arms, their exposed wrists white and veiny, and the bodies they belong to, and it's all happening so fast, the bodies and the wrists and then, into the center of the circle is heaved something that can't possibly be real, can't possibly exist like the wrists and robes and the flickering flame-tips on the wall-mounted torches do, but what choice does Miranda have but to believe what she's seeing: in the center of the dark, fire-lit circle stands, shrieking and enchained, complete with furious, red horns curved like a steer's and a pointed tail (God, please let that be just a tail) whipping around in a gorgon frenzy, a very human-sized *Banana*, its yellow "skin" browned in spots by some assumed physical torture (it's the only explanation for all those icky brown lumps and the open, oozing slits along its phallic abdomen) and obscured by the video transmission, which has grown fuzzier the closer this Banana — this Banana — this Banana — *thing*, comes.

This demon. This *Banana Demon*.

Because that's what this is, right? What else can this be but a demon? Cindi never has to say it and Miranda never has to come around to the idea. What she always knew was rooting around in the bushes at night, making them rattle, and what she had always thought punished unruly children post-tantrum, what kept her from staying out after dark and cheating on her exams, the thing that caused all that, could it really be a Banana? A FUCKING BANANA!? God does apparently have some sense of humor. God, that is, or the devil.

A robed figure comes forward into the center of the circle brandishing an enormous, bejeweled sword, like from some geometric table legend, moves their lips in apparent prayer, dips the sword into the flaming dumpster until the blade turns swollen and orange and black and glows, too. In one expert, practiced motion, the figure raises the sword to shoulder height and brings it down, slicing through the very air before slicing through the center of the writhing Banana. Miranda, half-sick, hopes horribly it's just some unfortunate kidnapped soul in-costume. But because its top half slides off of the bottom half with no blood, just a smattering of pulp, she can't possibly believe it to be so. The halved body sits on the ground for a moment, grimacing, and then disintegrates into a kind of wet sand, pooling on the ground.

There's a pair of loud beeps, and an over-eager Roomba enters the frame, headed full speed for the mush on the floor.

Cindi waves her hand and the feed cuts out. She turns to Miranda. "So, you see what I mean."

"What — what in G-g-god's n-n-name w-w-was th-th-that?"

"Most *Big Banana* employees, my dear. The whole R&D department, most of accounts, like half of the mailroom. And *all* of marketing. Well, not *all* of marketing. There are some straggling pencil-pushers in there, smiling faces like, oh you know, what are their names? Your roommates? Sweet girls, very nice, preeminently forgettable, certainly not demons."

"I just, just can't…this is all some kind of joke, right?"

"Miranda, listen to me. *Big Banana*, everything you said about them, all of it was correct. They're an evil corporation, *literally full* of demons. I was a figurehead, that's it. I'm not sure why they needed me but I, I had to…They made me an incredible offer. I couldn't say no. Maybe this whole situation is my punishment, but if it is, it should only be me being punished. They're run by *demons*, Miranda. The rest of the Board, all of them are just like that *thing*, if not in appearance then surely in attitude. They'll destroy anyone to get their way, I've seen it happen. And it's frankly *unjust*."

Miranda says, "I think my appendix is bursting."

"You're just freaking out. Deep breaths. Please, breathe, I know how frightened you must be."

But maybe she doesn't know exactly, because it isn't just fear gripping our dear Miranda, it's complete, horrifying, soul-sucking existential dread, like you might feel after you hit a pregnant pedestrian with your Prius. All of life and death, all the accepted rules of the universe that have hitherto governed life mercilessly retreat from before her, sucked from her brain as if by divine Dyson. Too many questions, too many vast, unanswerable questions about origin, about Christian Hell, about that preacher Caleb took her to see…

And yet, of all the questions she and we are both desperate for answers to, the one she actually asks is, "Why Bananas?"

Why Bananas, indeed. Cindi Lapenschtall, voice raspy from her own hyperventilation, goes off on a tirade about the fate of the universe's soul (which is long and rather rambling, but what she essentially says is this: Miranda, those demons you were always afraid of, they're as real as you or I. Why they chose *bananas* as their unifying symbol, well who in the holy Hell knows but Satan himself? Long ago, they trafficked in pelts, then people, then coal, now bananas. Who can trace their logic, or if they're even capable of logic? Nobody knows where they came from, how they're here, what they are, or what they're goal is, but don't be a dolt, you saw the damn thing, they're obviously bad news, and they're *here*, certifiably here; I've seen them flying, shape-shifting, sucking the aortic veins of livestock, doing all sorts of down-right demonic things, driving motorcycles, going to the dentist, and all of your worst fears are true.

But the scariest thing of all? Thus far in history, nobody has been able to do a damn thing about them. They wear their historical invin-cibility like chainmail. I've been inducted into an order — those kind folks you saw on that screen —, fast-tracked into their upper echelons, become privy to the losing battle they've been fighting for all of history, it seems.

But things are different now. I know they are. People can be reached on such a grand scale. All humanity can finally be united against a common foe. We don't know if we can beat them by force, especially with the extended length of their payroll, but I think that if we engage the culture correctly, if we let the culture take down demons as they might take down poorly-timed *Oscars* jokes or celebrity child molest-ers, if we are allowed to discuss and debate and argue and incite and *joke* about them, if we can make them another *ordinary* evil, we might destroy the very fright, terror, and taboo they peddle in. At best, we'll take away their power. At worst, we'll make them uncool. And to be uncool, unwanted, laughable…that's a form of powerlessness).

"They're going to announce a new CEO. Next Sunday…that big countdown timer on the Statler building? It'll go off and then they'll announce a sudden festival at the *Bash* to unveil the new figurehead they've chosen to lead them into the future or whatever, some poor sucker who probably got reeled in with the same lovely promises of wealth and influence and acceptance and pride that I did. Someone who'll sooner or later be pushed out of a building themselves.

"But you and me, we can start something. There's a whole plan in motion, you're just one part of it. I'm going to get another one of those Banana *things*, my friends and I will bag one up, and we'll livestream the whole thing, the show and the execution and it'll be me up on that screen personally blowing kisses to the crowd, and, and, and that's where you come in, because you're going to promote the hell out of the whole thing. You're going to go reactivate Gwami — I know, I know, but hear me out — you'll do that and then go live, stream the entire announcement, and the whole world will tune in because they haven't heard from you in so long, and because you're promising something *big*. They think the war between you and *Big Banana* is over; they'll bite the bit to witness the next battle live and die-rect. After *Big Banana* cuts their own stream, which they will, it'll be you who broadcasts the rest of the video to the world. You leave the technological aspect to me. I can get up on that screen, I know it. You just get in that crowd and stream everything through Gwami.

"Miranda Swami, you can be a part of the greatest *coup* in human history. Paradise fucking found baby, you ready?"

"Do I have a choice?"

"Good question! Ah, not really. This isn't your narrative anymore. You're just riding along, the eyes and ears. This was never really your story."

Nothing Cindi could possibly have said would please her more. What could be more relieving than stepping outside of her own story for a second into something grander, larger, more complex, where she can be a mere mechanism and not the mechanist?

It seems like the whole universe is chanting her name in cheerful solidarity of her newfound purpose.

"Gwa-Mi! Gwa-Mi!" it says in a voice that sounds like a thousand voices.

Miranda smiles in two worlds. "It certainly sounds like my story."

"What do you mean?"

"My name…"

"What about it?"

"Don't you hear? You mean, you're not doing that? Like the orchestra? Isn't this —?"

You remember our talk earlier? About how the cogs of the internet keep turning even when not observed? Well, suffice to say, they've been turning. Something rank grew in the petri dish overnight.

From Cindi, inside the goggles:

"Miranda, what is happening?"

From Judith LeMeur, upstairs:

"What in the holy hell is happening out there?"

From Miranda, inside the computer room:

"Oh my good God."

From a mass mob, outside in the street:

"Gwa-Mi! Gwa-Mi! Gwa-Mi!"

And then, Unknown, through a megaphone:

"GWAAAAAAAMIIIIIIII!!!!! WE KNOW YOU'RE IN THERE! COME OUT AND FACE US!"

Pulling the goggles up to her forehead, Miranda finds the room has caught an eerie orange-yellow fever, the surfaces lit up in bush-fire hues. Through the window, she sees the glow of their *actual torches*, a mob of people a few-hundred-strong, many of their faces masked, their many voices amplified by bullhorn.

From an open upstairs window, LeMeur shouts "I'm calling the police, you degenerate lowlifes!"

Then come her great, frantic footsteps bounding down the stairs. Judith LeMeur, Violent in her Nightie vs. 200 Bloodthirsty Internet Trolls.

Fight!

While the members of the mob cry for Gwami to surrender herself, while Cindi screams desperately in her ear — "If you need me, @ me! Whatever happens, @ me, and we'll come find you!" — Miranda tries to work out the logistics of squeezing through that back window there and then landing without any broken bones. In a flash of panic, Miranda stabs the computer's CPU with her left foot. It emits a death groan as the screen swirls to black.

Judith LeMeur screams back at the crowd through a slat in the door, the sound of her voice muffled. Some elected speaker, assumedly the mob's leader, offers retorts from the spiral staircase on the landing.

"Is Gwami the Seer in here?"

"Why in the…Seer be here?" comes LeMeur's voice.

"We were told by a trusted confidante that this is where we'd find her."

"Don't be a fu…you…"

"Don't call us names!"

Comments of that nature continue on. Miranda would stay and listen all day if she could, but it's clear now she misjudged the window's dimensions, and the hot, growing thickness in the air portends all sorts of badness.

Though the crowd's ringleader must see that a woman of LeMeur's age and temperament — "You think I'd *waste my time* with that politically-charged drivel?" — couldn't possibly be the Seer they've come to accost, and though the folks in "charge" of the march or protest or lynch mob, or whatever this is, are obviously considering retreat, some imbecile in the mass, feeling strongly about action in the face of uncertainty, hurls a rock through one of LeMeur's wide downstairs windows, which is cue for the rest of the mob to ignore their better judgment *and* the denials LeMeur keeps on screaming *and* the increasingly frightened yelps of their leaders to "Stop! Stop! Get back and stop!" and march zombielike onwards towards the house, pelting it with beer bottles and rocks and whatever else is nearby — uprooted plant stems and plastic-wrapped newspapers. And there's some gnarly Dubstep coming from a boombox in the center of the the mob — fights begin erupting within it — and the screaming and the throwing and the shouting increase tenfold as the crowd turns its relentless hunger inward towards itself, meanwhile all the windows up and down the block are lighting up yellow and orange as the residents within them — those not paralyzed by the classic Upper West Side fear of pandemonium — jam the lines of the local police precinct. All this happens while LeMeur becomes more desperate, nonsensically remaining at the door, trying to reason with the riot.

She's saying "I'm not Gwami! I told you, I'm not Gwami!" at anyone that will listen, dodging the debris of tossed banana peels (you can't make this shit up) before an idea overtakes her, something prompted by a few words she was told not a half-day ago, and the cries of "I'm not Gwami!" become "I'm not Gwami, but I know who is!"

"I'm not Gwami, but I know who is!"

"I KNOW WHO GWAMI THE SEER REALLY IS!"

The Mob Leaders, not so much struggling to restrain the riot as they are annoyed by the rapidity of its devolution, try quelling the crowd with their bullhorns. When some control returns, they allow LeMeur to continue, even bestowing upon her a megaphone with which to really get the message out there.

Which she does, going on to tell them all about the girl who stalked her here earlier, who came so rudely knocking on her chamber door, some NYU artist with a downtown gallery at the *Eldred Apple* Building— "Did you get that? El-dred App-el." who, upon being told more-or-less that she's never going to have a career in this town, offered up some very interesting information about a certain alter-ego that may be of some note to all of you.

And that is all Miranda will overhear.

While the stalling Judith LeMeur offers up that very same pertinent information, the girl in question outraces the mob to her apartment, having left the goggles in a panic and ducked out a back door, hopped over a fence and jumped on the nearest subway, home now and gathering up everything vital to her continuing survival — computer, phone charger, a couple of unread Marilynne Robinson books in the event of extended unplugged boredom, proper electric toothbrush, underwear, tampons, contact solution — and fleeing in a state of mental and physical disarray to Penn Station, where she'll board the next possible train south to New Jersey, where a bus, god-willing, will take her to a proper hideaway nestled deep in the crossed arms of the coast. There, sanctuary awaits her arrival.

Sanctuary, and maybe funnel cake too, awaits her at the Jersey Shore.

BANANAS!

7

In the eyes of the inexperienced, the salt air stings. It's so thickly dissolved into the oxygen here that it sticks to your clothes and your hair, your nostrils and your eyeballs if you aren't generous with your blinks. You'll notice those raised on the Shore all have this slight squint, long eyelashes, too. These are evolutionary traits, designed for life on the coast, helping residents get on with their business without going blind. It's dangerous to spend too much time on the shore if you're an out-of-towner. And you best not open your eyes underwater.

Once, Miranda opened her eyes in the surf off Long Beach Island and had to be bed-rested for a week, the result of some amoebic subterfuge on her system; and this was a girl who'd spent every summer on the shore, in that house off East Mermaid Lane, the one with the gravel driveway and the outdoor shower, the unfinished third-story addition wrapped to this day in a veil of industrial plastic. Every summer until she was ten, from Memorial Day to Labor Day, the Swami's would trade their beige Long Island castle for a more serene spot a stone's skip from the sea, slyly chosen by her parents for its distance from the Taffy Shops and townie bars that populate the island further north, away from anywhere that might attract youth or lasciviousness or life.

The Shore House was Mother and Father's summer reward to themselves. The two worked dolorously through most of the year, but in the warmth of the center season, they could stay mostly housebound, hosting only the most crucial of clients in the comfort of flip-flops and

Tommy Bahamas. While they enjoyed what was, for them, essentially just a change of scenery, the Shore meanwhile became the very spine of Miranda's childhood. From it grew swim lessons and conch collecting, arcade games and expensive sweets and staying up past bed time with her head poked out her bedroom window, listening to the surf.

In her 22nd year, these summer memories have taken on the qualities that all early childhood nostalgia aspire to: immensely sweet, immensely narrow in perspective, and immensely unlikely to have occurred as remembered.

Yes, once or twice a year, Henry, the summer help, grilled his Cajun Andouilles in the backyard, sending a singular smoky sweetness spiraling outward from the house to the surrounding streets, but in Miranda's mind, this is the way the house, nay her entire childhood, has always smelled. Every once in a while, she gets a rare whiff...and it takes her back. Oh, yes it does.

And only rarely did she see the fat orange cat licking itself in the sun atop a stone driveway post, but whenever she pictures the house now, the cat is always there, tongue on hind leg, semi-smiling, stretched out satisfied in the sun.

But just when that shore world was readying to open up its shell and reveal the shining, priceless pearl of pubescent experience within — she might've stolen hugely important kisses under the boardwalk, chucked beer bottles into the sea, and put out illicit cigarettes in clamshells, watched the sunset over faraway surf, a soft hand in hers — it was ripped from her. It's that very ripping which now tinges all her shore memories. In every familiar *whoosh* of briny air, in the *clopping* of sandals upon beechwood, in the funnel cake fragrance, the remembrance she *has* is accompanied by another, a remembrance of what she *ought* to have.

She was ten when Father informed her that LBI had become "unnecessary." Taking off summers was no longer financially feasible, and Caleb was too old to be interested in the same old summer shore shenanigans — he was busy with serious internships in the City. Tacitly, it was thought foolish to stick around the place for only Miranda's sake. They fired Henry. She'd never forgive them.

Every year thereafter, Miranda would have her heart re-rent by the inevitable conversations about potential buyers, selling the house outright or, no, putting it up for auction, which renovations were *absolutely necessary in this market* and which were frivolous, and on and on. But after Hurricane Sandy blew in and sank the local housing market, those conversations ceased altogether. As did the renovations. Right now, there's a space-age stove below wet, mildewed wainscoting. The outdoor showerhead, glimmering fresh silver, is barely held aloft by grimy, kasha posts. And then there's the plastic cocoon wrapped around the house's forehead like a surgical mask, a reminder to all potentially interested parties that something is wrong here.

Only to Miranda did the cracks, drafts, and rotted beams ever sing an endearing paean. To everyone else, the house was an eyesore, and thus, a nuisance. So, they abandoned it. Miranda, however, refused to.

As soon as she got her license, Miranda began escaping to the shore on all sorts of jaunts, for a day here, for a week-long residency there. Mother and Father weren't what you would call "attentive" caregivers. Comings and goings were never much remarked upon as long as responsibilities were taken care of and important events attended. Silence was what amounted to permission in the Swami household. If something was disagreeable, it was vocalized, otherwise; the least necessary communication was the best. Be concise, and don't ask for the same thing twice. So, Miranda was, and never did.

The driver stops a few blocks from the destination, at his passenger's request, letting her out onto Ocean Avenue. She remains motionless on the side of the road until his lights are far away and out of sight. Now that the street is empty, now that all nearby car noises have ceased, she moves into the center of the road, closing her eyes and tuning her frequency to the distant waves breaking on the distant sand.

The shore is something that, if you really love it, you don't want to share. The breezy solitude of its off-season is meat for loners. And it infects you. You simply can't get to *this* place, see *this* shore, it's greatest form, if teenagers are playing chicken with the beer trucks, if frisbees fly hither and thither thrown by unseen, uncoordinated hands, if the Sherman's and the Lee's and the Callaway's are all sitting around playing poker on their porches, guffawing while you try to have a God damn cigarette in fucking peace.

But before and after the season, the streets stay mostly deserted. You can stand right in the middle of Ocean Avenue and look up and watch the satellites slide past the stars with no fear of sudden vehicular manslaughter. There are periodic cabs, sure, and your year-rounders hustling to the highway en route to and from work, but they, a mere tenth of the summer population, are mostly manageable folk who keep to themselves. You'd hear their cars coming from a mile down the road.

Right now, it's totally still and you can stand in the road and feel that you own it and all the land around you. You can casually be absorbed into the shore itself, into the air and the waves and the faintest glimmer of funnel cake smell carried down from Seaside Heights by the breeze.

She'd stand there forever if she had the nerve. But when something in a bush rustles too forcefully, Miranda's senses steel themselves. Her heart begins to sputter, her shivering skin goes goose-pimply. She scurries away as quick as she can from the possibility of who-knows-what accosting her from the shadowy roadside brush. Lest she forget, there are new fears with which she must wrangle. She runs all the way to the house. She does not look back over her shoulder.

Thank God, the front door key is in its usual spot: inside a fake rock under the doorstep hydrangeas. She always has a latent anxiety that someone will have removed it, that she'll find the house resold or condemned or, worse still, containing her own family inside, the lot eating dinner at the dining room table. Mother will look up and see her through the window and whisper something to Father, who won't move so much as a muscle, and dinner will either go unbated as if nobody saw anything at all, or Mother will shout "Sweet*heart*," through the window, leaving Miranda no choice but to join her family for mealtime. Each possibility is somehow worse than the other.

As she fumbles with the lock, she notices a kitchen window she must've left open the last time. Here's hoping no colony of ants or hornets has claimed this place as their kingdom in her absence.

And what a solemn kingdom it would be. The house itself is a stone soldier, no stucco in sight. Slate slabs are your pathways around its circumference, and igneous pebbles of faraway volcanic origin fill in the empty space between shrubs and walkways. There's only a small square of sod in the back, a lone grass island adrift in a sea of stones.

It's a grey and austere and purely parental temple, the peace of which no freewheeling child could destroy. It's air of proscription was solidified in the abundance of rules written neatly on a chalkboard in the laundry-room. No jumping in the pool, no tracking mud or gravel in the house, no throwing balls or talking back. No yelling, demanding, or coming inside with wet feet. Voices down, towels folded, none of those pool noodles allowed because, inevitably, they'll fracture from time or careless teeth and leave us infested with foam.

Inside the house, the thematic austerity is further explored. Like so many seaside abodes, this one also takes its design cues from a ship's interior, although where many mimic a Hemingwayesque fishing boat — life preservers and coral and sandalwood pillars beside driftwood tables — Mother and Father went all in on the "Navy Destroyer" motif: slate walls and porthole windows too high up for juvenile eyes to peer through. Ships in bottles assembled in abstract countries are beached on every conceivable surface. A house like this demands awareness of one's elbows. It's not a welcoming place for children.

Maybe that's why Miranda's turquoise room, up the front hall stairs and to the right, is devoid of such seafaring paraphernalia, to coax her there and away from the fragile rest of the house. Its meager but sufficient space is filled some by a foam-cornered twin bed and the white woven rug of an indigenous ancestor, but mostly by the harem of stuffed animals lining the room like it's some Parliamentary Chamber. It's a *cushy* room, and nothing's ever changed within it except the amount and location of the toys. Miranda was always prone to falling, and Mother would not allow a single sharp edge within her space. Should she banish the girl to her room for tracking in mud *again*, she could rest easy knowing she wouldn't find her daughter face down on the new carpet with a bloody gash engraved into her temple.

Now, in the night, it's also the only room in the house in which Miranda feels safe. Even with the lights on everywhere, there is still an uncertainty *re*: potential hiding spots for horrible spirits. What could be waiting in the hall closet? Might some subzero spirit be holed up in the fridge? In her own room, Miranda is aware of all nooks and secret spaces. Nothing can sneak up on her here, whereas anything could be lurking outside her locked door. Bathroom breaks will have to wait until morning. The *Wawa* subs she forgot to take upstairs will remain disastrously uneaten. The bread will surely be soggy by sunup, the meat inedible; a true New Jersey Tragedy.

Even with her beat-up soul and general malaise, Miranda remains awake for hours. It's far too frightening in here with the lights off, and every excited pipe's *clang* within the walls nearly causes her to cry out in terror. She thinks she hears footsteps on the 2nd floor landing. She's convinced there are voices conspiring within the air ducts.

Despite dread's delaying it, Miranda is eventually soothed to sleep by the tumbling, onshore waves and the groan of distant acceleration on the parkway.

She soon wakes up in cold sweats. And then she does again.

In the morning, in the light, she skips stones, makes tea, and smokes on the front stoop. She tries reading a book on the patio, but can't stop imagining demons climbing over the fence, so she reads it on the beach (but what if they come out of the water?), reads it in her room, gives up reading altogether, takes a shower to calm her nerves, and makes more tea. As the sun sets on an unsettling but uneventful day, Miranda lays on the pebbles in her backyard, watching the sky squeeze color from itself like juiced fruit onto the horizon, its nightly exhibition of self-mutilation. She only feels safe with her back against the impenetrable Earth.

But the body is tired, and a surprise sleep whacks her like a whiffle-ball bat.

"Miranda? Miranda! Hey, Miranda!" a voice in her dream says, but it's too loud to be part of the dream, and she opens her eyes. In the glossy world of our freshly-awoken paranoiac, most any form would be frightening. Any individual looming over her would appear monstrous. Not only in their muddied, sleepy shadow, but in their intentions. Who knows what species of beast might be after her now? There might very well be three streets in the Upper West Side still aflame, and a mob could be marching on her safe space right now. They might have her goggles, they have her name. They could have the Twins hostage, forcing them to admit where Miranda goes when she isn't in the city (not that they'd know), ransacking her room for mailing addresses and phone numbers. The universe has swiftly instilled in her a kind of omnipotent fear: everything is dangerous, everyone is an unknown quantity.

But not him. From any direction, with any amount of mental or visual blur, he's familiar, unthreatening. An asshole, sure, but a well-known one.

They look into each other's' eyes, she squinting up at him, he wide-eyed down at her, and both begin to cackle. Wild people, they laugh and laugh and laugh, and he's got his hands on his knees he's laughing so hard, smiling so wide their cheeks begin to hurt. Like maniacs. Ranting, raving maniacs.

Look at those smiles. All teeth. Neither thought they'd ever smile at the other like that again.

These two, forgetting that they're supposed to despise each other, laugh together by the sod in the backyard, not knowing necessarily why they're having the reaction they are, but not wanting to question it. Sometimes, things just are just so nice that to examine them would be a small suicide. Besides, take it from me, the both of them could really use a friend right about now.

Finally, they're calm, settled into a shared sort of delirious joy. "What the hell are you doing here?" he asks.

"I should ask you the same question," she says between yawns, pushing herself up onto her hands.

"Let's go inside," he suggests.

"When did you get here?"

"Go inside and start a fire, I'll be in in one second."

And so she does. And then he is. This girl who hates taking orders, and this boy who can hold most any grudge unflinchingly close to his soul.

They're inside and sitting by the fire, their toes extended and dry beside each other's, and they wouldn't have to say a single word if they didn't want to, but lo and behold, they want to.

"I'm actually really glad you're here," he says.

"*Actually?*"

"Well, we didn't leave off on the best of terms. I've been, ahh, hesitant to reach out."

She sighs. "I'm sorry about that. I was under a lot of stress. It's been very hard."

"I know. I should've been more brotherly. I haven't been a good sibling to you. I'm not a good sibling to you. That much is clear."

"Thank you for your honesty."

"And you yours."

Ah, the easy silence of the soundly reunited. She lays her head on his shoulder, uncharacteristic, but she wants all of this feeling, this feeling of being close to a person. He shuffles nearer, hard for a man of his girth to do gracefully. The same flame licks both of their little toes. She confesses she could really use a friend. He says she has no idea how much he feels her on that. No idea.

"Things are changing for me really quickly," she says.

"Yeah, me too."

"Want to talk about it?"

He looks at her for a long time, his beautiful, big blue eyes and their lovely, unfair lashes batting lazily at her. "Not really," he says. "I don't know how you'd take it."

"Try me."

"Maybe later. Want to tell me your thing?"

"It's not really that important."

"You're a terrible liar. I'll start some dinner for us," he says.

"There's a sub in the fridge…" she offers. "Well, half of one." Just the mention of food has made her stomach rumble. A soggy half-sub does not seem the tantalizing meal it did earlier in the day.

"I actually have some stuff in the car. Was planning on being here all weekend. And you know I usually eat for two anyways. We can go shopping again tomorrow…if you're thinking about staying, that is."

"Not looking to leave anytime soon."

"Great news."

"You don't have work? I'm shocked."

"A bit of a lull. I expect it'll pick up in a week or so."

"Heh, same."

"I'm going to go start dinner."

"Make sure you let me lick the spoon." Good memories come bubbling back to her. The orange cat and the sweet smell of sausage and how always, always, always, Caleb let her lick the spoon.

Caleb, for all of his faults, is a marvelous cook, having spent a wandering year in France studying under Jean-Paul Clavellete. Quite a talent with tongs, special with a spatula, he flips and turns, braises and slices with an adept's precision. He was always an insanely helpful talent to have in a restaurant group, with equal-parts cultural knowledge and culinary skill. Of course, it made him kind of condescending towards the cooks, but no man is perfect.

Soon the house is hazy with the scent of roasting nutmeg, and a braising eggplant concoction spits little droplets of mustard over the nearby walls. He might have covered the pot before walking outside, but the allure of a cold beer with a much-needed comrade was too distracting from safeguards of sanitation. They laugh and drink out on the patio, the warm odor of baking spices wafting through a crack in the patio door, and Caleb gets suds on his chin as the kitchen gets another new stain.

Looking at him now, smiling and calm, whistling off-key, hair just slightly amiss, apron wrapped around his thick neck and hips, she can't help but love him through. He's got such humanity, such an obvious collection of shortcomings and inaccuracies that, defiantly, he smiles through. There's a charm to him, a finely-layered pheromone that emanates off his tucked shirts and cuffed pants, some trust-begetting thing. You look at him and can't imagine how anyone would ever wrong this guy, this guy who's, yeah, so often a prideful and selfish man, but always always so sincere about it. When he's prideful and selfish, it isn't something manipulated or fake, it's really him. Maybe that wouldn't be seen as a virtue in another generation, but in this world of Miranda's, that type of sincerity is something seriously sanctified.

They're singing along to acoustic covers of 90's songs, and Caleb lets Miranda try the remoulade. It's "quite bomb," and Miranda excuses herself to the upstairs restroom. It takes her a few minutes of rummaging through cabinets to find an adequate tampon, and in none of those minutes does she feel herself in danger. Nothing bad can happen while Caleb's here, she thinks. Beside him, she feels safe. Caleb, for all his faults, has and will always protect her. The thought makes her teary. She comes back downstairs.

She returns to a special moment: Caleb's back turned to her, spices simmering in the air, cold beer frothing on the countertop; Miranda feels that she's stepped out of her life. Hers is not a life of easy pleasures and safe smiles, of warm countertops and soft, familiar music. But there are smiles here. There are smiles here.

Caleb, not aware of Miranda's current dietary-restrictions but aware enough of her capricious culinary whims, stays away from possibly offensive meats and starches and gluten, keeping his own sensibilities out of this meal. There are none of his usual lardons and fried bread-crumbs, no sign of bocquerones or veggies cooking in rendered animal fat, just a simple, tasteful meal, brightly flavorful and innocent to even the most militant of herbivores.

Dinner comes and goes and, like so many meals, the complexities of the cuisine do little more than add depth to the details of the meal itself. If there were smiles when the food was bubbling, boiling, baking, now there are laughs. The hearty laughs of the mutually nostalgic.

"What about the swingset?" Miranda says through a giggle, a fat piece of cauliflower on her fork, nodes of broccoli stuck between her teeth. "And when, oh fuck what was his name? You know who I'm talking about."

"Dave Lipschitz."

"Dave Lipschitz! Yes! When he — HA HA HA — when he sat on the swing and the whole thing toppled over."

Caleb holds back his laughter respectfully, only barely concealing his smile. "And we told him he was too fat for the swings."

"God we ruined him over that."

"I mean, he *was* too fat for the swings. Clearly," Caleb says, slurping up a zucchini noodle.

"Jesus Christ. Poor Dave Lipschitz. We were so mean to him. Where do you think he is now?"

"I think…if I had to guess…I think he lives in suburban St. Louis, with a woman he *thought* he was going to marry but had merely impregnated; I think he weighs somewhere between 200 and 210 pounds, not altogether unreasonable for a man of his height, and I'm pretty sure he practices carpentry as his main gig, with a soulful business touching up antiques on the side." And to the blank, Miranda Swami stare he replies, "We're Facebook friends, he and I. No harm, no foul."

After dinner, the two walk along the beach smoking cigarettes, ashing them into the sand and burying the burnt ends with their bare toes. Yet, still, they walk.

"Have you spoken to them recently?"

"No. Have you?"

"You know how Mother is. Likes when I check in. It's a bi-weekly thing. At least."

"What a horrible fate hast thou befallen."

"You don't give her enough slack, Miranda. You do know you're too hard on her, right?"

"Maybe," Miranda says, lighting up again. "And maybe not. But in the very adult game of who's-going-to-reach-out-to-who-first, she still has the onus of all her years upon her shoulders."

"I think she misses you."

"Do you think that because you've surmised so, or because she told you?"

Caleb thinks about this for a moment. "Why wouldn't she miss you?"

Miranda shrugs, "I don't think she's ever missed me."

"You don't give yourself enough credit either. Do you hate *all* women like this, or just the ones you're related to?"

"Oh, shut up!" Miranda yelps, giving Caleb a push with her shoulder. "I hold my sex to a higher standard. We display constantly the capacity for things you can hardly even keep in your skulls."

"Amen to that."

"And how's Father?" For discussions of Father, Miranda might met-aphorically light two cigarettes.

"You know," Caleb answers, "he's him."

The comment hangs in the air for a while, neither one addressing it. The silence they fall into is not a comfortable one, not reflecting an absence of forthcoming speech, but because each party must process the best way to express what they both mutually know about this man who raised them.

Caleb proves braver. "He's a bitter man. I feel sorry for him."

Which is exactly the kind of thing Miranda wants to hear, for it gives her retort of "Yeah, tough life, what with the 7-figure income, the beauty queen wife, the fame, fortune and the two independent, successful kids, right?" a practiced, long-contained feel to it. But what she says next is completely off the cuff. "What do you think went wrong with them?"

"What?" Caleb says, taken aback by this brief and obvious crack in the Miranda Swami armor. By this point they've stopped at an aban-doned life-guard tower about 50 yards from the water's edge. It's obvi-ous Caleb is apprehensive about following Miranda up its ramp. She speaks down to him from six-feet-or-so above his head.

"They're both such...so...what's the word I'm looking for?"

"Do you want me to —"

"No! I got it. They're so...so...so *fragile*. It's like they want ev-ery reason to believe the world is a terrible, corrupt place, that if their lives don't follow the exact dictates they desire then everything will just fall apart or become awful or or...I guess I just don't understand why anyone would want that to be the case."

Miranda turns away from him, goes full silent-contemplative. "Miranda," Caleb calls to her, but she answers not, turns not, acknowl-edges not. He comes up the ramp and is next to her. He doesn't need to see the tear-stains beside her shoes, but simply takes her head into his chest, leaving it there, leaving her there, close. "Come on," he whispers, kissing her head, "let's go see about some ice cream."

They leave *Wawa* with two bags filled with every sort of ice cream treat: *Dippin' Dots* and *King Cones* and *Klondike Bars*, *Haagen Daaz* and *Ben and Jerry's* and *Magnum Bars*, too. All the goods laid out before them in the car, and Caleb's hardly paying attention to the road that peeks out from over the Escalade's big dashboard, and Miranda's laughing, squinting, and when she looks up through the windshield, it's just in time to catch something black and big darting across the road.

And Miranda fucking loses it.

"CALEB!"

Screaming, yelling, absolutely shrieking bloody murder, her yells so shock Caleb he almost drives off the road altogether. Swerving across the street despite there not being anything in the way at all, he shouts, "What the Hell is going on?!" which just incites Miranda more, incites her so much and so quickly it sends her into a full-blown panic attack, her face red and her bulging eyes swallowing forehead sweat, everything bloodshot and all the clothes constricting, she needs air so bad but out there is where that *thing*, where those *things* stalk and shuffle and watch and only in here, in this suffocatingly-small car compartment is she safe. Still the screams flee from her mouth like of their own volition, and nothing in her power can stop them. Caleb is angry and then horrified and then his very soul starts to shake. But he can see her sweating and, not knowing what else to do, puts the A/C on full blast, places his big hands on Miranda's shoulders, cooing quietly in her ear as they stall on the roadside. After a few minutes, she begins breathing more regularly, her hyperventilation reduced to just big breaths inward, and Caleb takes a proper break before asking, "Well what was that about?"

"I uhm, nothing."

"You can't have something like that happen and not explain. Explain."

"I don't want to."

"I'll sit here all night."

"Please don't do this."

"*Miranda*. It's important."

And, as he says this, she knows it is.

"I've been having nightmares."

Caleb considers his response. "Like, the old nightmares?"

"Yeah. Just like them. I don't know why they've come back. But I'm, like, terrified of dark places and shadows and corners I can't see around. I think it was a deer jumped across the road, or maybe it was just my imagination. It was like, like I was suddenly unsure whether I was awake or asleep and whether anything around me was real, and I looked over to the side of the road and I kept seeing all these eyes, horrible eyes, in the dark, and-and-and, I don't know, everything just got tight."

And Caleb only utters two syllables. "Oh-kay."

At the house, Miranda complains about being tired, and Caleb says, "Why don't we sleep up in Mother's room?" like they used to. Big California king bed, flat-screen TV, wonderful view of the ocean sunrise; together on opposite sides of the bed, in their respectively ridiculous pajamas (hers of cotton, his of silk), they sit watching old sitcoms. It's three episodes of *Community*, a handful of *Friends* and an obligatory pair of *Seinfeld's* before the younger sibling drifts to sleep.

Caleb needs to hear Miranda's slow, shallow snoring before he allows himself to drift off, too. For this, he turns on David Attenborough nature documentaries, sets a sleep timer for just after sunrise, and lets himself fall into nothingness amid a sea of soft pillows.

In the morning, Miranda will awaken to the smell of freshly-brewed coffee. Caleb, a man of creature comforts, has thought of everything.

On the beach, smoking:

"Miranda, what's wrong? You're far away."

At the grocery store, examining spices:

"Are you not going to tell me what's bothering you?"

Home in the kitchen, as things burble on the stovetop:

"You're too private for your own good. That stuff will eat you from the inside."

Caleb, perceptive as ever, clearly sees something gnawing away at Miranda's cool façade. His sister should be violently angry that her beloved *McGreevy's Toffee, Taffy and More* has been shut down to make way for something called *Banana Emporium*, for example, but there's nothing. All of that is too close, and she's somewhere far away. She can hardly even see it from where she stands, on an island in the middle of a rough black ocean.

Daylight saving time has come and passed, so it's pitch dark out by six. In the summer, the three extra hours of daylight allow you to sink into the end-of-day laziness slowly, softly, like settling into a hammock. But once it's late autumn — and winter is even worse — the night just crashes down upon you, an always startling, always disappointing thing. Zaps your energy away. The sun's shredded warmth dissipates, and on the shore, a wind always picks up. Miranda takes a cold beer out onto the patio. Caleb follows behind.

"Miranda, it's freezing out here, you need a jacket."

"Remember how Mother used to talk about demons?"

"You don't have blubber like I do; you're going to get hypothermia."

"You *do* remember, though, right? I mean, I don't know, but when she said those things to you, and maybe it was because you were older by then, it always seemed like an inside joke. 'Oh Caleb, better study for Algebra, otherwise the demons are going to take you flat out the window.' And you'd both have a good laugh about it."

"Yeah, I remember. You didn't find the whole thing as riotous?" Caleb feels sweat forming under his arms, but behind the soft leather of his black jacket, he's hidden from an exposé on his eccrine glands...

"It sounds so stupid. So, *so* stupid. But that shit has always stayed with me. They're going to come out from under the bed and in the closet and through the crack in the open window, going to get me, eat me up, punish me for my misgivings…do you know what she said to me once? I think I was five. *Five*. And she says for every bad thing I do in a day, the demons will come in while I sleep and take a bite off my fingernails, and that's how everyone will know I'm bad, because my stubby fingernails will never grow. She *said* that."

"Jesus."

"Yeah."

"Admittedly, that's psychotic."

"Five!"

"Five. Crazy. So, what? You never sleep with your door open?"

"Never. I can't sleep unless I know all the doors are properly locked. Sometimes, when my roommates get home late, I'll sneak out of bed in a panic to make sure they locked the apartment door behind them."

"Check under your bed for monsters?"

"And in the closet."

"And what do you expect to do if-slash-when you find something?"

Miranda thinks about this for a moment. "Hope the shock kills me outright, or at least keeps me from feeling what the beast is doing to me with its claws."

Back inside, Miranda stands by the oven to warm up.

"I should've worn a jacket," she says, shivering.

"How often did Mother tell you these things?"

"You're not going to let this go, huh?"

"I'm just…confused is all. With me, it was *always* a joke. It was never actually weaponized against me. I don't know, Miranda, I just want to know."

"It was pretty frequent."

Caleb seems genuinely taken aback. He's doing that thing he does where he places the back of his hand to his forehead, as if the heat of what he's heard is making him woozy.

"The cruelty of it…that's what really gets to me." He says it like he knows, like he was there, like he was exposed to half of what she was exposed to, like he ever got any side of Mother but the one that reflected the sun. All she got was darkness. When she got anything at all, it was darkness. Any and all of the darkness within herself — and it's there, she's seen it, has felt it, has felt its wormy body in her veins and its tinny whispers assaulting her over bowls of cereals and from the crevice between movie theater seats, knows the horrible things it thinks and suggests and the terrible influence it has over the weak and suggestive rest-of-her; she knows it — was inherited from all the shadows Mother exposed her to.

"It's okay," she says, having been told in mandatory therapy that blaming her Mother for actions *she* herself considered and planned and carried out is the kind of cop-out that sociopaths use to explain their murderous rampages, and sex offenders their stashing of kiddie pics. "She was doing the best she could. Well, maybe not…at least she was around."

You can't see the garage door from where Miranda stands, but you can hear it open, and you can hear a battalion of bootsteps march in, thick boots on tile. Miranda looks to Caleb, and Caleb pokes his head around the corner, and Miranda says, "Who is it?" but Caleb doesn't immediately answer. Maybe she should be more panicked, after all, there are clearly intruders here, trespassers, and who knows what they're intentions are? There might be demons afoot. But it smells so good and Caleb is so calm, and-and-and, and there are smiles here…How can anything bad happen with so much goodness in the room?

The intruders are not outwardly demonic, just a twosome in chef's coats, probably siblings since unrelated noses don't often share such pronounced ridges. They come into the kitchen, holding hotel trays wrapped in glimmering foil, visibly taken aback by what hegemony the dense, red-faced Caleb already has over the kitchen, *their* kitchen supposedly.

And then Jean-Luc's heavy Samoan body enters in backwards, dragging a huge white cooler like a child might drag his Red Ryder.

A shrill female voice, the bite of it sharpened by all the time it has spent correcting behavior, yells, "Please, Jean-Luc, you'll scratch the tile."

The big man, straight flexin', flips the cooler up into his arms without so much as a grunt, brushing silently into the kitchen and setting the thing down by the patio door. He nods politely at the two Swami children. He's known them for the better part of two decades, and still only ever a polite nod.

Then the female voice, bite withdrawn, shouts around the corner, "Surprise, young man! Surprise!"

And finally, everyone, we have tonight's entertainment:

Smiling like an idiot invalid, bedecked in so many jewels she refracts even the meager light around her, like some glittering peacock chimera, into the kitchen comes Heiress to the Klubelman Cookie fortune, Diana Klubelman Swami, better known to the house's occupants as Mother.

Well, Mother is followed further into the house by stoic Father, and she kisses Caleb, and gives some orders to the cooks (very on-brand), and then, only then, once she's kind of gotten comfortable in the space, does she turn to look into the living room, to the columns there, upon which leans a perpetually teenage daughter with half of her head shaved, the other half greasy and falling uncut past her shoulders, scrawny legs crossed at the ankles, arms folded aggressively, scowling, and with a mustard stain on her cardigan.

"Sweet-*heart*. What a *pleasant* surprise."

"For us all," Miranda snickers. Her heart, apparently wanting to see what's going on out there, has lodged itself halfway up her throat.

"Honey, *please*. We *just* got here." Father says, seating himself at the kitchen table. He must've come in with the *Journal* half-read because it's open and already on to the stock ticker.

"Arthur, you don't have to —"

"*Diana*," Arthur says, far sterner than necessary. Everyone in the room goes silent and still. "We *just* got here."

There's a very tense moment. Diana looks down at her dress. Miranda wants to scream so many things, but can't seem to find her voice. That has become a worrisome trend.

Miranda, will you be, ahem, joining us for dinner?" Mother asks, finally.

"I'm pretty sure Caleb…" she's cut off by a look from her brother. It's a pleading, begging look: *just leave it alone, it says, it's not worth it.*"

"You're pretty sure Caleb what, sweetie?"

"She's pretty sure I just made all this eggplant," Caleb says for his sister, drawing Mother's attention.

"Oh, just toss it. Victor and Ella here are from *Carpaccio*. They have a *Michelin* Star."

Suddenly wanting to skin herself, Miranda grumbles something quietly and leaves the room.

"Was it something I said?" Mother asks Caleb, who turns away.

"Surprise, indeed," Father says, then coughs, then asks Jean-Luc to put on some coffee.

"I think maybe I should bring Miranda some tea," Caleb says.

"Extra-strong, Jean-Luc," Father says. "Lots of cream."

Mother leans on the granite countertop as Caleb slowly removes his apron; Father flips to the sports section while Jean-Luc removes a bag of coffee beans from the cooler. Victor and Ella speak rapidly to each other in Italian, flipping through settings on the oven.

"So lovely to have the whole family together," Mother says, then looks down. She sighs and lifts up the hem of her dress. Someone has tracked mud onto the tile.

ⵑ ⵑ ⵑ ⵑ ⵑ

Thankfully, the door to her room is thick, sturdy oak, and with Pearl Jam playing on an ancient *Walkman* dug out of a pseudo-sock drawer, Miranda can just about drown out the conversation downstairs. But Mother's unusual voice has a way of circumventing even the best attempts to contain it. She won't be thwarted by mere music.

So she can hear Mother's cooing, sing-song voice through the headphones, through the walls, gushing about Caleb, laughing with Caleb, either talking to Caleb himself or simply babbling into the ether. No lack of listener will keep her from cawing about her beloved first-born.

Their only intended child: Caleb, the golden one, the tactical birth.

At the time of Caleb's conception, there was only one way for an up-and-up like Arthur Swami to reach the inner sanctum of American politics, and it mandated being straight and white and eminently likeable. In this case, the lattermost dictate required 1) a loving, personable wife and 2) a lovely, young child in her arms or belly. Diana Klubelman, a bit of high-cheek-boned old money, allowed herself onto Arthur's arm, thus checking box number one. Diana was drawn to the power game, asserting herself as a preternatural impresario to donors and snake-charmer to their wives. Her latent interpersonal power had remained dormant before Arthur, for despite all the hours spent honing a laugh and batting eyelashes at her reflection in the mirror, it's hard for even Upstate New York's elite to attract real glamour to their Hudson-side homes.

But everything Arthur Swami did dazzled. She would have undergone heart surgery for the man if it meant lunching with swankier people in larger rooms, but there was no need for that. As it happened, all he needed from her was to get pregnant. What luck, she had planned on doing that anyway. Check box number two.

Arthur's re-election was a cinch with a bun in his darling wife's oven; and though Diana's fatigue meant a sometimes separation from her beau, they were able to convene often enough on-camera and in print to craft Arthur the armor of the devoted pre-father. Meanwhile

Diana appeared just the kind of spunky, flush, first-time mother that lights something in the proverbial gonads, the perfectly game political wife, all hips and tits and joking about her swollen feet.

It was a pure symbiosis. To Diana, Arthur offered passage into an incredible new world, which Diana made ripe for his political conquest. To Arthur, Diana gave her body, which Arthur made the most beloved body, by husband and then constituency, in the great state of New York.

Caleb arrived a week premature, excited perhaps by his father's landslide victory the previous Tuesday. Strangely, wonderfully, conveniently, so much of the spotlight just beginning to shine on hot upstart Arthur Swami was repositioned onto his young wife, with the new baby in her arms, and the wonderful picture she painted of marital and parental bliss.

That spotlight only got brighter. She was in *Good Houskeeping*. She was on *Oprah*. She smiled, she laughed, she cracked jokes and danced. She told of Arthur holding a moist washcloth to her head while she lay in the throes of some feverish mid-pregnancy something-or-other. She embellished. She chided. She called the shots, she knew her place. She was superhuman. And she did it all while a golden-haired baby with Sea of Cortez eyes rocked placidly in her arms.

It was divine. Arthur wished nothing more than to go about his political wheelings from behind a curtain, and the more fuss Diana commanded on-stage, the less anyone seemed to care about him.

People wrote about her, they discussed her on daytime talk, they sent letters asking for child-rearing advice. To all those viewers, Diana appeared a quintessentially adoring mother, a being of such pure and unselfish affection that no matter her minor indiscretions, her ability as a mother, and thus the sincerity of all that adoration, couldn't be called into question.

Beside her in the glare of that spotlight was only Caleb. Every coo was remarkable; the world closed in around them. So bright that light was, it turned dark all else. There was only she and Caleb. Caleb and her. She loved him like you love life, like you love the idea of a gondola ride, like a sailor loves the land which ends a voyage, dropping to his knees to kiss the ground beneath him simply because it's there, and it hadn't been for so, so long.

But lo, love, even a mother's, isn't unending. With everything in her, Diana loved Caleb. Truly. Cosmically. With the scraps left, she supported her husband as he travelled the country, meeting potential constituents in such faraway places as Boise and Ketchum. By the time Miranda was born, "Mother" was just about barren.

Less an accident than an oversight, the pregnancy was a curious thing that became known to the doer as it became known to the watchers, too. We're 10 years post-Caleb here. Arthur is a fifth-term Representative and bearer of much power, power he finally plans to focus on a senate run. It's all happening, baby, finally happening. All possible futures are bright. All possible outcomes are known.

Diana ballooned almost overnight. Celebrities and politicians, everyone in the public eye can agree that the stressors of such a position might sometimes cause wonky body changes. Thus the weight gain was attributed to stress. And the professionally-done makeup, the already-messy circadian rhythm, the eating only when convenient, the long-ago hypothesis of her crack gynecologist that Caleb's difficult delivery probably left her infertile, all of these facts masked the truth of Miranda's subtle fomentation within her.

Then she's on the air with Amanda Washington, so kind-hearted and dark-skinned and ambitious, who's looked at her with this strange curiosity since she walked in, who waits politely until her guest has finished discussing her husband's views on the Second Amendment and says, "Excuse the shameless pivot, but we've spoken enough about your husband, you're as influential as he is —"

But the ever-instinctive Diana isn't at her first rodeo and juts in, "It's such a privilege to have the reach we do. And all our constituents in New York's *18th* know that *Arthur* and I have always used that reach to do good. That's why *Arthur* and I have been staunch supporters of animal rights and the right of *every person* to have a warm bed waiting for them at home." Cue the *applause*.

"Yes, yes we're all quite aware of your impressive successes in New York's *18th*. But, as I'm sure you've heard, there's talk that you're having another child. Would you care to comment?"

There! There! Stop the tape! Look! Okay, let's go frame-by-frame. Just for a moment, see the color dampening in her cheeks? The eyebrows slackening? She'd never do that on purpose. At this speed, you can really see her putting it all together: the snacking, the heaviness, the weight of her chest, the moods. And if you squint and look hard enough, there's her tongue teetering along the trench underneath her teeth, traipsing up top then retreating, only producing the first half-syllable of the word that's been ringing again in her head, heard from all sides as an omnipresent excuse for all of the above symptoms — "stress." In this rare but prime example, we see the conscious and subconscious minds coming to the same realization at that same time.

Cue these infinitely complex, minute mental reactions happening between nanoseconds: *if I say I'm not pregnant and I am, it becomes obvious the child was a mistake, and there's no recovery from that. But If I say I am, one of two options become available to me: either I have a little baby on the campaign trail, and the constituents flock for a glimpse of its forehead, or I have/fake a miscarriage, and the sympathy floods in through any open orifice, preceding teary letters and flowers from all the inspired would-be-mothers also struggling to conceive.*

A prodigious candidate's wife, she makes a calculated decision. "Well, I suppose the cat's out of the bag. This old dress wasn't as slimming as I thought. Yes, Arthur and I are having a second. Crossing our fingers for a little girl this time."

Well, she was indeed with child, and, unlike with Caleb, this pregnancy was a doozy long before labor. Diana was constantly bed-ridden, made invalid by sweats and fatigue and phantom fears rising like sauna steam from the very floorboards insulating her quarantined bedroom. With her hormones in such insane imbalance, periods of weeks or more passed where a creeping paranoia — paranoia of armed men, rivals of her husband, coming to attack her and kill Caleb — produced delusions so powerful, one even required a thankfully-unpublicized sedation.

Dealing with a wife both mentally-unstable and pregnant was strain enough, never mind the normal psychological taxation of an election cycle. Arthur slipped in conversation before slipping in the polls. And with his wife out of commission, there was nobody to help woo donors, no master of spin to correct his comments, no connecting cord to constituents.

Despite the best efforts of New York's *18th* to turn out, Arthur lost his senate race to the republican incumbent. And having given up his former chair in pursuit of a more gilded one, he found himself jobless. At least there was a brand-new baby girl to brighten his spirits. If only she'd have stopped crying, maybe she would have.

But she wouldn't, and Arthur Swami somehow fell further. In the weeks following Miranda's birth, some intrepid reporter Arthur had once privately called a "fucking stickbug" published a revenge piece about how inattentive Arthur was to his sick, pregnant wife during the campaign, causing a veritable landslide of popular opinion to bury any future political hope. Though Diana drew considerably sympathy because of it, Diana was not a candidate. The Swami patriarch withdrew from public life altogether. Left without many other options, Arthur became a Wall Street lobbyist. His wife just became bitter.

And it was all Miranda's fault, was it not? In a post-pregnancy daze, Diana had fitful fantasies of stepping back in time, going through with the fantasized backdoor abortion, faking a fall and forcing a miscarriage, being more careful with Arthur in the first place. For if any of those had been fortune's favored footpath, Arthur Swami could have been careening towards a presidential bid within the decade. She might've been Diana Klubelman, First Lady of the United States, a title that would have etched her into history's tableau, the ultimate dream of the ultra-rich.

Instead, she became a mother of two and a businessman's wife. So unexciting and uninspiring, totally bland. *Obvious.*

Miranda, from even before her birth, was to be sidled with all the failed possibilities her germination represented. She and Caleb, the Omega and the Alpha:

He a symbol of all that could have been,

She a symbol of all that wasn't.

Caleb was more than Mother's son, and Miranda less than her daughter. They were relegated to motifs, to plot points. Since this was decided long before Miranda could question her circumstance, there was little outrage to be had. There was simply this circumstance, one that worked out for her in some ways, did not in others, but meant that her relationship with her parents would always be cold and rather unpleasant.

No love lost now that they've all relegated to seeing each other only at the obligatory Seder, or even less actually, seeing as Miranda failed to attend even one night of 'A Very Swami/Klubelman Passover' this last year.

Maybe if she stays up in her room long enough, they'll just forget about her, content to bask in Caleb's afterglow and then leave, and everyone can avoid the terse, awkward conversation. If the clinking glasses and the hushed chortles, the *clack-clack-clackclack* of Mother's acrylic fingernails on granite, are any indication, she might already be an afterthought.

They'll be gone after tonight. Just make it through the night, she repeats, and the days are yours again. She turns onto her side as if to doze off, but there are footsteps on the stairs, and her blood freezes.

Face it, kid, they were never going to leave you up here.

The stepper on the stairs, announcing themselves, flicks the light on and off and on and off from the switch outside. Now, let's be real for a second: who in their right mind puts a light switch *outside* a room? This ridiculous architectural quirk, ubiquitous in every room on the second floor, was the bane of most every bathroom visit, producing a fear that cruel Caleb might bathe her in darkness, leaving her locked inside and alone as he made crunching, gnawing demon sounds outside the door. What epitomizes their relationship better than that?

"Come in," she sighs, and the brazen intruder, stripped of his apron, wearing a familiar suit of blue wool, hair slicked and attitude all-business, walks in, looking down at his phone.

"Dinner time, Miranda." His eyes bounce flamboyantly around the room. He seems to recoil at the smell.

"Yeah, okay."

Though that should be enough, Caleb stutters at the door. "Miri," he says, resurrecting that decrepit old nickname again, "we're okay, right?"

"Sure, Caleb," she says. "Why wouldn't we be?"

He takes a step into the room, entirely without permission, and grazes his finger over the walls. Because her dresser boldly blocks his circumnavigation of her room, Caleb stops in front of it, picking up the dusty family photos that are its crown, rubbing his thumb over them and smiling sadly. He looks up at her. "I just…you know I had no idea they were coming. This whole thing, I've got no fingerprints on it."

"Caleb. Really, I know. Let's just go and get this over with."

"You don't have to stay if you don't want to," he says quickly, almost desperately.

"Yes, I do," his sister says, brushing past him into the hall, and down the stairs, and into the kitchen.

She moves so fast he can barely say, "Wait." He certainly doesn't have time to say the rest. For a moment, Caleb stays planted by the bureau. Slowly, he glances around the room, at the bed and the open notebooks atop it and all the stuffed animals. Did you know they all have names? He used to stand in this room and listen for minutes at a time as Miranda would introduce him, personally, to all the cotton-blooded dinosaurs and lemurs and panda bears she kept here. This is a world preserved, a world as it used to be. He leaves the room with the light still on, achingly aware of the symbolic significance.

It's been more than a year since the family was together, and the time away shows on her parents' faces. Arthur's recent commitment to CrossFit couldn't sojourn the ceaseless marching of age, the crinkles and creases of so many practiced grimaces and squints now folded into his face's fabric. Who's to say when the younger Arthur, always trim and painfully well-groomed, finally surrendered to the greyblack stubble growing wild over chapped lips? Good for him, at least he's given up thoroughly. At least he's sincere about it.

And Mother. Her Mother. Ah, Her Mother. Her Mother's latest ballgown a waterfall of indigo and Swarovski crystals, she dresses like the queen she might have been, or once was. Mother's obsession with sparkles and tails was, in Miranda's early youth, a fascinating and endearing quirk, something princess-like she'd wanted to emulate. Although when imitation, too, failed to get her mother's approval, she gave it up, mimicry as a whole, leaving the braggadocios outfits to the professionally braggadocios.

But was her face always this thin? This gaunt? Instead of drooping with time, it's tightened, so taut her skin just barely cloaks her bones. So sharp are her shoulder blades, so fatless is her pretty neck, so slight is the hair that flows down her back, all the greys within defying the best efforts of expensive dyes to mask them.

"Let's start with the soup *now*, perhaps?" Mother calls vaguely to the kitchen. The male chef promptly sidles tableside, ladling heaps of a mauve chowder into bowls while his female compatriot follows with a grater and some pungent amber cheese.

Caleb nudges Miranda with his shoe under the table. "I thought we weren't allowed to wear shoes inside?" she whispers to him.

"When yours are made of Italian leather, Mother will let you wear them inside, too."

"I hate you."

"A *lot* of fennel," Mother suddenly *exclaims*, putting her spoon down, introducing rather early the criticism portion of the evening.

"I think it's great," Caleb says even louder, hoping the chefs will hear. "Fennel and lavender, and dukkha?"

Father grunts. "It's fine," said without a hint of levity.

Miranda isn't hungry anymore.

"Such a sweet surprise having you both here," Caleb says finally. "You didn't have to do all this."

"We just wanted to say congratulations before the whole world was nipping at your heels. We wanted to be with you while you were still ours," Mother pontificates, spoon spelunking through the soup. "Your brother is pretty impressive, huh?" she says to Miranda.

"*Oh yes*," Miranda says. "*Such* a specimen."

"Miranda, don't be rude."

"Yes, Father. Sorry, Mother."

"Miranda's doing well, too, if you didn't know," Caleb says. "She just had an exhibition at the *Eldred Apple* Building. Very big deal."

"You knew about that?" Miranda asks softly.

"Yes! Miranda! Of course!" Mother exclaims, mistaking antecedents. "So sorry we couldn't make it out, dear, but you know how autumn is for your father. And how *was* your Apple show?" Mother makes a show of her apology.

"Fantastic, actually."

"Well, that *is* wonderful. And classes are going…well, I mean your grades aren't being, ahem, interfered with by the Apple business?"

"Of course not, Mother. I'm on pace to graduate a semester early.

"Well, well, sweetheart, that *is* quite the accomplishment. And to what do we owe the pleasure of *your* being here this evening?"

"I come down here sometimes," Miranda mutters. "It's usually quiet."

Cue a hallmark Swami Family Silence™.

"Well we have *two* things to celebrate, then! To Caleb's promotion and Miranda's scholastic excellence! My wonderful children, *huff*, how lucky am I? *Ahem*, are *we*?"

With minimal enthusiasm, Father looks up from his soup, glass in hand to match his wife's, and says "Here, here."

"But *really*, Caleb," Mother says, defining her toast, "this is such a crowning accomplishment. At 33, no less. *Wunderkind!*"

"Mother, please." Caleb interrupts, "Really, let's talk about something else."

Mother's eyes narrow a bit, and she locks hers with Caleb's. He looks down at his soup, and Miranda sees all of this. Something is amiss.

"Miranda, dear. Caleb *did* tell you about his big news, didn't he?"

Miranda shakes her head, no. One of the difficulties in being a man Caleb's size is people are kind of always looking at you. A separate issue for men like him, with Adam's apples like that, is that it's really difficult to *gulp* discretely. As such, his gulp is not discrete, and everyone is looking at him.

"Mother," he says quietly, "please."

But Mother is still speaking to Miranda. "I was under the impression that Caleb had shared his successes with you, *like we discussed*, but I suppose not. Caleb would you care to, perhaps, illuminate your sister on the latest?"

Miranda feels the temperature drop like twenty degrees. The shivers begin in her toes and crawl upwards, freezing the sweat under her arms and on her brow and even her eyes are cold.

"Mother, *drop it*." Caleb commands.

"Caleb!" Father yells, startling the chefs in the kitchen. How effortlessly he can commandeer a room. "You do not speak to your mother like that."

"Arthur, it's fine, really. Caleb, *I'm sorry*, I didn't realize how —"

"No, this is ridiculous. He's a grown man." Father swoops in like the angel of death, his scythe slicing the air, unaware and unapologetic, simply doing his duty, matter of fact and straightforward, separate are his actions from their consequences. He neither stutters nor slips as he says blankly to Miranda, "Your brother has been made CEO of his banana company."

"Ba-na-nuh cum-pen-ee?" Miranda hears herself saying slowly. It's a wonder she can even hear at all; there's a hundred thousand nuclear devices detonating at once in between her ears. A noise somewhere between a steam engine and a comet breaking up upon entering Earth's atmosphere, that's the underlying sound that life (perhaps in perpetuity) adopts.

"There, was that so difficult?" Father asks Caleb.

"See, honey? It's *okay*. Your sister is so happy she can hardly speak!"

"Ba-na-nuh cum-pen-nee?" The words repeat again and again in her head, sad, bored, metronomic, building speed and clatter like motorcyclers in a circus dome. She's not totally sure if she's speaking or simply thinking, and whatever control she has traditionally had over her eyes and mouth has been lost. She sees, at once, every inch of the room, and also the skeletons of the things in it; colors flash and her mouth hangs slack as she speaks. *This is it*, she thinks, *I'm dead*.

"Mer-an-duh, puh-leeze, don't fuh-reek ow-wut," Caleb says in slow-motion, but it's not really in slow-motion, it's just that time has completely collapsed. Miranda experiences her own birth and death, feels in her spirit the decay of all things, and the growth of mushrooms upon the wet, dead log.

"Suh-wheat-*hart*, wuh-hut is thuh mat-ter oo-whith yuh-who?" Mother's voice, even slowed and numb, still bites.

Time, having finished flourishing for Miranda, returns to normal, which is hyper-speed by comparison, and Miranda juts her chair back into the serving elbow of the male chef who yells, "*Aghhh,*" or "*Mamma mia!*" or some other Italian outcry of surprise as his large cauldron of ashy, cream-covered pasta discards half its stomach onto the floor. The chef looks around mortified, the daughter looks around defiant.

"Jesus Christ, Miranda!" Mother shouts.

"How long?" she asks Caleb, directly, without edge, without emotion, as if she were asking when the delivery guy was going to get here.

"Miranda, come on," he pleads with eyes and voice and forehead. She thinks maybe if she looks at him long and hard enough, he'll explode, splattering Mother and Father and all this frilly fucking food with the world's most traitorous blood-'n-guts.

"Miranda, please, you're being —" Mother tries to say.

"How *long*!?" she shrieks, inflamed by her brother's evasiveness. Mother and Father sit silent, either stunned by the goings-ons or aware that something is happening completely over their manicured heads. The chefs pick up the pasta with large tweezers.

"Since June," he says. Blunt as Professor Plum with the candlestick in the parlor.

"This whole time you were there?…And with Cindi Lapenschtall… you were *there*? With Gwami, too? At that church you were already *there*? You didn't tell me that you were there why didn't you tell me that you were there why wouldn't you tell me that you were *there*!?"

Caleb doesn't have a response, but that's okay, she doesn't want one. She knows she has command of this room, totally and inconsequentially, that if she flexed her might in this moment of weakness, she could get to the very root of so many things: how long he's been there, exactly what he knows and what he wants, exactly how much blood is caked onto his hands–Cindi's and Gwami's certainly, and whoever else he had to bully, bludgeon, or bury to get that penthouse corner office. Caleb has never been the kind to puff out his chest in moments of tense confrontation, turning over by default like a submissive house pet. If she were a brash and brutal creature, she would take this moment to destroy him, destroy whatever ripped remnants of his soul still hang around his chest; she would reveal her alter-ego to Mother and Father and use the shock of that exposé to emphasize exactly the size and scope of Caleb's betrayal. She would craft an off-the-cuff thesis statement on how she was right about her brother, about how all the coddling and care going into his raising turned him into a selfish, entitled, self-serving, insular, careless, sociopathic, pathetic, milquetoast piece of shit, *asshole*.

But Miranda isn't brutal nor brash. She's none of those things. She's much more like her mother. Even if she wishes she weren't, Miranda is in fact her mother's daughter. Her inherited brain calculates right now a thousand possible responses in half-a-nanosecond, factoring into its decisions nothing more important than this: *Big Banana* is Gwami's mortal enemy, they smote her and will smite Miranda if they can; and if it's true, if Caleb really is their *new CEO-to-be*, if he too is dealing in forces stronger and darker than any he could imagine, if he's been there for so long and if he had *any* hand in the situation with Cindi and Gwami, then *they could*, then they can, then they will. They most certainly will.

Miranda's entire life has thus been compromised. From two fronts she must flee: from the mob and the militia both. The enemy knows everything there is to know about her, how much money is in her bank account, the contents of her crawlspace, the phone numbers of everyone she's ever met. A very distant threat of violence against her has become incredibly real and violently close. Her responses right this second might, should Caleb have truly morphed into the worst possible version of himself, decide whether she'll live to see the morning. Or the one thereafter.

There is no more time for shock or anger or existential dread. After she gets somewhere safe, maybe. Now demands calculation.

So, Miranda takes a deep breath, relaxes her shoulders, and says, "I'm so sorry everyone. I don't know what came over me. Caleb, that's amazing. I'm so proud of you, you're going to do great. Mother, Father, you should be proud of him. I'm happy for us all. It's a great day for the Swami family. Cheers," and she raises a glass.

Here, here.

The family goes on with its meal, making polite talk about politics, about the new wars, about the coronation of Caleb Swami. He engages in long, sincere, apologetic stares at Miranda, who looks back and smiles with her eyes, like nothing's wrong, like nothing's ever been wrong in her life.

Miranda makes a very convincing show of eating. Look! She really chews and swallows!

"Excuse me," she says, "Just need to use the restroom." She leaves the kitchen, the chef comes over to fold her napkin, and she heads upstairs, esoteric familial code for which type of bathroom trip this is. How proper she is, how polite.

Polite talk continues in the kitchen, polite contained laughter and polite fork movements. Downstairs they eat Pappardelle, a very polite and proper type of pasta, while Miranda politely packs her bags, politely tiptoes into Mother and Father's room to grab a few things and down to ground level, managing sufficient silence as she opens the front door, her backpack digging into her shoulders, her heart weirdly calm.

By the time they even notice she's gone, she's already in an *Uber* the *Wawa* cashier called for her, *en route* to catching the 10:14 northbound out of Manahawkin. She left her phone on her bed, on top of a note that says *Fuck You, Caleb* in black Sharpie. In her tip-toeing, she unflinchingly stole twelve-hundred dollars in cash and a debit card from Mother's purse on the bed. And she left her room light on, too; someone will have to go up there and turn it off.

She'll be long gone when Caleb, forlorn, stands in the doorway, a flush of orange light behind him, and stares out onto the empty street. Mother'll call after him, asking what's wrong, but he'll pretend not to hear. Slowly realizing his sister is gone, he'll return inside, leaving the door open a smidge, letting in a draft as if to demonstrate his true level of distress. Miranda's gone he will tell them. Mother might stand and make a show of making a fuss, but then she'll sit back down, eat a marinated olive and tell herself it isn't her problem. Father will see something unsettling in the paper but will decide against sharing it. Caleb will feel very alone, and then quite upset, angry, furious, even, and then he'll push the whole thing away.

"So, guys…how was the trip down?"

And Miranda will be sitting on a train, flipping through the money she's managed to make off with, counting it like it isn't real, counting it in public, and then switching to a bus and then falling asleep. In her bumpy dreams, there's a great open field, green and yellow with patchy banana trees and an endless blue sky shining down upon them. But storm-clouds start to convene from the west, the faraway sky lit blue and yellow and orange with primordial lightning. The ground below begins to swell and recede like a belching belly, and fissures like salt-flats open within the very earth. Alerted to danger by the fissures and the lightning, hundreds of laborers, sweaty and dirt-caked, stand up from their knees, look out from behind the trees, wiping their foreheads with their forearms, bountiful baskets of unripe bananas on their hips.

"¿Que es eso!?" A deep male voice shouts, and dozens of screams follow suit. Crashing towards the workers is a sky that has turned hellish by approaching flame, orange and crimson, and bright burnt splinters from charred trees rise up in the ash clouds before descending like hail. Running bodies caked in Vesuvian soot explode out from the thick smoke as those beings, the Banana Demons from Cindi's video, begin to crawl out of crevices in the Earth, ridiculous looking, somewhat, but so terrifying now that they're whole, uncut, unchained. There are hundreds of the beasts altogether, and with them literally pouring from the earth, the fire gets brighter, hotter, and the lightning strikes closer and closer, the storm rushing in with maniac speed. There are demonic snarls and so many pleas in Spanish for "*¡Dios, por favor, salvame! ¡Salva mis niños!*" So close the fire gets she can feel its flame and then it's overtaken her and the heat is so real and so incinerating and there's another *crash* of thunder.

The vividness, the smell and the heat, all of it is forgotten. The whole dream fades right away. Miranda opens her eyes as the bus comes to a halt at Port Authority, the sewage smell and dazed fluorescent glow waiting to greet her as she steps off. Outside, the city is enveloped in a fog either precluding rain or deposited by it. All the raincoats and hoods and umbrellas on the passersby obscure their faces, and Miranda takes the opportunity to hide hers, blending in totally as she makes for Grand Central.

On the way, Miranda stops at an ATM, correctly guessing at Mother's bank pin. In deciding how much money to withdraw, Miranda has a few things to consider. Will she ever see her parents again? Something in her blood says this is a far more dangerous business she's involved in than her mind would like to let on. How much money does one need to live at a hotel for a week? Without her phone, Miranda can't check rates, but it's better to be on the safe side, right? And with taxis, trains? Where is the cut-off between petty larceny and felony theft?

Miranda takes more than she was planning to, but in time Mother and Father will understand. At the very least, they will not see each other until after Miranda has helped end this current iteration of the world, and by then, who knows? Maybe hers will be the most famous face in Long Island. And you can't put a price on that.

Surely in that regard, Mother will understand.

Less than four hours after she left the dinner table in Long Beach Island, New Jersey, Miranda Swami steps into the brightly lit atrium of the Westchester Hilton in Rye Brook, New York, some 132-miles away.

The Woman at the front desk asks for her name, and Miranda, who'd been thinking about it, tell her it's Samantha Obama. Nonplussed when Miranda refuses to put a card on file, the clerk eases off when she drops a couple hundred dollars in cash (and a little extra for your kindness, ma'am) on the counter between them.

"That'll do for collateral?" Miranda says sweetly, quietly a master of the smiling-with-her-eyes thing.

"That should be fine," the woman says in a much friendlier tone, putting the money into her back pocket, but who'll ever know? She's the only one on duty.

"Here's your key, Ms. Obama. Say, I'm sure you get this all the time, but are you related to —"

"Cousins. By marriage. I do get it a lot."

"Wow. Say hi for me, *heh heh heh*, enjoy your stay."

"I hope to. Oh, uhm, actually, sorry, but do you have a computer I can use?"

BANANAS!

The maids here leave chocolate on the pillows when they finish cleaning. Isn't that nice? And the soap is molded into a seashell shape. Even this far inland, there's a certain charm in that.

Miranda is just trying her damndest to focus on the little things: the chocolates and "gently folded" towels, the soft lilac scent in the lobby, and the quiet overhang by the entrance under which any number of cigarettes can be smoked in peace. It's the endless ice from the machine in the hall and the faintly nostalgic smell of community pool chlorine spread out all over the second-floor. And the children who jump about the place in their swim trunks.

Upon arrival last night, Miranda-cum-Samantha Obama lumbered with her heavy heart to the hotel computer, tucked unobtrusively beside the then-defunct *Starbucks*, and sat for nearly twenty minutes in front of the screen, debating what the best way to "@" Cindi would be. At the end of a long, mostly inconclusive rumination, Miranda decided to walk along Occam's Razor, simply @-ing Cindi Lapenschtall the word *Hilton* from her own private account, the progenitor, @msgothkid666. Not really in the business of questioning Cindi Lapenschtall's methods, she simply put her trust in the process and in the woman herself. Either Cindi or *Big Banana* are going to find her here, hiding in this hotel. In the meantime, she might as well enjoy it, right?

And so, the little things.

The bouncy bed, for example, the soft beige wallpaper, and the way exhaustion waited until she was safely atop a bed before coming upon her so suddenly and so completely. The sleep that refuses to be interrupted by any earthly stirring, not the raucous rumbling of nearby highway trucks nor the unseasonal mosquito feeding periodically on her earlobe. The small ocean of gummy pillows around her, that's another thing. Miranda slept through the night and woke, early and refreshed, into Day One of her interval/internment *here*, at the Westchester Hilton.

It strikes her early in the day, as she skims *Big Banana* news on the lobby computer, that remaining here until the day of the announcement isn't mandatory. Perhaps it would be better to keep moving, to make a wide berth around the City instead of remaining stationary. Cindi would be able to find her wherever she is, surely. Despite all the headache it would cause, Miranda knows leaving this place would be for the best, and the sooner the better. She knows it on the stairs and she knows it back in her room, and she knows it as she lay back down into the scintillating embrace of the pillow, knowing the thing but actively ignoring it.

Those thoughts of self-preservation prove not long for this world. They fade slowly and finally fizzle fully, pushed away because, simply, Miranda is *tired*. She doesn't want to keep running. She's been journeying for weeks now, unstoppable and unflappable in her resolve; well she finished the job, found the Woman with the Red Hair, got her next steps, and now she wants to rest, to idle, to hang around and chain-smoke and for just a short while worry only about *here*, divest herself from *next*. This, after all, might be the final week of this world as she knows it. Her and Cindi's actions could very well have huge unintended consequences. Will they inadvertently usher a demon army into their earthly realm? Will *Big Banana* topple overnight? Will Miranda be driven underground, like Cindi, destined to a hideaway life as an enemy-of-the-state? Miranda isn't sure how this story ends, so while it's still possible, she wants to bask in a known quantity. Just to see what it's like.

She wants to drink sugary gingerbread coffees in a *Starbucks*, wants to return home to a room that's unpopulated, with a bed devoted to her form alone, with walls she can't hear others through. She wants to eat bacon in the morning and ice cream before bed and just, for the love of God, spend a moment not caring just about the world or its soul or how a band of demon marauders are twisting it, pulling it apart, suckling at its fresh drippings. She wants to feel like any old person, for a moment, and not like Miranda Swami.

It's what she thinks she wants, at least.

Day One passes without much to mention. It's hard to fear any-thing evil or supernatural in a place so blasé, comforting, and blandly commercialized as a multinational hotel chain. Something about the aerosol smell and the focus-group-tested uniforms, the stock-photos of grass and the Empire State Building and smooth blue stones by the elevators in the lobby…it just doesn't seem like the unruly forces of hell can walk free in such a sanitized space. There are no dark corners in a hotel like this, no illicit alleys where horrible things occur. There's a shadowy foot-and-a-half beside the first-floor vending machines, but everything else is brightly-lit, is security-camera captured, every act carrying with it a threat of litigation and an excess of liability.

For breakfast, she has a bellhop materialize with bacon and toast, but since the knock on the door nearly scares her half-to-death, lunch sees her trekking to a nearby *Denny's*, because what bad shit happens at *Denny's*? Too much commercial cuisine leaves Miranda feeling generally icky, so "dinner" is eaten in small installments, each course plucked from the nearby vending machines: a first-course of pork rinds and *Nilla Wafers*, an entrée of salted peanuts and *Pop-tarts*. Her stomach stays strangely civil the sugar and salt. And then the ice cream. She's prepared for the knock this time.

And how nice it is, for just a day, to give in to the classic commercial consumerism of the able-bodied American. This weekend will see her toppling a stalwart of capitalism, so can't she just, like, leave her principles on the mat outside for one measly evening? The eventual good outweighs the current bad.

In bed at night, after ensuring her door is locked and out-fitted with the proper do-not-disturb documentation (the chocolate, though a nice surprise, is too weak a treat to overcome her fear of unknown intruders in her private space), Miranda settles into bed in a black room, allowing any interested ideas into her tired mind.

The first thoughts to enter are of Cindi, and the offhanded remark she made the last time they spoke. "@ me," she had said, and Miranda had. What is the woman doing now? Is she assembling a crack team to infiltrate the hotel and come rescue her? Is she spiraling into a depression, thinking that Miranda is in some terminal danger but unable and/or unwilling to come physically deliver the girl to glory? Or has she not noticed at all? Has Miranda's quiet plea gone unread and unseen? Does Cindi sit somewhere poolside, Mai Tai in hand, basking, like Miranda, in this last week of normalcy before the world illegalizes the color yellow?

Thoughts of Caleb, which waited patiently outside the door for those of Cindi to finish with her, finally get fed up with the extended wait and bust in, rushing up and buffeting Miranda with the totality of their weight, heft, and rank smell. *Wrangle us*, they cry, *wrangle with us, please*!

Oh, they wrangle alright. And at the end of their tussle, this is what the two parties come to agree on:

Caleb Swami isn't an especially smart man. He's not an ambitious man, and he's not overly lucky. These are things she understands now. What Caleb Swami is, more than anything else, is impatient. Miranda knows her brother is not evil, either. Evil is an absolute, and Caleb is nothing absolutely. This she knows. The man who held her on his shoulders once, who lifted her up so she could grab that apple there, that really red shiny one, Caleb, on that branch riiiiiiiight theeeeeerrreeeeeeee, he couldn't be evil. There are wholly evil acts that do not completely tarnish a person's soul, and there are evil people with malintent spread throughout their blood vessels. There is a difference. It's unclear if Caleb also knows there's a difference.

Caleb Swami impatiently waited for success and fame and a positive-self-image to beget him. But he simply could not wait for these things to accrue in their usual fashion, and so made his life a race after them, maintaining the cold, simple goal of collecting them as soon as possible. If that pursuit ruined his relationships, so be it. If it alienated his sister, that's fine; she would understand.

And that's the worst part about all of this. That's the horrible rub. She does understand. As soon as the initial anger and hysterics gave way to more complex thought, she knew she'd understand. She, who looked in her mailbox and under her desk for a scratch-and-sniff letter. She, who looked *everywhere*. Esau sold his birthright for a mess of pottage. Miranda fears on her darkest days she would sell hers too, and mayhap for far, far less.

She does not hate Caleb for what he did, but she feels him leaving her, whatever strands of care that remained from before. He's cut himself off from her; this was his doing, though she cannot help but feel his absence. The place on her heart where he sat, fat and satisfied, has been freed from his crushing weight. This feels both liberating and very, very lonely. But that's okay. That has to be okay.

Despite their best efforts, the Caleb thoughts do not destroy her. They do not strike fear into her heart, not do they succeed in jumping her bones with electric anxiety. Despite all the power they promised when they rushed in, they merely sapped energy, sapped care, sapped a little more life from a body already drained of so much. They leave her thinking what a slog this whole ordeal is for body and mind alike. They leave her thinking that whatever she does next, it will be with more care for others than Caleb, in his life's one meaningful decision, showed for his only sibling, the girl he lifted up for apples. The girl who reached for the one riiiiiiiight theeeeeeerrrreeeeeeee, all shiny and red.

Day Two is more eventful.

Miranda is woken late by a phone call from the Front Desk.

"Ms. Obama — oh I love saying that — good morning! You have a visitor downstairs in the lobby. She was asking after your room number."

"Uhm, okay, can you ask her name?"

There's a silence. "She says her name is Cindy."

Jesus.

"Okay, uhm, yeah, tell her I'll be down to chat in a bit, thank you."

"Yes'm," and then, further from the receiver, "She says she'll be right down."

As Miranda stalls, brushes her hair and applies mascara, as she brushes her teeth for two, three, four, five! minutes, she tries to keep her mind from ruminating on all the possible situations waiting for her in the lobby. She tries quashing them through unrelated action, and is surprisingly semi-successful. It's only with slight sweats, with her teeth quietly crunching on the inside of her cheek, that she dresses and takes the stairs down to the lobby.

Once down there, Miranda is at once accosted by…accosted by… accosted by? Absolutely no one? Neither Cindi Lapenschtall nor any other Cindi is obviously waiting for her. There's an older man in a tan jumpsuit resting in a chair beside his tennis-balled walker, and a pair of bored looking hotel employees man the front desk, presumably in the event of a sudden check-in rush. Otherwise, the lobby is deserted. This means either A) something has happened to whoever wanted to see her, B) someone is playing upon her a horrible prank, or C) this was all a ruse to lure her face out of hiding.

But honestly, whatever.

Her response to each of these scenarios would be the same, to pack her things right up and immediately leave the hotel, walk to the nearest bus station and head out on the road to nowhere, but just as she's about to turn tail back to her room, a gentle Porter, an older gentleman with a Friar John ring of hair and one rusted-silver hoop earring, kind of half-jogs over to her, taking the big strides of the blessedly long-legged. "Samantha Obama?" he asks her, seeming out of breath, like the simple act of getting to her was its own sort of exhausting adventure.

"Yes?"

"Your visitor had to go. She asked me to give you this note."

Within a sealed envelope, on a small piece of hotel stationary, is a scribbled note in near-calligraphic script reading, "*One quarter-mile down the road, past the second McDonalds, is a picnic table aloft in a small glade. Meet me there.*" The note is unsigned.

Miranda takes a few absent-minded steps outside, deems it too cold for a mere cardigan, and returns up to her room for a winter coat. So as to prepare for an ambush, she packs her meager things and hangs 'em on her back. This might be a one-way trip.

Past the first McDonalds and then on to the second, past that and Miranda espies a short dirt path cut out of the resiliently plump pine thicket in the woods beside. Unable to spot the glade from outside the wood, it only takes a few steps onto the trail for the clearing to reveal itself, a conspicuously carved-out little flat with a picnic table and a dripping water pump. There is indeed someone waiting for her here, but it's not Cindi Lapenschtall as she had hoped, nor is it the trench-coated Banana Demon she feared. It's someone distinctly other.

You want proof that our fair heroine has been changed by her journey thus far? She goes towards the table-sitter freed of all anxiety, every bit of her having quietly acquiesced to the principle of whatever-hap-pens-next.

"Hello?"

Contrary to what Miranda momentarily believed might happen, the Woman does not, upon closer inspection, reveal herself to be Cindi Lapenschtall in disguise. The figure seems quite content remaining a prim and proper type of older woman, a bit younger than Mother, who's matched the lines in her face with those in her outfit, producing an appearance at once austere and wizened and a tad off-putting. She looks ready to shush someone crunching on cashews at the library. Her two sharp, inquisitive eyes tell stories of harsh judgments passed. They look up blankly in Miranda's direction. A phantom streak of blonde hair fissures an otherwise homogeneously oil-black head. Miranda says "Hello?" again, and again, and after the woman refuses to answer this third request for salutation, Miranda simply sits on the bench in front of her.

It's not my story anymore, Miranda tells herself. *I'm at the whim of the plot. I do not move it; it moves me.*

(Which is about half-true.)

The woman takes those eyes of hers and uses them to look Miranda up and down, like scanning her for some defect. Not so unlike Mother at all. An obnoxious Bluetooth headset hangs from one of her ears. Although she doesn't speak or move or even blink (freaky old thing), faint murmuring voices coming from the headset make it clear this woman is taking orders or receiving information. Or perhaps she's just lost in a podcast.

From out of her pocket: the woman takes a facsimile headset.

From out of her pocket: Miranda takes a cigarette.

"I suppose you want me to put this thing on?" Miranda asks, lighting up. The woman looks on blankly, pushes the headset further across the table. 'Great,' she says, smoke billowing from between her front teeth.

Two things happen after Miranda hooks the Bluetooth into her ear and says, "Okay, so what's all this about?"

1) Cindi Lapenschtall's unmistakable red velvet voice saunters into Miranda's ear, saying "Oh! Oh! Miranda! You've come! Are you okay? Is everything okay? Sorry it took so long, we had to get to you quietly."

2) The woman across the table begins, with about a quarter-second delay, mouthing each individual word Cindi says in Miranda's (and assumedly her own) ear.

So, Miranda is staring at this Mother-like lady speaking with a slight lag, like some half-telepathic circus performer, wondering in order of importance: How did this woman get so good at such a specific task? How does she know Cindi? Is Cindi reading off a pre-written script?

"Okay," Miranda says, "this is trippy."

"What is? Oh, Linda? Yes, odd I imagine, especially if it's your first time seeing it. Please understand though, it's absolutely necessary. We have no idea if people are watching ya'll from afar or whatnot. After as much time underground as I've spent, you learn to cover even your most farfetched of bases. I know it's, like, completely effin' paranoid, but just go with it. Linda is a trusted advisor and a dear friend. I trust her with my own life.

"Now, is everything all right? We saw you trying to get in contact and had your location traced. *Big Banana* isn't the only one with hands in puppets."

Miranda nearly blurts out something about Caleb, but is it her place to spew such news? Wait, fuck, *of course it is*. The only question is, how much does Cindi already know? And if the answer to that is "not a whole lot," how will she react when she's told? "Yeah, I'm physically okay, but, uhm, my brother —"

"Yeah. Your brother," Cindi says, hesitating. "Don't trouble yourself with that right now, there will be plenty of time."

All this while good ol' Linda mimics the voice in her ear. If Miranda only looks at the woman through her peripheral vision, it appears that

Linda is speaking in Cindi's luscious warm butter voice. Spooky; she wonders how someone even goes about practicing this.

(A flashback plays, in black and white, of a little girl, the least-nuclear member of a four-part, 50's family; father's just got home from work and is putting his first one back while mother makes dinner, Jimmy is practicing his violin and everything is quiet except for *Leave it to Beaver* on a tiny TV; the girl, eyes wide, looks to the screen with complete pre-adolescent reverence, her mouth moving in close time with her beloved friends on the screen as she relives an adventure she's had the good fortune to have already experienced two, three, four times now. Father coughs and mother drops a glass onto the linoleum floor, shattering it; Jimmy breaks a string, but still the girl watches, her eyes beautiful and blank and unblinking.)

"Do people actually spy on you from afar?" Miranda asks after a quiet moment, carefully ashing her cigarette into a small concavity of grey fluid on the table.

"People do all sorts of odd things, whether they have malicious intent or not. SO many crazies out there, all with their own well-researched and fully hashed-out mental machinations. Whenever you have any kind of success — as I'm sure you know — there's always bound to be a lot of, uhm, uhm — Linda what word am I thinking of?"

Out loud, Linda says, "Vitriol."

"Vitriol! Yes!" Cindi shouts, which is weird to watch because it means Linda says and then mouths the word *vitriol* in rapid succession. "Yes, much vitriol, surrounding especially all the facets of my person. Add into that mix the very real and present power of *Big Banana* and, and, and it just helps to be safe. Let's not dwell on all that though, not when — wait, did you hear that? Is someone else there?"

If Miranda hadn't been looking directly at Linda in that moment, she wouldn't have seen her eyes just-barely widen in surprise. This is a woman/puppet/pawn/caregiver no doubt accustomed to Cindi's moments of sudden emotional turmoil, and nothing, certainly no shrill shriek of paranoiac panic in her ear, will disturb her clean facial façade for more than the briefest immediate reaction.

Displaying what can only be described as a superhuman, possibly supernatural sense of hearing (or perhaps the Bluetooth amplifies the sounds going into it), Cindi says "I think there's someone else in the wood."

Miranda starts asking, "How could you possibly —"

But a sharp laugh and a hand on her wrist cut Miranda off mid-thought. Out of Linda's otherwise stoic mouth comes this folksy kind of hooting laughter, the laugh and the warm touch of her fleshy fingers preceding the rest of her bizarre and sudden metamorphosis.

At once, Linda's face loosens, her shoulders drop, her entire demeanor becoming light-hearted and laugh-heavy. Miranda's never seen anyone with control over their skin like that. Octopuses once in a David Attenborough documentary but never a person. Linda's lolling her head to the side as if under the calming spell of some joke, some soft monologue delivered by an honored guest. Her eyes curve upwards in a gesture of kindness and ease. She'd fool any lie detector, or anyone versed in facial recognition, let alone the two jamokes strolling over right about now.

It's a father — or appears to be — with his young son, both of them in tan fishing vests and waders, both with bucket hats and armfuls of fishing supplies. Dad's got a tackle box, sonny's got the rods. "Hey! Hey, yes, hello ladies! Well, look here Tyler, some luck; perhaps these nice women can help us. How are you two? My boy and I are supposed to be on or around Wampus Pond Park? Seems we've gotten a bit lost."

And Linda's voice, well, it's like fresh-baked cookies, and with a smile to match. "Oh, you poor dears. Well, Sheila and I would love to help you, but we're from out of town. Don't know the area too well. Can't offer you directions, but maybe a bite to eat perhaps?" From around her feet, Linda lifts up a previously unseen Little-Red-Riding-Hood picnic basket, open on one side to reveal a bounty of red grapes, wrapped cheese, and a chopped baguette, salami and chorizo and the promise of *more* underneath.

The boy yelps "Ooo! Ooo! Daddy! Can we —"

"Oh ho ho," the father says, patting the boy's head with his off-hand. "That is *very* sweet of you ladies, but we should be going, right Tyler? We want to get *some* fishing done today, don't we? All the best to you two. Enjoy your picnic!"

"And you two enjoy the lake…if you can find it!" Cue sitcom laughter, cue slow-walk away, smiles all 'round, dad grips son by shoulder, zoom in on the queer wholesomeness of the entire interaction, and, finally, cue the cuteness lingering on Linda's face as her voice reverts back to its harsh normalcy. "We can't stay here; you have to go back to the hotel."

"Is everything okay?" Cindi's voice says on the headset, but Linda's mouth makes no moves to mimic it.

"We're going to walk to the parking lot like we're old pals," Linda says sternly, "and if we run into our friends out there we'll simply say we forgot something in the car, then go on our merry way."

"Wait — what's happening?"

"Miranda!" Cindi says sharply into the headset. Is that a hint of genuine worry or just Miranda's imagination? "Please be quiet and listen to Linda. If she smells something, then something smells. We need to get you inside and to safety. Something is afoot."

As they walk, Linda maintains her posturing warmth, moving slowly, leaning on Miranda's arm as if for support, her beautiful blue eyes looking every which way. As Miranda looks down to the deliciousness poking out from the picnic basket's mouth, she realizes her stomach is rumbling, the gnawingly empty thing. The sensation of a stomach nibbling at itself keeps Miranda from fully appreciating what Cindi is saying in her ear.

"— same method available to us, possibly. Hard to tell, since everyone we get on the inside ends up being cooked over an open fire or torn apart by wildebeests, so we stopped sending people inside. We had this one guy with a pager programmed to send out automatic pings in time of trouble. They lost him in Richmond and finally, after a wild goose chase of epic proportion, picked him up somewhere in Bali. He'd been drawn and quartered by a quarter of rabid, detusked pachyderms kept on a nearby farm. All I'm saying is, if we were able to find you, I guess they might be able to as well. Gotta get you to a safer location, but don't worry, it's all good for now. They don't ever act impulsively. Bureaucracies move slowly. We've got the upper hand there."

When they part in the parking lot, it's with Linda encouragxing Miranda to keep the picnic basket. Supplied with a sufficient alibi, Miranda prepares to head back to the hotel, her hungry stomach in a dreadful knot.

"Just get back and wait for us to contact you. We will. Don't be afraid, you're in good hands," Cindi says, prompting Linda to offer her own soft, flabby hands up to Miranda's eyeline for examination. "And keep the basket, a proper meal will make you feel better."

In Miranda's brief absence, the hotel has become a hotbed of activity, what with a recently-arrived wedding party, a hundred-or-so-strong, having taken over the lobby. Elegant suits of beige and white and black, and the elevator stinks with enough hanging hairspray to tear a fresh hole in the local Ozone. Miranda just hopes they won't be too loud, she could use a rest. Fear and mal-information take a lot out of her apparently.

As Miranda returns upstairs to properly stew in her expectations — to hear again from Cindi, to meet again this Linda, to get on with the events to come five days from now — she hopes to God the new guests won't be too loud.

Tearing into the picnic basket, Miranda finds hard Italian sausage and wedges of aged Manchego cheese. There are a bevy of red-and-white striped napkins, a too warm bottle of Chenin Blanc, and two types of bread: long, smooth baguette, and a sesame-seed crusted sourdough loaf. It's as close to a home-cooked meal as she will have for some time.

Surrounded by charcuterie scraps, Miranda spends the rest of the day waiting to be contacted. Every time a phone rings in another room, Miranda's sweet little heart skips a beat. She waits and waits and waits, too nervous to nap, too manic to make headway into anything good on TV.

Night crashes down upon WestChester county Like an *Acme*-brand Piano, and Miranda thinks, after all this time, despite all that's happened, really truly absolutely believes, in every part of her system, she's been forgotten about by a very busy universe.

She opens the door, letting in all the patiently waiting thoughts. *Please, only one of you at a time*, she begs. They ignore her intonations.

Some hours later, it's midnight, and Day Three begins the same way Day Two ends: with Miranda still wide awake, thinking about demons. It's not the thoughts that are keeping her awake, not solely at least, but that the returned wedding partiers have decided that simply being loud isn't emphatic enough for their ends. If the well-traveled sonics of their celebration are to be believed, they may have devolved back from their humanity to some primitive ape-like state. Someone is very clearly playing trombone.

Bottles breaking and the loudest of thumping beats, coming from not just rooms on this floor or the next, but from every one around her. The screaming and the swearing and the laugh-filled prank-knocks upon all the doors down the hall. No girl could sleep; a walrus couldn't catch z's with this racket.

Where are the authorities? Who is in charge of busting hotel hallway bangers? Does a hotel itself have any real power to diffuse this situation? Especially if their guests are high-rollers getting raucous on an expense account, they'd probably just sacrifice the comfort of their less well-endowed clients, fucking capitalist bastards. Whatever options are at their disposal, they've obviously chosen *inaction* from the quiver upon their backs, letting this band of cumberbunded ruffians do whatever they like in the rooms they purchased and the halls they most definitely did not.

By the time the sun comes up, Miranda has only half-heartedly flirted with sleep — "So…what do *you* do for work?" — having spent most of the night watching *Friends* reruns, then the informercials which replaced them, and now, *coming up at 7, the day's first traffic reports, only on A-B-C Morning News at 7.*

The partiers are semi-tamed but still engaging in serious chandelier-swinging shenanigans when, as if a sudden-onset black hole has sucked them all from the premises, the wild yellers, swingers and noisemakers all go silent. A strangely juxtaposed quiet returns to the Westchester Hilton, one that forces your sonically-salient senses to focus on the sounds that remain: the heater bustling in the Key of D, the squealing tires coming to rest in the hotel parking lot.

Miranda stays in bed for a few hours more, trying to coax her body into late-game REM, but it's to no avail. She takes a hot shower and orders some yogurt and a coffee up to her room. There are quiet sirens in the parking lot. With her piqued curiosity overruling any power of self-preservation, Miranda opens the blinds, looks out the window, and sees that the hotel is *inundated* with police. Dozens of cop cars flash as the officers beside them loll about, a hand on their holsters, a hand on their hearts. Meanwhile, the weird cops on horseback trot in circles, probably positive they look nearly Napoleonic.

Holy shit, she thinks. *That's* what must've happened: so many people must have complained without success to the front desk, and one concerned citizen must have finally worked up the courage to call the local authorities, who came around in sufficient number to kill whatever wildness had overtaken the hotel's denizens. The bastards must be getting rounded up from every conceivable room — "Anyone with a tuxedo is going down, *hard*!" — and it wouldn't be surprising if a few officers *knock knock knocked* on her own door pretty soo —

Knock knock knock.

Look at that, right on time.

Miranda opens the door, expecting the arrival of either the authorities or her breakfast, but does not in any universe expect to see Linda, certainly not a version of her dressed as a hotel maid, pushing a cart full of cleaning supplies, towels and bedsheets into the room.

"Does '*do not disturb*' not mean anything anymore?" Miranda says, unable to resist.

"No time," Linda says, "Just get your things and hop onto the cart. Down on the bottom there. As quick as you can."

Stealing glances at Linda as she robotically culls her things together, in a prolonged post-wakeup daze, Miranda sees in the steel-veined woman a gripping, truly terrifying nervousness. This worries Miranda greatly, sending her colon shooting up into her esophagus, prompting her to increase even the already great speed at which she brings her things together.

Would she need a toothbrush where she's going?

"You'll have to curl up, but don't worry, you'll fit, we tested it," Linda says, helping Miranda squeeze her form and backpack both onto the cart's lower platform, which, when shielded on all sides by towels and hanging bedsheets, is actually quite cozy. She's like a café cat, all bundled up into herself.

The creaking cart begins bumping around as it is moved down the hall, and the slam of the door behind her means they're out into the world, the cruel, hostile world. Then, quietly, Linda starts talking.

"They know you're here. Or, they know someone of interest is here. We don't think they know it's you. It was wise to check-in under a false name, slows them down. They're going through the hotel real slowly, taking their time, not letting anyone in or out, doing sweeps of entire floors before moving up, and also — Oh, no sir, my apologies, I'm off-duty. Just give the front desk a call and they'll be happy to…oh okay, sir…yeah you too. Okay, I'm going to stop talking, don't want to appear suspicious. Just hang on, it'll all be over soon. And whatever you do, do not come out until I personally tell you it's okay. I will do so by saying the words *Fat Marge's Lovely Antique Pies For Sale Here*, and you will know by my saying those words that I'm not under duress. If anyone tries to remove you from the cart without hearing those words first, make a run for it or play dead, whatever you think is best, but that's a last resort."

Shit, Linda really sounds out of breath. Miranda, trapped in the cart and in her head, has no concept of how far they travel, just that they keep steadily moving forward, now slightly downhill, now apparently into a shaky service elevator, down some ramps, and judging by both the low rumbling of a nearby engine and the shaking metal beneath her, up a truck ramp into the back of some vehicle.

Linda does not say another word, not of good luck nor parting advice. The cart is stopped, the nearby footsteps distance themselves and disappear, and there's silence. Miranda dares not speak Linda's name, although God knows she wishes to; a profound comfort would come with knowing her guardian angel remains over her shoulder. In reality though, all her pent-up emotion is just looking for an escape. She just wants to cry out.

There's a jolt as the vehicle begins moving. There are muffled voices in conversation somewhere outside her immediacy, both of them dark and gruff and too low for their stray syllables to enter Miranda's ear properly. Onward she goes, slow movement. The bumps of potholes and short stops of sudden suburban stop-lights. The rolling streets of a way forward.

But forward to where?

The rumbling intensifies, the engine beneath her growing impatient and enraged as more of its power is called upon. For so long,

Miranda nearly sleeps, wakes and nearly sleeps again, the general tur-
bulence of the truck taking on a soothing, regularized gait. There's a
comfort in this, a strange comfort Miranda would never have guessed
she'd find in such tight quarters. It's nice to be assaulted by respite
instead of anxiety. And assault her it does: she's warm, she's sleepy, she
really truly believes she's safe.

Then there's a sudden, sharp turn, and Miranda feels the cart nearly
tip over. She has to shift her weight quickly and drastically to keep
the thing on its four wheels. Each consecutive bump takes on a more
violent force, and the once comfort recedes from around her. Her back
and elbows slam into the cart's plastic posts, and when the truck again
jerks, Miranda-upon-pushcart is sent hurtling from wherever she is in
the carriage to the other side, smashing into the wall with a loud and
shocking slam.

Whatever this vehicle is, it feels like it's traveling at light speed and
is hitting every possible celestial pothole along the way. There are fresh
bruises forming on her elbows and shins. It seems entirely plausible
she has left Earth, that Cindi, by way of certain safety, has set up a
Moon base, or perhaps something on the near side of Mars. Miranda
would not be surprised to find herself in some strange alternate reality,
Cindi's triumphant hiding spot being in a world that does not know
who she is.

Amidst the barrage of bizarre thoughts, the truck begins slowing,
and the rough ride smooths out. Soon everything slows to a standstill.
There are noises, the same muffled voices speaking again in just-barely unintelligible verse. A door nearby is opened and shut with a metal-
lic *clang*. Fresh, cold autumn air flings itself forward in-to Miranda's
temporary prison.

There are footsteps; The footsteps are close, close, closer, and the
shadow of a hand approaches the cloth nearest to Miranda's face.

Linda's soft voice coos *"Fat Marge's Lovely Antique Pies For Sale Here."*

Her hand helps Miranda from the cart, though Miranda proves too heavy and it's only her head and shoulders which emerge from her hiding spot. The bright light enters into and burns her eyes, purifying them by fire.

The light slowly settles, and with each cone in Miranda's eye coming around to the idea of daylight, fall foliage emerges into further definition. Through the opened back of the truck (she's in a U-Haul trailer), Miranda sees she's been brought to the middle of a red-and-orange-tinged wood, well-crunched leaves all upon the ground and lichen loose upon all the tree branches she can see.

Moving to the middle of the leaf-lined scene is Linda, out of her maid outfit and into a long yellow robe, like a monk's, with big open wizard sleeves that hide her conjoined hands within. Apparently, she feels Miranda can remove herself from the cart without any further help.

More figures in the scene include a bald man in a similar robe conversing with a falcon on his shoulder, a very tall woman with a waterfall mane of hazel hair standing with her back turned to Miranda, and further off, a pair of yellow robes coming closer, two pairs of dirty brown feet sticking out from beneath them. Miranda, scrunching herself in all sorts of twisty new directions, succeeds in removing herself from the cart, and jumps to her feet, stretching and standing straight up, arms overhead. Just then, as the tall woman begins to turn around, the blood either rushes to or from Miranda's head. Her vision goes black, and both she and the world topple right over.

The world is all white, all warm, and a hand brushes Miranda's hair from her face. The ground beneath her is hard and it's cold but the hand is warm, and so is the light from above.

"Am I dead?" Miranda asks, able to hear the dynamics of her own voice.

"Yes," comes another voice, luscious as fondue and thick as dark chocolate.

"Really?"

"No, not really, Miranda, God, you're *very* much alive. Just give yourself time to adjust." The hand continues removing strands of sweat-caked hair from Miranda's head before moving down along the length of her body. Miranda's daze isn't relegated to just her aching skull, but has spread throughout her nervous system, rendering so much of her body immobile and unfeeling.

But as the hand moves down her body, hovering just above it, Miranda can feel its heated reiki energy radiating through her, a warm pathway of minor electricity that snakes down her shoulder and torso, to her forearm and onto her hand. Sensation returns, softly at first, just a recognition of temperature, which gives way to goosepimples and shivers, to the warm throb of the bruises. The magic hand stops over her own hand, and takes it within itself. The hand is hard and rough and calloused and large enough to grip her full mitt, could rip it into bits should it wish. Miranda extends a finger up and feels long, acrylic nails capping the fingers, smooth as dried glue.

A gentle pressure is applied to her back, and Miranda feels herself lifted from the cold ground upon which she lay, the cold wet ground, and onto two feet that miraculously do not give way under her weight. Vision comes back in a rush, smacking her all at once with its breadth, knocking into her head with fully saturated colors, with mid-after-noon mist, with soft light upon stubborn leaves swaying gently in the winteresque wind. She looks upwards, but a perfectly-positioned sun eliminates the bulk of the forest she expected to see. It also silhouettes the entire torso of the person standing before her, leaving only their yellow *Chuck Taylors* and brown leggings and cross-stitched belt and the bottom of their *Versace*-looking vest to assist in possible identification.

"Miranda," coos the voice. Her own name, never sounding sweeter, slithers into the cleft within her ear, curls tightly and nestles itself in, the warmth of the word feeling like a tiny fireplace in her head. Miranda feels light, feels lit up from within.

She knows this voice now; it's completely unique, and not unfamiliar. As the identity comes clear into Miranda's mind, so does the face it belongs to. The head upon which it rests moves in front of the sun, projecting around itself a Christ-like corona. Nothing could be more fitting.

The last time she saw *this* face, Miranda was dressed like a dragon. Though not in ballgown, though not dolled-up, though not surrounded by fans, Cindi Lapenschtall nevertheless projects a radiant, queenly beauty. She's redwood tall with shoulders somehow both mega-dainty and NBA-broad; Miranda's never seen a body shaped or shapely as hers is. Never has she seen a body you could so easily fall in-love with, so delicate where you want it to be — that slim neck — but such strong secure hands and ankles and sunlit eyes sharp as uncut diamond. Miranda — who, I swear, never gets this way — turns beet red, and blushing, turns to face the dark-skinned queen of any reasonable person's dreams.

"Hi," Miranda putters, the word falling flat, a misshapen paper plane crafted with the best of intentions.

Cindi doesn't say another word, just slowly wraps Miranda in a long hug. Cindi's breath is on Miranda's neck, almost like she's nuzzling, while her big hands seem liable to stretch all the way across Miranda's back. Miranda's no small-fry, standing a solid 5'7", but she's never felt so small as in Cindi's embrace, like a little bean, like a string-bean, like a sun-struck fern wanting desperately to curl.

"Come with me," she says, her voice like velvet and her hand all over Miranda's.

As Miranda walks forward, she hears herself saying "Where's Linda?" but it doesn't seem like it's *her* actually saying it, but instead the words come out of that body, *that* one, all the way up there, walking five or six feet in front of Miranda proper, that body that looks like hers but seems somewhat robotic, like a husk, like something remote-controlled.

In answering, Cindi doesn't look at the body, but back at Miranda's soul, which floats a few feet behind her form. "She's inside, but that doesn't matter. What matters is you aren't totally in your body right now. Don't freak out, this kind of thing happens here. Scared me near to death the first few times I got that way, all distended and what-not. Just focus on your body, focus hard, and the whole thing will go away in time. It's the runes."

"Runes?" Miranda says, but no voice comes out. She's so far away from her body now, she can't will it into creating words, so it's just following Cindi along dumbly, a vessel dragging a leashed soul around by its heels.

Cindi directs the body with two hands on its shoulders, moving it forward through some thick trees towards a cave's shallow mouth, one hidden by brush and branch. A great hiding place in the buxom warmer months, this place must become far-less accommodating for *Cindi and Co.* in the spry, timid winter. Still, it makes a sick sense that Cindi would be holed up in a cave somewhere in, presumably, the Upstate New York woods, in a place you'd have to be dumb-lucky or whip-bright to find her in.

Into the center of the cave Cindi steps, lowering herself to the ground. Miranda tries to will her soul forward so as to see what Cindi is doing over there, succeeding herself forward only a few paltry feet. The reduced distance lets Miranda see the blue candle between Cindi's legs, and the light and the fuse and Cindi stepping back and a subtle, courtly flame reaching the candle, hitting the wick with a burst of blue starlight, and, finally, the spreading of said starlight all through the ground and onto the walls, where symbols like hieroglyphics burst with ambient cerulean light all around the cave mouth and far, far beyond, revealing the cavern's hidden, deep throat, all lit up like a constellation, like constellations litter the walls. And they do. While obvious now that the cave only appeared shallow, Miranda could never have guessed it would stretch so far inward, down into the Earth's belly. And the light stretches on, way way down into the cave until it reaches a faraway crescendo, an overwrought sunburst of ocean blue in an assumed ante-chamber some ways away.

Something about the light maybe, or else it's Cindi's cold stare which sends Miranda's soul *whipping* back into her body, the spir-it-substance collision forcing Miranda's rejoined form forward with such lurching force she falls to her knees. Her kneecaps hit the cold stone and come damn near to cracking outright.

"Ooooooh! Shit, shit, shit. Miranda, I am *so* sorry. I *always* forget that happens. Come on, Cindi, come on and think!" yells the former CEO of *Big Banana* — *Time's* Most Influential Person in the world last year — as she smacks herself on the head six times in quick succession, as if to shake awake some snoozing synapse. Then she looks forward. Linda, wearing her head-to-toe monarch yellow robe, steps forward from within the cave's far recesses.

"How is she?" Linda growls, her voice made warbly and rugged by the echo of the cave walls, an echo that, for some reason, only *her* voice seems able to coax from the ether.

"Good," Miranda says, looking dazed, "just my knees are bothering me a bit."

Cindi helps her to her feet and shifts most of Miranda's weight onto her own shoulders, carrying the girl further into the cave, towards the big bright blue beyond.

"I thought maybe you were going to get vaporized out there," Cindi says softly in her ear. "I had a somewhat sinking feeling you were too good to be true."

"I don't suppose you have some kind of magic salve to mend my knees, do you?" Miranda says, pushing slowly off Cindi onto her own power, grimacing in what is a much more severe pain than she wants to let on. She relapses somewhat. That or she doesn't want to totally lose the feeling of Cindi's skin upon her own.

"I have some CBD lotion somewhere in my bag."

"Not exactly what I had in mind."

If she weren't in such medically profound pain (seriously, how hard did she fall?) Miranda might be driven into a starry-eyed trance by the cavern they finally come into. Situated at the end of the long, blue-lit, glow-worm tunnel, is a huge Parthenon space, covered soil-to-scalp in the same unintelligible Betelgeuse markings as the cave mouth. Cindi follows Linda dutifully, mimicking her very footsteps even. Miranda draws close to Cindi, puts a hand on her arm and feels the muscles rippling underneath. A little something in her swoons.

Linda takes a slew of slow steps forward, and eventually stops before a conspicuously bare patch of the rock wall, about person high, about as wide as someone coming forward for a hug.

It takes only Linda's soft handprint on the wall to send a shockwave through the chamber, one that reverberates through and then up and back down the walls, as the barren section of rock crumbles to the floor, the stone dissolving into a glittery dust as it reunites with the Earth below it. "Watch your step," she says to Cindi and the scintillating Miranda behind her, the latter woman freshly settled into her throbbing knees and now able to stand on her own. Perhaps she milked her suffering an extra moment to stay longer on Cindi's arm. She can't remember having ever felt this specific combination of intimidated, turned-on, and reverent. At least not about a person. It's a strange mix of sanctified and sinful.

"Come, Miranda. Come sit over here," Cindi says, allowing Miranda through the crumbled rock and then ushering her towards a long marble table at the center of a great, empty hall. Cindi is much too nonchalant about it. I mean, it's like a castle was carved into the cave system! The long tapestry-wrapped hall stretches on for a few-hundred feet, starting here, with the crumbled rock entrance on this side of the room, and culminating way over there in a raised dais that would well-fit a throne, but which now deifies only a pair of intricately-molded black torch-holders. All lit up and painting the room a fiery, sensual orange, they stand guard over the two-pronged hallway splitting off to the east and west of the hall's northernmost section.

Approaching the table, Miranda sees it's an unbroken extension of the slate stone floor underneath it, as if the table was carved out of the room. A real chicken-or-the-egg situation. A gilded red and gold dressing flows down the table's exact geometric center, falling to the floor in elegant rumples.

"Linda, will you fetch us a beverage? Miranda could probably use some electrolytes." Linda bows solemnly and leaves the two sitting at the corner of the rectangle table (these are the only two chairs around it anyways), darting through a lip in the rock at the room's midsection and into an unseen part of the complex.

It's altogether unclear whether Cindi's overall cool demeanor is reassuring or freaky. Miranda tries not to betray much of the uncertainty welling up within her.

The torches on the wall shine with an almost fluorescent brightness, and with a moment to examine her surroundings, Miranda sees that the tapestries on the wall tell a continuous story, each one displaying a segment of what looks to be a great prolonged battle between a half-naked swordsman and all manner of kooky flying and crawling and slithering things.

"So, is this like your secret demon-slaying base?" Miranda asks sardonically.

"I need to talk to you about your brother."

Miranda gulps. She feels her eyes become hot with latent, unwanted tears. She simply nods. She did not expect this, not so soon, and can only nod.

"So, *you* know then," Cindi starts. "That's good. That makes my life a *lot* easier. I'm so sorry. I knew, but I didn't know if…so I didn't want to bring it up until…I don't know. Anyways, you're going to meet some people. And it's important you don't say anything about it. Nobody else knows. Nobody knows except for you and I, actually."

"— My parents," Miranda chokes out.

"Oh, well, *and* your parents I guess, and the Board of course. You have to understand how sensitive this information is. How powerful it is that we have this information. And how powerful your brother is going to be."

Miranda takes a couple of deep breaths, and after a few starts and stops finally says, "He's such an asshole."

Cindi shakes her head. "He's not an asshole, Miranda, you just don't understand what they can do to a person. No, no, don't say anything. I know…I know, but I need to say this quickly. Your brother is at the mercy of powers much stronger than he is. Much stronger than I was, and I was one hundred times more prepared for this than your brother was. I knew all about your brother. We met in passing a couple times, and I always recognized something in his eyes, something that wasn't there with anyone else I worked with. Even some of the lowlier employees, the very much humans, they lacked a certain *commitment* to their employment. Do you understand what I'm saying? Caleb was willing to give up everything for that position, and if they did to him what they did to me, they found him at his weakest moment, they pounced upon his uncertainty and his fear, because that's what they do.

"And now they're going to name him their CEO, although God knows what they have planned for him after. If we do this right, if we can pull this off successfully, we may be able to save him. Otherwise, I fear, the all-too-powerful forces are going to have their way with his weak, empty soul."

All those words, and their intrigue, pull Miranda from her emotion. Stone-faced, she admits "I, like, 60% understand. You keep talking in these vague undertones, and I need clear answers. Are we —"

But she's interrupted by Linda's return. Upon a jewel-encrusted silver tray sit an orange can and a steaming mug full of a dark brown liquid. "Tea-time, Mistress," Linda says to Cindi.

"I hope you like Fanta," Cindi says, handing a can to Miranda, "Go on, the electrolytes will be good for you. If you'd prefer something else —"

"No, no. This is perfect. Just perfect." Miranda sips her first bit of soda, feeling the acid bubbles attack the open wounds on the inside of her mouth, then go off pillaging the rest of her throat. She coughs while trying to say "So, where exactly are we?"

Cindi shoots Miranda an appreciative look, a *Thank you for playing along with my ridiculous request* kind of look, before saying "I can't rightly tell you that. Not that I don't trust you implicitly; it's just part of an oath I took. Certain things I can't divulge. Breaking a lot of rules just having you here. I promise, I'll answer what I can."

"Totally, yeah, cool." There's an awkward silence as Linda takes up a place against the nearest wall, standing board-straight against it, unmoving and unblinking and unspeaking. Unlistening, though? Cindi, despite gushing about Linda in the past, seems on-edge. "Personal bodyguard?" Miranda says, motioning her head towards Linda.

"Helper. Bodyguard in some ways. Part of my staying here entails having an escort. It makes sense, I promise."

"Sure, yeah, totally. Makes as much sense as any of this. I mean, what are we doing right now? Are we inside a fantasy novel? Secret club, magical runes, demon-hunting…magic doors? Are you about to tell me I'm some long-prophesied warrior? The only one capable of stopping the demons and restoring balance to the world?"

"No, no — oh Miranda — don't be preposterous."

"Oh, thank God, because actually this is like —"

"*I* am."

"What?"

"What you said. That's me. *I'm* the long-prophesied warrior capable of stopping the demons and restoring balance to the world."

Cindi just lets that hang in the air for a moment, perhaps expecting it to have a more physical effect on Miranda than it does. Nope, nothing to see here folks.

"Oh. Oh! Uhm, wow, totally. Cool," Miranda says, disassociating and suddenly very tired. "Honestly, that's not even very surprising. Were you like working undercover for *Big Banana* and they found you out? Or —"

"No, I'm sad to say. I'll avoid specifics, but to get to the top of that company you have to do a very bad thing. It was a near-total sacrifice of myself that made me the eventual vessel for the work I'm doing now." Cindi grabs Miranda's hands with a sudden earnest and fervor. "This is a story of redemption, Miranda Swami, and I'm nearing the end of my arc."

"Oh, well, Mazel! Where, uhm, if you don't mind me asking, do I fit in? Am I just a courier? A helper a —"

"Possibly. I'm not rightly sure yet. Depends how you interpret the prophecy. You may either be my greatest friend and ally — a true Samwise —, or my foil. We're here together in the middle of the arc, destined to become friends and confidantes and possibly even lovers —"

"Lovers?"

"And while we will ultimately succeed in our mission here — Yay! — it will have one of two effects. Either we will become a two-headed monster, together vanquishing the great beasts in their well-guarded dens, or all of this will only serve to create in you some untamable evil, which it will eventually be up to me, and me alone, to destroy. We are either Gilgamesh and Enkidu or Obi-Wan and Anakin."

"Woah. Heavy. Your prophecy is *that* specific? I guess it's nice just to be prophesied about at all. But you know we're not in a story, right? *Right?* If you really believe all that, then aren't you a slave to your own destiny? Why bring me in at all if you know I'm just going to turn heel and betray you?"

"But Miranda, I *don't* know. All prophecies are open for interpretation." Cindi takes a long contemplative pause. Miranda wants to light a cigarette but is concerned about the ventilation in here. This seems like a good conversation to have within a cloud of smoke. "All of life is an endless story, the battles and set-pieces laid out before us, waiting for us to walk into them. Everything is predestined, pre-written, outlined and sketched-out and decided for you, in some manner. No matter how you fight, it will occur as it must. But really, don't let that get you down if you can help it. It'll all *feel* natural. And if they've done a good job, you'll have your own totality and opinions and a head full of ideas you might even be able to convince yourself are your own.

"Right now, I need you, Miranda Swami. We'll do this together, overcome *this*, and then deal with that. One problem at a time. One arc, one central conflict; save the rest for book two."

Sensing her exhaustion, Cindi abruptly offers to take Miranda to her room, with Linda pulling up the trio's rear. The cave system, past the great hall, opens into a sequence of narrow, ornately decorated hallways, covered floor to stalactite-tiled-top with red and gold and lacy accents, the rugs and tapestries hella baroque, and ditto all the shelves holding Grecian urns, so intricately designed Keats would have a stroke trying to wax poetic about them. She tries and fails to keep from making eye contact with the dozens of portraits hanging about the walls, the high lords and ladies (presumably of the demon-slaying variety) looking generally snooty and disapproving; Miranda wonders if they change their faces depending who walks by. That'd be a fun, imaginative detail! The long, uncut rug underneath her feet appears, like the tapestries in the hall, to tell a lengthy, textile story of some hero's journey, though Miranda in not wanting to trip only looks down every couple seconds. Here the hooded hero wades through a river; here they've let their long locks out from under their hat and, well look at that, it's a woman! Can't you see the circular curves on her chest?

"Ya'll are really big into your prophecies, aren't you?"

"It's nice to be told what you're going to do…who you're going to be," Cindi says, looking back at Miranda with a tall smile. "It's hard to have all these choices before you. It was hard for me. It's always been hard for me."

They come to another fork in the hallway. To the left, an unfurnished alcove guarded by a thick wooden door, all strong oak and wrought-iron and requiring a serious siege vehicle to ram through. To the right, an equally bare stretch of hallway, under an abbreviated ceiling, with a sequence of blasé, balsa-wood openings every few feet, the barest and basest of doors. Cindi takes Miranda's shoulder and urges her on. "Second on the left, if you please."

The "room," lit up by torch-light, is scarcely more than a hole in the wall. A stone slab sticking horizontally out is the room's only furniture, a sleeping arrangement made tolerable by a memory-foam mattress-topper thoughtfully laid over it. There's no obvious bathroom in the tiny space, although there is a small ledge where Miranda can and does place her things. Perhaps, should she need to pee in the middle of the night, a toilet will appear in some sudden moonlight. Or she can squat over a hole leading down to hell. That'll show the demons below.

A glistening chamber-pot in the corner of the room portends a much lamer fate however.

Cindi leaves her to sleep, a sleep that arrives in short bursts, leaving always before it will envelop her totally. Like in the Program, there are no windows in this underground sanctum. Besides the torch burning and crackling on the wall, there is only darkness, only silence, the totality of it punctuated by far-off footsteps and the tiny canoodling of rats, hopefully in the next room over.

Hours later (probably), right when she's finally gotten to sleep, Miranda is quite literally shaken awake. Her still-strained eyes at this uncertain time are only half-open, but nevertheless recognize the tall wisp of Cindi standing over her, breathing real close, the burning torches coloring her face like an oil-painting. Miranda's abruptly-awoken brain cannot quite comprehend A) why this woman is standing over her, or B) where she even is right now, let alone all the other questions and comments that come with sudden consciousness in an unfamiliar place. But Cindi is smiling and obviously excited and says in a flurry, "Hey, come on, you have to get up. We have to go see something!"

She grabs Miranda by the hand, very literally pulling her out of bed and out of the room. This cat's got kitten energy. It's fortunate Miranda slept in her clothes, as it doesn't seem Cindi is very concerned with her companion's possible indecency. Cindi, of course, is immaculate. It's one of life's great mysteries (and well-documented as such) how she gets her hair to wave as gently as it does, especially in as dingy and dry a place as this. Maybe her room is nicer. The chosen one's digs probably have a private bathroom and walk-in closet. Maybe there's a *Versace* outlet somewhere down in these tunnels.

Soon Miranda is saying something about coffee, about *god my stomach is rumbling*, but is ignored and ignored again. Finally, she shuts up. Cindi is either too preoccupied for conversation, or too tongue-tied by the threat of it. The thick silence lasts until the two reach the great hall, where, in a line by the resurrected rock wall, four men in yellow robes stand at proper attention, each with a specific facial signifier that identifies them from their compatriots.

There stands Scar and there Eyepatch, Gold Tooth and Hook Nose, all utterly disinterested in Miranda, but boy howdy, do they fall *right* to one knee–and with such fervor! — at the approach of their God-queen, Cindi Lapenschtall.

"They're off to put Phase One of our master plan into effect," Cindi starts explaining. "Capturing one of the Bananas and bringing it back here is of prime importance. A difficult task but necessary, and not our first time at it. We'll be broadcasting everything from a command center within these caves. You may rise," she says, and the men do indeed rise. "Go," she commands them, and they obey, leaving through the again-busted cave wall. The hungry blue glow of the far-off runes soon swallows the men clean up. The rock, understanding its place in this whole thing, builds itself back into a wall.

"Oh shit, so you were serious about all this?"

From a shadowy corner unseen, Linda makes a snickering sound. Surprised, Miranda turns to face her, and is surprised further still to find the woman smiling, a kind smile, one Miranda returns.

"Oh yes. Serious as a stroke. Come on, now you're up, I want to show you something else." Cindi says. "Linda will stay here and keep guard."

Linda nods slightly, brushing her robe aside as she turns, exposing the great silver broadsword hidden beneath her robes. At this reveal, she looks at Miranda and winks. For the first time, Miranda thinks *hey, maybe I could get used to this place.*

Poor girl, she won't have much of a chance to.

"Are you sure I'm allowed in there?" Miranda asks, hesitating before another doorway, this one somehow more bedazzling than the others. A door made of pure gold, as shimmery and heart-stopping as you might imagine so much precious metal might be. It has no handle, no accents, is simply a mesmerizing slab of solid wealth placed carefully in between some stone. And it takes Miranda's breath away.

"As long as you are pure of heart and pious of mind."

"Well…hopefully my good looks will be enough."

The door gives way with a slight push. In fact, Cindi opens it with only her index finger, indulging in the serious strength her extremities seem to command.

A gorgeous door, and behind it, a room to match. Mammoth. That's a good word to describe it. A truly titanic hole in the Earth big as a basketball arena, one that doesn't seem even possible congruent with the cave system's otherwise understood dimensions. Maybe she actually is in another world. Immaculately wood-paneled, and with bulging bookshelves rising up from floor to ceiling, this Library of Legend must be home to millions of tomes. Are those clouds all the way up there? And if you should require a selection from up in the stratosphere, fear not. Skyscraping ladders on monster truck wheels lay periodically the shelves, like tests of courage, though a sign by each cautions users to wear a harness, for the house isn't apparently liable for on-site accidents.

"All the world's literature not fit for the common man," Cindi says in absent-minded admiration, hands on her hips. "Too much power is in these pages for the average, reticent human. Answers and secrets galore, unauthorized biographies of history's *intelligencia* and co pendiums of all the world's shadow beasts. Summoning rituals and Dionysian dances; I've barely scratched the surface of what's here, or so I've been told. This whole complex, all of these caves, it was all built off of this, the Library."

"So the Library *preceded* all of this?" Miranda asks, incredulously scanning the spines of anything at nearby eye-level. Their titles are in Wing-Ding (or look like it), and when she runs her finger over their exposed mid-sections, a strange gossamer residue sticks to her skin.

"A remnant of some old civilization, an old branch of an organization like ours. People have been interested in creating a compendium of the occult as long as there has been occult. My predecessors found it hundreds of years ago, but some of these books are eyewitness catalogues of civilizations older and more advanced than anything else on record. Here, watch this."

Cindi takes a few steps forward to a lamp-lit reading podium atop which a dense book of runes sits open. "Happened to leave this open last night," she says, flipping the pages for a few moments, lost in thought, eventually letting forth an "Ahah!" as she finds what she was after. Cindi begin moving her hands tepidly through the air, as if she's trying to remember a past life as an orchestra conductor. Small, semi-silent words sneak forth from her lips. A few moments of this, of

Miranda looking on nervously, and Cindi brings her hands together in a thunderous, reverberatory clap. The air goes freezing cold, and atop the spell-book forms a black-and-purple portal about Chihuahua-wide. Miranda hugs herself tight, her teeth chattering, watching in awe and horror as something completely, ridiculously, parodically fantastic happens before her eyes. The portal shakes and churns and passes through it, like an interdimensional kidney-stone, three action-figure-sized skeletons, all in mariachi regalia, with a guitar, trumpet, and tambourine respectively.

"Eee-hee-hee!" Cindi yelps, jumping up and down, clapping in excitement. "I did it! I did it!"

As the skeletons play a little Mexican marching tune, Miranda leans against the nearest wall, fanning herself with a free hand and slowly turning purple. Cindi does a little jig, for the skeletons' sakes, until their finish their song. Cindi showers the bowing band with applause. Again, the portal burbles and burps, making a show of its incontinence before swallowing up the songsters. The portal closes, taking the cold with it, belching a wave of warm, swampy air into the Library. Cindi turns back to her audience.

To her dismay, however, Miranda isn't pepped-up and excited by the little show of magic, but is shaking, looking pale, lips going indigo, eyes glazed a bit over, the teeth inside that closed mouth of hers finding and biting the nearest possible clump of gums.

"I really can't do this," Miranda says suddenly, quietly. "I don't want to do this. Why did you bring me here? Why are you making me see all of this?"

"Oh, come on! That was supposed to be *fun*!" In awaiting a response, or at least a smirk, Cindi seems to realize the gravity of what Miranda is struggling with. "It gets easier," Cindi says at last, "but I know it's a shock at first. Tears down everything you think you know and forces you to build it back up into something new."

"This isn't what I wanted for myself. Getting mixed up in all of this…I didn't know it was going to be so —"

"So, what? Extraordinary? Fantastic? Otherworldly? Come on! Miranda! This is an adventure! And it's not *that* bad. You weren't going to sit behind that screen all your life, were you? Were you really going to paint away your days? Get a Graphic Design degree? Go work for a start-up? You were never meant for that. Think of this as, like, going to Thailand! It's a culture shock at first, that's all: the food is weird, the language is incomprehensible, but then you learn how to say 'Hi' and 'where's the bathroom?' and it gets better. This is normal. What you're feeling is normal. Pretty mountains, tuk-tuks. You get used to it. It will settle into normalcy. Life always becomes itself. Everywhere, under any circumstance."

"Did you *come* here," Miranda asks, staring deeply into Cindi's eyes, those opal eyes with their long, mascara-blackened lashes, "or did they bring you here?"

Cindi exhales what seems like a week's worth of air. "Miranda, can I be honest with you?"

"If you think I can handle it, sure."

Cindi smiles sadly, knocking her knuckles against a near bookshelf. "I don't mean to be presumptuous, but how much do you know of my life story?"

"Well enough. I've read the *Vogue* piece. A few times. Many times. Start with whatever I wouldn't know."

"Well, let's see, let's see. After I started transitioning, there was an assault, and then another assault in college, and then a third rather grisly one outside of a bar in St. Louis, where I was living at the time. After the third, I knew if I didn't get above *that* world, I was looking at a short life. You know the statistics, I assume. I needed to become untouchable. So, I started the fund with money from a second mortgage, and compounded that with a small inheritance my Aunt Shelly left when she passed. I built it slowly, but, anyways, all of that is well and good and documented, and if you were interested further, I could craft you a pretty compelling reading list. The more esoteric thing I'm getting at is I always felt there was some*thing* watching out for me, guiding me, some force, some power, and at the time I called it God. Ever since I started building a staircase out of the shit that was my life, it seemed like the world was being manipulated for my benefit. Big gains when everyone else was failing. And I mean *everyone*. Interest from all over the place; people shoving their money in my face. That's true! That actually happened! I was always reluctant to think that 'God' was actually looking out for me, but I knew there was more than sheer happenstance at my sails.

"And for the record, I'm not devaluing what I did. I *literally* built my fortune from nothing, from word-of-mouth, from little bits of wealth and trust here and there, hiring one employee at a time. I did that. I pulled myself up into a better life."

"But?"

"But…I caution you to suspend your disbelief."

Carefully, Miranda says, "I'm pretty open to new information at this point."

"Yes, I know. There's no easy way to say this, so I'll just say it: I met the one who claimed to have been manipulating things. And honestly, what he said all checked out. All the suspicion, the apprehension, the feeling that I was taking advantage, not of God, but of some dark force…

"I was approached by the Devil, Miranda Swami. The God-Damned Devil." Cindi says his name with hard, furtive eyes and a mouth wholly uninterested in cracking any knowing, half-disbelieving smile. It remains taut, hard, discomfiting. "I met the Devil, and he told me it was *he* who had been there for me, had been looking out for me, had taken a special interest in me, and me alone. He said — this is what he said — he said he wanted to give me a platform, so I could make positive change in my community, in the world, wanted to make me so famous and powerful it would normalize everything that I am, my transition and my gender and my color, on a world stage. He said he had that power; he said he could make all of my dreams a reality. All my *other* dreams. That's a direct quote. 'My *other* dreams.' He said he was interested in *justice*. In reparations. And all I had to do was sign away my soul. He said he'd do the rest."

"Yeesh." What else *can* you say after someone admits to selling their soul?

"Yeesh, is right! But think! Think, Miranda Swami! It was giving *my* soul, *my* little life, *my* own eternal whatever in exchange for the uplifting of my entire community. All of my communities! It was a selfless act, I swear. It wasn't ever about me, even for a moment. And that doesn't make me a saint, and it doesn't make me worthy of reverence, it's just a fact. But that was his fatal miscalculation. It made all the difference.

"Now, I don't pretend to understand the politics of soul-selling, but something about that selflessness, in hindsight, must have, if what I've been told is true, negated part of the deal. Because there I was, CEO of *Big Banana*, with all of my other dreams a reality, but for some reason I wasn't the soulless, easily-manipulatable monster they needed me to be. Or the one they thought I would eventually become. I learned from some well-calculated eavesdropping that I was an almost-Biblical-level disappointment. When I realized that things were going to go south for me and fast, I started investing in the infrastructure of the Program, the one I used to find you. And when I caught wind that my death wasn't just being discussed, but was imminent, I executed my plan. I made a big public spectacle — at your show — and then disappeared outright.

"My friends here found me soon after. They won what was essentially a race between them and *Big Banana's* bloodhounds to sniff me out. That was not part of my plan, but it was welcome nonetheless. That was my second act break. They brought me here and installed me with the technology and confidence I needed, got me up-to-date on all the necessary prophecies, had me take an oath or two, and then, well, then I sent you a text. You've been a part of the rest."

Miranda sits in silence for a while, awaiting the arrival of a witty response. And then it comes to her. "Pretty cool you can get out of a deal with the Devil on a technicality."

That fact stays with Miranda for days, mostly solitary days, as Cindi's time is spent dealing with some snafu in her otherwise fool-proof plan to topple the world's fastest-growing company. A technicality. A bloody technicality. That is just *classic* morality for you. Somewhere Nietzsche's ghost howls with laughter.

While Cindi is off in other, members-only rooms of the underground sanctum, Miranda spends her time in the Library, tracking down the few books written in comprehensible English and having a hard-enough time deciphering their contents.

If what she reads is to be believed, Abraham Lincoln had a twin brother he struck down in childhood like Cain did Abel, Marilyn Monroe and JFK were reincarnations of two eternally-spawning soulmates (who may or may not now inhabit two elderly rhinoceroses in the Atlanta Zoo), the War in Korea was fought in actuality over a space-stone upon which a tiny, hyper-advanced civilization lives to this day, and horses in the first few centuries B.C. could be coaxed into a very mangled, slow but still understandable version of human speech. That characteristic was bred out successfully by the early French. The world around her, it seems, has been more subjectively set down than she had appreciated. Salinger wrote eight otherwise-lost sequels to *Catcher in the Rye* discussing the other members of the grain-based baseball team, and Virginia Woolf's lost notes detail how, against the advice of close confidantes, she spent the last decades of her life researching a secret Spanish treasure hidden somewhere in the Sierra Nevada. Some say she hid a codex leading to the bounty in later publications of *To the Lighthouse*.

Two nights before Miranda is to be in New York for the announcement, Cindi enters the Library, coming upon Miranda suspended in a make-shift hammock, reading about how the pre-Reformation Catholic Church drove faeiries out of Great Britain in the years after Columbus set for America. Riveting stuff. Actually makes a lot of sense.

"I have to leave," Cindi tells her.

"So soon? Is everything okay?" Miranda asks.

"That's what I'm off to find out," Cindi responds, looking very regally into the middle-distance. "When it's time to take you back into the city, Linda will come for you. Best of luck, Miranda Swami. I'm sorry to skedaddle so unceremoniously. Until we meet again."

Cindi extends her long fingers for a shake, and her grasping of Miranda's hand is like wrapping it in a soft, luscious blanket. Miranda feels tears in her eyes, tears from nowhere, about nothing, but tears nonetheless. Perhaps her tear ducts understand more of her hopes than she does. After all, they might've been lovers. Cindi said it was possible. Cindi said.

They share a longing look, a direct plea sent from one pair of eyes into the other's, both woman feeling briefly all the infinite other *thems* turning and pushing within themselves, ones in just slightly askew situations with just slightly askew emotions and outcomes, before the electric spell is broken. Cindi turns quickly to leave.

"Wait!" Miranda calls. "I keep forgetting to ask: why did you pretend to be Lakshmi?"

"What?"

"In the Program. I met someone who was impersonating my friend Eric Lakshmi. That *was* you, right?"

Cindi thinks for a moment. "I'm sorry, I don't know what you're talking about. The nature of the Program is that, within, it's very difficult to track people down. I didn't know where you were until you showed up on my doorstep. And just in time, might I add."

"Interesting. Cool."

"Until we meet again, Miranda Swami. It's been very nice being so close to you. I wish you the best of luck if/when we take our rightful place as foes."

"Likewise, I guess."

In her room, Miranda is suddenly crept upon by two old friends. Depression and Anxiety take her into a series of darkness-and-delirium induced daydreams. You've had this happen to you, too, I'm sure. In places of certain special darkness, where time ceases to move in any calculable way, the machinations of your mind seek to fill the nothingness with sensation, intense enough at times to produce trancelike-visions. And in a place of such magic and power, no less, those kinds of visions are worth something immense.

In her head, a simple train of thought about Fake-Lakshmi's identity leads her subconscious mind, dead-tired and already sick of the sudden solitude, to create before her a familiar desert of red and beige and sandstone. Half-asleep somewhat, but more like she's astral-walking, Miranda sees herself climbing to the top of a huge red-stone pillar jutting straight up out of the Earth. She ascends a winding path around the spire's edge until she's standing at the very top, balancing on one sturdily-planted foot, looking out as the planet below her exposes its curvature. Dotting the far-off land are all the world's nation-states, scribbled over by their bold-faced names, each with well-defined black borders. Within every plot is, say, a towering mountain covered in poplar fur or a rainforest milieu with a lemur head poking around, a distillation of each area into its sexiest geographic feature.

O'er yonder is a burbling, bubbling volcano. Two polar bears frolic in the snow down south.

But in the faraway distance, a gargantuan black cloud slowly obscures the lands underneath it. The cloud seems to shake with laughter as it sends enormous yellow thunderbolts down to the Earth, incinerating every nation they strike. *Crash-bang-zap-boom*, and a mountain range is blown to snow-capped smithereens. *Crash-kaboom-crunch-krinkle*, and a field of poppy flowers turns to cinders.

The lightning continues floating forward, quicker and more severe in its manner as it does, and while Miranda wants to run, she can't seem to move her legs. Not a great time for dream logic to kick in. She looks down, focusing her will into movement, directing all her energy into the simple art of stepping. But when she finally does gain a little control over her leaden limbs, it matters not. The ramp she followed up here has disappeared. She's trapped atop the spire.

When she looks up from her shoe-laces, it's to come face-to-face with bad news. The storm cloud is upon her. It has left so much destruction in its wake, the world appears nothing more than a blackened mass of burnt toast and red-hot ash. With the thundercloud so close, Miranda can make out its details. It's taken the shape of a head and face.

Which wouldn't be that terrifying excepts it's Cindi's head and Cindi's face. And when Cloud Cindi opens her mouth, things are destroyed underneath her. The cloud-head-of-Cindi-Lapenschtall comes close, hangs over Miranda, and opens wide, saying *aaaaaahhhhhh...*

A violent barrage of lightning rains down upon her, shocking the world, flooding it with bright, electric-blue light. Yellow and red from instant fires, and Miranda can't open her eyes with all the smoke.

There's coughing and so much dust but still the lightning rains down, still it must destroy, still it desires a further-flung world turned to dust.

And then nothing. It all stops. The air lightens, and the slick bright of a sunlit day washes over Miranda's shut-tight eyes.

Opening them, she finds herself still somehow standing. The world below her smolders, but she is literally above all that. The spire was somehow unperturbed by the rumbling doom. The cloud has dissipated, and the sky is a beautiful robin's egg blue. Two sing-song swallows soar above her, and then someone coughs.

Miranda looks over and almost dies of shock. A human-sized Banana, twisting devil's tail behind it and two yellow wings squelched tight against its body, sits next to her, its legs hanging off the edge of the spire, looking out at the world. It clears its throat, removes its derby hat as if in reverence.

"Say, that was a close one, wasn't it, kid?" The Banana says this, looks up at her, seems to contort its face halfway between a grimace and a scowl, and as it does so, the hallucination vanishes.

Miranda wakes with a sudden jolt and a deep intake of breath. She is, in fact, panting. And someone has refreshed the torch upon her wall. Her door, she sees, is cracked open, and after taking stock of her body, ensuring it is currently safe, she stands upright, following the leaking light into the hallway. Stoic as a statue, Linda waits for her, in normal-person clothes, a smart mix of blouse and blue pants, of flats and a fleece.

"You've been asleep for two days" Linda says, which can't possibly be true. "It's time."

In a few minutes, Miranda will say goodbye to these caverns forever, heading out into early morning sunshine with un-brushed teeth and uncombed hair, letting fresh sunlight kiss her gently on the cheek, the soft shine of a known world.

Within the half hour, she will be blindfolded in the back of an Escalade en route to further civilization.

By 11:30, she'll be on a train for New York City, an unlocked and untraceable phone in her pocket, purchased for her with plenty of 4G by some fine folks that slay demons and live in caves. By 4PM today, the world will cease to show its usual face, will act with unusual candor, will display different colors.

A New World and a New York await. Miranda hopes she'll be brave enough to face them, limber enough to enter them both at once.

Having imagined it a hundred-thousand times, Miranda has a rather strong preconceived notion about what exactly will happen when Gwami the Seer opens her eyes after such a long sleep. The accounts will reactivate, and as if by celestial snap, the world will affect a golden hue. A shockwave will burst forth from the epicenter of the event, a ripple in space-time causing momentary migraines in any passerby as it shoots outward, and those affected will just *know*, the information silently but successfully shared, that Gwami the Seer has returned to life. It will be spoken of in hushed tones by teenagers and then louder by the ten o'clock primetime anchors. It'll be national news within an hour.

Only it doesn't happen anything like that.

Shoulder to shoulder, jostling back and forth with all sorts of yellow-clad zealots, Miranda can't keep her fingers in precise enough position to accept all the necessary terms and conditions let alone input all the necessary passwords. And some of them are *intense*. Digits, symbols, ancient hieroglyphics, emojis, there is no price too high for security. Only right now, she's paying it.

Someone's elbow hits her hand hard and forces a sequence of renegade *3's* onto the screen. People are animals. People are savages. If only she could've done this before she joined their march, but alas, that would've been impossible.

Reviving Gwami the Seer earlier might have set off alarms, would have notified any interested parties that Gwami was transmitting again, but though a new device, one located right here in New York City. If Cindi is right and *Big Banana* does have everyone in their pockets, that subtle information alone might have given them an opportunity to mobile forces against her. With Cindi (and, you know, the world) counting on her, Miranda couldn't take the risk. But since the timer on the Statler Building is in its final hour, she's betting the company has neither extra time nor energy, fully focused on ensuring the unabated success of this, *Big Banana's Big Day*.

And if she were to do it outside of this enormous mass of humanity, one that has already accepted Miranda into its girth, they might be able to pinpoint her location still, send an assassin or satellite laser to take out the lone human occupying the certain slat of space from whence the resurrection occurred.

She's cutting it close time-wise, she knows, and she's surrounded on all sides by folks who probably won't like what it is she's plotting right now, but these are small sacrifices to be made *en route* to a world *sans* bananas. And so, she types away.

The great horde's ebullient brand loyalty more than makes up for the lack of bananas Miranda has experienced in these last few blissful weeks. Like football fans at a tailgate, the downtown marchers wear their college allegiance on their sleeves, literally. The streets are a swarming sea of tall banana hats and yellow vests yellow jeans yellow shoes yellow blinking sunglasses with LED bananas dancing around the lenses. Banana ice freezing the more lucrative necks, banana ice sold by yellow trucks with ouroboros lines snaking around their exteriors.

This is the spirit of the *Bash* extended outward. It is a solar system of bananas. Manhattan, at least the southern half of it, has become *Big Banana's* private island, private playground, private prison. *Hmm*, she thinks, *those are all pretty damn good metaphors*.

Ducking off into a side street and pressing herself close to the wall, Miranda quickly and quietly sends small defibrillator shocks into Gwami's lifeless online body. Her Instagram, her Twitter, her Tumblr, the entire connected limbic system of Gwami the Seer begins to jerk, twitching across the enormous internet expanse. As each reloading screen sends her to a new-but-oh-so-familiar timeline, Miranda looks up, awaiting the world's changing color, seeing if the people passing by start reaching into their bags for Advil.

But it doesn't, and they don't.

And maybe that's because — boy oh boy — her follower count has *suffered*. While it was obviously inconceivable to reach Gwami's full former followers count count right from the start, neither she nor Cindi could have imagined the actually awful effects of her extended inactivity. It's *bad*. She has maybe a 20th of the followers she claimed at her height. Even that number is optimistic. And judging by the profile names and activity logs of those who've stuck around, most of them are either unmanned bots or one-off Twitters some teenager made for, like, their dad, pre-stocked with all the "necessary" follows. This is bad, bad because the entirety of the plan rested on enough people hearing that Gwami had returned, cautiously craning their necks to see what she was up to and, lo and behold, she's got a live stream going? Maybe I better tune in, you know, to engage with "the culture," a culture that very quickly and forgivingly latches on to their old, familiar teet. But this, this will not do.

Makes sense, though. When you're inactive, after all, you're boring, and while general following habits are highly-individualized, there is one constant between all users: nobody follows boring shit. Boring old inactive Gwami hasn't been moving the cultural needle, wasn't provoking or prodding or contributing to the wave; she was just sitting there, dead as a morgue stiff, turning blue and putrid and puffy. Nobody wants to look at that.

Thus, Gwami the Seer is revived with only the most dedicated (or least aware) followers as witnesses.

Thus, the mob joining her downtown jaunt towards the *Bash en* larger and larger *masse* probably have little idea Gwami has returned to save them. Miranda has an inkling that, no matter how long she waits, the the world will contentedly keep its current coloration. The frolicking folks around her do not seem dazed nor now knowing nor armed with strange new certainty. Nothing's changed. *Big Banana* business as usual.

The good news, however, is there's a certain *palpability* in the air, a general expectation of coming content that means people will *all* be armed with their phones, and *all day*. Thank *Big Banana* for that, for this small part in their own sabotage. Word will travel quickly. All these people with their phones, and the crazy part is that nothing's even been officially announced yet, it's just that the countdown timer is ticking closer and closer to *00:00:00* after having spent weeks filled with more well-defined integers. The vague promise of *something* is apparently all it took to get these fine New Yorkers off their asses and into their finest, yellowest clothes, enough to get them marching down the streets of Manhattan Island on a windy autumn day, preferring a nice walk in the breeze to the mobbed subways below.

Although she would love nothing more than to remain locked-in to her own phone, watching her follower count slowly rise the way she used to, watching the world slowly come to realize that there's a Lady Lazarus in their midst, Miranda feels she has no choice but to shut the phone off for now, sucking the life from the thing with a smooth two-button press. There will be no tracking today, or at least not right this second. She posts an innocuous *"hey, is this thing on?"* out into the world, and then it's off for real this time. The dopamine desire for likes drains from her brain, and Miranda, hands stuffed in pockets, shuffles along with the rest of the crowd.

It will remain unbeknownst to her until after this whole thing is over (but not long after) that it didn't take long at all for *Gwami's Resurrection* and *Big Banana's Mystery Alarm Clock* to claim their rightful places as dueling top stories, the two trading blows at the tops of tabloid sites. The world tunes in to this clash of the titans; the primetime anchors order their PA's to update the teleprompter ("Yes, Gavin, right the fuck now!").

Miranda, meanwhile, is just doing her best not to be trampled.

The crowds, which were already hard to move through or breathe within, suddenly start flooding in from up out of the sewer grates and the subway stations, fully gagging the sidewalks. When the mere walkways are unable to contain their girth, they create a traffic nightmare in the streets. And this is a dangerous crowd, pulled along indiscriminately by its own mass. A cracked skull underneath their yellow Yeezys would feel like nothing more than a pavement bump; even if they had the decency to look back on what they'd just flattened, the swarm would have already covered it up. The only option is to stay moving, eyes up and forward.

Gazing upon a veritable sea of yellow, Miranda fears her utter lack of spirit might invite violence.

The crowd:

bedecked in so much yellow you might think they grow such threads as leopards grow spotted coats, and with the frenzy that comes with deindividuation.

She, Miranda Swami:

wearing, you know, normal people clothes, jeans and shit, with a spindly black scarf over her dainty neck.

The crowd:

bananas.

Miranda Swami:

decidedly not.

An easy enough fix: Miranda throws fifty dollars into the hands of the nearest pushcart operator and says, "Gimme all I can get for this."

To her torso:

a t-shirt with an arrow pointed up to her face, and scrawled in blocky yellow writing, *Going Bananas Right Now.*

To her domepiece:

a trucker hat bedecked in Andy Warhol's famous *Velvet Underground* bananas, almost certainly reproduced without permission.

To her neck and arms:

plastic-gold links shaped like bananas. If she shakes herself around, she jingles.

At an adjacent *Banana Republic* (who've really leaned into the trend), Miranda ditches her dark jeans for bright yellow sweatpants and her black flats for neon yellow, steel-toed boots. Prepared, she is, to kick some teeth in with flair. She comes out of the store looking as much a fanatic as the rest. Sliding some banana-shaped glasses over her eyes, Miranda goes full incognito. Wow, what a powerful feeling, this being completely disguised, completely at ease, completely a part of the trend.

O God, O Christ, it feels good to be a part of something so big... even if it's only a ruse. With renewed confidence, she dips into and out of empty pockets within the crowd. She stops to greet a policeman. Someone lets their unleashed dog come lick her hand. O strange new world, that has such people in it.

Around her, the hundred-thousand voices speaking over each other blend into a single continuous, cacophonous yelp. Mixed up in the smattered sounds are police sirens, and the first hint that she has arrived at the *Bash* proper are the spinning yellow lights of the smoothly ululating police cruisers around its circumference. Yellow lights? Come on. So on the nose. No idea how they convinced the city to oblige that one, *or* the yellow police barricades, the yellow license plates, the yellow paint splatters dotted deliberately on the otherwise manicured sidewalks. Very un-NYPD. Ditto the yellow helmets on the officers, ditto their waving, yellow, metal-detecting batons. All the better to defend the innocent with, my dear.

The mass of bodies is soon squished into a straight line, into a dozen straight lines, the lot of them becoming a hydra's mass of snake necks making their way slowly into metal-detecting lanes. Policepeople in obfuscating visors bark orders through megaphones, but with all the noise and all the voices, it sounds like they're just barking, grunting. Miranda gets shoved from the back and shoved again, is nearly crushed between a couple of overweight gentlemen with their phones up, one with a child on his shoulders.

At the front of the line, a masked militiaman, — neon-yellow vested and with a *Here-to-Help* badge declaring their commitment to the crowd's safety —, waves over her with a baton. When it begins beeping down by her phone-carrying pocket, as it does with everyone, Miranda's insides start to freak out, and she can feel the coming on of an anxiety attack. But there's no anxiety at the *Bash*. There are no bad feeling in the *Bash*. Those things have been focus-group-tested away. She's waved through the gates.

A few steps inside, and a clown hands Miranda an ice cream cone, then goes cartwheeling off to find some new girl in need of a sweet treat. Miranda is honestly too entranced to really appreciate the gesture.

There's some screaming and carrying on from out in the crowd behind her, and if Miranda were to look back to the entrance, she'd see that all of the lanes into the *Bash* have been unceremoniously closed off, that the massive gathering of people who lollygagged a few moments more than she are being denied entrance, being told that the *Bash* is at capacity, being told to come back another day. Judging from the shouts and snarls, humanity out there is breaking down, threatening to dissolve into a full-fledged animal riot. People really love their bananas.

But she doesn't turn around. She can't. Because after hearing so much about it, seeing it so many times from afar, hating it so senselessly for so long, after sweating and swearing and creeping towards it all day in the crevices between taller and fatter and more fanatical folks, Miranda is finally experiencing the *Bash*.

The *Bash* is creativity as its most pointless: meandering, and, thus, brilliant. It is creativity untethered to the real — it exists a world away from the practical, from mortgages, paperbacks and jury duty, from the structured and deliberate thought of the unwealthy. Creativity is almost always a matter of wealth, as wealth allows for free imagination unrelated to the rote requirements of survival. You might have all the world's poetry pushing up through your pores, but if you spend 18 hours a day working two jobs and the other six blustering through sleep, it will matter not. The *Bash* is an imagination let loose and then manifested via means. It is the crossbred offspring of enviable affluence and maddening vision.

The five square blocks that comprise its area swell with the *Totality of Banana*. It overtakes Miranda like a sudden fever. The crowd parts as if to let her experience it all at once. Food carts sell frozen bananas in cups or cones while dwarfs in banana costumes get juggled like bowling pins by beefy circus performers on stilts. There are costumes upon costumes and custom banana peel bracelets woven by wrinkled Guatemalan transplants in paint-splattered smocks. Banana earrings and belts and home décor all for sale at everyday low prices, and a yellow, plug-in Toyota encircled by velvet ropes. MC's with yellow hair lead street-corner charges in the *Cha-Cha* and *Electric Slides*. Somebody hands her a balloon; someone hands her a pamphlet on agricultural regulation. Fire dancers and an exhibition in a heated tent called "Musaceae from Around the World." All the streets painted yellow and ditto all the faces of the children. A caged lion lazes in human clothes, or, wait, is it a caged man covered in fur? Things appear and disappear as if in a delirium, exposed and swallowed up by the pulsating, swirling crowd as they run and jog and skip hither and thither. The fever dream continues, here revealing a trio of magicians pulling bananas out of any passing handbag, and there someone in a yellow body-suit is scaling a building with suction-cup hands. The encircling skyscrapers are all covered in anthropomorphic banana graffiti six-or-seven stories-high. If this is a nightmare, it is a particularly xanthaphobian one. And it's all perfectly primed for the posting.

Click clik click click. Flash flash flash click.

Some kids pass around an illicit flask. Someone ignores the No-Smoking signs. A gaggle of too-human policemen apply their visors, blocking their eyes.

Even if you were completely taken by the desultory nonsense blitz-krieging your senses, as Miranda is, it'd still be impossible not to notice the gratuitous police presence. I mean, there is law enforcement *everywhere*. So many cops; the bored beat walkers without purpose indulge in the food stalls while their ranking officers wear aviators and lean angrily upon their car windows. That is to say, even those with authority seem unsure of their role, such is the sheer glut of them. And all in yellow. Is this normal for the *Bash*? Even in an omnithreatening world, this seems redundant.

Mixed-in with the throng of law enforcement proper are a bevy of less intense, yellow-vested folks, like who manned the metal detectors, motorcycle-masked and militia-like, dragging along dogs trained to grow feverish at a stray sniff of explosives or ecstasy. Even this many years later, the phantasm of 9/11 hangs over any public gathering, a phantasm made more solid by Parkland, by Newtown, by Las Vegas. Madmen don't need a grand gesture to leave a mark anymore, just a doorman caught unawares and an open window somewhere far, far away. Makes all this hyper-local security seem superfluous. Surely, some should be setting a perimeter, locking down every one of the 686 windows peering down upon the *Bash*. Perhaps they are.

There used to be such strength in numbers, now there's just vulnerability.

Maybe they know she's here.

Someone walks past smoking an illicit joint. The dogs curiously decline to notice. A man drops his turkey-leg and snickers at himself. A woman get ketchup on her Mink and howls. Somewhere, church bells ring.

Overcome by stimuli, Miranda is hardly aware of her movement, or that she's part of a phenomenon, but mindlessly follows the crowd forward, pushing past the slower sorts, ducking under fat arms and sneaking past wobbly children as her subconscious leads her and everyone else forward.

Somewhere on the way she gets a whiff of expensive men's cologne. And this has two profound effects.

1) It reminds her that nearby, probably hyperventilating into a paper bag, is Caleb, her blood-relative and once-confidante, enjoying his final moments before becoming the most famous person in the world. Does *he* know she's here? Does he know *she's* here to watch his life's work be destroyed? Does he know that she'll be the instrument of his destruction, the way he was the instrument of hers?

It is to be justice, at long last.

And

2) Miranda realizes how quiet everything has become. That, and everyone's stopped moving.

The whole crowd has just stopped. Everything has stopped. The police sirens and the barking, sniffing dogs, all of it observing an impromptu moment of silence. Miranda looks around her, at all the individuals, big and small, short and tall, dressed for summer and fall, but catches nary a stray eye. They're all looking down at their phones. Miranda alone gazes up to the sky, to the cobalt cap of the Statler-Abramson Building, to a countdown timer which no longer displays numbers, but displays instead a web-address.

Some people in the crowd begin whimpering. A man takes his presumed wife into his arms and begins kissing her forehead, tears of joy streaming down both their faces. Miranda — fuck it — bites, flips a switch and imbues her phone again with computing power, revealing herself to the world, sure, but the temptation to visit *www. BananaTime.com* is too much.

It's only a yellow background and a message in Impact. **TODAY IS A VERY IMPORTANT DAY**, it reads, **AND WE'RE SO EXCITED TO SHARE OUR BIG NEWS WITH YOU. TO EVERYONE AT THE BASH, WE WANT TO THANK YOU FOR YOUR LOVE, YOUR SUPPORT, AND YOUR PRESENCE IN SUCH A TRYING TIME. WE AT BIG BANANA LOVE YOU TOO! WE WANT TO SHOW YOU JUST HOW MUCH. COME JOIN US AT ZUCCOTTI PARK (FOLLOW THE SIGNS) TO BE A PART OF OUR NEXT CHAPTER.**

FOR THE REST OF YOU OUTSIDE THE BASH, DON'T WORRY, WE LOVE YOU TOO! TUNE IN AT 4PM TO OUR BIG BANANA LIVE STREAM AS WE UNVEIL TO THE WORLD OUR NEXT C-E-O.

EXCLAMATION POINT.

(WE'RE FREAKING OUT TOO). (sic).

The people in the crowd, those that aren't debilitated by emotion, look around at each other, desperate to make knowing eye contact with everyone else lucky enough to have shown their brand allegiance early enough and on the right day. Smiles of *we did it*, and *how great is this?* pop up on bearded and bandaged and bespectacled faces. The rigorous part is over, all that love and lust for the brand, and here is its reward. An event of wild geopolitical importance will be happening *here*, *now*, for a teeny-tiny audience. They were doing it all for some until-then unknown incentive, but now that it's been revealed to be bragging rights, they can relax. That's what they were hoping for all along.

Police cars begin encircling the *Bash's* perimeter, blocking off any wayward entry-ways, discouraging the dissatisfied masses with less luck from trying to squeeze over, under, or around the barricades.

There's the initial emotion, there are the shouts of joy to God himself, and then, when the sensational dust has metaphorically settled, the members of the crowd, some hand-in-hand, some resting their heads on their neighbors' shoulders, begin shuffling softly towards Zuccotti Park, herded there, in fact, like sheep. Miranda's just going with it, whatever. She already had the ending spoiled for her.

After much shuffling, Miranda's body comes to rest, along with all the others. Caught tight in the midsection of a bloated crowd hundreds of people over capacity, all the anxious feet and paperweight phones are almost too much to digest for as middling a stomach as the *Bash's* nucleus, the mediocre Zuccotti Park. Less known as a park than a well-manicured median where once Wall Street was Occupied, it is in reality one of those mid-street islands of elevated grass strips and stone benches that exist hardly for pleasure, moreso to honor some hero cop from the 50's.

The park and surrounding streets are laid over with a turf triangle which points all incoming fanatic feet forward to a platform at its nose. This particular stage, raised just a few feet off the floor, is a people's stage, a stage surrounded by security, sure, (armed forces with riot-controlling cannons and visors and all of them white of skin and yellow of shirt), but so near to the ground to almost imply that, yeah, if the guards weren't here, you might walk right up onstage and shoot jive with the new CEO, whoever it may be, and all the big brass of *Big Banana* would look at you from their twelve thrones at the back of the stage and smile in approval.

Two metal bars erected on the leftmost side of the stage support a massive LED screen, presumably one that will broadcast all the happenings up-front to those in back.

And because *Big Banana* basically owns the trademark on onanism, two enormous, gilded yellow *B's* flank the stage, glittering with lights that, come dusk, will be lit bright enough for even the astronauts to look down upon and worship.

By this point, most of the phones, including Miranda's, are busy getting the best-angled picture of the stage possible. The feverish mass, desperate to claim official ownership of this singular experience they're about to share, must make sure *everyone* is aware. So many phones, and so close together, all so obviously the centerpiece of their owners' attention. It's time, then. Now. The realization swoops in from above. Time for Miranda to reach her hand up Gwami's back and into her mouth and make her speak.

She logs in. She begins the end. She aggro's the final boss. She posts.

"*Get your fill of the new and improved @GwamitheSeer at #thereturn, broadcasting live and direct from the Bash #BigBanana #BananaCEO #BBCEO #EasterinAutumn.*"

And just like *that*, the world acquiesces to a golden hue, a shockwave seems to burst forth from her phone, a ripple in space-time itself, and everyone in the crowd — faces looking at their phones and then up and around them — just knows, the information silently and successfully shared, that Gwami the Seer has *properly* returned to life. And by now, it *is* national news.

Almost immediately, Miranda starts seeing all these poor souls looking around the crowd, hoping maybe to spy someone with curiously familiar facial dimensions, the saboteur source of a quite cryptic little message apparently emanating from within their canary cohort. The interaction is immediate, the curiosity unabating. More and more faces pop their eyes up and around. But Gwami isn't *really* there with them, and her puppeteer looks just like the rest, peering up and down from her phone just as they do theirs.

Maybe Gwami's post added some urgency to the event, because the feedback falls away from the speakers, a line of lights sighs to life across the stage, and the music is hushed. With the sun stopped high in the sky, pausing where it will have the best view, reflecting soft orange off of the speakers and the building sides, it starts. And just like *that*, Gwami ceases to be the center of attention.

All these poor people, where are they supposed to direct their eyeballs?

Up at the stage, of course. Gwami was only ever going to be a momentary distraction. And when the Board comes out, the place goes, only somewhat figuratively, bananas. There should probably be more security. But despite their deficient numbers, despite the bull-moose energy of the crowd, the security forces remain stolid as the Board takes the stage; all the bastards are wearing yellow, waving open-handed at the crowd, making this feel like some bizarre college commencement *sans* the robes and diplomas, *avec* the self-satisfied smiles and practiced, camera-ready poses.

Adelaide Ansley blows kisses to the crowd, showering everyone with her love. What a sweetheart. Dominic Lambrusco, muscles surging underneath a too-tight tee chosen by a PR intern, drops to one knee and high-fives all the fans pushing wildly against security, desperate to lay hands on this man, this sex symbol, he who's worth somewhere in the ballpark of $600 million, most of it acquired in arms dealing, sure, but who cares? This isn't a *Washington Post* exposé, and *look at those arms!*

MaryJane Kant and Dolly Meyers shoot t-shirt cannons, while Derek Cassiopeia throws handfuls of yellow confetti out towards the audience. Originally, he was to throw dollar bills with Cindi's face on them, but there was fear this would confuse the simple crowd, causing a premature panic. There was time allotted for panic later.

Adelaide Ansley approaches a microphone, hushing the crowd with an open palm before saying with rockstar cadence, "Thank you all for coming! Thank you for your love and your support! Cindi would be proud. But we're done mourning Cindi. It's time now to *celebrate* her legacy!"

That's exactly what the crowd needs to hear, because they as a mass swing their limbs skyward and some even start speaking in tongues, their eyes rolled back in their heads, possessed by some strange profligate force, and anyone with a hat throws it up in the air like they've just graduated. In a way, they have.

Dominic Lambrusco is handed another microphone. "Cindi was the greatest leader. She taught us what it takes to lead: integrity and responsibility, insight and humility!" His sharp-cheddar voice echoes through the city square. A woman nearby swoons. It is unclear whether anyone catches her.

Miranda hears the man's words and thinks of her brother and scoffs.

"The first thing we asked ourselves about any candidate was this: would Cindi *like* this person? Would Cindi *respect* them? If they weren't *indebted* to making the world a better place, then surely she would not."

For such canned, corny remarks, they really incite some latent Dionysian thrum in the crowd. Someone beside her rips their shirt off, and Miranda understands too late that the gathering has assumed an increasingly sexual vibe — there's all this screaming, and sweat too, and straight-up moans if you listen hard enough. Or maybe her imagination is compensating for what are, really, just the innocent, exulting wails of an otherwise pleasant dithyramb.

There are more prepared remarks; there is a slipshod slideshow about Cindi's effect on the company and on the Trans community, though, curiously, there are no activists or celebrities interviewed. The rather meditative tone of everything onstage clashes with the crowd's wild spirit. To be fair, these people would continue on to ever more feverishness no matter what actually happens on stage, but the proceedings still seem rather tone-deaf, rather carelessly designed, rather out of character. It's a misfire. On the biggest stage, at their biggest moment, *Big Banana* misfires.

Something is definitely amiss, because with *Big Banana*, nothing ever is.

The Board settles into their back-of-stage thrones, smiling and whispering to each other, posing unassumingly for pictures, looking at the slideshows and advertisements — whatever it is up on that screen — seeming all too tranquil while the crowd is almost literally gnawing at its own arm. Can't they hear the shrieks? Can't they even comprehend what it is they're doing to these people? Or, shit, is this like Christmas for them? Must be. A bunch of godless capitalists made uninhibited and exposed by their false idols…sounds like something a demon would be into.

Though it's daylight, and though even the rowdiest demons would be intimidated by this crowd, something fearful bedevils Miranda, something that makes her stare compulsively into all the open spaces between bodies and pray fervently that Cindi will appear *soon*, take over *soon*, cause a big enough commotion to break the mob monotony; this waiting is unbearable. It's a dangerous, deathly thing she's involved in, and she can't escape the certainty that worse things are yet to come. For here is a crowd excited, and the excitement has turned into sex, and sex left unchecked always turns into violence.

A video starts playing, recollecting *Big Banana's* history. There's triumphant music, and some, like, back-stage and unauthorized videos of the Board members engaging in such family-friendly activities as *Going to the Water Park* and *Eating Ice Cream in the Green Room*. It's unclear if anyone but Miranda appreciates the bizarre juxtaposition between the innocuous schtick on stage and the sweaty, yellow Woodstock wildness of the crowd below. Nobody, even the Board, seems really sure of what's to come next. Most of them are just sitting there, waiting. Naomi Freemen is very conspicuously checking her watch…and checking it again. As if she has somewhere better to be.

The video ends, and it is in the great spreading silence that follows, the kind of silence which precedes something, that Gwami finally goes live. Miranda raises her phone up like an offering, joining the 600 others recording the very same thing.

Miranda watches as Agatha Wolonksy, standing motionless and cold behind her golden chair, suddenly looks up, her own phone screen raised in Miranda's direction, transparently trying to place the now-live Gwami the Seer in the crowd. A man in a suit hurries over to her, and they exchange whispers; those whispers travel through each individual Board member to the front of the stage, where Adelaide Ansley, a nanosecond of actual panic flashing across her face, takes a standalone mic in hand and breaks the inaction.

"Okay! Who's ready to meet our new C-E-O?"

The sex sounds turn to snarling, and huge swaths of the crowd swirl together in violent mosh-pit typhoons. Bodies *slam-bang-boom* collide. Fistfuls of hair fly away in the breeze. Teeth enter hands and two women begin hollering, their necks nuzzling against one another's.

"Woah, woah, woah. I'm sorry, I couldn't *hear* you. I saaaaaiiiiid: Who's ready to meet our new C-E-O?"

People are dropping to all fours, are literally beginning to howl. Dads bounce kids with blood-shot eyes on their shoulders. A foursome nearby starts taking off their shoes.

Adelaide continues on unabated, speaking in ambiguities about the promised candidate. With each forthcoming sentence, oddballs in the crowd begin to, like, transcend the riot and freeze, looking towards the stage with eagle-eyed intensity, rapt by some unspeakable force, perhaps the same one that's just now supplied Miranda with body-shivering chills.

It's unclear where they came from or when exactly they approached, but a horde of the yellow-vested, white-masked miltiamen have gathered at the back of the stage. Miranda's body shouts at her brain to *get out of here*, but she can't reasonably move backwards and point the camera up at the same time. Whatever is going to happen will happen with her in the center.

Agatha Wolonksy begins whispering to a man with an M16 at the back of the stage — is that legal? — when a shrill gasp erupts from the center of the crowd, timed perfectly with the huge screen's schlocky slideshow cutting to a grainy static, and Miranda is already streaming, thank God, to like *90,000* viewers right then (they showed up out of nowhere, and *all together*), and now the giant screen begins to distort, displaying, instead of the *Big Banana* logo swiveling coolly, a dark room in grey, surveillance-camera style, and everyone's cameras point either towards the disturbance in the crowd or at the screen.

Cindi's familiar, semi-lascivious voice begins speaking all muffled and coarse from out of the speakers, the crowd quiets somewhat, straining to hear, and nobody even realizes that there's tear gas rising up from the ground until it's already in their eyes and their mouths. They hardly even hear the rubber bullets until they or their neighbor or their wife gets smashed in the neck and back and thighs. The shirtless guy beside Miranda gets hit in the eye, and all at once reality cracks.

And then, all Hell breaks loose.

For a moment, everything stops — the coughing and groaning and flying elbows, and even the bullets hang in mid-air. This unnatural pause brings a sound, a low moan like an *ohhmmmm*, produced as the tectonic plates below ground strain to break their temporal restraints. The *ohhmmm* rises in pitch and volume. You can almost hear the sound expanding and expanding and expanding, enveloping more and more frequencies within it, before, all at once, contracting into itself. *Zwwooooosh*. The ensuing screech is too acute to be heard properly, but it breaks all the nearby windows, ravages all the nearby eardrums. Small shards of glass begin falling from above, a bloody snowfall of broken, yellow windows.

Was that an EMP? She still has service, somehow, so unlikely. And all this smoke? Is it Napalm or something? Agent Orange? Whatever it is, it envelops all of the *Bash* before anyone's bearings can conceivably be gotten. Trapped inside the cloud, breath becomes scarce and reduced to *gasping*. The grit and dust and glass and horrible ash stick to any open eyeballs or sweaty forearms. The collective headache is unforgiving.

Somewhere inside the helter-skelter, Miranda keeps her phone hand-high, capturing as much of the twisted carnage as she can. Her free hand grabs blindly at a nearby shoulder, using it to propel herself forward. She takes a thrashing arm to the face but regains momentum as she rushes forth through smoke then around a pair of trembling, embracing figures and forward, forward, and the smoke even seems to be thinning when *thunk*, her stomach collides with a police barrier, sending her harshly to the ground. Her phone falls flat upon her nose, and in her scramble to pick it up, she sees her own face looking back at her.

An already terrible moment has been made worse: Gwami the Seer's face has been revealed to the entire world.

And the fucking balls on our heroine, I swear to God: she smiles. *Wide.*

In a world of less chaos, less hostility, less bizarre, Miranda might begin a much-entitled freak out. But adrenaline, good adrenaline, won't let her leave this immediacy, grabs under her shoulders, raises her up to her legs and with a final push, lifts her onto the hood of a nearby police car. For one moment, thrust into a random pocket of clean air, she can point her phone clearly onto the pandemonium, catch her breath and wipe her eyes. In its gratuity, such overflowing chaos tends to look muted, as violent, churning waves do from far onshore. 180,000 people are watching the world crumble through her eyes. It takes all her willpower not to start reading all the comments scrolling like automatic wildfire up and down her screen.

With the mayhem transforming the landscape into one stunned *tableaux vivant* of blood and screeching frenzy, it's the stage, still calm and in such stark contrast to the rest of the landscape, that draws her attention. On that stage she thought she might see the Board frozen in panic, and at their vanguard, Caleb standing worried, looking for her, spying his sister in the crowd and sending his army of personal security forward to rescue her.

She's half-right. On the stage, standing just where they were, like automatons, *are* the Board, only they've changed their clothes, slipped into something more comfortable, more uniform, these drab yellow jumpsuits, like the militiamen were wearing, jumpsuits that tighten thick around the ankles and around the neck leaving only shiny hands

and faces and soot-blackened feet exposed. And behind the Board is —
what in tarnation? — the Board? Another nearly complete set. Twelve
all in a row. And behind *them*, another Board. Again!

Stripped of their yellow shirts and white visors, the militia-
men-cum-Board-Members seem equally inhuman, their empty faces
betraying no emotion, no thought. Miranda, though she has felt much
new sensation recently, finds herself diving to new, never-before-seen
depths of pure terror. The few remaining rules of the world have collapsed to dust atop her toes. As rows and rows of Board Members like
rows and rows of shark teeth march forward into the smog with military
precision, Miranda knows there's only one directive she can cling to:

Survive, god damn it.

Survive to tell the motherfucking tale.

Escape becomes all-important. Miranda turns to run and steps
right into the/a Dominic Lambrusco, who smashes a rifle butt into the
bridge of her nose. There's no time to react, only to drop her phone and
fall backward through an undergrowth of flailing limbs onto the turf
below. The floor skins her cheek; blood trickles from her nose *drip drip
drip* onto her left hand and the tear gas swells in thick billows but *sniff-
sniff-sniff*, there's something else sulfuric and semi-noxious mixed in
with its vinegary odor. Miranda looks up expecting to see the sun, but
it has hidden behind a building for safety. It's only the cobalt point of
the Statler-Abramson Building visible in the sky overhead. On its face,
the web address has vanished, replaced instead by a yellow smiley face.
Beneath it, Chinese Restaurant Bag encouragement: *Have a Nice Day.*

Then the smoke, voracious, comes forward to eat the sky and eat
Miranda too, and it does and everything goes black.

Life reeks of sulfur, burnt rubber, boiling tires.

Miranda's legs feel as if they've been blasted by shrapnel. She begins
to crawl, desperate for movement of any kind.

A pair of crushing black boots sprint by, kicking dirt and street
water up into Miranda's face. If they had been but two inches to the left,

the boots might've sank through her skull as a heavy spoon crunches through the shell of a soft-boiled egg.

She pushes herself to her feet, but balance is hard to maintain when you can't see the sky. Which way is up? Screams and shouts, absorbed and refracted by the smoke, seem to oscillate in and out from everywhere at once. Sightless, accosted by shrieks, and disoriented like a big wave surfer thrown under, Miranda lurches around wildly, scrambling for a handhold that might keep her upright.

Only able to open her eyes for split seconds before the ash cakes on and leaves them stinging, she moves blindly, her hands flailing in front of her, here smacking someone in the face, there cracking their knuckles against the mirror of a parked car. She pulls herself along with whatever she can grab, resting on door handles and trying, when her eyes are open, not to look off into the distance, for in the boiling light within the smoke, all things come to look strange, harrowing, horrifying.

She makes herself flat against a building, and through an open scar in the fog, she sees three of the Board members moving robotically forward. The one in the middle, a facsimile of Fausto Gutierrez, the guava-fruit heir — a man whose metaphorical plastic insides she once filled with buzzsaws that really spun — drags an unconscious woman by her ankle, the lady's head smacking against each and every upturned asphalt boulder. An Arthur Haynes-copy beside him stops, sniffs, begins to look towards Miranda, but the smoke rushes to fill its former gash. When it opens again, the girl is gone.

Something *caws* from above, and Miranda finds that if she stays low, almost in a duckwalk, she can move with her eyes open. Ash and charred bits of building matter drift indolently to the ground, interrupted only by the *quaking crash* of a window-washer's lift that couldn't quite hang on. One such contraption falls some twenty feet in front of her, sending her hurtling back, sending metal chips shooting out like burst grenade shrapnel, sending up a cloudburst of flame that splits the smoke.

The action draws the attention of some meandering, marching Board members, two Adelaide Ansleys and a Dolly Meyers — *sans* expression of course, but if you came close enough you could see their pupils vibrating wildly within their iris prisons — who approach through a flame-scorched circle in the cloud, inspecting the lift for blood or other human gore they can lick off for further fuel. Miranda, lacking a better option, plays dead under some slashed rebar wires. There's sufficient blood smeared on her face, and though the footsteps get close, perhaps that too-convincing blood is why they eventually step away.

Despite her fear, Miranda's clothes are hardly even damp, for the air is so dry and acrid with chemicals and fire-heat that the sweat wicks away as it forms. Her throat has become sandpaper. Her eyes can't produce tears at any fixed, normal clip so they produce as much as they can whenever possible. Miranda runs through more smoke, bent low as possible, crying and bleeding and coughing and coughing, and gagging and coughing some more.

In a clearing in the center of the street, three ropes descend down from above the cloud.

Miranda spots them first. The relief is insane, the confusion terrific, but why would her body care about its mind's hesitancies? This is an escape, a friendly helicopter full of stand-up National Guardspeople here to airlift medics in and the wounded out. She runs to the ropes but stumbles on a raised brick, tripping and sliding down the pavement on two now-skinless elbows. She looks back up at the ropes.

A white man with brown hair and a purple, swollen eye has the same idea she did. He limps frantically over to the rope, grabbing it with both hands, wrapping his arms around it tight like it's his mother, and tugs. It pulls up, a fishing hook reacting to a hit.

And then there's this awful, unforgettable noise. The noise of a high-speed blender, a smoothie maker, a *Magic Bullet* or *Robocoup*... an efficient and merciless destruction.

And the falling charred remnants of building and tree and scaffold add the chopped-up bits of a white man with brown hair and a purple, swollen eye to their feather-falling ranks.

Another person rushes forward to the rope and Miranda shouts "NO!" but the smoke comes in with calculated force to obstruct her vision. The smoke that's been doing her plenty favors, sparing her from harm best it can, keeps her now from witnessing this fresh horror. Her elbows busted up but adrenaline keeping them from being a concern, Miranda pushes herself back and back and back; the smoke cloud, be it out of concern or torment, follows and follows and follows.

For how long or how far does the smoke let Miranda push herself back before it tires of the game? It might be ten blocks, it might be two; might be taking an hour or thirty seconds. The smoke has long since blocked out the sun and the light, and her phone is by now smashed into pieces. All possible windows have been shrouded over.

Backwards, she rises and steps and falls and crawls and then drags herself, tripping over small fissures, tumbling into a slight sinkhole, the very Earth keeping her from collecting her bearings. The sky and the planet both seem to be in on some gag, some prank that takes away first her legs, then her arms, then her mind. Her hand passes through something wet and pre-mushed. If Miranda weren't so preoccupied, she might be bothered to wretch.

Things start to fade away. The thoughts go like when you're smoking a cigarette; eyesight next, a mask tightened over her face. And, god forgive her, she lets it happen.

It's not acquiescence to death necessarily, but a letting go of her own story threads for a second.

For there is a plot, a plot that's moving.

And that plot *requires* her. Right?

And something *has* been looking out for her this whole time. Her work here, she knows in her soul of souls, is not done.

The smoke overtakes her, gets right up into them nostrils, and blots out her thoughts.

Whatever the smoke is doing, she'll let it. She's been left with no other choice. The mask sets upon her eyes, and the last thing she sees is yellow. Bright, putrid yellow. And everything smelling oh so sweet.

When she comes back to life, it's just in time to see two beakless birds with human teeth swooping down to steal a clementine out of her cracked, bloody hand, but she doesn't protest. She lacks the willpower, and besides, the birds look ornery. Best avoid a scrap and preserve her energy, lest the next interloper threaten more than the fruit she carries.

Wait! Listen! What has happened to the screaming and sirens and the insane cackling cracks of straight-up clefts opening in the Earth? It's all quiet, all dissolved into a single, underlying thrum. The dull roar of the city, she finds, is her only companion.

The circling birds, squawking and hissing at each other as they fight for the last of the citrus skin, leave for another target further away. Soon they're gone into the smoke and haze, somebody else's problem now.

So, she sits alone in what appears to be the debris of a ruined fruit stand, unaware of how she got here, praying for mercy from the birds, wishing there were a more varied selection of produce around her than the meager corpses of kiwis, smushed tangerines and, of course, bananas. Aloe leaf would be nice for her cuts. But she makes do with the kiwis. Even after they've been crushed and smattered, their insides smashed and their outside charred, they're still the best things she's ever tasted. She would eat the spines off a cactus if it meant an end to the gravel throat and the stomachache.

No matter the circumstance though, she refuses to touch the bananas, which are all strangely intact.

Although weirdness has been coming at her pell-mell, the atmosphere here is somehow calm. The smoke, or something in it, has kept her from immediate destruction. And taking her here? Icing. The fruit cart, compared to everything else around her, seems an oasis. The smoke is definitely clearing, or at least lightening, and if she looks up, she thinks she can make out a suggestion of blue sky. A blaring police siren flashing blue and red and yellow explodes out of the nearby smoke, screams past the cart — only it's light visible — before disappearing, sound and sight alike, into the further cloud. Now tell me? Would *that* happen in Hell? (maybe)

Miranda shuts her eyes, still stinging from the soot. She tries to relax, tries to breathe, licks kiwi guts from her bloody fingers. But those birds, their squawks become shrieks, aren't content to stay gone: they return with a full phalanx of their hungriest cousins. The time for repose has passed. Safety will have to be found elsewhere. Slowly, Miranda backs away, further from the pushcart until her back is against a building on the opposite side of the street. The birds circle and swoop and, wisely, also stay away from the bananas.

Above her, the awning of *Len's Chinese Grocer* glows red, unperturbed and nary scratched. It actually makes sense that these lesser Chinatown supermarkets would be spared; they're so tight and cramped and never air-conditioned, and it's likely any wayward hellion would think it had already been tagged by other, earlier demonic forces. But *Len's* is fortuitous, for it grounds the girl. This is, in fact, a grocer Miranda has visited many a time, for the owner, whose name is Yu and has a gold front tooth, is happy to sell cigarettes at a lower-than-the-state-minimum price, and when Miranda has been particularly tight on cash/not talking to Mother and Father, it's to *Len's* she treks, getting *Parliaments* and *Takis* for whatever spare change she has in her pocket. *Len's*, she knows, sits on an oft-trodden street in East Chinatown. Hell might have boiled over, but it's boiled over onto the same New York that was here before.

A formal exit route at long last presents itself: amble along east — if you hit *The Doughnut Plant*, you're going the wrong way — and get to the East River Park. Maybe she could catch a ride from there to the Palisades on a passing barge.

Tears come to her eyes; she's never felt so fully a New Yorker. God Bless the Grid.

Miranda looks into *Len's*, smushing her eyes to the glass. Though hampered by ambient smoke, she can just about discern that the rows of shelving are all empty. In kind of a half-trance, she tries the door, finding it open but the store inside lacking her friend. If she were a more courageous type, perhaps she would call his name softly, finding him huddling for safety in the walk-in freezer behind the storefront, enlist him in her journey and gain a welcome compatriot in her stroll through Hell. But Miranda Swami's trying to get the fuck out of dodge; it's just maybe a smoke would help steady her hand.

Surely Yu won't mind if she walks quietly around to the back of the register, selects a pack of *Parliaments* — or, you know what, maybe two packs — smacks a ten-dollar bill upon the counter, and lights up right then and there, in the soft sepia light and orange glow of mid-street cinders.

One cigarette indeed steadies her nerves, the next clears her head, the third sits heavy in her stomach. Lighting the fourth, she exits *Len's*, trying and failing to keep the *ding-dong* door-chime from ringing as she does so. She closes the door softly, turning back out to the ash and knowing, just knowing, that with the bloody scars on her cheek and the limp cigarette hanging from her mouth, that she looks fucking *cool*. Some things just don't change with each generation's fresh morality, and one of them is that a badass, beat-up, bloody broad with a fire stick in her mouth is going to look dope as hell. And she knows it.

Something about her appearance imbues Miranda with confidence as she walks quietly east towards the water. The walking along goes great at first, and the strange outline of horrible things, perhaps not wanting to fuck with her, seem satisfied staying in their shadows; only their silhouettes can be seen through the haze, and only if Miranda actively looks for them. She should have taken a water bottle from *Len's* too. She's prepared to smoke her throat bloody.

Maybe it's her imagination, hmmm probably not, but doesn't it seem like the fog is lifting as she moves further east? Maybe it too is now afraid of getting in her way. Does this mean everything is going to be okay? She hears a the unmistakable squeak of a Prius horn, which means maybe normal New York is returning from its holiday, and are those subway screeches she hears from down in the grates beneath her?

As if it were watching her, wait until she could find some bit of self-assuredness and safety in the smog, a new, sinister sensation slithers out from the smokescreen. Miranda feels in the silence behind her a presence. A chilling presence. You too know this feeling, of something unseen watching you, its eyes upon your neck. It's worst when alone in the dark, when nothing is there to distract you from the indelible *nearness* of the watcher. Miranda, all good things sapped from her, refuses to turn and face *it*, for facing it might make it real. She lights another cigarette, but can't steady her hands. It falls from her quivering lips, landing with a sizzle in a puddle of grey liquid. Fearing what immobility might force her into confrontation with, Miranda continues on, repeating the prayer of the child who's heard midnight footsteps outside her door, who hides underneath her blanket thinking *If I can't see it, it isn't real.*

If I can't see it, it can't hurt me.

Just a few more blocks.

She stops finally, finding herself panting from absurd fright, but there it is, dogging her, the same feeling, the same assurance by her autonomous nervous system that she's being followed. Something in the delirium is tracking her steps.

Then, it's like someone takes a balloon to her arms: All the hair raises, puppeteered by unseen static, and she feels in her stomach what's about to happen, so she turns, turns to see a figure coming at her slowly from the dusk. But it's not running at her, nor is it trying to hide or pounce, and, oh thank heavens, oh thank the Lord, it's a man. It's just a man! Threatening on any other day, the idea of a white man approaching her on a dark and deserted city street is, right now, rock-candy sweet. Hardly threatening at all, it's an elderly street vendor, in a white smock and pants and capped by one of those old diner-style *Back to the Future* hats. A wonder he's survived this situation at all. Even more curious is the spotless, nondescript hand-trolley he pushes. Perhaps he has come, has followed her, this emissary of good, to bestow upon her harmless Earth treats, ice cream or dirty water dogs or honey-roasted cashews with the sweet street smell they give off. Perhaps he is here to spur her onward, another plot device to push her towards the end of this arc.

"Hey!" Miranda screams, waving her gnarled arm, utterly incited by any company at all.

The man comes closer, and closer still, smiling with rotted yellow teeth (*weird*), white hair hanging like stalactites from his ears and nose (*gross*), and attached to his cart is a solitary balloon (*kinda lame*), a balloon that's mylar yellow (*oh no*) and very much in the shape of a banana (*oh my god*).

The static returns, and the man, smiling as he does it, takes a hand from behind his back, a hand clasping a slick, black pistol, and points it at Miranda.

This is *so* American: even when a portion of the country has *literally* been consumed by Hell, the most immediate danger is still some old, white man flaunting his second amendment rights. So typical.

Right when the gun goes off, the actual single nanosecond amongst the billions every moment, Miranda is pushed forward, physically pushed as if by cosmically strong shoulders, her full weight thrown towards the old man's old legs. The bullet whizzes by. She can actually hear it sizzling through the air as it passes, taking a chunk of her ponytail with it. Her nostrils will catch whiffs of burnt hair for the rest of the day. But her own heaved shoulder with the man's knees, which *crack* in a brittle, elderly way — his poor legs already so arthritic and problem-riddled, aside from the very new and debilitating medical issue of having a full-grown woman smash down upon them at top speed.

She gets back up and starts running, a new kind of adrenaline coursing within her plasma, and she's not running like before, not running to get away from *some*thing, but running to get away from *every*thing, running with speed enough to jerk out of her paltry skin altogether.

There is no direction or sense in her escape, only fever. She can still hear, or imagines she hears, the creaky wheels of the handcart and the *clop-clop* of her would-be-assailant's clogs on nearer and nearer pavement, and it doesn't matter what gargoyles and mutants and marching satanic soldiers she sees, for she's lost herself in the steps, in the unflappable fog, running, running straight without the option or desire to stop, the *clop-clop* behind her camouflaged now by an abrupt wail of car horns and the soft creak of their chassis being pulled along, sounding close but not quite *here*. A subway rumbles below, sending a ripple through the very Earth. It's also become quite windy.

And still her legs churn, apparently operated by a different motor than the one controlling her spent, swaying torso. Her brain is so full of unchanneled signals, so many neurons firing simultaneously, that it's a wonder she can even manage consecutive, alternating steps. Still somehow enveloped in the cloud, it's unclear whether the smoke has continued growing in volume or if she is dragging a personal portion of it with her.

Fear of this magnitude dulls time's edges, whittling away at the seam between moments until everything, structurally unsound in the first place, collapses. Although tempted to believe that time has stopped outright, Miranda is already wary of temporality's treacherous tricks. Her feet keep moving, the concurrent sounds materializing and disappearing in rhythm with her footfalls, so time spurts forward still;

her thoughts still move from left to right. This metronomic motion couldn't happen outside of time. Nor in death. The safeguarded knowledge that somehow, despite everything, she's clung to life is enough to keep her moving forward, forward, forward for God knows how long, forward until the subway's rumbling becomes distant and the *clop-clops* die away and a new smell enters into her sweaty, smoky olfactory glands, glands so damn happy to be whiffing something even the slightest bit different: freshness.

It's the kind of freshness that comes from trees; trees with prickly branches bursting intermittently into the canopy of the thinning smoke. Trees that are harbingers of new circumstance, as merciful daylight and blue sky finally appear through an aperture in the cloud's apex. The blue above, with a graceful power, swoops down to street level and blows away the last ardent haze. It's the breath of a watchful God commanding the smoke to dissipate. And the smoke, powerless to this wind's whims, obeys.

Miranda stops short, nearly falling over, as all the adrenaline within her, no longer necessary, flees fully through her toes. Swaying, she holds herself steady against a mailbox, sucking in as much air as possible with every breath. The smoke in her eyes has left the world blurry, but even with the details smudged she can see color, greens and beiges and birds-eye blue.

She can now see the trees for more than just their branches. Their woody stems exploded through the sidewalk cement long ago, hoping for a prolonged taste of the same, sweet sun that now kisses Miranda's cheeks, that falls flat on her outstretched tongue, tasting like butterscotch. A bird flies overhead, not some sooty midtown gull but a forest songbird, a lark or robin or a cardinal, all but the latter grossly out of season. Along with the freshness comes a chill, a welcome chill, one that dries the sweat on Miranda's upper lip and begins to evaporate the ocean in her underarms. She wishes for sturdier boots, for a more robust collar. Ah, the familiar wishes and complaints. From this, she knows she's back in New York.

But this is a different facet of New York, green and brown and not grey, with real residences, a few stories at most and thin, thin like parodies, thin like the suburbs, thin like stilted cabanas along the shore, the home less the focus than the *terroir*. How can this quiet, birdsong place be contained in the same city, nay province, as the overflowing garbage cans and typhoid vagrants of Midtown, or as the smoke-spitting barges parked and belching along the south harbor? It's too green, too pristine, too still.

The symmetrically-spaced mailboxes have family names on them. Miranda imagines the Montana's and the Sheehan's and the Richard's all safe in their houses, watching today's events unfold on the 65" in their family rooms and not out in Manhattan personally dodging Hell. If they're even in Brooklyn that is. Actually, it doesn't seem like anyone is in Brooklyn.

On second thought, it might really be *too* green, *too* pristine, *too* still.

It's like Brooklyn after a plague, like the population fled something sinister, leaving all their belongings behind, their bread unleavened. Toys and trikes lie overturned in the yards, cars have been left running beside paid parking meters; perhaps there's been a mass Christian disappearance, and she's solely, Judaically been *Left Behind*. A liquor store with an open door is without discernible leadership, and a subway station staircase transports no commuters.

If Miranda had any capacity to fear left in her, she might very well fear. But only clear, present danger would exhaust her final reserves now, not this total but tolerable weirdness. So, she walks forward with less anxiety than she might otherwise have, approaching a far-off tree line with no emotions whatsoever except a desperate desire to relax, reach the firework canopies, of green and red and yellow and autumnal orange like molten nickel, and just relax there. There's no other park this could be than Prospect Park, mammoth and densely-forested, replete with cool patches of moss and crabgrass where a weary girl can lay her head. She'd do anything for a nap.

If her senses hadn't spent the day so overwhelmed, perhaps she would see Him sooner. Like from the other side of the street, where she stops to look both ways for sudden, speeding traffic. She doesn't even see Him as she passes, for He's on a bench to her right, and she's only focused ahead, on the trees and the nearest pathway into them.

"Miranda Swami?" He says, the voice like gravel parting underneath a snake.

Something in His voice restores her to normalcy, and she turns to see Him in his full effect: a man, sitting alone on a bench behind her. Under the outstretched arms of an old, very weepy willow, He sits, this man, this first presence felt since exiting the smokescreen. Her heart begins to beat, for some beings carry in their very vibe a kind of warning.

But it's not like she can ignore him, because events were always going to deposit her here, with Him. It was always a mathematical certainty that they'd both be here; every incident in the universe has conspired to this point, to this meeting. To this turning point.

The man, statuesque until now, shuffles a bit, rustling the ends of his long tan trench-coat against the leafy debris on the sidewalk. A shabby, brown derby hat shields his face, and it's pulled pulled down low, so as to an old-timer engaged in a park-side afternoon *siesta*.

He finally looks up at her. He's got these great green eyes, two illuminous, unblinking emeralds with facets to spare, and fetid, yellow skin like rotten flan. What could conceivably be deemed a "smile" appears on the bottom half of what could conceivably be deemed his "face" (though his whole body is kind of his face) revealing rows of tiger-shark teeth, all serrated and gleaming and that's when Miranda *gets* it.

She's crossed a certain point. She *has* aggro'd the final boss; she never stopped to buy potions.

She knows this man.

"Miranda Swami!" he shouts.

And not a man at all.

"You've made it! I was beginning to think —"

Him and his ilk have haunted her dreams a-thousand-and-one times.

" — you had lost your way. Or met an, ahem, unfortunate end over there."

Does he know the torment his fruity friends have caused her?

"A pleasure to see you again," he says.

Who are we kidding, of course he knows. It's his business to.

This literal, and very much alive, banana demon, a truly Big Banana, extends his gloved hand for a shake, but anyone could see the half-hidden claws trying to poke out of the fingers. Miranda's hardly in control of the hand that takes the Banana's. Turns out there was indeed some fear left over. Here, it is, put to good use.

"It's been a long time coming, Ms. Swami. A long time. My *friends* call me A.B. And you look like you could use a friend," he grumbles, his voice like a silty mudslide.

As a matter of fact, she could.

"I know *we* have sort of a reputation to the contrary, but I won't bite, I don't even have a digestive tract. "These," he says, knocking on his jagged teeth with a fingernail, "are just for show. I promise. I just want to talk. Here, sit," he says, moving over, making space.

Smooth-talking as always, A.B. has lured another one, folks. The girl, as if in a trance, meanders to his side, exhales, and thus, accepts her fate.

BANANAS!

10

Let's be clear about something: Miranda has never been the best judge of character, preternaturally eager to eat from outstretched hands, regardless of their contents. Too trusting. She has been, however, cagey with her friendship in these past years, after certain extended palms that seemed to offer her compassion and understanding instead held, upon closers inspection, only self-doubt and negativity and anxiety and pills and mental health degradation until a not-so-accidental-overdose-type-deal ended all that, so yes, although looking into the glassy green eyes of this creature, a creature renowned for evil, causes some cautious voice within her to scream "RUN," something in his offer still appeals to her true nature.

And besides, this is a being of ineffable power, one that might have used all manner of subterfuge to finagle her into a mutilating scenario. But it didn't: instead, it came to her as it is, grotesque and unfamiliar and frightening, but also sincere. It's here purely as itself. And that goes a long way.

Anyways, there's only really one small part of her that wants her to engage with the Banana, but that's the part responsible for sympathy and decision-making, so engage she does. Her first breath beside the beast fills her nostrils, nay her very soul, with the sweet, fetid aroma of old banana.

"So, what's this all about?" she asks. "What do you want?"

"We'll get to that, Miranda Swami, have no fear. For now, just take a load off. My colleagues have been chasing you all over the city, and I'm sure you're quite tired. Can I get you anything? Coffee?Tea? FantaColaCoffee?SevenUpHotTeaSprite?"

"Uhm, I'm actually okay, thanks."

"Your prerogative," A.B. says. Apparently, the beast has a thirst himself, or else just wants to show off, for he snaps his fingers and in his hand appears an amber-tinged bottle of perspiring, cold Kombucha.

"That's a nice trick," Miranda says, thinking how good Kombucha actually would be right now, "do you do it at parties?"

"Don't be too impressed. I can make things appear, but it doesn't work the other way. And only non-biodegradable plastics. In other words, I can create garbage, I just can't take it away. How's that for hellion humor? The *Boss*, curse his soul, loves that kind of stuff. 'Humor: it's a demon's greatest weapon in the struggle against untrusting humans,' that's what I was always taught."

"And your boss is the Devil, right?"

"Yes, indeed. Now, I'm no slouch myself, mind you. When I'm not out meeting with important clients like yourself, I have quite far-reaching authority over a number of departments. I don't mean to brag, but there are only a few individuals with more power than I have. Most have names you'd probably recognize. If you like, I can get into our whole hierarchy, tell you what makes Azazel tick, though be warned, it's somewhat arcane. Ah, you'd be bored to death by it. Believe me, sister, if there's one thing unique to my kind, it's our love of bureaucracy. Bureaucracy, lovely thing, is confounding, illogical, irritating at worst, maddening at best, causes gridlock, *ahhhh*, just our cup of tea."

"With *Big Banana*, you mean?"

"Oh, everywhere. We've got plenty of other operations — diversification is the key to a sturdy portfolio — and if they're hellish in design, they're fiendishly bureaucratic, you can count on that. Corporations, government agencies…take, uhm, the DMV for example:

what efficiency-minded human would've invented that fucking night-mare?" A.B. says, laughing, though it comes out sounding more like a burp. The cloud of yellow gas escaping his mouth neither confirms nor debunks the notion. "Goodness me, my apologies. Must've eaten some bad brimstone, been coughing up sulfur all day."

Miranda is too distracted to smile.

"That was a joke," A.B. clarifies.

"I can't believe the DMV is actually —"

"Let me stop you right there. Don't go trying to guess everything we've got our claws sunk into, it'll drive you mad. And you wouldn't be the first." Then in a whisper, "*Marlon Brando.*"

"Why are you telling me all of this? Why tell me any of this?"

"Because I want you to trust me, Ms. Swami. That's my style. I believe in honesty and direct communication. You're a smart girl, you have a keen nose for bullshit. So I'll be level with you, because that's what I'd want if I were sitting where you are. That's what would work for me. And the straight and narrow of it, Miranda, is that I have your best interests at heart."

"Everyone says that."

"Kid, I'm not everyone," he says. As if to prove it, A.B. groans, strains, and eventually pushes two enormous, ochre bat wings, equipped on their surface with sharp scales, through the light fabric of his jacket, allowing their diseased, yellow plagiopatagium to lift him a few feet into the air. "Do you know why I'm here? Do you want to take a guess why *I'm* here, *me*, a suit more-or-less, and not one of my more vicious colleagues like the ones, say, from across the river? Nasty creatures, by the way, I'm truly sorry about all that. But, uhm, well that's the nature of bureaucracy, yeah? There's always going to be some departmental overlap. You were never in any real danger, I made sure of that. Surely you remember all the good times we've had together? The thunder cloud, the talking cactus, that weird balloon merchant. Not sure who's terrible idea that was. Got bloodied up right good at the end there, you did though, yeah?"

Flashes of horrible things attack Miranda's subconscious and lay for mini-moments in front of her eyes. She can't think of a good response. The Demon hovers up into the air and around to her other side, adopting a levitating lotus-position, his little wings needing to perform only the slightest of flaps to keep his assuredly hollow body airborne.

"Maybe, Ms. Swami," he continues, "you've realized certain occurrences that have, in the not too distant past, seemed too good to be true, certain fortuitous acts of fate. Information sprinkled at the correct moment, a certain, shall we say, *push* forward when the route ahead was nebulous?

"I can't take complete credit, but you should know that many strings had to be pulled, and many favors called in, to get you safely to this bench today. But that's why they've assigned *me* to your case, someone with authorization, someone with real power, not some boring, bastardly corporate drone, some number-crunching intestine muncher. You're an important client, and that designation comes from all the way at the top. I'm here, Miranda, all of this has been done because, and pardon my language, we're not fucking around. We need you, Miranda Swami."

"Need me? Need *me*? Need me for what?" Miranda asks, half-concerned, half-intrigued, soothed from her shock by the surprisingly stimulating siltiness of the winged Banana's voice. Despite her instincts, despite all the self-preservation-related alarms blaring within her, Miranda likes this guy, this thing, this Banana. He's a straight-shooter he is, and if he's truly as important as he claims to be, and if he's really come down to Earth to speak with her — with little old her? — why that's pretty gosh darn flattering to boot.

"Come on," A.B. says, "nobody's up and around today what with all the craziness across the harbor. People quaking in their houses and bomb shelters and doomsday vaults and such. Let's go for a walk, I want to show you something." The Demon leads the way.

Halfway into a more densely-forested part of the park, A.B. must feel he's not being followed. "Look, I'm not gonna hurt you okay?" he yells over his shoulder. "You gotta trust me!"

"Forgive me, I'm just now realizing the insanity of following a literal demon into a deep, dark wood."

A.B. turns in the air, exasperated crow's feet stomped into the skin beside his eyes. "Look here," he says. A pouch manifests in the creature's abdomen, a pouch in which the demon's knowing claw rummages for a moment before producing from its depths a small white business card. He takes it by its corner and flicks it forward, all wrist. It spins like a ninja star, seeming to rend the very air, before sticking its northwest corner into the telephone pole to Miranda's left. "Read it."

Cautiously, she removes the card from the wood.

Mr. Avery "A.B." Banana
26 Nassau Street, Floor 26, Ext-817
Sr. V.P., Devil's Advocacy

"You see there?" he says, "I'm obviously not one of the violent demons! We don't issue them business cards is what I'm saying. I myself am a proud Devil's Advocate...Oh come on! Not even a little smile? It's supposed to be funny! You know, not all of us are even capable of humor. Most have no need for it. If I were anything like them, interested in gnawing at your gizzards and sucking out your stomach through your throat — which isn't even the worst of it, by the way — I'd be licking your blood off my claws by now. I surely wouldn't be here cracking jokes. I mean, look at you: exhausted as can be, no witnesses anywhere, what's stopping me? Only my honor, my title, my directive, *capeesh?*"

Okay, well, *hrmph*, that's fair. She's been satisfactorily swayed, but doesn't quite want the demon to know, so still she stays a few feet back of the hulking, floating thing. A.B., curiously, casts no shadow upon the ground below him.

Miranda:

adequately assuaging an increasingly-anxious amygdala.

A.B.:

not minding her distance as long as the girl is following and accounted for.

"So, what does a VP in Devil's Advocacy actually do?" she asks.

"Can't figure that out yourself?"

"I try not to assume."

"How admirable." A.B. scratches the back of his head, saying, "How do I put this? It's a big, wide world out there. My Boss, for all his power and insight, is often too busy to himself do all the little things that need be done for the good of our organization. I quite literally advocate for the Devil, here on his behalf, at his *behest* — and yes, I repeat for emphasis, he mentioned you personally. Are you following me, dear?"

"Not really."

"I'm saying I was assigned to your case, so I'm here to make mine."

"Your what?"

"My case."

"Case for what?"

"For your *soul*, Miranda Swami! Don't be dense. We're *Demons*. I work for the *Devil*. We want your soul, or some of it, and it's my job to convince you why that's a good idea."

"Oh...shit. Another capitalist, huh?"

A.B. raises his claws, palms forward, beside his face. "Guilty," he squeaks, smiling.

"Well, best of luck with what I can honestly say will be one hell of a tall task," Miranda says, lighting a cigarette.

"You'd be shocked how malleable morality can be."

"So, just to get everything straightened out, for my own sake: the

Devil, *your* boss, wants *my* soul, and so he's sent you here to try and convince me. This is a sales pitch?"

"Yes."

"So: you're going to gain my trust, hit me with all sorts of razzmatazz, and then, at the end of this, I'm supposed to sell you my eternal soul."

"Well, I want you to at least be thinking about it. And, mind you, it's not so cut and dry. These words 'eternal souls' and 'heaven' and 'Hells' and all that…without going into too much detail, they're misleading. Trust me. Honestly, for someone with as keen a nose for bullshit as Gwami the Seer, I'd be shocked if you bought into such a hardened Judeo-Christian narrative."

Miranda is close behind A.B., sure, but something's obviously wrong. Her eyes are faraway, staring into a middle-distance that might as well be another universe. Her feet can't keep a straight line. "So, they…they do know…" she says under her breath.

A.B only catches the end of her little muttering, but nevertheless knows what she's melting down about about. "Know what? That you're Gwami the Seer? Yes, Miranda Swami, we all know. Even before your little exposé today during that live stream — which we were *all* watching by the way. Remarkable work, even if it was all for naught. But, I digress. Surely you remember we have a certain someone's *brother* as our new CEO."

Miranda slows in the center of the lane, a certain slant of light shining a diagonal down her face from temple to throat like a scar, and she's blubbering. Tears from God-only-knows-where just pouring from her eyes. She's not heaving for breath, she's not even sad. She just can't seem to stop the aqueduct eyelids.

"He's not worth it, kid. Take it from me, he's an asshole."

"What did you just say?" His comment causes Miranda to stop altogether right in the middle of the asphalt. A.B. doesn't seem to notice.

"His willingness to give it all up," the Demon continues, "well it was great for water-cooler talk. *That* was a big job, done front-to-back by the *Boss* himself. Likes to show off his stuff, now and again, put on a show, set an example. We've all watched the tapes: flawless execution, I mean really, truly inspired work.

"Not totally your brother's fault — no man is an island, of course, and Ol' Lucifer's persuasive powers are well-documented — but you should know what we think of him. That kind of smarmy, slick-thinking type guy…well, even we Demons have our preferences."

A.B. turns around to face Miranda, who still stands stoic, unmoving and unblinking and expressionless some ways back. "Miranda? Miranda, what's wrong? Are you okay? Are you frozen solid?"

Nobody, but nobody, and I mean *nobody*, has ever confirmed her suspicion, the one she's had her whole life, the one she posits to anyone that'll listen, that her brother *really is* an asshole. Everywhere he went he was coddled and lauded, put on pedestals and given clout for his queerness, for his business acumen, for his grades and his extra-curriculars, for all sorts of things that Miranda never cared too much about because, when you cut all that extraneous fat away from the core of him, he's always been this: a beating, pulsating, undulating asshole.

And here was proof. Unbiased proof from an objective figure, a figure whose *job* it is to judge such things. A.B. floats over to Miranda's side. In perhaps the first ever recorded instance of a demon compassionately *touching* a human, A.B. lays his hand on her shoulder. God, how good that feels.

"Don't think too much into it," he says, "He'll get what's coming to him. That's what we're here for."

"What do you mean?"

"What do *you* mean?"

"You said 'That's what we're here for.' What *are* you here for?"

"Well, we're not *evil*, Miranda. You can believe the old narratives if you want, but like I said, that's never really been your style. We punish evil. That's kind of what Hell, if that's what you want to call it, is all about. My ilk and I, we're agents of *justice*. All this dealing in souls, it's in pursuit of a balanced world, where good is encouraged and evil punished. That makes sense to you, right? Why else would we be able to make such change on a world we're borne outside of? We are the system and we are the failsafe. Don't be afraid of us, we're everywhere. We have to be."

"Yeah, but..." Miranda seems to lose her train of thought. She almost starts a phrase three times, but stops each time in a pout, her sentences not communicating what she'd like them to. And right now, her words are too important for imperfection. "I'm not saying you're an idiot," she says finally, "I'm really not...but even an *idiot* could see that this 'agent of justice' shit is propaganda. Do you really think *the ACTUAL Devil* cares about justice? Don't you think, maybeeeeeeeee, he just gets off on fucking lives up on Earth, safe in some cosmic cave somewhere while his underlings do his bidding?"

"You're a tough cookie, you know that?"

"We're negotiating over my literal soul, dude. You wanted a layup?"

"There's that patented Miranda Swami fire. I like it. I love it, in fact. Most people cave by now, you know? They get dazzled by me or by the drink trick or by their own imaginations. You impress me. Or, should I say, you *continue* to impress me."

"Yeah, well, I've seen some shit. You're not going to shock me out of my complacency that quickly."

"No. No, I guess not. Here, my wings are tired, let's sit for a while." A.B. floats lazily over to a bench at the edge of the paved path. No semblance of the surrounding cityscape is visible through the growth and underbrush. Without city sounds, you can really get lost in tthe quiet of mid-autumn, the cold-snapped twigs and patter of frantic chipmunk-feet making final preparations. A Human and A Demon share the world's stillness.

"I want an answer."

"About the justice thing?"

"Yes."

"Well, and I can't stress this enough, it's not really up to me. I just collect the souls I'm asked to collect, you know? I just do as I'm told, advising when I can. Maybe that's not a great excuse, but I don't get to decide what I do or do not believe. For instance, I know your life story pretty well, but it's not for me to consider whether you deserve what you've gotten, whether you've been good or not. That's really a question for the boys in accounting."

"So, your whole existence rests upon willful ignorance?"

"It's not willful ignorance, it's faith. Well, you and I can call it faith, but really, these are things I know. Demons are different from your kind, we don't question ourselves or our circumstances; it's not in our codex to do so. We know the facts of our existences, and there's no use questioning them, since it's not like that'd do to change anything. We're like computers, just combinations of algorithms. And you know what? Things are easier this way. You want to call it a deficiency? Fine. You want to say it makes me less alive than you? That's fair. You want to say it makes me easily manipulatable? It does. It certainly does.

"But I have a purpose, a real purpose, the same purpose as the rest of my kin, a purpose that binds me to my brothers. We're all of us in pursuit of the same things, in cahoots about the same situations, believers in the same ideals. I don't have the luxury or curse of questioning myself, but that's okay, because none of us do. Does that answer your question? I know I'm an agent of justice, so I must be. And that's okay because we all are."

"I didn't mean to upset you," Miranda says, noticing that her companion is shaking, that small trickles of yellow liquid have begun to discharge from open-mouth sores pouting all over his abdomen. "Are you okay?"

"Yeah, yeah I'm okay. I just, well, this is what happens when I start *thinking* about these things. My body has a physical reaction. You know, it's not easy being a Demon either. Knowing about free will but not being able to experience it, that's a special kind of hardship. It's like having a word on the tip of your tongue for your entire life. It would drive you crazy after a while, *if* you thought about it too much."

"Tough lot."

"Sometimes. Sometimes."

They sit in silence for a moment, and a stray breeze blows black hair across Miranda's face.

"So, is that your pitch?" Miranda finally says, impatient. "I should make a deal with you because you *think* you're an agent of justice, that it's somehow my cosmic duty to universal homeostasis to do so? I have to say, Mr. Avery —"

"My friends call me A.B."

"A.B., then…I have to say, not a great pitch."

"Sweetheart, I haven't even started my pitch yet."

"Well, by all means, I'm ready when you are."

"Absolutely, and if you'll direct your attention to that small patch of grass right there, we can begin."

Miranda looks forward to a conspicuously bare patch of grass within the great thicket ahead, everything a tangled mesh of branches and resilient buds except for this empty spot.

"Watch."

The sun, at its current angle, shines through some of the branches, casting a shadow on the bare ground. As the seconds pass, and the sun moves minutely forward, the shadows on the ground, disparate lines, begin to bend, then start to connect, to converge. The sun passes ever-so-slowly through the fishnet branches as a picture begins to present itself: a pentagram of perfect dimension and exact circular construction comes together out of the dark lines, reliant on the predictable path of the sun for its eventual completion.

"And here we go."

Without warning, red light bursts up from the pentagram, and like a flashbang, momentarily blinds Miranda, who opens her burnt, raw eyes to see a Hag standing in the circle, a Hag like those of swamp legend, all warts and shriveled skin, warped fingernails that curl at their tips, clad in a black, dusty frock. The creature makes a stink-eye at Miranda, then turns to A.B. and nods.

"Abby," she says, pleasantly surprised, "what a pleasant surprise." Her voice is deep, guttural like a rumbling stomach.

"Jacko, how are we?"

"Who's the girl?"

"A client."

"Terrific. Ma'am," the Hag says to Miranda, tipping an invisible cap. The creature cracks her neck, a sound which echoes through the forest, before leaping into the air, and all of spacetime seems to bend as her whole mass swirls into a single point, crunching into itself and then blasting back out in the form of a crow. It *caws* a parting *caw* and presently flies away over the trees.

The pentagram, per the sun's automatic directive, loses its previous proportionality, becoming more and more oblong and finally unrecognizable, before passing out of existence entirely, spending its last few moments of life as the same scattered array of light lines it was before.

"Miranda Swami, you have no idea how much magic is hiding in all the corners of the world around you. No idea. It startles even me sometimes."

Miranda Swami, meanwhile, is having trouble catching her breath. It wasn't immediately apparent to her companion that she was gasping at all. In a beggar's intonation, she asks, "What...what, how?"

"This spot can only be used like that, as transport, very rarely. It's existed here for millennia, and yet you're the first human soul to see it. Imagine that.

"Miranda, I know you've seen some things, and I know you've been privy to some awful frights. I know about your meeting with Cindi, and I know about all the things you read in those dusty old books she keeps in that silly little cave she likes to hide in. I know all of it. I know everything you know, and I want you to now know this: you don't know *anything*.

"Beings you can't comprehend with agendas you can't understand hide in plain sight all around you. But that's okay. You weren't *meant* to know that much. You humans are simple creatures by design. Your job is to remain earthbound, to affect change here, to enjoy this simple, lovely place for all of our sakes. My point in bringing you here is to ask you to let go of your preconceptions, about *everything*. There's so much you don't understand, about souls, demons, sales — you name it. Oh, don't make that face, is this so surprising? Take, for example, your roommates, your pretty little roommates, your *strictly inferior* roommates; how do you think they got where they are? Working for *Big Banana*, money coming out their ears, *enjoying* their fruitful days and not fretting about their futures…"

It takes Miranda a moment to put the pieces together. As she does — *when* she does — her jaw begins a reflexive descent.

"And your parents in their pretty house. Your father with all that political goodwill. That always seemed a little *too* ridiculous, yeah? Why would *anyone* trust your old man to lead them? I mean, you've always been able to see right through him, ever since you were a kid. And Mother is, well, you *know* her. How come so many people love her as they do? You see where I'm heading?"

A cold bitter wind blows straight down Miranda's throat. Speech eludes her. She thinks of Caleb. As if involuntary, she thinks of Caleb.

"Him too. As you know. But if you had any idea what was done for him, how *much* of our maneuvering it took to get him where he is now, well, you'd be…you'd just be floored. People always assume they're the only ones, that meeting with us, dealing with us is somehow reserved for a special chosen faction of humanity. But the fact is that everybody sells their soul, or a part of it, sooner or later. That's the way it works. Some take the Cindi Lapenschtall route, and have a permanent effect on the world. Some are happy exacting revenge on an ex-boyfriend, because that's all their soul is worth to them. It's dicey, ain't no way around that. Nobody discusses it, either because they're scared or guilty or whatever, but this is the way the world is turned. It's the way justice is applied to everyone: the good, the bad, and otherwise. Sometimes it's confusing, and sometimes its effects seem strangely counterintuitive, but everything is figured out in accounting. It all makes sense in the books. You just have to put faith in the system.

"Listen. I'm a trustworthy guy: I've been as forthcoming and transparent with you as possible. I wouldn't screw you on this. Get a jump early, use what we're offering to live a better life, to bring more good to the world. That's why I brought you here, showed you all of this. Because I want you to have a leg up, Miranda. Because we're able, for a limited time, to *offer* you a leg up. What you've just seen today, none of it was ever meant for human eyes. Know that. But I wanted you to step into my world so you might allow me to step into yours. Know that I believe you could be good, do good, help maintain balance for the rest of your days. I want to *invest* in your soul, Miranda Swami. Let me put my money where your mouth is, so to speak. And don't worry about all that after-lifey type stuff, okay? Let me just say this: it's nothing like it says it is in the book. Just be a good person, don't murder anyone, and soul or not, you'll be a-okay. All right? There. That's my pitch. How do you feel? What do you say?"

Miranda can sense, even at that moment, that her forthcoming reaction will have far-reaching, perhaps cosmically-significant, effects. Every adjective every noun every subject-verb agreement she's ever uttered or considered or seen on a standardized test appears before her in a grand matrix; processes beyond her control whittle them down one by one, until the chosen sentence leaves her mouth:

"I need to think about it."

Which is true, she does.

"That's great, Swami, really great. Just consider it. Really consider it, that's all I ask. It's not like we're going anywhere, no matter what happens with everything across the water. I warn you though, your soul might not ever be as valuable as it is now. Call with any questions, okay? Super. Here, again, is my card."

A.B. snaps his fingers. The sharp sound is the cue for hundreds and hundreds of business cards to explode skyward in a continuous stream from an adjacent sewer grate, like water spouting from a busted-up fire hydrant. A.B. sticks his hand into the paper pell-mell, pulls out a single card, and hands it to Miranda as the deluge reverses course, diving back down into its subterranean home.

"That's one of my favorites. Rule #1 of sales (write this down): always leave 'em on their ass. Been nice talking with you, Miranda Swami. It really has been. Let's not wait so long until next time."

On that, A.B. extends his wings and blasts into the air, becoming in a matter of moments no more than a brief yellow speck on a darkening horizon.

Miranda looks towards the sky until she can no longer make out the imaginary point where A.B. might be. Some cirrus clouds rush in and do their measly best to block out the sun. She turns the card over in her hand, finding on the back some writing scrawled in crayon. *Subways are all closed. I'd walk. A.B.*

Certainly uncertain about whether she'll take A.B.'s long-term advice, she decides to take this bite-sized bit, hugging herself close and hustling out of the park, trying to phonelessly orient herself in the direction of the Brooklyn Bridge, wishing for warmer clothes. She'd love to ask someone for directions, but all the Bodegas are boarded up, all the terrified families still huddled tight in their homes.

"Well, that's that, then," she says out loud, a button line that seems to have been said in someone else's voice. It's amazing what the motor muscles manipulating the mouth may mutter when unaccompanied. She walks and walks and eventually takes a left at the edge of the park, walking along this, the last visible treeline before the city reverts back from its primordial forest form to its standard concrete and mortar. A breeze knocks some shriveled berries down to the sidewalk. Are they edible? Better not find out.

Miranda, two roads diverged before her, one berried and one not, hopes for the best.

EPILOGUE

In the end, "justice" proves to be a wily beast, one that shape-shifts, that burrows and crawls and camouflages, readying itself for the pounce. Who knows what kind of sick, prolonged justice called for *Big Banana's* rise, and whether the company's ultimate downfall was a part of it all along?

In the not too distant future, unknown sources will leak to the press that the entire CEO Announcement, and the violence that followed, was a kind of frighteningly savvy media ploy intended to drum up both controversy and sympathy for the "agricultural" giant known as *Big Banana*. Intrepid reporters, their well-trained noses following the faintest whiff of blood, will thrust their way past all the company's public denials into their legal and financial records, publishing their findings that, yes, not only was the *Bash* well over-capacity and quite under-staffed at the time, but all those police officers? The yellow-vested riot controllers standing on cop cars? Most of them were on the payroll of some shadowy shell corporation that stunk of mercenariness. It was intentional violence.It was staged. Those deaths, those injuries, that pain? So real, but so artificial.

The same press and public sentiment that pushed *Big Banana* up to its apex will simply step aside and let them skid back down. In the online age, all good will is semi-Sisyphusian.

Twitter, Facebook, all the various *Times'* and *Posts* and *Heralds* and *Journals*, anything with a subscriber count will run merciless streams of stories proclaiming the fall of *Big Banana*, willing it into existence, spooking even the most resilient shareholders into mass selloffs. *Big Banana* will be driven into the ground in a matter of weeks. Ever seen a company's stock tank 50% in a day? Nobody else had either. Some will call it Black Tuesday for Tropical Fruit Conglomerates, but that won't be entirely true. *Del Monte* will go up five points. And three for *Chiquita*.

People will ask how a company famed for its marketing could have blundered so brazenly. Maybe, they'll say, it was the doings of that new CEO they trot out to take the blame for the company's missteps. Poor guy, he'll spend the entirety of his 15-minutes looking like he's been hit by a bus, hair amess, eyes aflame, red cheeks and red irises and a bulbous neck squeezed into a button-down two sizes too small. Most companies in *Big Banana's* position would have fired the guy responsible, or else made him a stooge for the shareholder's stake, but they'll keep shoving him onto TV and into press conferences and Reddit AMAs, and he'll continue apologizing. Almost like they want the world to watch him squirm. Interesting. All other targets for blame will *poof* vanish into thin air. The Board, the oh-so-famous Board, will retreat into obscurity, and the sweaty guy in the poindexter shirt will get hit with more-and-more concentrated vitriol. First, they'll spit and throw insults. Then tomatoes. And finally, it'll be old VHS's and stray rebar pulled from the company's far-reaching rubble.

But all of that is still some weeks away. There will be plenty of time, time *ad infinitum*, for the truth of *Big Banana* to enter the national bloodstream. The antibodies *are* coming. But now, as New York City officials try to clear up the flotsam of the announcement gone wrong, calm constituents, *and* dispel rumors that the eight-hour media blackout was part of some conspiratorial, 9/11-truther type coverup, Miranda, like so many others, is utterly unaware of the fall to come. Her mind is on other things.

It's important you see what happens when Miranda finally gets home, well after dark, having made the entire journey from Brooklyn on foot. Wrapped up in hugs from her roommates, their outpouring of pain and anguish and shock needed an outlet and then found one, soot-covered and bloody, walking into the kitchen.

They will not be able to speak to her at first, too afraid of saying the wrong thing, paralyzed into silence by the now universal knowledge that the girl they met in GD303 is in actuality one of the internet's most sanctified voices. She's an idol. And they know they've slandered their idol, they know she remembers what they said about her — at first deifying and then despicable — and wonder if she'll hold a grudge. If she's, like, literally gonna hold a grudge rn, they're gonna just, like, die. Or whatever.

It's Miranda who speaks first, who asks point-blank, "Were you watching?"

But, duh, of course they were. "Everyone was."

It takes all of her restraint not to dwell on the carnage she must've shown them, the destruction done by Demons, and wondering, if they *were* watching, how they aren't quaking in their boots, huddled under their beds for safety; how the entirety of New York City isn't under their beds right now. "That's good," Miranda decides to say, "that's what I wanted."

Then, the Twins, the initial battering ram interrogation having breached the etiquette barricade, launch questions at her, assault her with the latest news, filling in the gaps in a story which personal experience had heavily redacted. Even as they bounce around the room, talking of *Big Banana* and the black cloud of smoke over the *Bash* and the friends that they haven't heard from and all the conspiracy theories getting airtime right now on CNN, flinging truly sincere emotion hither and thither, Miranda cannot keep her eyes from wandering down to their chests, wondering how much or how little of their souls are truly theirs.

For the first time perhaps ever, she *really* looks at them, not just through them, or around them. Famously beautiful, famously charming, socialites supreme and Instagram darlings in a certain set. Now exactingly examining, Miranda can make out the faces that their faces usually hide. The strained eyes, the city grid of reddened blood vessels within, the black, makeup-smeared half-moons below them, the smiles propped up by too-taut chins, the same smiles that ballast their ever-cheery disposition. Miranda looks briefly to the TV, where 24-hour news coverage tries in vain to mask its lack of insight into the day's horrible happenings.

"Are you two happy?" she asks them suddenly.

And — Jesus Christ, guys — they're so, *so* quick to say yes. Desperate to say yes. How couldn't they be? Everyone is *always* happy, right? When was the last time you asked how someone was and they didn't look right through you, saying how good they were, work is, the husband is, the kids and the fam, too, before you even finished asking? In other cultures, you know, they wonder how Americans can use "How are you?" as a greeting and expect nothing but smiles and pleasant lies as a response.

"Hey, how ya doing?" you say to the doorman, the grocery store clerk, the barista, the bartender, the new coworker, your god-damned asshole brother on the phone.

"Good."

"Good."

"Fine, thanks."

"Great."

Always always always. And after a couple of generations, that kind of thing seeps out from its place as a conversational nuance into the national psyche itself.

The Twins *are* quick to say they're happy, but, actually, don't they wait a half-second too long? Just on the tips of their tongues, their words must meet some kind of impeding force. A force that suggests

they just sigh and say, "Well, no. Actually, maybe? I'm not sure really…
but perhaps we need to redefine happiness. I'm comfortable. I'm chasing ambition, and I'm proud of myself, but I'm not sure any of those things make me 'happy' in the conventional sense. I've sacrificed traditional happiness for the sake of these other things, and those other things help me go on."

It's Katie who gives in to the force. She says it. She looks right in Miranda's sooty, yellow eyes and says exactly that. Kathy looks at her first like she's gone mad, then resigns herself to a fate as the one who *didn't* say it. Katie looks at Miranda and finishes, "I've — we've — sacrificed traditional happiness for the sake of these other things, and those other things help us go on." Then she wonders aloud, "But does that make us bad people? Does that make us wrong? *Everyone* does some form of that; everyone sacrifices important stuff for other… other…other, uhm, *stuff.*" Kathy looks at her sister like *please stop*, but Katie keeps going on, practically shouting, "We're *millennials*, the entire world around us is collapsing into the ocean! There's no way to be happy. 'Happy,' *pffffttt*. Nobody is ever going to look at the pretty leaves on the autumn trees again. Nobody will ever again get any *real* pleasure disappearing into their video-games and art projects, cuz we're all just staving off this *thing*, all these *things* that are coming for us. So, you know what Miranda? And Kathy can speak for herself, but I'm most certainly *not* happy. Not at all. But I'm after something, I'm getting by, I'm doing it. And it's worth it for me because *everyone* is doing the same thing. Because I know I'm not alone.

"Because I know I'm not alone."

A few days later, as the dust finally settles on the *Big Banana* debacle, as further answers finally start to be sought, Miranda takes a train out to Crown Heights. In Zen mode, she wanders the streets, half-startled by the amount of life present on a normal, unterrorized Brooklyn day. Why it is that so many in Manhattan assume the outer parts of their fair city are wastelands of silence and open space? Every leaf pile is occupied by leaping children. Sidewalks are cluttered with strollers and chatting moms in athleisurewear. Women in sweat-wicking shirts power-walk in pairs down the pavement in Prospect Park. An old man offers bread crumbs to pigeons; the birds peck their lunch from right out of his old, cracked hands.

In the geographical and ideological center of the park, on a familiar bench, a girl waits. A certain slant of light matriculates through the trees and a certain yellow being, his eyes perhaps a bit sadder, his skin a bit more rotten, emerges from thin air.

"You're back," he says, conjuring a smile. "I'm glad you called."

"I am, I did." the girl says. "I think I'm ready to make a deal. And quick, before I change my mind."

A scroll appears in mid-air, a subtle *poof* of smoke puffing out around it. A.B. whips his tail around to his hand, preparing to use its black tip like a pen. "And what exactly are the parameters you're interested in?" he asks.

"I want this all to go away. Take it all away. Take Gwami, and send me back to Earth with the rest of the people. I want them to forget about me. I want to be with them, among them. I just want to be like them." And in a quieter voice, she says this: "I just want them to like me."

And A.B. says, "With what funds would you like this accomplished?"

And Miranda says, "Take it all, what do I care? You know you'll get it eventually, why wait? All it's doing now is weighing me down."

That very afternoon, Miranda packs her things into two grand suitcases and leaves the apartment to its other two denizens. She does not know when she'll be back. NYU would probably call her, tell her she's missed too many classes to graduate on-time, if, that is, they could reach her. She left her phone in the apartment. A subtle slip of the tired mind.

She'll never return to NYU. Not as a student, anyways. She's content for now, sleeping back in her childhood room, with the old pitter patter of her parents' feet on the tile a floor below her. She can't sleep until they come upstairs themselves, the old night owls; she too much likes to listen to their muffled movement.

She's never felt at all close to them before, *ipso facto*, she's never felt this close to them. And all she had to do for that nearness was sell her soul. Because, and this is totally true, Miranda didn't gain anything in the soul-selling transaction. She wanted an escape from a mind and a life that kept her from others, and she got it. She wanted off of her unassailable pedestal, and she got her wish, cast down with the go-getters and the yes-men, all of 'em kissing ass and doing menial work for a few bucks, and maybe finding a warm one to love here and there. No more upkeep of an unclean soul. No more worrying about purpose, what the cosmic consequences of her actions might be. She's given herself over, *finally*, allowing the plot to whisk hr away, letting the Unmoved Mover do what it will with her life.

All of those people, and all their ordinary, easily-deconstructed rat race wishes, suddenly they don't seem so silly anymore. She didn't want them to be silly. She never *wanted* them to be silly. Miranda Swami was tired of hating everything. So, yeah, maybe she'll wear yellow a time or two. And the world will keep turning. Maybe she'll bartend on Fire Island for a summer, and the world will fail to notice whatever amount of great art Miranda Swami does or does not produce. It doesn't really matter. Her life will become simple, and that will be its own kind of art.

Miranda isn't here to answer to the universe. She's not here to answer anything, or to anybody. If she dares not disturb the universe, perhaps it will dare not to disturb her.

She has joined hands with the rest of the world, all of them having sold their souls (and what *is* a soul?) for a chance at normalcy, for a chance at what all the normal people want, for a chance to feel normal themselves. She is not better than these people, and never could be. She sees this only now, linked together in the inexorable chain of the soulless. She's picked a side; she's stopped fighting everyone, and started fighting alongside them.

Because amidst the bustling hive of people going about their business is the true soul of humanity. And that soul, a larger and more decadent prize, is up for grabs as well. And all the sellers of all their souls, all the fighters of all the wars, all the big ideas who clean restaurant with a toothbrush, they will forever remain contemplating their souls — complete or not so — as they look out into the dark, be it the dark of the wood, the dark of the city, or the dark of their closed eyelids, wondering, adrift in the throng, if anyone among them is truly happy. Wondering if they really had to sell their souls to be so. Wondering why there isn't a better use for their souls hiding in plain sight. Wondering, perhaps, if there is. If there may be.

BANANAS!

Bananas! was set in Adobe Garamond Pro.
The font size is 10.5 points.
Book cover and design by Jessica Richards.

CPSIA information can be obtained
at www.ICGtesting.com
Printed in the USA
FSHW011816210820
73171FS